ENDGAME

Born in 1983, Daniel Cole has worked as a paramedic, an RSPCA officer and most recently for the RNLI, driven by an intrinsic need to save people or perhaps just a guilty conscience about the number of characters he kills off in his writing. He currently lives in sunny Bournemouth and can usually be found down the beach when he ought to be writing. Daniel's debut novel *Ragdoll* was a *Sunday Times* bestseller and has been published in over thirty countries.

Also by Daniel Cole
Ragdoll
Hangman

ENDGAME

DANIEL COLE

TRAPEZE

First published in Great Britain in 2020 by Trapeze
an imprint of The Orion Publishing Group Ltd
Carmelite House, 50 Victoria Embankment
London EC4Y 0DZ

An Hachette UK Company

1 3 5 7 9 10 8 6 4 2

A CIP catalogue record for this book is
available from the British Library.

ISBN (Paperback) 978 1 4091 6886 7

Typeset by Born Group
Printed and bound in Great Britain by Clays Ltd, Elcograf S.p.A

www.orionbooks.co.uk

Dear reader,

> 'I don't want to just reset everything at the end of each book like an episode of *The Simpsons*.'

I've been saying that since those first daunting interviews promoting *Ragdoll*. But it feels more relevant now than ever, having just finished work on book three in the trilogy, incorporating all of the history and sense of consequence that entails. I believe I've achieved a depth to these characters and drama to their relationships that I couldn't have by writing standalone novels. And while I've tried to accommodate new readers in both *Hangman* and *Endgame*, there's no getting around the fact that the books will mean so much more to you having seen the story through from the very beginning.

I also have a bit of a geeky side and love spotting 'Easter eggs' and subtle references hidden in my favourite movies and TV shows, knowing that only the most loyal fans will ever know they're there. It makes a fictional world feel just that little bit more real, and these books are littered with them accordingly.

This is not the end of *Ragdoll*, not by a long shot. I always wanted these first three novels to be about this particular team at this particular point in time. They overlap. Their stories interweave. They are a trilogy . . . But that's not how the real world works either – life has a tendency of coming back to loosen whatever neat little bows we may tie. I already have the bones of book four in place, and I'm incredibly excited about this and the fresh direction in which the series is heading.

After all, it's just one big story.

As always, a huge thank you to the readers and even huger apology for my complete lack of social media interaction; it's just not my thing. But you keep me in a job. This book is for you, and I sincerely hope you enjoy reading it as much as I enjoyed writing it.

So, without further ado: ladies and gentlemen, the final part in the *Ragdoll* trilogy, *Endgame* . . .

Daniel Cole

'Don't mistake me for the hero . . .
I'd kill every last living thing on earth to save you.'

PROLOGUE

Monday 4 January 2016

11.13 a.m.

'Once upon a time . . . Not anymore.'

A snow-capped suburbia scrolled past the grimy windows, the weak sun warming the leather interior as they juddered towards their destination.

'But you are him, right?' the man in the driver's seat pressed. 'You're William Fawkes?'

'Someone's gotta be,' sighed Wolf with genuine regret as the dark eyes in the rear-view mirror watched him, occasionally flicking back to the matter of the road ahead. 'It's just up here on the left.'

The black cab pulled up, engine spluttering as it idled over someone's driveway.

Wolf paid the man in cash, not that it mattered anymore, and climbed out onto the quiet street. But before he'd even had a chance to close the door behind him, the vehicle accelerated away, spraying him with icy sludge as the taxi and its swinging appendage disappeared round the corner. Rather regretting tipping the intrusive snitch, Wolf supposed it had probably been wishful thinking that the £1.34 bribe would ever procure the man's silence for long anyway. He wiped his trousers with the sleeve of the long black coat that had once belonged to Lethaniel Masse – the Ragdoll Killer – a souvenir from a past life, a trophy of sorts and a reminder of all the people he should have been there for.

Successfully smudging the wet spots into dirty streaks, he realised he was still being watched. Despite losing two stone and growing an impressively scraggly beard, Wolf's imposing size and bright blue eyes betrayed him to anyone attentive enough to give him a second look. Across the road, a woman was staring at him as she fussed over a pram and the baby presumably concealed somewhere beneath the pile of blankets. She took out her mobile phone and held it up to her ear.

Managing a sad smile in her direction, Wolf turned his back to her, entering through the gate behind him. An unfamiliar Mercedes, only identifiable by the badge poking up through the snow, sat grandly neglected on the gravel, and the familiar house itself had grown a third bigger since his last visit. Knowing the front door would be unlocked as always, he didn't bother knocking, stamping the snow off his shoes before stepping into the mournful gloom that had permeated the hallway despite the cloudless sky outside.

'Maggie?' Wolf called, voice breaking just for being back in that house, for taking a greedy breath of the air inside – laced with dying books, floral perfume, ground coffee and a hundred other things that evoked unsolicited memories of simpler, happier times. For this was the place where he felt more at home than anywhere else in the world, the one constant he had been able to rely on ever since first moving to the capital. 'Maggie?!'

A creak upstairs broke the silence.

As he started to make his way up, light footfalls hurried across the floorboards above.

'Maggie?!'

A door opened: 'Will . . . ? Will!'

No sooner had Wolf reached the top stair than Maggie threw her arms around him, very nearly relocating their reunion back down to the hallway.

'Oh my God! It really *is* you!'

She was embracing him so tightly he could barely breathe and then all he could do was squeeze her back as she burst into tears against his chest.

'I knew you'd come,' she sobbed, voice trembling. 'I can't believe he's gone, Will. What am I supposed to do without him?'

Detaching himself from the embrace, Wolf held Maggie at arm's length to speak to her. The unfailingly immaculate woman was in her mid-fifties, her running make-up and dowdy black clothing actually making her look her age for once. She had let her dark curls hang loose, when she normally would have tied them up into a vintage style that had inevitably come back into fashion.

'I don't have much time. Where . . . where was he?' he asked, struggling with the first of many uncomfortable questions that he needed answering.

Her shaking hand pointed towards a splintered door frame in an uncarpeted section of the landing. He nodded and gave her a gentle kiss on the forehead before stepping up into the latest addition to the house, while Maggie held back, loitering on the threshold of the bare room. Wolf regarded his friend's final project proudly, finished to the exacting standards he applied to anything that concerned his grandchildren. It was to be their new room when they came to visit, a way to spend more time together now he had retired.

A wooden chair lay upturned in the centre of the room, beneath which a dark red stain had soaked into the porous floorboards.

Wolf had convinced himself that, once inside, he would be able to remain impassive, to treat the situation with the dispassionate efficiency he would any other crime scene . . . But, of course, he had been wrong.

'He loved you, Will,' said Maggie from the doorway.

Unable to hold back the tears any longer, Wolf wiped his eyes to the sound of someone crunching across the gravel outside.

'You should go,' Maggie told him urgently, ignoring the polite knock. 'Will?' Hearing the front door creak as somebody let themselves in, she hurried to the stairs to intercept, her expression relaxing as a blond-haired, rat-faced man made his way up: 'Jake!' she sighed in relief. 'I thought you were . . . Never mind.'

Wolf watched suspiciously as the two of them embraced like old friends.

'Got you a few bits and bobs,' the man told her, handing over the shopping bags. 'Could you give me a minute with him?' he then asked, shattering the pretence that this was merely a social visit.

'Go ahead, Maggie,' Wolf told her.

Looking uncomfortable, she headed downstairs to put the shopping away.

'Saunders,' Wolf greeted his ex-colleague as he stepped into the room.

'Wolf. Long time no see.'

'Well, you know, I needed some me-time,' he quipped, hearing a vehicle pull up out on the street. 'Didn't think the two of you knew each other.'

'We didn't,' shrugged Saunders, remaining a safe distance away despite the civil conversation. 'Not until . . . all this.' He sighed heavily. 'Mate, I am *genuinely* sorry about Finlay. I really am.'

Nodding his appreciation, Wolf's eyes returned to the stained floorboards.

'What are you doin' here?' Saunders asked bluntly.

'Needed to see for myself.'

'See what?'

Wolf lowered his voice for Maggie's sake: 'The crime scene.'

'Crime?' Saunders rubbed his face wearily. 'Mate, I attended myself. He was found *alone* . . . in a locked room . . . lying next to the weapon.'

'Finlay wouldn't kill himself.'

Saunders looked at him with pity: 'People never fail to surprise us.'

'Speaking of which, you got here awfully quickly.'

'Was on my way over anyway . . . when the call came in.'

Wolf had never much liked the loud-mouthed detective constable back when they'd worked together but was now beginning to see him in a new light. 'Thank you for looking out for her.'

'It's no trouble.'

'So . . . how many are out there?' Wolf asked him, as if enquiring the time, the atmosphere in the room changing instantly.

Saunders hesitated. 'Two out front. Two out the back. One sat with Maggie and, all being well, one three feet away from us behind that wall.' He turned to the open doorway: 'Honk if you're horny!'

The sound of a clip being loaded into a semi-automatic rifle answered from the landing.

He smiled apologetically and then removed a pair of handcuffs from his pocket. 'I promised them you wouldn't run. *Please* don't make me look stupid.'

Wolf nodded and slowly got down onto his knees. Raising his arms, he interlocked his fingers behind his head and stared out through the snowy window – the last vista his mentor would have seen before the end.

'Sorry, mate,' said Saunders, stepping forward to secure the handcuffs round his wrists. 'Suspect in custody!'

'Will?!' Maggie called from the kitchen as her house flooded with armed police.

Heavy boots were climbing the stairs towards them, Maggie's footsteps following them up.

'Would you do something for me?' asked Wolf, looking from Saunders to Maggie as the last of the officers filed in through the broken doorway, barking customary orders as they secured him: 'Don't tell her I'm back yet.'

'But, Will—' she cried, desperate, yet unable to place a foot inside the room in which her husband had been found.

'It's all right, Maggie. It's all right,' he assured her. 'I'm not running anymore.'

CHAPTER 1

Monday 4 January 2016

11.46 a.m.

Thomas Alcock was distracted by the muted television as he made himself a cup of tea.

'Arse!' he whispered, slopping boiling water all over the work surface . . . which then dripped accordingly onto his hand: 'Cocking piss bums!' He winced in reserved agony, shaking off the pain without taking his eyes off the screen.

On Sky News, a helicopter circled the site of the devastation that had befallen the country's capital a fortnight earlier. Where it eclipsed the sun, a dark shadow swept effortlessly across the rubble below, at least two others in its company at any given moment – like vultures gathering over a fresh carcass. Apparently the airspace ban over the city, which had caused untold misery and disruption over the festive period, had been lifted, allowing the world to finally appreciate the extent of the destruction.

A disaster narrowly averted, but not without cost.

The explosion, contained to a set of underground toilets at the top of Ludgate Hill, had prompted a routine evacuation of the surrounding buildings while structural engineers carried out their checks. After one eagle-eyed tourist noticed fresh cracks to St Paul's Cathedral's west front, emergency restoration works were commissioned. But before the scaffolding had even been erected, they lost the north tower to the concrete below. And then, over the course of three days, column after column had broken off, like legs buckling under the weight, until the enormous portico inevitably crumbled away – an iconic monument slowly dying of its wounds.

It was a surreal image: a missing jigsaw piece.

It took Thomas a moment to realise that the colourful border surrounding the area was in fact a mountain of wreaths and flowers stacked high against the fences: a tribute to those who never resurfaced from Piccadilly Circus, to Constable Kerry Coleman, to all of those lost in Times Square – a touching but short-lived gesture in the sub-freezing conditions.

He sipped his tea.

Flashing lights pulsed distractingly over the yellow subtitles as what was left of the Christmas tree in the other room reminded him it was still there, the piles of unopened presents beneath collecting pine needles. Stroking Echo absent-mindedly, Thomas's mind returned for the umpteenth time to selfish thoughts: how thankful he was that no one he'd known had been among the dead or injured, how fortunate he felt to have his girlfriend back in one piece and, shamefully, how he secretly hoped that the horrors of the past month, culminating in a national-security incident and capped off with the untimely death of a dear friend, might just be enough to tip her over the edge, to persuade her to leave it all behind, to appreciate what she still had left and be satisfied with her lot.

Baxter's phone started buzzing loudly across the kitchen table.

Diving across the room, Thomas answered it in an irritated whisper:

'Emily's phone . . . I'm afraid not. She's still asleep. Can I take a—. . . Wednesday . . . nine a.m. . . . I'll let her know . . . OK. Goodbye.'

He placed the mobile down on top of the oven gloves in case it went off again.

'Who was that?' asked Baxter from the doorway, startling him.

She was sporting one of his baggy jumpers over her tartan pyjama bottoms, the homely attire a welcome change to the thirty-five-year-old detective chief inspector's usual get-up. Thomas felt sick all over again as he looked at her, at the toll the job had taken on the woman he loved. Her top lip was stitched together. Two of her fingers were splinted to one another, protruding from the sling she was reluctantly wearing to support her injured elbow, while her ruffled dark brown hair was hiding the majority of the scratches and scabs that still covered her face.

He forced an unconvincing smile: 'Want some breakfast?'

'No.'

'Just an omelette?'

'No. Who was on the phone?' she asked again, holding her boyfriend's gaze, confident even that much conflict would be too much for him.

'It was your work,' he sighed, angry with himself.

She waited for him to elaborate.

'A Mike Atkins calling to inform you that you have a meeting with him and the FBI on Wednesday morning.'

'Oh,' she replied dazedly, scratching Echo's head when he jumped between the work surfaces to dribble on her.

Thomas couldn't stand seeing her looking so fragile and down-trodden. He walked over to embrace her but wasn't convinced she'd even registered that he was holding her as she stood there limply.

'Has Maggie called today?' she asked him.

He let go: 'Not yet.'

'I'll go over . . . in a bit.'

'I'll drive you,' Thomas offered. 'I can just sit in the car or get myself a coffee while you—'

'I'm fine,' she insisted.

The curt response actually lifted Thomas's spirits a little. Somewhere, hidden deep beneath the broken surface, was that familiar acidity to Baxter's tone.

She was still in there. She just needed time.

'OK,' he nodded, smiling kindly.

'I'm gonna . . .' She finished the thought by gesturing upstairs. 'But I'm fine,' she muttered as she headed for the hallway, Echo trailing close behind. 'I'm fine.'

The hedge might have looked like any other hedge had it not been for the flash of bright orange hair bobbing in and out of sight behind it.

Alex Edmunds's first assignment as a private investigator had been a modest affair, leading him to a piece of wasteland-cum-shopping-trolley-cemetery opposite his local Sainsbury's. But now, with his mark squarely in his sights and the only exit blocked by his team, the welcome buzz of the chase started to return.

He made his move . . .

His target bolted, faster than he'd been expecting, fleeing straight towards his trap.

'PI 2!' he yelled into the Toys R Us walkie-talkie. 'PI 2, prepare for intercept!'

'Do I have to?'

'*Please!*' panted Edmunds before watching his plan unfold like a well-rehearsed piece of choreography, his fiancée appearing from nowhere ahead of them, blocking the path with the pram.

Skidding to a halt, their payday deliberated for a moment and then scrambled up what appeared to be the tallest tree in London, knocking snow from the upper branches as he ascended out of reach.

'Balls!' grimaced Edmunds, holding a stitch as he stared skywards.

'PI 1, ferrets can climb trees,' Tia's distorted voice informed him as she wheeled Leila over. 'What now?' she asked, no longer requiring the walkie-talkie.

'This is . . . This is all right,' Edmunds told her confidently. 'He's trapped.'

'Is he, though?' she asked him, removing the cat box from the back of the pram and placing it on the frozen ground.

'Right, I'm going up there,' said Edmunds decisively, expecting her to protest.

She didn't.

'Up the really big tree,' he clarified.

She nodded.

'OK, then,' he nodded back. 'Stand a safe distance away just in case I fall . . . and die.'

'How about . . . back at home?' suggested Tia.

'Sure,' he shrugged, a little surprised she would want to miss out on all the excitement. He stepped up to the tree and took hold of a thick branch above his head. 'This is fun, though, isn't it? Getting to spend a little more time together?'

Tia didn't respond.

'I said . . .' he tried again after sliding back down the trunk. 'Oh, you've gone.'

She was already halfway up the bank.

'Well, *I* think it's fun,' Edmunds mumbled to himself. 'OK, Mr Scabs,' he called up into the branches. 'Your reign of terror ends here!'

Wolf was snoring loudly.

He had been confined to the room in Hornsey Police Station for over three hours, two and a half of which he'd spent enjoying the most restful sleep he'd had in weeks. When a door slammed out in the corridor, he awoke with a jolt. Briefly confused by his unpleasant surroundings, the handcuffs clinking against the metal chair at his back served as an adequate reminder of his eventful morning. A little annoyed at the inconsiderate door-slammer, he was now quite desperate for a wee and a couple of minutes' pacing the limited floor space to wake up his left butt cheek.

As he attempted to flex out the encroaching cramp, the sound of heeled shoes clicked down the corridor towards him. The door unlocked and a dashing man in his fifties entered the room, his bespoke suit jarring with the taupe walls.

'Huh,' Wolf greeted the well-dressed stranger. 'I thought you were a lady.'

The silver-haired man looked perplexed, deep creases forming across the leathery skin of his forehead.

'But you're not,' Wolf informed him helpfully.

A hint of a smile appeared on the man's face. 'And there was me worrying needlessly that your detective skills might have suffered while you were AWOL.'

He pulled up a chair and sat down.

'Speaking of which,' started Wolf, suddenly reminded of something. 'And I don't want to sound petty or anything, but I *did* still have fifteen days' annual leave to take when the whole Masse thing . . . *happened*. I don't know if there's any way to—'

The man cracked a bemused smile, stopping him mid-sentence, his ice-white teeth almost glowing against his orange-tinted skin.

'Yeah, you're probably right. We'll sort it out another time,' Wolf nodded, puffing out his cheeks when a strained silence ensued.

'You don't recognise me, do you, Will?'

'Errrrrm . . .'

'This is Commissioner Christian Bellamy,' announced a regrettably familiar voice from the doorway as Commander Geena Vanita entered the room.

She was wearing a relatively tasteful ensemble by her standards: a black jacket covering a commendable amount of the clashing garments beneath. Perhaps it was too much daytime television, maybe just where his mind was at, but if he were to categorise the outfit, he'd have gone for 'Teletubby funeral wear'.

She was still talking.

'I'm sorry. What?' asked Wolf, completely missing everything she'd said next, his mind wandering onto far more pressing matters: Dipsy – heroin OD.

'I said: "It was only a matter of time before we caught you,"' repeated the diminutive woman.

'You *do* remember the part where you didn't actually catch me, right?' asked Wolf. 'Because I *distinctly* remember giving myself up.'

Vanita shrugged, already formulating the press statement to announce his capture. 'You say tom-*a*-to. I say—'

'Shameless propagandising?' he suggested.

'Look, we're not your enemies, Will,' interjected Christian before they could continue bickering. But on noticing the glaring match taking place across the table, he decided to amend his statement: '*I* am not your enemy.'

Wolf scoffed at that.

'You know, we've actually met before,' Christian continued. 'Admittedly, a long time ago. And . . .' For the first time, the effortlessly suave man's composure faltered. 'We *both* lost a dear, dear friend this week. Don't think you were the only one.'

Wolf regarded the man sceptically.

'So . . .' started Vanita, 'William Oliver Layton-Fawkes.'

He winced.

'Now that you've been caught—'

'Surrendered!' groaned Wolf.

'. . . you're looking at a *pretty* lengthy prison sentence to atone for your rather considerable list of offences.'

Wolf noticed Christian frown disapprovingly in his subordinate's direction as she continued.

'Withholding evidence, perjury, failing to attend when requested, actual bodily harm—'

'Aggravated assault at best,' argued Wolf.

'The list goes on and on,' Vanita finished, folding her arms in satisfaction. 'You've managed to wriggle your way out of so many messes over the years, but this time it looks like your sins have finally caught up with you. Have you anything to say for yourself?'

'Yes.'

She waited expectantly.

'Would you mind scratching my nose?' he asked her.

'I beg your pardon?'

'My nose,' Wolf repeated pleasantly, the handcuffs jangling at his back. 'Would you mind?'

Vanita shared a look with Christian and then laughed. 'Did you *even* hear a word I said, Fawkes?'

Wolf's eyes were watering.

'You are going to prison for a *very* long time.'

'Come on, please,' said Wolf, unsuccessfully attempting to rub his nose against his own shoulder.

Vanita got to her feet: 'I don't have time for this.'

She'd made it as far as the doorway before Wolf spoke again. 'Léo . . . Antoine . . . Dubois.'

Vanita paused, one foot out of the room. Very slowly, she turned back round:

'What about him?'

'Nose first,' tried Wolf.

'No! What about Dubois?'

'Pardon my ignorance,' interrupted Christian, 'but . . . *who*?'

'Léo Dubois,' huffed Vanita, recalling the multi-agency fiasco she'd had the pleasure of not thinking about in years. 'It was a big case for the department: murder, human trafficking, drug smuggling. Fawkes was involved, so, unsurprisingly, an unprecedented mess.' She turned back to Wolf when he yawned loudly: 'What about Dubois?'

'Current whereabouts, names and images of his entire network, account numbers, the name of the ship en route to our shores packed to the rafters with sex workers . . .'

Unconsciously, she took a step back into the room.

'Oh! Vehicle registrations,' he continued, 'money-laundering services . . . and I'm *pretty* sure he's hacked someone's Netflix account.'

Vanita shook her head: 'The desperate promises of a captured man.'

'Surrendered,' Wolf reminded her.

Christian remained quiet, noting the abrupt change in his colleague.

'I feel I've horribly misjudged you, Fawkes,' said Vanita theatrically. 'The sceptic in me always suspected you'd gone on the run simply to save your own arse after commissioning the services of a serial killer. But it turns out, all this time, you'd actually taken it upon yourself to single-handedly bring down a notorious crime lord!' She laughed at her own wit. 'This is ridiculous! You can't expect anyone to believe—'

'I expect you to believe,' Wolf cut her off, 'that from the *moment* I left that courtroom, I started putting provisions in place to get my life back, in preparation for this moment right now, to present you with an offer you couldn't possibly refuse.'

'Oh, I can refuse it,' snapped Vanita, apparently forgetting she wasn't in fact the most senior person even in the three-person room. 'So, at no point did Dubois happen to recognise the man who tried for months to put him away? He wasn't suspicious in the slightest?'

'He was suspicious plenty,' Wolf told her. 'But there's nothing like having your face plastered all over the papers to instil a little truth into a story . . . I'm going to need you to scratch my nose now.'

She opened her mouth to refuse.

'Just scratch his nose, will you?' barked Christian, eager to continue.

Looking indignant, Vanita removed an expensive pen from her pocket and held it out in Wolf's general direction, making no effort to hide her displeasure.

'Right a bit,' Wolf instructed. 'Bit more. Oh *yeah*, that's it. You're in the wrong profession, you know?' he told her, before adding: 'That's just a completely unrelated statement of fact, by the way, nothing to do with your scratching skills.'

Leaning back in his chair, he smiled victoriously as Vanita dropped her favourite pen onto the table for somebody else to pick up.

'What do you want, Fawkes?' she asked through gritted teeth.

'No prison time.'

She laughed out loud:

'It's public knowledge what you did. At least some of it, anyway. The very best you can realistically hope for is a police-friendly wing.'

'So it's the public we're worried about, is it? Hence the relentless manhunt you conducted to find me,' grinned Wolf. 'Apart from it wasn't so much "relentless" as it was "leisurely", and not so much a "manhunt" as it was a "browse".'

Vanita tensed up.

'A month. Minimum security,' he offered.

'A year,' countered Vanita, somewhat overstepping her job description; however, Christian didn't raise any objections as he watched the negotiations bounce across the table like a spectator at a tennis match.

'Two months,' suggested Wolf.

'Six!'

'Three . . . but I have conditions.'

Vanita paused: 'Go on.'

'No one tells Baxter I'm back but me.'

More than happy to avoid any interaction with her irritable detective chief inspector, Vanita considered knocking a week off Wolf's sentence in gratitude; instead, she feigned a reluctant nod.

'And . . .' he continued, 'this is *probably* the opportune moment to tell you that during my time infiltrating Dubois's crew, I played a part in a group beating of a rival sex trafficker, who wound up in ICU with life-threatening injuries.'

'Jesus, Fawkes!' said Vanita, shaking her head.

'He made a full recovery, though!' Wolf added quickly.

'OK. I'm sure we can work with that.'

'So we went back and shot him.'

'Anything else?!' groaned Vanita, nearing the end of her tether.

'Yes. I'm going to need a suspended sentence,' said Wolf, deadly serious.

'But of course you are!' she replied sarcastically. 'And, just out of interest, how long do you fancy?'

'As long as it takes.'

'To?'

'To work one final case,' he told them, all cockiness and mischief gone from his voice.

'You're wasting my time, Fawkes,' said Vanita, again getting up to leave.

'Hang on,' Christian jumped in, speaking for the first time in minutes.

Glaring at her superior, Vanita obediently sat back down.

'Which case, Will?' Christian asked him.

Wolf turned to address the commissioner:

'The murder of Detective Sergeant Finlay Shaw.'

No one spoke for a few moments while they processed the bizarre request. Christian cleared his throat and raised a hand just as Vanita was about to respond:

'Will, it was suicide. You know that . . . I'm sorry but there is no investigation for you to join.'

'You were his friend?' Wolf asked him.

'His best friend,' said Christian proudly.

'Then answer me this,' said Wolf, meeting his eye. 'Is there even one conceivable scenario you can dream up in which Finlay would *ever* have left Maggie?'

Realising she was no longer part of the conversation, Vanita kept quiet. She hadn't even known for certain that Finlay had been married.

Christian sighed heavily and shook his head. 'No. Not one. But the evidence is . . . It's indisputable.'

'Surely, as his friend, you can't have a problem with me verifying that beyond any possible doubt? Then I'm all yours,' promised Wolf.

Christian looked torn.

'You can't *seriously* be considering this?' Vanita asked him.

'Would you just be quiet?!' snapped Christian, before turning back to Wolf: 'You would *really* put Maggie through this?'

'She'll understand . . . if it's me.'

Christian still looked uncertain.

'Come on. What have you got to lose?' Wolf asked him, for the first time letting his desperation show. 'I confirm it was a suicide; you get Dubois.'

He watched the commissioner turning over the options in his head:

'OK. Do it.'

Vanita got up and stormed out of the little room, leaving the two men alone to talk.

'I'll have the file brought over to you along with a signed copy of our . . . agreement,' smiled Christian with a twinkle in his eye. He slapped Wolf affectionately on the back, just as Finlay used to, no doubt leaving a bruise that his mentor would have been proud of. 'So, where do we start?'

'We?'

'Think I'm letting you do this alone? This is Fin we're talking about!'

Wolf smiled. He was beginning to like Finlay's oldest friend.

'So, where do we start?' Christian asked again.

'We start at the beginning.'

CHAPTER 2

Monday 5 November 1979

Bonfire Night

5.29 p.m.

Christian opened his eyes, only to be blinded by the bright light dangling from the corrugated roof. Shifting his weight to turn away, he felt the floor flex beneath him. He raised a hand towards his aching jaw, smacking himself in the face with a heavy boxing glove. Piece by piece, things started coming back to him: he and his partner had been sparring . . . Losing miserably, he'd gone in for a reckless uppercut . . . and missed . . . He remembered his opponent winding up for a left hook . . . and then blackness.

Finlay's unpleasant visage appeared above him. The twenty-four-year-old Scot was built like a tree trunk, his shaven head almost as knobbly and unsymmetrical as one. He had a flat nose, which tended to change direction with each visit to the gym:

'Get up, you girl,' he taunted in his rasping Glaswegian accent.

Groaning, Christian sat up in the centre of the ring:

'You're supposed to be teaching me, not just beating the shit out of me!'

Finlay shrugged, the muscles moving beneath his skin weirdly reminding Christian of his date the night before, the young constable shifting in her sleep under the sheets when he snuck out of her room.

'I *am* teaching you,' Finlay told him with a smile. 'Next time, you'll duck.'

'You're a prick, you know that?'

Chuckling, Finlay pulled him to his feet.

'How do I look?' Christian asked in concern, as he intended to take their attractive co-worker out again after their run of night shifts.

'Wonderful,' grinned Finlay. 'A bit more like me.'

'Christ! You should've just put me out of my misery,' Christian told him, earning himself a final winding blow to the kidneys.

Almost three years younger than his partner, Christian was the polar opposite of his appointed best friend: a handsome and popular young man. He wore his sandy hair in a shoulder-length style like the pop stars off the television. He was intelligent, when he wanted to be, but was lazy and more concerned with chasing women than criminals, if truth be told. The two men did share some common ground, however: an 'army brat' upbringing, an uncanny ability to attract trouble and a shared aversion to their new chief.

'Come on. Shift starts in an hour,' mumbled Finlay, undoing his gloves with his teeth. 'Let's see what *utter* bollocks the boss has in store for us tonight.'

'I know this might sound like utter bollocks,' started DCI Milligan through the hanging haze of smoke that mimicked the smoggy Scottish capital outside. The arching pole of ash clinging to the end of his cigarette finally snapped off, dropping onto his trousers.

'Maybe it sounds like bollocks . . . because it *is* bollocks,' suggested Christian.

Milligan wiped the ash into a grey smudge and turned to Finlay. 'What's he saying?'

Finlay shrugged.

Milligan turned back to Christian. 'We cannae understand you, son. What country are you from again?'

'Essex!' replied Christian.

Milligan watched him suspiciously for a moment before continuing. 'You two shites are on surveillance of the shipyard tonight. End of.'

'Can't French and Wick do it?' complained Finlay.

'No,' replied Milligan, who was rapidly growing bored of their company. 'Because French and Wick have been posted at the truck stop.'

'Where the deal is *actually* going to take place,' huffed Christian.

Milligan either ignored or didn't understand him.

'This is a waste of time,' said Finlay.

'In which case, you two idle shits are going to get paid for sleeping in a car park all night. Everybody wins! You are excused.'

'But—'

'You . . . are . . . . excused.'

At 7.28 p.m., Finlay pulled up outside one of the side entrances to the shipyard. Parking inches from the metal gates, they had an unobstructed view of the floodlit warehouses, a wall of multicoloured cargo containers stacked like giant Lego bricks, and a lone forklift truck abandoned for the night, their reflections trembling in the dark River Clyde beyond.

The first raindrops struck the windscreen, blurring the colours together, distorting shapes like paint running on a canvas. They watched the shower intensify into a torrential downpour while they tucked into their Wimpy burgers and first warm beers of the night – a stakeout tradition, much like the department's unmarked Ford Cortina. After eleven years of service, the clapped-out vehicle was probably as recognisable to Glasgow's criminal element as a patrol car with the sirens blaring, but who were they to argue with the wisdom of those higher up the food chain?

'Why is it,' started Christian between mouthfuls, 'that us two always get the shit jobs?'

'Politics,' Finlay told him wisely. 'Sometimes you just need to know whose arse to kiss in this job. You'll learn . . . Plus, I'm pretty sure Milligan's a horrible racist.'

'I'm from Essex!'

Finlay decided to change the subject: 'How's it going with the hairdresser?'

'She found out about the masseuse.'

'Oh,' said Finlay, taking another bite of his burger before continuing: 'Client of hers?'

'Sister of hers.'

'Ahhhh. So, how's it going with the masseuse?'

'Didn't take kindly to me seeing the constable.'

'Right. So, how's it—'

'It's going well,' said Christian. 'I'm taking her out again on Thursday. I think that *Mistress of the Apes* flick is on at the pictures.'

Finlay raised his eyebrows but didn't vocalise his concerns over his friend's appalling choice of date movie. He reached into his shirt pocket and proudly produced a cassette tape.

'No! Come on! Not Status Quo again!' complained Christian. 'Please not Quo!'

The clunky mechanism swallowed it whole and hissed a static prelude through the speakers . . .

It was Quo.

An hour had passed.

'Sean Connery?' tried Christian, cracking a window to avoid suffocating as they chain-smoked their way through the evening.

'How the *hell* did you get Sean Connery from that?'

'Literally all your impressions sound *exactly* the same!'

Finlay look rather offended. 'I'll have you know I've been told I've got a very good ear for accents.'

'And perhaps you do,' said Christian. 'I'm saying it's your mouth that's letting you down.'

'OK. Try this one . . .' said Finlay in irritation.

Listening carefully, Christian closed his eyes as he wracked his brain.

Finlay repeated it a little slower.

'Sean Connery?'

'Oh, fuck off!'

The flimsy hands of the dashboard clock read 9 p.m. when the first colourful explosions started lighting up the sky.

'I spy . . . with my little eye . . . something beginning with . . . "F".'

'Fireworks?' asked Finlay in a bored tone, feeling reasonably confident, seeing as they'd already had 'fence', 'forklift' and himself.

The various booms and crackles were just about reaching them through the crack in the window.

'Yeah . . . it was fireworks,' sighed Christian, as he searched the glovebox for something else to do.

Finlay looked around the car. 'OK. I spy . . . with *my* little eye . . . something beginning with—'

They both jumped when there was a loud bang against the roof of the car, heavy footfalls bending the thin metal above their heads. A tall figure then proceeded to stomp across the bonnet before scaling the metal gates. Both Finlay and Christian watched open-mouthed as the mullet-haired trespasser scrambled over, landing acrobatically on the other side of the fence. Pulling a pair of bolt cutters from his rucksack, he broke the chains and started dragging the large gates open.

All of a sudden, the rain was sparkling, a set of headlight beams illuminating the scene from somewhere behind them. Realising that they were now worryingly conspicuous, Finlay and Christian slumped lower in their seats, watching five dark figures pass within inches of the passenger window, followed by a black van. The sound of the engine was drowned out by the rain as the vehicle rolled at walking pace into the shipyard.

Finlay groped blindly for the radio. Over the dashboard, he could see the group fanning out as they approached the largest of the warehouses. He held the clunky handset to his mouth.

'Crystal?' he whispered, having heard his favourite dispatcher's voice over the airwaves throughout the evening. 'Crystal!'

The sound of tyres spinning on wet tarmac cut through the rain as the van accelerated aggressively towards the warehouse, building enough speed to smash through the enormous roller doors. The team on foot hurried in through the opening to the stutter of automatic gunfire.

There was a static click over the radio: 'Is that you, Fin?'

'Aye. We're down at the Goven Shipyard and need backing up pronto.'

There was an explosion from somewhere inside. Clearly, the microphone had picked it up because the dispatcher's friendly tone turned abruptly efficient. 'Backup en route to you now. Out.'

Finlay had just replaced the radio when a second explosion blew the mullet-haired man out of a first-storey window, his floodlit form a crumpled heap on the ground.

'Whoa!' laughed Christian, already practising the story in his head to rub in their colleagues' faces.

But then, unbelievably, the broken body swung out an arm and struggled back up. The man retrieved his weapon from a puddle and hobbled back inside.

'Someone's keen,' said Christian, finishing his burger.

Finlay turned to him angrily: 'How can you be eating right now?'

Christian shrugged innocently: 'We going in, then?'

'Yeah. Why not?' said Finlay, winding down the window to stick the magnetic light to the roof.

The fireworks in the distance continued to shower over the city as he switched the engine on and Status Quo's 'Rockin' All Over the World' fired back up. Hitting the sirens, they sped towards the warehouse, no real plan in place bar the hope that the presence of one police unit might indicate the imminent arrival of more.

'Mullet-head's back!' warned Christian as the man staggered from the building, weapon raised as he spat bullets at the approaching Ford Cortina.

'Put your *bloody* foot down!' yelled Christian as the car was peppered with fresh holes.

'It *is* bloody down!' Finlay shouted back as he spun the wheel, sending the car into a skid, inadvertently swinging the back end into the gunman.

There was a sickening thud as the limp body rolled towards the river. The vehicle spun to a stop, its one surviving headlight illuminating the bloody corpse twenty feet from where they'd hit him. Both breathing heavily, Christian and Finlay glanced nervously at one another, realising that they had perhaps bitten off more than they could chew on this occasion . . . Over the raindrops exploding against the damaged bonnet, they watched the gangly figure reanimate once more.

'What the hell?!' gasped Christian, appalled.

With trembling arms, the long-haired man pushed himself up onto his hands and knees.

Finlay revved the engine threateningly.

'Hit him again!' yelled Christian.

Despite a disgustingly obvious broken arm, the sodden man staggered to his feet. Swaying slightly, he stared at the two concerned faces gawping back at him through the cracked windscreen. And then, without a moment's hesitation, he turned round and dived into the dark water.

'Huh,' nodded Finlay, eyes still fixed on the river. 'You know, whatever they're paying that guy, it's not enough.'

They climbed out of the car and ran over to the destroyed doors.

An eerie quiet had settled over the warehouse as they peered in. The black van was visible among the debris in the loading bay, its rear wheels still spinning uselessly a foot off the ground. A metal staircase scaled the back wall up to a solid-looking door.

'Looks clear,' whispered Christian.

Tying his hair back into a ponytail, he hurried over to the van. A quick glance into the empty cab revealed that the accelerator had been wedged down with a rod. He waved Finlay over.

'Up?' his partner suggested.

'Up,' nodded Christian.

They climbed the staircase to an oval metal door that wouldn't have looked out of place on a submarine, a jet of cool air whistling out through a single bullet hole in the glass.

'Airlocks,' frowned Finlay, waving his hand through the escaping air.

He had to fight to pull the door open, hearing another slam elsewhere in the building as they entered a clinical corridor. Two bodies were slumped against opposite walls. One was clearly a member of the infiltrating team, the other dressed from head to toe in protective overalls.

'Stay behind me,' hissed Finlay, relieving the first corpse of its weapon and then systematically checking the open doorways as per his training: industrial weighing machines, money counters, flatbed trolleys.

They pressed on, walking against the indoor breeze as the pressurised air continued to leak out, when there was a deep boom from somewhere below them.

They both froze.

'That didn't sound good,' whispered Christian.

Finlay shook his head: 'Let's make this quick.'

They hurried to the end of the corridor, where a second airlock door blocked their path. Taking hold of the long handle, Finlay heaved it open. Christian stumbled through the doorway as a wall of air rushed past him, the imbalanced pressures attempting to equalise. Struggling to hold the heavy door open, Finlay edged through the gap before letting it slam violently behind him.

'Don't worry about me . . . I got it,' he said sarcastically, but his partner didn't answer. Christian was staring in awe at the bags of off-white powder piled five feet high and the bricks of neatly stacked cash beside them. Finlay made his way over and handed Christian the weapon. He tore a small hole in one of the bags, licked his finger and then spat it out on the floor: 'Heroin.'

'How much is here?' Christian asked him. The most he'd ever come across on the street was a kilo.

'Dunno . . . Thousands.'

There was another rumble underfoot. On noticing the warming glow dancing across the wall, Finlay approached the door to investigate, feeling hot air pouring in through the opening. Peering through the small window, he could see a metal walkway spanning the upper level of the warehouse. The deformed door swung freely as he crossed the threshold and hesitantly approached the roar of a fire in ecstasy.

The moment he stepped out into the open, he had to shield his eyes from the heat radiating off the inferno. What once had been a state-of-the-art manufacturing lab was now no more than a collection of tanks and canisters taking it in turns to ignite, cremating the assorted bodies scattered across the floor below: laboratory staff, infiltrating team and what appeared to be casually dressed security alike.

Realising that the soles of his shoes were melting into the metal, Finlay sprinted back towards the room, closing the broken door behind him as best he could.

'Problem?' asked Christian, looking worried.

'Fire.'

'Big?'

'Pretty big.'

'Shit.'

'Looks like we missed a hell of a firefight. Everyone's dead.'

They both turned back to their career-making find.

'Which is the priority?' Christian asked his superior officer. 'The drugs or the money?'

Finlay looked torn, bubbles forming on the wall behind him.

'The drugs or the money, Fin?'

'Drugs. We take the drugs.'

Christian looked tempted to argue, when the sound of shattering glass prompted him into action. 'I saw a trolley back in one of the rooms.'

Finlay nodded and hurried over to the pressurised door. Straining with the effort, he held it open enough to allow Christian through, his eyes drying out as the hot air rushed past. Moments later, Christian returned, wheeling one of the corpses on top of the flatbed trolley, its dangling hand trailing along the floor.

'He was a drug dealer!' he said defensively on seeing Finlay's disapproving expression. 'Now he's a doorstop.'

Christian unceremoniously dumped the dead body in the entranceway and tried to ignore the stomach-turning crunch it made when Finlay released the door to help him load up. Ninety seconds later, they tossed the final bag onto the flatbed, sweat pouring down their faces as the warehouse became a furnace.

'Go! Go! Go!' yelled Finlay when Christian allowed himself one final look back at the mountain of money cast in orange light as the fire stalked them through the collapsing building.

Christian and Finlay were both coughing up black phlegm when the first of their colleagues came speeding towards the inferno. Having exhaustingly moved the bags a safe distance from the blaze, they were sitting on the tarmac watching fireworks go off above their bonfire. Finlay hadn't said anything when he noticed his partner's hands shaking, the burn to his own left arm throbbing painfully in the cold rain.

A car door slammed.

'We're up,' he told Christian, getting to his feet.

Adopting their positions either side of the record-breaking bust, thumbs up and grinning widely, the warehouse roof collapsed in on itself behind them. The iconic black-and-white photograph circulated the national press for days – a PR triumph for the Robbery Unit, for Strathclyde Police as a whole . . . proof that heroes did still walk among us.

CHAPTER 3

Wednesday 6 January 2016
9.53 a.m.

'A man is dead, Chief Inspector!'

'A lot of people are dead . . . after what happened,' replied Baxter calmly, before turning venomous, 'and for some reason *you* people seem intent on wasting everybody's time worrying about the only person out there who deserves to be!'

Her meeting with the FBI was going about as well as expected, the monumental mess left in the wake of her last case someone else's problem to clean up: a suspect executed, a missing CIA agent, a blizzard-cloaked crime scene and a large area of Central London blown to hell.

'Do you have any information on Special Agent Rouche's current whereabouts?'

'To the best of my knowledge,' she answered evenly, 'Agent Rouche is dead.'

The interview room's buzzing heater billowed out uncomfortably hot air as their incessant questions continued.

'You had a team search Agent Rouche's house.'

'I did.'

'You didn't trust him, then?'

'I didn't.'

'And you feel no residual loyalty towards him now?'

She hesitated for the briefest of moments: 'None whatsoever.'

The moment the meeting in the next room adjourned, Wolf got to his feet and headed towards the door.

'And where do you think you're going?' asked Saunders.

'I want to see her.'

'I'm not sure you're *totally* grasping this whole "under arrest" thing.'

'We had an agreement,' said Wolf, turning to Vanita.

'Fine.' She dismissed him with a wave of her hand. 'It's not like this mess could get any worse.'

'Surprise!'

Wolf's forced smile started to ache in the protracted silence. The stale smell was yet to follow the liaison officer out of the interview room as Baxter stared at him from across the table. Although she remained silent, her huge dark eyes betrayed the innumerable emotions jostling for position behind her calm exterior. It was like waiting for a fruit machine to stop spinning.

Shifting uncomfortably in his seat, Wolf brushed his wavy hair out of his eyes and picked up the file in his lap. The handcuffs jangled against the metal table as he placed it down in front of him.

'Five quid says she hits him,' Saunders bet Vanita as they watched from behind the relative safety of the one-way mirror.

She closed her eyes and muttered something in Hindi, currently surrounded by the three biggest headaches in her life.

'No deal.'

Reaching across the table, Wolf switched off the microphone to the eavesdropping viewing room and dropped his voice to a murmur. 'I, errrm . . . I know I'm probably not your favourite person right now, but I can't even tell you how good it is to see you.' He shot an irritated look towards the mirror, willing their audience to give them a few minutes' peace. 'I've been really worried . . . with all that's been going on. I should've . . . Maybe I could have done something.'

Baxter hadn't moved a muscle while Wolf fumbled his way through his sentences.

He cleared his throat before continuing. 'I went to the house. I saw Maggie.'

Baxter's expression flickered.

'Don't be cross with her. I made her *promise* not to tell you. Long story short: I've made a deal . . . with the commissioner. They're going to let me work one last job . . . My last job. They're going to let me find the person who did this to him . . . to Finlay.'

Baxter's breathing had quickened, eyelids fluttering over moist eyes.

'I know what they're saying,' Wolf continued carefully. 'I've looked through the file and I get why they're saying it. From the outside, everything adds up. But you know as well as I do they're wrong.' His voice began to crack. 'He wouldn't have left her. He wouldn't have left you . . . He wouldn't have left *us*.'

Baxter now had tears rolling down her cheeks.

Wolf pushed the file across the table towards her. Scrawled over the photocopied front page:

Baxter's Copy

'Just look over the file,' he said softly.

'I can't,' whispered Baxter, breaking her silence.

Wolf flicked through to an annotated page as she got to her feet.

'But here it says that—'

'I can't!' she snapped at him before rushing out of the room.

Rubbing his face wearily, Wolf closed the file. He got up and dropped it into the confidential-paperwork bin behind him. Walking over to the table, he switched the microphone back on to address the large mirrored window. 'Just in case you missed that: she said, "No."'

Baxter exited the Tube station and entered a Tesco Express.

Sporadic patches of snow still lingered as she trudged along Wimbledon High Street, compacted round the bases of frozen lamp-posts or cowering within retreating areas of shade. On reaching the entrance to her block, she automatically selected Thomas's house key, habit revealing where she now considered home. She climbed the stairs with two heavy shopping bags but paused when she reached the top landing, the door to her apartment standing wide open. Setting the bags down, she approached cautiously. A short-haired woman walked out, zipping her jacket up over a veterinary nurse's uniform.

'Holly!' Baxter sighed in relief.

'Emily!' the woman greeted her enthusiastically, but knowing better than to attempt to make physical contact with her stand-offish school friend. 'I didn't know you were coming over.'

'No. Me neither.'

'Had a bit of spare time before my shift, so . . .'

'Coffee?' offered Baxter, having just stocked up.

'Would love to if I wasn't already late. But catch up later?'

'Sure.'

Stepping aside to allow her friend past, Baxter collected up the shopping bags and entered the apartment. She half expected Echo to come skidding round the corner and into the bookcase in greeting, before remembering that he was at Thomas's with the majority of her possessions.

It felt strange being back.

The hallway smelled like a hospital: antiseptic perfume to cover an infected musk. An assortment of plasters and bandages littered the kitchen worktop alongside half-empty bottles of medication. She carried the bags over to the fridge to start unloading the shopping when there was a heavy thump from the bedroom.

Baxter froze, vaguely named Vegetable Couscous Medley in hand.

The bedroom door slowly creaked open.

She stood back up, watching the hallway anxiously.

Suddenly, a half-naked man staggered out at her, a hungry look in his eyes. Horrendous wounds had been carved deep into his chest, crusted and yellowed where his body was failing to heal itself. Thick bandages pulled taut over his shoulder as he raised his grasping arms towards her.

'Lovely,' she said, tossing a bag of McVitie's Hobnobs Nibbles across the work surface.

'We're letting it breathe,' explained Rouche as he ripped the bag open greedily. 'Thank you!' he added, like a child forgetting their manners.

'I thought you might be asleep,' said Baxter as he slowly made his way over, holding his ribs and wincing with every step.

'Not the Vegetable Couscous Medley again!' he complained on spotting it in her hand.

'Stop whining! It's good for you,' she smirked.

She crouched down to place it in the fridge, allowing her smile to drop in her few seconds concealed from view. Rouche looked worse than ever. His pasty skin was wet with sweat. Every movement seemed to take intense planning and concentration so as not to injure himself further, and his heavy eyelids suggested that he'd had another night in too much pain to sleep. Even his salt-and-pepper hair looked a little limper and greyer than it had the day before.

Smile back in place, Baxter stood up: 'How'd it go with Holly?'

On the night of the blizzard, she had screamed at Rouche to stay conscious, forcing him back up onto his feet and away from his own crime scene. Less than twenty metres from the man he had killed, he'd collapsed in the shelter of a weeping willow that slumped over the banks of St James's Park Lake, not one of the countless emergency-service personnel aware of his presence in the whiteout.

Hours had passed before she could safely return for him. With a panicked but accommodating Thomas in tow, they had struggled to walk Rouche to the car. While Baxter tended to him in the back of the Range Rover, Thomas had driven them out of the city to Baxter's

Wimbledon apartment. Having no one else to turn to, she had risked everything by phoning a friend she hadn't spoken to since excusing herself from a hen do over a year earlier. Without hesitation, Holly had headed over, via her work, on the most limited of information. A veterinary nurse at the London Animal Hospital, she had spent the entire night at Rouche's side, made him comfortable enough to rest and cleaned his extensive collection of horrific wounds.

'*What?*' asked Rouche, too busy eating.

'Holly: how'd it go?' Baxter asked again.

'Says the antibiotics aren't working and I'll be dead in a fortnight if I continue to deteriorate like this,' he informed her quite cheerily, riding a Hobnob high. 'How'd it go with the FBI?'

'They want your head.'

Rouche stopped chewing and swallowed his mouthful:

'Can they wait a couple of weeks?'

Baxter tried to crack a smile, but it barely materialised.

'They're not going to stop looking for me,' he told her sincerely.

'I know that.'

'Look, Baxter, I—'

'Don't even bother saying it,' she cut him off.

'But if they find me here—'

'They won't.'

'But if they do—'

'They won't! We're not talking about this again!' she snapped. 'Get back to bed. I'm cooking you the Vegetable Couscous Medley now just for being a dick!'

She watched him fondly as he shuffled towards the bedroom door. Opening the fridge, she hesitated, shook her head and then selected a chicken tikka masala to heat up for him instead.

Back at Thomas's, Baxter heard the front door slam.

Abandoning her futile efforts to waft smoke out of the kitchen window, she elected to simply drop the whole pan into the rose bush instead. Her grand plans of cooking him a surprise dinner had gone the way of most of her plans lately.

'Hello!' he greeted her, frowning at the twig in the corner of the lounge on his way through, which shed another dozen pine needles just in the few seconds he was looking at it. 'Something smells' – he started to choke – '*good*. What are we having?'

'Vegetable Couscous Medley,' Baxter informed him, hoping the microwave wouldn't ping while he was in the room.

He looked a little disappointed.

The microwave pinged.

'How did your meeting with *the Feds* go?' he asked.

'Pretty bad.'

'Oh . . . Well, how was Rouche today?'

'Pretty bad.'

'Oh . . . And the rest of your day?' he tried hopefully.

Baxter's mind wandered: Wolf in handcuffs; her crying in a toilet cubicle; the stink of the infection eating away at her friend; consoling Maggie when she'd stopped by that afternoon . . .

'Pretty bad,' she answered, on the verge of tears again.

Dropping his satchel to the floor, Thomas rushed over to hold her.

She rested her exhausted head against his chest while the microwave beeped again.

'Want fish and chips tonight?' he asked her soothingly.

'That would be nice.'

He gave her a squeeze and headed for the door.

'Pour us some wine. I'll be back in fifteen minutes,' he told her.

Baxter smiled and followed him through to the lounge to the tap of pine needles on wrapping paper. He paused in the hallway.

'I know that today was hard. But it's done now. It's over, isn't it?'

She nodded: 'Yeah, it's over.'

Thomas smiled at her.

As the door clicked shut behind him, Baxter went back into the kitchen and poured herself a drink. She sat down at the table and pulled the creased file, fished from the interview-room bin, out of her bag and started to read.

It was *almost* over.

CHAPTER 4

Thursday 7 January 2016

8.08 a.m.

Wolf was trying to ignore the whispers and endless glances in his direction as he waited outside DCI Simmons's old office in Homicide and Serious Crime Command. No matter how long he stared at Baxter's name on the door, it looked wrong – a prank that he and Finlay might have pulled back in the day.

What had management been thinking?

What had Baxter been thinking?

'Morning, William!' Janet, the cleaner, greeted him. 'Cold out.'

A little surprised, Wolf nodded in agreement. Apparently the fact that he'd been on the run for the past eighteen months had completely passed her by. He allowed himself to enjoy this fleeting moment of normality, sitting outside the boss's office, making small talk as though none of it had ever happened. He concealed the handcuffs as best he could while she changed a bin bag beside him.

'How's Gary getting on at uni?' he asked her.

'Oh, he's a gay now!' she answered in delight.

'OK!' Wolf beamed back. 'And what's he studying again?' he asked, hoping to make the moment last just a little longer, but before she could reply, the door to the office opened and he was beckoned inside.

Wearing another sharp suit, Christian was already sitting at the desk. He gave Wolf a wink as he took a seat beside him.

'Your information panned out,' announced Vanita, assuming her seat behind Baxter's desk. 'An operation to round up Dubois and his crew is in progress as we speak, and the French coastguard have already intercepted the ship . . . Our deal stands.'

'Shall we uncuff the poor lad, then?' suggested Christian.

It looked to cause Vanita physical discomfort to hand over the key. Christian did the honours and then had to fake a coughing fit to disguise his laughter as he watched Wolf cuff her purple handbag to the frame of the desk.

'The paperwork is being prepared,' she informed Wolf, who looked up innocently, 'and should be ready for you to sign tomorrow. I expect you to check in with me *every* morning and afternoon. And, seeing as this arrangement cannot go on indefinitely, I'm imposing a timescale of five days to produce something tangible.'

Wolf went to argue.

'Much as it pains me to say,' she continued, 'you are a good detective, Fawkes. If you haven't found anything by then, then there isn't anything to find.'

He looked over to Christian for guidance, the wiser, more experienced man adopting Finlay's role in his stead. He nodded.

'Five days,' agreed Wolf.

With the white sky threatening to snow again, Baxter was sporting her ridiculous bobble hat and matching gloves set. Knocking on the flimsy shed door, she dislodged the home-made sign, which dropped face down onto the wet grass. There was a crash from inside, before Edmunds's confused face peered out, not expecting any visitors in his own back garden.

'Baxter!' he smiled, embracing her.

'Tia let me in,' she explained, stepping into the Alex Edmunds – Private Investigator nerve centre.

Edmunds picked up the stool he'd kicked over for her. 'I would offer you a coffee or something, but the hose froze up about a week ago,' he apologised. 'Did you want to head inside?'

'No, I'm fine,' Baxter assured him. 'Anyway, I'm actually here in an official capacity.'

'Oh? Aren't you still signed off work?'

'Yeah. Couple of weeks,' she said without elaborating further. She glanced around at the pictures of a particularly angry-looking ferret pinned over maps of Manhattan and crime-scene photographs of a burnt-out car, two ghostly figures still sitting inside. Feeling ill, she turned away. 'Case closed on Mr Scabs, then?' she asked, aware of Edmunds's ridiculous first assignment.

'*Actually*, at this particular time, he still remains "at large" . . . But I'll get him,' he said confidently, rubbing the enormous bruise on his thigh. 'Official capacity?' he prompted her, keen to change the subject from his inability to apprehend a small mammal. 'Are you here to arrest me?'

'Nope,' said Baxter, handing him the crumpled file. 'I'm here to *hire* you.'

After kicking off their shoes in the hallway, Wolf, Christian and Saunders received their obligatory rose-tinted kisses from Maggie.

Despite Wolf's protests, Saunders's involvement in the original investigation meant that they were stuck with him for the time being. However, on their journey out to Muswell Hill, he had learned that on the night of Finlay's death, Saunders had point-blank refused to leave Maggie's side until Baxter arrived to relieve him, which had raised Wolf's slowly building opinion of him yet another notch.

Wolf removed his coat and draped it over a kitchen chair, while Maggie prepared them drinks to a backing track of stilted conversation. When Christian and Saunders eventually headed upstairs, he held back to speak with her.

'If you need anything, you call to us. I don't want you up there today.'

She nodded and he squeezed her tightly, more for his own sake than hers. Following his colleagues up to the landing, Wolf approached the broken doorway, only to find two familiar faces already waiting for them inside.

'Fuck're you doin' 'ere?' asked Saunders, blissfully unaware of how many apostrophes he'd just squeezed into a five-word question.

'Swear jar!' Maggie called from downstairs. 'She made me promise not to tell you!'

Wolf caught the flicker of a smile cross Baxter's lips.

'Knew you'd come,' Wolf told her, but she didn't respond.

'Edmunds,' he said frostily.

'Wolf,' he replied, cooler still.

'Edmunds, this is Commissioner Christian Bellamy, an old friend of Finlay's,' said Baxter. 'Christian, this is Alex Edmunds, a private investigator,' she introduced him proudly.

The two men shook hands.

'Saunders,' said Saunders, offering his hand.

'Yeah,' said Edmunds in confusion. 'We know each other.'

Saunders looked blank.

'We worked together for, like, six months . . . The Ragdoll Murders?' Edmunds reminded him.

Still blank.

Suspecting it easier to just shake his hand, Edmunds just shook his hand.

'All right, Saunders,' said Wolf, stepping back to give him space, 'you're up.'

Removing his notebook, Saunders hesitated and then walked over to the damaged door to push it closed.

'The first of January, twelve thirty-five a.m., Detective Blake and myself get the call to back up a Constable Randle on a suspected suicide. We arrived at twelve fifty-six a.m. to find' – he cleared his throat – 'the body of a sixty-year-old male, positioned face down in the centre of the room, a single bullet wound to his left temple, a nine-millimetre firearm on the floor beside him.'

No one spoke, each occupied with their own thoughts as the dark stain on the floorboards dominated the room.

Saunders turned the page. 'Once photographs had been taken, the firearm was bagged for evidence. Forensics state only the victim's prints were present, consistent with him being left-handed, ballistics confirming it *was* the weapon the bullet had come from. On arrival at the scene, Constable Randle had to force entry to the property. On discovering an upstairs door locked, he then opened that by force as well, causing the damage seen round the doorway.' Saunders flipped another page. 'The body was discovered alone in a locked room, the only window secured from the inside . . . Conclusion: suicide.'

Wolf moved over to inspect the window, factory plastic still covering the lock from where it had never been opened.

'No note?' he asked.

'None discovered,' replied Saunders. 'As is the case in seven out of ten suicides.'

'Where was Maggie during all of this?' asked Edmunds, who was yet to finish reading through the file.

'With friends,' said Saunders. 'At a party in Hampstead.'

'Finlay hated New Year,' Wolf and Baxter chimed together.

He smiled. She didn't.

'So, who called it in?' Edmunds asked them.

'Finlay did. Using the landline in the hallway.' Saunders referred back to his notebook. 'At seven minutes past twelve, the Silent Solutions protocol was employed and a unit dispatched.'

'He didn't say anything?'

'No,' replied Saunders. 'But God knows what state of mind he must've been in by that point.' He looked to the commissioner expectantly.

'He seemed fine to me,' Christian smiled sadly. 'I was here with him earlier in the evening,' he explained. 'We put a pretty sizeable dent in a fresh bottle of whisky.'

Baxter recalled the crime-scene photographs, the low-quality bottle lying upturned on the floor – his retirement gift from the department.

'What did you discuss?' Edmunds asked Christian. 'If you don't mind me asking.'

'What do all old friends discuss when they get together at the holidays? Reminiscing about our adventures, who won which fight, the girls who broke our hearts,' he smiled. 'I missed a call from him just after midnight, which I will never forgive myself for. A few minutes later, I received this . . .'

Christian held up his phone:

Take care of her for me

'At which point, I panicked, jumped in a taxi and made my way back here as fast as I could. I arrived a few minutes after they'd kicked down the door,' he told them, staring at the floor as if he could still see Finlay lying there.

'He used his mobile to try to call you,' started Edmunds with a puzzled expression. 'Texts you from it. But then goes *downstairs* to phone 999 from the landline . . . Why?'

'I don't think he wanted Maggie to find him that way,' answered Christian, his voice breaking.

'And the landline would've made it easier to track the call,' added Saunders. 'Finlay would've known that.'

'Talk me through the door,' said Wolf, looking at the chunks of plaster ripped from the surrounding wall.

'This was intended to be the grandkids' new room, so there was no lock on the door.'

'But you said—'

'I know what I said,' Saunders interrupted him. 'Sealant. He'd sealed the door in place round the frame and floor, which is why it was so difficult to get in. Look, Wolf, with all due respect, this isn't going anywhere. He was found in a *completely* sealed room basically holding the weapon. It was suicide, mate.'

'It's not suicide until *I* say it's suicide,' Wolf spat back at him, conscious of Maggie downstairs.

Saunders raised his eyebrows at the others.

'Can you *not* hear yourself, Wolf?' Baxter asked him. 'You sound proper nuts.'

Admittedly, it was an insult, but at least she was talking to him now.

'He topped himself. I know my job, Wolf,' said Saunders, confidence in numbers.

Towering over his unimposing colleague, Wolf squared up to him.

'Will!' said Christian in the same tone Finlay always used to talk him down.

After a tense moment, he backed off and turned away.

'If you don't want to be here, Saunders, get out.'

Ill-advisedly, Saunders shoved Wolf in the back as he walked away. 'You think I don't care about this?!' he shouted. 'You think I don't want to be wrong?!'

Wolf had a dangerous look on his face as he turned round to face him.

'Finlay and my old man used to work together. Didn't know that, did you?' said Saunders. 'So when him and my mum split up and he decided to go and sit in the garage with the car engine running, guess who came to tell me the news, who stayed with me the entire night, who told me it wasn't my fault . . . I *do* fucking care!'

Wolf nodded in apology.

'Forgive me for asking the blatantly obvious,' blurted Baxter. 'But whose gun was it?'

Saunders picked his notebook up off the floor. 'No idea,' he answered. 'Beretta 92. Serial number filed off. As I already said, the only prints were Finlay's. I did speak to a mate in SO15 who reckons the gun's thirty-odd years old at least. It had been fired on numerous occasions, three bullets still in the clip . . . Could've come from anywhere.'

'And yet, for some reason, Finlay decided to keep it all these years,' said Edmunds, pondering out loud.

'I'm trusting you all with a little discretion here,' started Christian. 'But you don't get to mine and Finlay's age without collecting a few souvenirs along the way. Back in our day, things weren't as stringently recorded as they are now.'

Another silence descended over the room as they each attempted to negotiate a way around this looming dead end.

'OK. Can I get this last bit out the way?' said Saunders, looking sick. 'The autopsy showed several mild health issues. Nothing to worry about, just the usual old-person stuff.'

Everyone glanced in Christian's direction curiously.

'What?' he asked them.

'No other injuries that couldn't be attributed to general DIY bumps and bruises,' continued Saunders. 'Cause of death: a single gunshot to the head, bullet retrieved from the skull,' he finished uncomfortably. 'So where do we go from here?' he asked Wolf.

In the brief pause that followed, they heard Maggie pottering around in the kitchen, no doubt preparing them another round of drinks.

'They won't release his body until we sign off on this,' said Baxter. 'The longer we drag this out, the harder we make it on Maggie.'

'It takes as long as it takes,' said Wolf.

Baxter huffed and shook her head.

'The gun,' he mumbled, distracted. 'That's where the answers are, one way or another. Finlay kept it all this time for a reason. We need to work out what that reason was.'

'Your plan?' Saunders asked him.

'You get the gun and the bullet retrieved in the autopsy out of evidence. Tell forensics to run every test they can dream up. Any information they can give us might help,' Wolf instructed him. 'Baxter, you focus on Maggie. She'll talk to you. Even a subtle change in Finlay might be significant in some way. The usual stuff: anything that was playing on his mind, any old jobs that had resurfaced in his thoughts . . . And, more importantly, you need to find where he'd been stashing a live firearm all this time.'

She nodded curtly.

'I've already started looking through some of Finlay's past case files, but I could use some help,' he told Edmunds, who looked to

Baxter, but she didn't argue with the logical delegation of tasks. 'And, Christian, we'll keep you in the loop. We'll be coming to you to fill in the blanks that *might* have been omitted from the official reports, if that's all right?'

The commissioner nodded: 'Anything I can do to help.'

'One of Finlay's old stories is missing its murder weapon,' said Wolf. 'Let's work out which one.'

CHAPTER 5

'Fin! On your left,' hissed Christian. 'Your *other* left!'

They crept up to the peeling door of Flat 19, where a shiny lock had been placed over the gouged wood beneath. The entire building stank of week-old rubbish and urine. Even the light seemed reluctant to enter through the cracked window at the end of the corridor.

Leaning against his burnt arm, Finlay swore a little too loudly. Christian looked at him in exasperation.

'You need to get that looked at,' he whispered across the doorway. 'Let me see it.'

'Now?!' Finlay whispered back, pulling a face. 'Why do you always do this?'

'Do what?'

'Try to dispense medical advice on everyone you meet.'

'Everyone who?'

'Everyone, everyone!'

Christian reached for the cuff of his partner's short-sleeved shirt.

'Get off!' mouthed Finlay, slapping his hand away: 'Nice watch.'

'What can I say?' grinned Christian, admiring his new timepiece. 'I was in a celebratory mood.'

Still basking in the glory of his temporary celebrity status, Christian lapped up every drop of the adulation lavished upon him, while Finlay shrugged it off with a mixture of humour and self-deprecation, eager for a return to normality.

'What do you need a flashy thing like that for?' Finlay asked him, displaying his own modest example. 'Mine came from Woolies and works just fine.'

'It's four minutes slow.'

'Oh,' said Finlay, taking his hand back as Christian regarded his own ostentatious purchase.

'Was it Oscar Wilde who said: "The very last purpose of a gentleman's watch is to tell the time"?'

Finlay looked blank: 'I have absolutely no idea what that means.'

'No . . . Me neither,' admitted Christian, and they both sniggered.

'We doing this, then?' suggested Finlay.

While the burning warehouse was collapsing in the shipyard, a carjacking had taken place in nearby Whiteinch, the description of the injured assailant matching that of their mullet-haired suspect. The stolen Austin Princess had been found on Mathieson Terrace in the Gorbals with enough blood and fingerprints decorating the interior to keep the lab busy for weeks. But the vehicle's proximity to several of the city's most notorious addresses had, at least, given Finlay and Christian somewhere to start looking.

From there, using some less-than-official channels to source their information, it hadn't taken long to pinpoint the distinctive man's location: Brendall Towers on Cumberland Street, little more than a colossal squat house for addicts to while away their lives and for prostitutes to conduct their business.

Stepping out in front of the uninviting door, Christian limbered up, rolling his neck and shaking out his arms.

'First time,' he promised Finlay, who looked from his partner to the doorway and back again.

'Third . . . Loser picks up the tab tonight?'

'You're on.' Christian took a deep breath. 'Police!' he yelled, booting the lock with all his might, not that the door seemed to

notice. Limping slightly, he ignored Finlay's bored expression and
went to kick it again. 'Police! . . . Son of a *bitch*!' he complained,
slumping against the wall.

'Think he's heard you coming yet?' joked Finlay, who stepped
up, baton raised. He was just about to hammer against the wood
when he thought he'd try the handle instead, which twisted freely
in his hand as the door swung open.

'Shut up!' snapped Christian as he hobbled in behind his
partner.

The rancid room wasn't improved any by the dead body
sprawled across the floor. Lying on its front, the recognisable
hairstyle was on full display, a fittingly lethal-looking hunting
knife embedded in its back.

'Well, that's a crying shame,' said Finlay insincerely as he looked
around the poky bedsit.

There were clear signs of a struggle: furniture in pieces, broken
glass underfoot. Flies were buzzing in and out of a blackened pan
on the stove.

Christian looked a little disappointed: 'So, he *can* be killed.'

'Looks that way. I'll do the honours, then, shall I?' huffed
Finlay, patting down the man's corpse. He pulled a wallet from
his back pocket. 'Ruben de Wees,' he announced, unfolding the
foreign driving licence. He walked over to join Christian by the
window to appreciate their view of refuse bins and kitchen staff
on a cigarette break. 'He was Dutch apparently . . .'

Christian made a disinterested noise.

'Till he popped his clogs,' Finlay added, watching his friend
shake his head while simultaneously trying not to laugh.

'Right,' said Christian, having his fill of the uninspiring vista.
'Let's go call this in and . . .' He paused. 'Errm . . . did you at
any point happen to check for a pulse while you were feeling
him up?'

Confused, Finlay turned back round.

The body was gone, a trail of bloody spots disappearing out
through the door.

He turned to Christian in horror. 'He had a huge *bloody* great knife sticking out his back!' he said defensively, as they bundled through the door and into the hallway, following the bloodstains to the stairwell.

'I'm thinking,' panted Christian, clearly enjoying himself as they raced down the stairs, 'we try a wooden stake to the heart next time!'

Somewhere below, a heavy door slammed shut.

Less than ten seconds behind, Finlay and Christian burst free of the gloom and into the dazzling greyness, the building having spat them out into an alleyway. Their resurrected suspect was only twenty paces away as he staggered towards the High Street with the hunting knife still in situ.

'Excuse me, Ruben?!' Christian called after him. 'This has got to be one of the saddest escape attempts we've ever seen!'

The flagging Dutchman summoned the strength to give them the finger.

'That was rude,' laughed Finlay.

They started ambling after him as he slowed a little with every agonising step, lurching out onto the busy street to an appropriate chorus of screams and panic. Taking their time, Finlay and Christian emerged from the alleyway to restore calm.

'Move back, please!'

'Give us some space.'

'Could somebody phone for an ambulance?'

They shook their heads pityingly as the man started crawling away, his broken arm dragging uselessly along the pavement, while the traffic on the main road rushed past as normal. Finlay's digital watch beeped, announcing four minutes past a new hour as the Dutchman dropped to the ground.

'Be my guest,' Finlay told his partner, gesturing to their suspect.

But as Christian stepped forward, he struggled back up to his knees, groping blindly until he grasped the handle of the deep-rooted blade.

'I *really* would leave that where it is!' suggested Christian, ignoring Finlay's smirk as he dispensed yet another invaluable piece of medical advice.

The man cried out in pain as, bit by bit, he started to work the blade free.

'Whoa! Whoa! Whoa!' yelled Christian, running in to restrain him too late.

The man lashed out, hair whipping across his face as Christian fell back onto the pavement, holding his hands over a deep gash in his side.

'Stay there, Christian!' ordered Finlay as the Dutchman wobbled back onto his feet, a constant trickle of blood pouring from the corner of his mouth.

Finlay raised his baton.

'Stay back!' the man warned the watching crowd. He glanced behind at the busy main road, realising that he could beat the number 7 pulling into the bus stop . . .

. . . but not the Citroën 2CV overtaking it.

There was a hollow thud as the tyres squealed, tangling the man's limp body up in the wheels as they rolled him out of human form.

Finlay took a few seconds to process what had happened. Moving on autopilot, he stepped out into the road to stop the traffic, before escorting the Citroën's dazed driver to the kerb. He crouched down beside Christian. 'You still with us?'

'Yeah, it's nothing,' smiled Christian, looking pale.

Slapping him heartily on the back, Finlay returned to the car. Reaching under the chassis, he handcuffed one of the twisted arms to the metal bumper.

'What are you doing?' Christian called over to him. 'His head's the wrong way round!'

Lighting up a cigarette, Finlay took a seat on the edge of the pavement, eyes fixed on their deceased prisoner as sirens approached in the distance. 'Aye . . . but I'm not taking any chances.'

Finlay shuddered as he watched the doctor sew up Christian's wound. The way that the skin tented just before the hooked needle punctured through was mesmerising, despite making him feel quite ill.

'An eventful week for you two,' noted the doctor, muffled by the bushiness of his own moustache. 'That should do it,' he said, trimming the remaining thread before admiring his handiwork. 'Beautiful.'

Christian looked down at the damage. 'Beautiful' apparently meant looking as though you had a piece of Hornby train track glued to your side.

'Cheers, Doc,' he said, underwhelmed.

'Let's take a look at you, then, shall we?' said the doctor, turning to Finlay. He peeled off the dirty self-prescribed bandage, which stuck in several places to the two-day-old burn. He pulled a face: 'The next time you receive third-degree burns, *perhaps* consider popping in to see us.'

'Will do,' nodded Finlay.

Pulling off his gloves, the moustached man scribbled some notes.

'I'll have a nurse come and clean that up,' he said, gesturing to Christian's large stitches, 'and do *something* with *that*,' he added, tutting at Finlay on his way out.

Christian stared down at his impressive injury. 'That's gonna leave one hell of a scar,' he grinned.

'This is the greatest week of your little life, isn't it?' said Finlay as the curtain pulled back and a beautiful young nurse entered, tray in hand, dark curls springing out from beneath her white hospital hat.

Transfixed, Finlay thought she looked like autumn personified: her singed-chestnut hair, rosy lips and sparkling blue eyes. Christian shot him an approving look, not that he noticed, unable to tear his eyes away from her.

'So, which one of you is Finlay?' she asked.

She sounded like the queen.

'Come on. That wasn't a hard one. Finlay? Any takers?'

'Yes. I . . . am Finlay,' he said, attempting to suppress his harsh Glaswegian accent.

Christian gave him a strange look.

She collected up what she needed from the tray, smiled sweetly and then clipped him round the ear.

'Gah!' he complained.

'Doctor's orders,' she told him unapologetically. 'In future, don't leave things. It just makes more work for us.'

'Shite!' he grimaced, unsure how she'd managed to make it hurt so much.

'And no swearing!' she added. 'Nurse's orders.'

Taking a seat on the bed beside him, she smelled of strawberries and chocolate, forcing Finlay to fake a cold when he sniffed the air a little too obviously.

'Don't you recognise us?' asked Christian as she dabbed at Finlay's arm.

'Should I?'

'Suppose not. It was only the largest drugs bust in Scottish history . . . Not like it was a big deal or anything.'

She looked up at Finlay inquisitively.

He held his breath, regretting the cheese-and-onion pasty he'd had at lunch.

'The fire at the shipyard,' she said, recalling the front-page story of the *Herald*. 'Something along the lines of . . . within fifteen minutes, you two had recovered five years' worth of heroin.'

'They exaggerate,' said Christian modestly.

'Oh?'

'Yeah . . . In fact, it only took us about ten!' he grinned, making her laugh.

She smiled up at Finlay. She was the most beautiful thing he'd ever seen. Holding his arm up, she wrapped a bandage round the fresh dressings. 'He's a one, your friend, isn't he?'

'Certainly is,' replied Finlay gruffly, suspecting their definition of 'a one' didn't quite align.

'OK, Fin,' she said. 'You're all done.'

Turning her attention to Christian, she wore a wry smile as he lay down obediently on the bed.

'I am *all* yours!' he told her eagerly.

'It was a pleasure!' blurted Finlay. 'To meet you, I mean.'

The nurse looked back at him, a little surprised to be confronted with a formal handshake. Christian huffed impatiently as she removed her gloves to take Finlay's rough hand.

'But it was an *honour* meeting you!' she said with a mischievous twinkle in her eye. 'I'm Maggie.'

CHAPTER 6

Thursday 7 January 2016
2.21 p.m.

Wolf made a strange snort-cough.

Edmunds glanced at him over the top of his case file. After a few moments, his eyes dropped back to the task at hand. But then Wolf started to chuckle, reading through the official report of Ruben de Wees and his inexcusable hairstyle's prolonged demise. Watching him impatiently, Edmunds wore an expression even Baxter would have been proud of.

'Sorry,' said Wolf. 'Finlay's been telling me this story for as long as I can remember, but it still makes me laugh.'

Rolling his eyes, Edmunds returned to his yellowed pages while Wolf treated himself to a stretch, filling the quiet with a series of groans and yawns as he regarded the Homicide and Serious Crime meeting room. The two grotesque photographic reconstructions of the Ragdoll had been taken down long ago, but apart from that, very little had changed. Even the crack in the glass wall was still there.

'I never did apologise about your head, did I?' asked Wolf.

Giving up, Edmunds tossed the file onto the table: 'No. No, you didn't.'

Wolf opened his mouth . . . but then just shrugged.

Edmunds laughed bitterly.

'Come on. Out with it,' said Wolf, turning his chair round to give Edmunds his undivided attention. 'Speak your mind.'

He watched Edmunds chewing over the words in his head.

'You think I'm a bad person? This is some sort of . . . *moral* issue you're having?' guessed Wolf, as though he wasn't entirely sure he was using the word correctly. 'OK. Yes, I did *inadvertently* commission the services of a deranged serial killer.' He raised his hands in surrender. 'That one's on me. Did I purposely hinder your investigation in order to protect myself? Well . . . yeah, I suppose I did that too. Did I *almost* beat said serial killer to death well after he'd given up? Uh-huh. But . . .' He looked lost. 'What was my point again?'

Edmunds shook his head and picked the file back up.

'If it makes you feel any better,' continued Wolf, 'the second this is over, Vanita will have me arrested. The bad man will pay for his sins.'

'That's not it,' mumbled Edmunds.

'Say what?'

'I said: "That's not it"!' he snapped. 'I mean, it is. I think you're an evil piece of shit who deserves to rot in a cell for what few good years you still have left . . . But that's not it.'

Wolf was amazed by how much he sounded like Baxter.

Edmunds closed his eyes and exhaled deeply.

'The Ragdoll case was mine,' he explained, a little embarrassed. '*I* was the one who turned the archives upside down looking for Masse's past victims. It was *me* who proved that the Faustian Murders were real. *I* was the one who saw you for what you really were . . . *I* did it all.'

Wolf listened patiently as he continued.

'You had your glory case. It was an unparalleled mess, granted, but you, William Fawkes, hunted down and captured the Cremation Killer. You, Masse and the Ragdoll investigation was *my* moment . . . and you took that from me.'

Edmunds felt a weight lift. It was the first time he had admitted out loud that his anger burned with a more selfish hue than he'd been professing.

Wolf nodded, not in the least bit surprised by the admission.

'You're the smartest of all of us.'

'Don't patronise me.'

'Because you got out,' he continued. 'This job is . . .' He puffed out his cheeks. 'It's no good for anyone. It's a drug, an addiction you know could kill you at any given moment. You get so obsessed with the highs that you stop noticing it tearing every other aspect of your life apart until there's nothing left.'

Neither of them spoke for a moment, the truth in Wolf's words returning their thoughts to Finlay and the certainty that, whether by foul play or his own hand, the job had contributed in some way to his untimely death.

'I wish I'd had the guts to leave before it was too late,' Wolf told him sincerely. 'Now it is.'

'It's easy to say that when you're not the idiot chasing ferrets around Sainsbury's car park for your first pay packet.'

'And investigating the possible homicide of a colleague for your second,' Wolf reminded him.

Edmunds watched Wolf's face grow dark as his thoughts returned to Finlay and the case file he had found so hilarious only minutes earlier. He had spent the previous eighteen months fantasising about tracking Wolf down, dragging him from whatever hole he'd been hiding in and before a court of law to stand accountable for his actions. He had imagined his colleagues and the media heralding him the hero that they should have all along, building Wolf up into some sort of phantasm in his head. But now, watching him seek desperately for meaning, for demons that probably weren't even there, he just saw a man who had lost everything.

'What?' asked Wolf when he noticed Edmunds staring.

'Nothing.'

They both returned to their work.

'Sorry about the head,' mumbled Wolf.

'Don't worry about it.'

Saunders was trying to breathe through his mouth.

The air in the forensic lab always had a bite of metal and death to it. The shiny utensils and bleach-streaked floors felt a little too immaculate, like a bloodbath hastily wiped clean.

'Shit,' said Joe, the bald-headed forensic medical examiner, slopping coffee over himself as he entered. 'That's gonna stain.'

Saunders watched him wipe at a small spot on an apron soiled with dried blood, brain matter and God knows what else, before realising he had a guest.

'Dammit,' he spat on seeing Saunders.

'Afternoon to you too.'

'Sorry. I was hoping you'd be the elusive DCI Baxter,' grinned Joe. 'Could've left the dirty apron on,' he lamented out loud.

Saunders didn't even want to imagine what that looked like.

'Wouldn't get your hopes up, mate,' he told Joe. 'From what I can tell, there's a bit of a queue forming there.'

Ignoring the comment, Joe set his coffee down and started rummaging through the box that Saunders had booked out of evidence.

'My favourite!' he exclaimed. 'Repetition of work! So, you want me to reconfirm that all the forensic evidence supports suicide?'

'No,' said Saunders. 'We want you to find us anything to suggest that it *wasn't*.'

'In a locked room?'

'Yes.'

'With no sign of a struggle?'

'Yes.'

'And he was holding the weapon?'

'Yes! Just find us something!'

Suddenly, Joe looked deep in thought, as though something were troubling him.

'What is it?' Saunders asked hopefully.

'What did you mean when you said: "There's a bit of a queue forming there"?'

Christian only had time for a 'walk and talk' as he marched between one meeting and another. Wolf and Edmunds were waiting for him outside the lifts and had to skip the pleasantries as they hurried across the atrium.

'Are we sure the invincible Dutchman was the only person to escape the warehouse?' Edmunds asked him.

Christian smiled at the memory. He had recited the story as many times over the years as Finlay.

'As far as I'm concerned, yes,' he answered as his entourage held doors open for them. 'Unbeknown to us, the entire laboratory was already an inferno. There was a blueprint knocking around. Perhaps it was in the file? Basically, all but two of the exits would have been unreachable, and I'm positive we'd have seen anyone trying to get out down our end.'

'The infiltrating team were armed with automatic weapons,' said Edmunds. 'But an assortment of others were recovered from the fire. We want to work out whose were whose. Anything come to mind that might help us?'

'Nothing, I'm afraid,' shrugged Christian. 'I'd guess that the Dutch would have all had matching equipment. They seemed well kitted out, if memory serves. So you could probably make an educated guess.'

'But do you think it's possible that—'

'Look,' Christian cut Edmunds off, to the horror of his minions pausing to address him. 'I think you're barking up the wrong tree here. I was there. I was with Fin the whole time. I'd have known if he'd come away with anything more than a badly burnt arm. There was no reason for him to keep anything from that job. You've got the wrong case . . . I'm sorry.'

'Sir.' A young man with a sycophantic smile approached them. 'We *really* do need to—'

Christian glared at him.

Almost bowing, the man grinned as if he'd just been given a treat and backed away.

'Wolf, a moment in private?' asked Christian.

Edmunds gave them some space.

'A word to the wise: that document Vanita's having drawn up has so many workarounds and loopholes in the wording, I'm not convinced it's going to be worth the paper it's printed on.'

'I'm sure that's just an oversight on her part,' quipped Wolf.

'Quite. Well, with your blessing, I'll have someone "in the know" go over it with a fine-tooth comb.'

Wolf nodded appreciatively, receiving a slap to the back as Christian headed into his next meeting.

Avoiding the upstairs of her own home, Maggie had set to work packing away the Christmas decorations. Before leaving, Edmunds and Saunders had made a meal out of carrying the dying tree outside, sharing far more expletives (courtesy of Saunders) and blood (courtesy of Edmunds) than strictly necessary. While Maggie carefully tissue-wrapped the more fragile ornaments, Baxter unstuck the remaining decorations from the ceiling.

'How are you holding up, sweetie?' Maggie asked her.

'Fine.'

She continued packing up her box, looking a little more her normal self, her dark curls tied up in Finlay's favourite style.

'I told you he'd come back,' Maggie smiled.

'You did.'

'For you.'

Baxter ripped a chunk of paint from the ceiling along with the glittery snowman.

'He came back for Finlay, no one else,' she told Maggie firmly.

'You detectives,' the older woman laughed. 'So good at spotting things in everyone else but blind when it comes to each other.'

'Where are these going?' asked Baxter, changing the subject as she dropped the snowman and piece of ceiling into a shoebox.

'In the garage, please.'

Carrying the boxes through the house that seemed so large and empty all of a sudden, Baxter wondered whether Maggie would even want to stay there once this was all over. Entering the chilly garage, she stopped briefly to admire Finlay's old Harley-Davidson. Using a broom to bat down a worryingly large cobweb, she pushed the stack of boxes against the back wall and got up to leave, when she spotted something she recognised.

Lying at the top of another open box, the aged photograph had captured her, Finlay, Benjamin Chambers and Wolf somehow managing to enjoy an office Christmas party. Sadness washed over her as she looked at the happy faces of the two friends they had lost along the way. Peering inside, she realised the box contained the contents of Finlay's work desk, cleared out on his retirement a month earlier. Lifting it off the pile, she placed it on the floor to go through the items one by one: the accumulated crap of years of collecting.

There were other photographs: the grandchildrens' school pictures, Finlay and Maggie outside the Vatican, a black-and-white photograph of a young Finlay and Christian posing beside a tower of white powder while a building burned in the background.

She set it to one side.

She found colourful scribbled drawings, bits of stationery, a certificate to confirm that he had (eventually) passed the Met's political-correctness training and a letter, dated 1995, informing him that he would be supervising a trainee named William Layton-Fawkes. Smiling, she then paused on unfolding a torn scrap of card scribbled in Finlay's recognisable handwriting:

How do you still not fucking get this yet?

I don't just love you. I unreservedly, unremittingly and hopelessly adore you.

You are mine.

And none of these fucking people, none of the horrible shit that's happened between us, not even these fucking bars, are going to keep us apart, because no one is ever, ever taking you away from me.

Frowning, she read the note again, sensing the desperation behind the words. Although feeling a little guilty for having seen something so personal, Baxter couldn't shake the niggling doubt that this obscenity-filled declaration of love had not been penned for Maggie.

Almost wishing she hadn't found it, she folded the note in half, picked up the black-and-white photograph and shoved them both into her back pocket.

CHAPTER 7

Friday 8 January 2016

7.05 a.m.

'What's the time, Mr Wolf?'

Wolf groaned and pulled the scratchy blanket up over his head. He heard the cell door unlock, followed by the sound of footsteps negotiating the obstacle course of dirty washing and case files he'd left strewn across the floor.

The intruder cleared their throat.

Slowly pulling the blanket away from his eyes, he was greeted by a familiarly creased face smiling down at him: George was the mild-mannered custody officer at Paddington Green Police Station, the six-by-ten-foot cell Wolf's temporary home for the duration of the case.

'Didn't think you'd want to miss out on breakfast,' said George, handing him a tray of slimy brownish eggs and cardboard toast.

'You didn't?' asked Wolf, suspecting there was something very, very wrong with the chicken responsible.

'Don't play with your food,' the older man told him, while looking around at the mess their guest had made of his limited space. 'Think you might have a bit of a tidy-up before you head out?' he suggested.

'No time,' mumbled Wolf through a mouthful of toast as he stood up to pull his trousers on.

George averted his eyes: 'This isn't a hotel, you know.'

'I know that,' said Wolf defensively, tossing the custody officer his damp towels before wincing at the bitter coffee. 'Two clean ones, please, when you've got a moment.'

'Right away, *sir*.'

Rummaging through the files on the floor, Wolf eventually found the one he was looking for. He placed it on the bed and picked up a crumpled white shirt.

'How's your ironing?' he asked optimistically.

'Neither am I your mum.'

'Worth a try,' smiled Wolf, tossing it onto a pile and stumbling over the mess into the corridor.

'Aren't we forgetting something?' George called after him, following him out, footprint-marked folder in hand.

Still tucking himself in, Wolf hurried back to the doorway. He swapped the folder for his coffee cup and then planted a kiss on George's wrinkly cheek.

'*Ah!*' the custody officer complained, wiping his face. 'I'm not your mum!'

Wolf grinned: 'See you tonight!'

'What time shall I expect you?'

'You're not my mum!' Wolf reminded him as he disappeared round the corner.

An exasperated George collected up the half-eaten breakfast. On his way back out, he hesitated and then, with a hefty sigh, scooped up the pile of shirts that needed ironing.

'Where's Christian?' asked Wolf, taking a seat. 'He was meant to be here.'

A smug-looking lawyer was smiling at him, which experience had taught him was never a good sign. Vanita closed the door and joined them at the table.

'The *commissioner*,' she said pointedly, 'is otherwise engaged.'

Wolf flicked through the wedge of paperwork in front of him. 'He wanted someone else to look over this.'

'I can't see why that would be necessary, and, clearly, neither did he, seeing as he isn't here,' replied Vanita. 'Mr Briton drew up the papers himself.'

'That's what I'm worried about,' Wolf told her, leaning back in his chair to regard the man sitting opposite. 'My dad only ever gave me one decent piece of advice. Would you like me to share it with you?'

'No,' tried Vanita.

'*Never* trust a man who smiles before eleven a.m.,' Wolf shared anyway, pushing the papers away from him. 'I don't like lawyers.'

'That's fine,' grinned the man.

'Therefore . . . I don't like *you*.'

'Also fine.'

Wolf leaned in closer. 'Want to hear the story about the last time I was in a courtroom with too many self-righteous lawyers grinning at me?'

The smile dropped.

'I won't be signing anything until I get a second opinion,' said Wolf.

Vanita had clearly been anticipating the response. 'Then I regret to inform you that our "agreement" is no longer in place.'

She looked to the slick-haired lawyer, who collected his documents and stood up for dramatic effect.

'The Metropolitan Police thanks you for your tip-off regarding Léo Dubois,' she told Wolf, opening the door to two uniformed officers, who entered the room, handcuffs at the ready.

'Look, Mr Fawkes, it's quite simple,' started the lawyer, his arrogance returning with the arrival of the officers. 'No signature means no agreement. No agreement means you are a fugitive again. And being a fugitive again means you will be arrested immediately and thrown on the mercy of the courts.'

'Alternatively,' started Vanita, unfittingly filling the role of 'good cop', 'sign on the dotted line, spend the next few days looking into the death of DS Shaw and retain your investigation into Dubois as a bargaining chip . . . It doesn't sound like a hard decision to me.'

She produced a beautiful new pen from her blouse pocket and held it out. The lawyer slid the paperwork back in front of him, open on the signature page.

Vanita had him over a barrel and they all knew it.

Wolf took the weighty fountain pen from her, sticking it straight into his mouth as he reread the incomprehensible final page one last time before scribbling his name at the bottom.

'Happy?' he asked her, offering her back the wet pen.

'Keep it,' she told him, collecting up the signed document, her possessions and her beaming lawyer before marching out of the room.

With the others not due until mid-morning, Baxter had been the first to arrive at Maggie's. She had used the extra time to help with the cleaning, an excuse to thoroughly search the house for anywhere that Finlay might have stashed a weapon from his house-proud wife.

At 10.38 a.m., she heard the letter box snap and went through to collect the pile of post from the doormat. Finlay's newspaper had been pushed through, along with a Domino's Pizza menu, three cards – no doubt expressing sympathies – and an envelope with bold, red writing plastered across the front:

FINAL DEMAND. DO NOT IGNORE.

Placing the other post on the sideboard, Baxter took the threatening letter into the kitchen. Deliberating for a moment, she came to the conclusion that she wouldn't be doing her job if she didn't look into every possible lead.

'Cup of tea, Maggie?' she called down the hallway.

'Please!'

Balancing the envelope face up over the spout, Baxter switched the kettle on and began preparing their drinks.

The glue clung desperately to the paper as she carefully pulled it apart to remove the credit-card statement covered in red print. The

sole transaction was a transfer from another card, and she gasped
on reading the outstanding balance at the bottom of the page.

'Jesus, Finlay,' she muttered, feeling ill.

With a new-found determination, Baxter set to work searching
every last inch of the downstairs rooms, logic dictating that this
illuminating demand for payment must have corresponding counterparts to explain the crippling amount of debt that her friend
had accumulated. Pulling up a chair to check on top of the kitchen
cupboards, she found only lint and dead spiders. She discovered
an entire feast of out-of-date food occupying the topmost shelves
but nothing more. Climbing back down, she prised the kickboards
away from the bottoms of the units, creating a cloud of dust.

She then moved into the hallway and inspected the basket of
fire logs before looking beneath the shoe cabinet. Confident she
had already thoroughly searched the living room, she opened the
door to the cold garage. Able to disregard the boxes that she
and Maggie had packed themselves, she shuffled past the pristine
Harley-Davidson to reach the adjacent stack.

She turned back to the motorcycle. Maggie had always hated it.

Crouching down, Baxter ran her hands over the custom satin-
black exhaust shields, the vinyl backrest, finding nothing out of
place. She climbed onto the seat, inspecting the analogue dials
before feeling her way down the bike's metal curves for something
. . . anything.

The seat rocked ever so slightly beneath her.

Jumping back off, she traced her fingertips along the padding
until she located a catch. One satisfying click later, she was able
to lift the top of the seat completely away to expose the storage
compartment inside.

One by one, the team arrived at the house, each claiming a spot in
the crowded kitchen to consume their mandatory drink and freshly
baked croissant. Saunders had been thoughtful enough to bring
another shopping bag of essentials, which he unpacked into the
cupboards while Edmunds buried his head in a file as per usual.

Christian was regaling the room with a story about Finlay and him once losing their trainee constable for two whole days, Maggie laughing along as though she'd never heard it before. Baxter was only half listening as she waited anxiously for an opportune moment to share her discovery with the others.

The front door rattled, interrupting Christian's flow, and Wolf appeared in the kitchen doorway. He gave Baxter a wink in greeting, presumably intended to annoy her, which of course it did. But determined to deprive him of the satisfaction, she just smiled back sweetly, which looked to confuse him no end.

Embracing Maggie, Wolf turned his attention to Christian. '*Thanks* for earlier.'

'You are very welcome.'

Wolf faltered: 'That was a sarcastic "thanks", as in "Where the hell were you?"'

Now Christian was stumped.

'This morning . . . with Vanita,' clarified Wolf.

'Yes, I know. I sent Luke . . . my lawyer,' said Christian, frowning. 'I spoke with Geena about it first thing . . . He wasn't there?'

Wolf shook his head.

Christian puffed out his cheeks: 'That woman is a piece of work. You signed it?'

'Had no choice.'

'I'll sort it.'

With the conversation reaching its natural conclusion, it became impossible to ignore the reason that had brought five past and present homicide detectives to their old friend's kitchen. Taking her cue, Maggie excused herself to meet a friend for coffee.

The moment he heard the front door close, Wolf jumped straight in. 'Strathclyde Police are dragging their feet with some of the old case files,' he told Christian. 'Think you could put a bit of pressure on them?'

'I'll call them this morning.'

'Saunders?' Wolf prompted.

'The gun's back with the lab, along with the rest of the evidence. I checked in an hour ago: so far, nothing to suggest anything different to before.'

'Tell them to keep looking,' instructed Wolf. 'Edmunds found something interest—'

At that moment, Baxter pulled the stack of paperwork out from behind her and tossed it across the table, the capitalised red lettering against the white paper silencing Wolf as effectively as a bloodstained rag.

'Finlay was going under,' she announced.

Even Edmunds resurfaced from his file, this latest development taking precedence.

'There's at least a hundred grand's worth of debt there,' she explained.

Something made her glance in Wolf's direction, but she immediately regretted doing so: he looked as though the bottom had just dropped out of his world.

'From what I can gather,' continued Baxter, 'Maggie has no idea.'

Christian cleared his throat: 'Does she . . . have to?'

'They're talking about repossessing the house. Most of it looks to be her private healthcare. There's the extension, of course, and then a final flurry on that new car out on the drive.'

Wolf picked up one of the overdue bills and turned to Christian. 'Did you know about this?'

He shook his head.

'Has anybody looked into Finlay's life insurance yet?' asked Edmunds.

'Would they even pay out on a suicide?' Christian asked him.

'Depends,' replied Edmunds, regarding the tower of debt in front of him. 'Normally after a certain period they will.'

Wolf screwed up the bill and dropped it to the floor: 'This doesn't prove anything.'

'Stop it, Wolf,' mumbled Baxter.

'He could've—'

'Just stop, Wolf.'

'But what if—'

'Will!' she yelled in frustration. She met his eye and held his gaze for the first time since his return: 'It's over. You need to accept this. You *need* to let him go.'

Looking around at the defeated expressions on the faces of his colleagues, Wolf snatched his coat off the worktop and stormed out of the house, slamming the front door behind him.

'How much?' asked Maggie in a strained whisper, the teacup rattling against the saucer in her shaking hands.

She had returned home to a silent house to find Baxter waiting for her, a pile of paperwork sitting ominously on the kitchen table.

'A lot.'

'How much, Emily?'

'A lot. It doesn't matter,' Baxter insisted. 'I had a look through Finlay's insurance documents . . . and I'm pretty sure it'll all be taken care of.'

Maggie stared blankly into space. 'He always told me it was covered by our private healthcare.'

'He wanted you to have the very best.'

'I'd rather have him.'

Baxter refused to cry again. It felt as though she'd spent half her waking hours in tears of late.

'Do you . . . do you think that's why he . . . why he . . . ?'

Baxter nodded and had to wipe her eyes.

Maggie started absent-mindedly flicking through the pile, exposing the aged photograph of Finlay and Christian in front of the burning warehouse.

'Sorry. That's not meant to be in there,' said Baxter guiltily, having taken it without permission.

Maggie handed it over with a smile, remembering how she'd bandaged up her husband's arm the first time they ever met. But then she frowned and picked up a tatty piece of card decorated in Finlay's clumsy handwriting:

How do you still not fucking get this yet?

Baxter leaped from her seat and reached across the table, but Maggie held the brief note just beyond her reach, her brow furrowing as she continued to read.

'Maggie, don't!' she gasped, knocking over her tea as she struggled to free her long legs from the bench.

But it was too late.

Maggie's eyes darted down the eight scrawled lines and then she folded it up, handing it back to Baxter.

'I am so, so sorry . . . Wait, you're smiling!' said Baxter, confused.

'I was just thinking: that would have been four pounds in the swear jar and a clip round the ear if he was still here.'

'He . . . wrote that for you?' asked Baxter.

'Oh, most certainly not. I've never seen it before.'

'But . . .' Baxter was bewildered by Maggie's apparent disinterest in her husband's impassioned outpouring of love for an unknown third party. 'Aren't you . . . *upset*? Not that I want you to be.'

'No, dear.'

'Curious, then?'

'No, dear. Whatever this is, I'm sure there's a perfectly reasonable explanation . . . I'll get a dishcloth for that,' she said, standing up from the table.

'But it's written in his handwriting!' blurted Baxter, unable to help herself.

'Oh, undoubtedly.'

'So how can you not want to know?'

Maggie laughed and took hold of Baxter's hands, sensing that her friend needed to hear that Finlay was still the man she believed him to be. Reverting effortlessly into the maternal role that she had been deprived the past week, Maggie welcomed this fleeting return to normality.

'Emily, if there is just *one* thing on this earth I know for certain

. . . that I would stake my life on without a breath of hesitation . . . it's that Fin loved me just about as much as anyone can love another person.' She squeezed Baxter's hands tightly and then smiled. 'Now, how about another tea?'

CHAPTER 8

Friday 9 November 1979

11.10 a.m.

Christian groaned in frustration.

He sat up and slapped himself in the face to prevent returning to his daydream.

'I can't get that nurse out of my head,' he shared as Finlay drove them along Glasgow's Cochrane Street, dirty drizzle collecting on the window, the depressing scene luring his thoughts elsewhere. 'What was her name again? Megan? Mandy?'

'Maggie,' replied Finlay gruffly, bringing his word count for the day up into double figures.

'Maggie!' Christian nodded. 'Of course. Beautiful Maggie with the magnificent arse!'

Tensing, Finlay had to bite his tongue as they rolled towards the address scribbled on a scrap of paper and propped up against a dog-eared map book.

'Ooooo! She's nice!' remarked Christian, gawking at someone out on the street, as usual treating the journey as some sort of urban pervert's safari.

Finlay had had enough. 'There's a lot more to her than just her "magnificent arse"!'

Interest piqued, Christian glanced back at the woman they'd passed.

'Not her!' snapped Finlay angrily. 'Maggie!'

Christian looked utterly lost: 'You mean like . . . *boobs* and stuff?'

'You really are a complete gobshite, aren't you?!'

'What's got into you?'

'Nothing.'

The queue of traffic slowed to a stop at the junction.

'Oh! Hang on a minute,' said Christian. 'I know what this is: *you* like her!'

Finlay ignored him.

'You do, don't you?' he laughed out loud, enraging Finlay further and earning himself a swift thump to the kidneys. 'I'm sorry. I shouldn't laugh,' he said, rubbing his side. 'I guess I just think you should play to your strengths.'

'Meaning?'

Christian smirked: 'Meaning . . . that if she came equipped with a dog and a white stick, you might *actually* stand a hope in hell.'

That comment justified a proper punch to the gut.

Winded and spluttering, Christian bent double, resting his head against the dashboard just as the windscreen cracked above his head.

Finlay looked uncomprehendingly from the eviscerated headrest to the innumerable fault lines snaking across the glass, all blooming outwards from a single circular hole.

'Fin!' yelled Christian, dragging his partner down as three more bullets impacted their patrol car's metal shell in quick succession.

There were shouts out on the street as people ran for cover.

Finlay and Christian looked at one another as they cowered beneath the dashboard.

'Get us out of here!' Christian yelled at him.

Sitting up as much as he dared, Finlay crunched the gearstick into reverse. He stamped on the accelerator, ploughing them into the van behind, the collision shattering the weakened windscreen across the bonnet and dash.

There were two more metallic pops as the gunfire resumed.

'Go, Fin!'

The gears grated harshly, the wheels spinning against the wet tarmac as Finlay pulled them out of the stationary traffic and onto the other side of the road. Barely able to control the damaged car, they jumped the kerb and careered across George Square, slamming into the bronze statue of Thomas Graham.

Head bleeding, Christian reached for the radio on the glass-covered floor. As he held it up to his mouth, the guts of the main unit dangled uselessly from the other end of the cord. 'Guess we're on our own.'

'Well, we can't stay here,' said Finlay.

He attempted to force his buckled door open, the bent metal refusing to budge, while Christian's exit was blocked by the base of the statue.

'This way!' shouted Christian, using the temporary reprieve from the shooting to clamber out through the absent windscreen and over the sparkling bonnet.

Finlay followed his partner out into the open square, buildings surrounding them on all sides, the church-like tower of the city chambers an ominous omen against the dark sky as they each took cover behind a tree.

'We need a phone box!' panted Finlay.

'Other side of the square,' Christian called back as the gunfire returned. 'What the *hell's* going on this week?' he yelled over the noise.

'Karma,' replied Finlay, as the gunman paused, shooting his partner a look that might as well have been an accusing finger.

'*Nah*,' laughed Christian. 'Don't believe in it.'

Gunshots echoed between the buildings once more.

'Why don't you go out there and tell *him* that!' Finlay shouted back.

The branches overhead trembled in time to the thunderous cracks, the dying leaves falling like auburn snow around them.

'Hey!' hissed Christian.

Finlay was peering up at the countless windows that looked

out over the public space as the few remaining civilians retreated to safety.

An eerie quiet had descended over the square.

'Hey!' called Christian, louder this time.

'What? I'm thinking.'

'Listen . . . He's firing in sets of eight. Then there's a pause as he reloads.'

'Fantastic.'

'I can make it,' Christian told him.

'No . . . You can't.'

Tying his hair back, Christian stared longingly at the phone box on the other side of the square.

'I'm going for it,' he said decisively, getting into position as the gunfire started again.

Dirt sprayed up from the concrete around them as wasted bullets littered the deserted space.

'We sit tight!' shouted Finlay. 'Help will be coming!'

Another pause.

'Next set,' whispered Christian.

'You won't make it!'

The gunman began firing once more, his aim improving as pieces of bark splintered off the trunks beside their heads.

'That's five!' called Christian. 'Six!'

'Christian!'

'Seven!'

Finlay risked exposing his arm as he grasped for his impulsive friend too late.

'Eight!'

Christian sprang to his feet and sprinted across the open ground.

'You stupid . . .' Finlay cursed him, watching, as another sharp crack filled the air.

There was a cry of anguish and Christian dropped to the wet ground.

'Christian!' yelled Finlay, unable to move without inviting the same fate himself. 'Christian?!'

'Nine!'

'What?'

'Nine!'

'I cannae hear you!' Finlay shouted to him. 'But that was *nine*, you tosser!'

'I'm hit!'

'What?'

'I'm hit!'

'Are you hit? I'm coming to you!'

Braving the gaps between cover one at a time, Finlay reached the final tree, where he could see fresh blood glistening on the ground. He had at least ten metres to cover to reach the statue that Christian had crawled behind.

The silence had returned, the quiet as calming as a shark disappearing back underwater.

Reaching for the biggest rock he could find, Finlay pitched it in the opposite direction, covering the short distance in seconds as the sound of his distraction filled the enclosed square. Christian was lying in a puddle of his own blood, holding both hands firmly over his right buttock.

'Told you you wouldn't make it,' said Finlay helpfully, looking appalled. 'Did you get . . . shot in the arse?'

'There's a *lot* of blood!'

'Well, you got shot in the arse!' reasoned Finlay.

There were sirens approaching from the south.

'We need to stop the bleeding,' groaned Christian.

'I'm not going anywhere near that!' Finlay told him, but Christian didn't reply, having just lost consciousness. 'I hate my life,' he muttered as he reluctantly placed his hands over the hole in his partner's trousers.

Watching the windows above anxiously, it slowly dawned on him that this clash between a madman with a rifle and his reckless friend's pasty posterior might well be the best thing to ever happen to him . . . because it might just lead him back to Maggie.

On bursting through the doors to A&E, Finlay spotted her, every bit as beautiful as he remembered. Even the half-filled bedpan in her hands couldn't detract from that.

'Gunshot wound!' the younger of the two ambulance men announced proudly, attracting Maggie's attention as they rushed through.

Removing his hand from his friend's buttock, Finlay gave her a bloodstained wave.

'What happened?' she asked, hurrying over.

'Shot,' mumbled Christian, face down on the stretcher. 'In the arse.'

'And *this* one refused to let go of it the entire way in,' the other ambulance man informed her, eyebrows raised. 'We did point out that we could handle it, but he insisted on coming.' As they reached another set of double doors, he turned to address Finlay: 'We've got it from here.'

Finlay watched as they rolled Christian into another room.

'I think it's sweet you wouldn't leave his . . . *side*,' Maggie told him.

'Aye. Well, he's my best mate, isn't he?'

'Come on, then, let's get you cleaned up at least,' she said, leading Finlay down the corridor as he struggled valiantly not to stare at her bum. 'I'm sure he's going to be fine.'

'Who? Oh, Christian! I hope so.'

They reached a basin, where she gently washed his hands under the tap, revealing a fine web of lacerations spun by the shattered windscreen. He was reasonably confident that his palms should have been stinging but was unable to feel anything beyond her delicate hands in his.

'It's funny this happened,' he started nervously.

'Funny?'

'Not like *funny* funny. I just mean . . . I'm glad.'

'Glad?'

'Yeah.'

'That your friend got shot?'

'No. I didn't mean that bit,' he clarified.

'I should hope not.'

The burly Scotsman was blushing like his teenage self asking Jessica Clarke to the school dance. Had she said yes, the memory might have been of more use to him as he struggled on, committed now. 'I meant *this* bit . . . Getting to see y—'

'Maggie!' A flustered nurse had appeared in the doorway.

Finlay shot her daggers.

'They need you in Majors, right away!'

'Sorry!' Maggie smiled at Finlay, drying her hands as she hurried out after her colleague.

'I'll . . . I'll wait for you, shall I?' he called after her, hands dripping down the corridor.

'For me?' she laughed, turning to walk backwards, unable to stop. 'As if you'd leave his side!'

'Whose? Oh, Christian's!' he realised as she was swallowed up by the swinging doors.

Finlay tucked the evidence bag into his pocket, doubtful that they'd learn anything useful from the bum-blood-smudged bullet. He stamped on the dying embers of yet another cigarette, his fourth during the conversation with his chief inspector while pacing the hospital car park.

An initial search of the premises lining George Square had turned up two empty casings, presumably missed during a hasty clear-up, pinpointing the vacant floor that the gunman had selected as his vantage point. They discussed the distinct possibility of the incident being in some way linked to the shipyard bust four days earlier, and then the equally plausible prospect of the attack being directed at Strathclyde Police in general. Finlay and Christian had been driving a marked-up patrol car and there had been a dramatic spike in unprovoked violence towards uniformed officers over the preceding months.

They had concluded that, in all likelihood, they would probably never know either way.

Promising to pass on the insult-ridden 'get well soon' message from the department, Finlay headed back inside, to find Maggie laughing uncontrollably at something Christian had said. Neither noticed him standing in the corner.

'What are you up to back there?' asked Christian in mock concern.

'Never you mind,' Maggie told him, still grinning as she removed the bloody bandage. 'Looks like you'll have to stay the night.'

'You don't even want me to buy you dinner or anything first?' asked Christian, peering back at her playfully.

'At the hospital,' she clarified with a smirk, purposely removing a layer of skin along with the old tape. 'You have a night of peeing into bottles, hourly blood pressures and hospital radio's "Love Hour" ahead of you. Enjoy!'

'And would *you* happen to be working tonight?' he asked her.

'Nope.'

He lay back down on his front, sulking: 'Shame.'

'For you maybe. I'm going out.'

'Out? Out where? A date?'

Maggie continued with what she was doing as though she hadn't heard him.

'With who? Is it serious? Boyfriend? Fiancé . . . ? You still there?' he asked, genuinely unable to feel anything much below his waist.

'I am. I'm just waiting for you to ask a question that's actually any of your business.'

Finlay cleared his throat.

Maggie looked up at him guiltily.

'How's our boy?' he asked.

'Irritating.'

'Hey!' complained Christian.

'But he'll be fine.'

'Good. So we're on for next week, then?' Christian asked her.

Finlay felt as though he'd been punched in the gut, but then his partner looked to him.

'Maggie and some of the girls are coming along to our *work night out.*'

Finlay looked blank: 'Our what?'

Rolling his eyes, Christian turned to address Maggie. She raised her arms in exasperation as the bandage dropped off, reintroducing his bare buttocks to the room.

'So we're on?' he asked her again.

Feigning annoyance, she huffed in resignation: 'Yes. I suppose we're on.'

CHAPTER 9

Friday 8 January 2016
12.43 p.m.

Unlocking her Audi A1, Baxter climbed inside, trying to ignore the missing paint and damage to the front bumper that she still hadn't done anything about since driving into a wall a fortnight earlier.

'Sorry, Blackie,' she said guiltily, patting the dashboard.

She had stayed with Maggie for two further rounds of tea before making her excuses to leave, having found the morning far more emotionally draining than she let on.

It was all Wolf's fault.

They had each accepted the devastating news of Finlay's death with the custom display of stoic reserve, whatever they might have been feeling in private, and had channelled their grief into something positive: assisting Maggie and the family with anything they might need. Cue Wolf blundering back into their lives with his usual grace, bringing with him his own unresolved issues packaged up as questionable theories and delivered with just enough conviction to spark hope in each of them: hope that Finlay hadn't felt as though he'd had no one to confide in, hadn't embraced *her* farewell for a heartbeat longer than usual knowing that it was the last time.

She whispered a curse word on realising that she was crying again. Flipping the sun visor down to check the damage to her make-up, she noticed a figure approaching with the lumbering gait of a far larger man, the wind billowing his coat out behind him like a superhero's cape, undoubtedly the very reason he was wearing it. She watched as Wolf opened the rickety gate fortifying Maggie's front garden before letting himself into the house.

'Son of a . . .' she hissed through gritted teeth, throwing the car door open.

Stomping into the hallway, Baxter heard heavy footfalls crossing the landing overhead.

'Wolf!' she yelled up.

Maggie appeared in the kitchen doorway, quite reasonably wondering who was in her house.

'It's fine, Maggie,' Baxter told her, already heading up the staircase. 'Wolf!'

She reached the top of the stairs to find him sitting in the centre of the bare room with his back to her and his head in his hands.

'What are you doing here?' she asked, stepping up through the broken door frame.

'Thought I'd missed something . . . Hadn't.'

He had placed the upturned chair over the bloodstained floor-boards, adopting the exact position that Finlay must have chosen for his final moments, an air of defeat surrounding him.

'I meant, why did you come back at all?' Baxter asked him. 'We were doing just fine without you . . . We were better off without you.'

Wolf looked up at her. He nodded.

'Well?' she pushed him.

'I just . . . thought I could help.'

'Help?' Baxter laughed bitterly. 'All you've done is prolong the misery for Maggie. As if she's not been through enough!'

'He wouldn't kill himself!' Wolf argued, raising his voice, but even he didn't sound as though he believed it anymore.

Baxter hurried over to shut the broken door.

'Shhhh! You . . . are . . . ridiculous,' she told him. 'And you *do* belong in prison. You know you're not the good guy in this story, don't you? You're not the misunderstood hero. You're not some burdened soul searching for redemption. You're just a *fucking* mess of a human being clawing at the lives of everyone around you on your way down.'

Although quite used to being on the receiving end of Baxter's tirades, Wolf looked a little taken aback.

'Fuck you, Wolf,' she spat. Unable to handle his bright blue eyes looking up at her like a lost puppy, she turned back to the door and twisted the handle.

She tried again.

'Shit.'

'Problem?' asked Wolf.

'No.'

There was a loud snap.

'Shit!'

'Let me try,' said Wolf, getting to his feet but looking decidedly less confident when she handed him the broken brass handle. 'I've got this.'

Moving aside, Baxter folded her arms.

Wolf stepped up to the door. He looked from the handle in his hand to the hole that it had vacated and back to Baxter, who made a 'well, get on with it, then' gesture at him. Deciding on a plan of action, he turned back to the obstructed exit, raised his hands and then thumped against the wood as loudly as he could. 'Maggie! Maggie!'

A few moments later, they could hear movement on the other side of the door: 'Will?'

'Maggie?' Wolf called through. 'We're locked in here.'

'Oh dear.'

'Is the handle still attached your side?'

'Yes.'

Wolf waited, but nothing happened: 'Maggie?'

'Yes?'

'Could you turn it?' he asked patiently.

'Oh yes.'

Nothing happened.

'Are you able to turn the handle?'

'Yes.'

Still nothing happened.

'Maggie?' asked Wolf, his voice turning suspicious.

'Yes?'

'*Will* you turn the handle?'

'No.'

The sound of her footsteps disappearing down the staircase cut through the frosty silence within the room. Wolf turned back to Baxter and smiled.

She looked quite cross.

'She'll let us out after five minutes,' he told her confidently.

The front door slammed.

'Ten tops.'

The Mercedes's engine started up in the driveway.

'Bollocks.'

He moved out of the way when Baxter marched over, jamming her fingertips into the gap where the handle had once been. When that had no effect, she crouched down and attempted to prise the door open from underneath. Using her full weight to pull against the frame, she succeeded only in creating a large crack that worked its way down the plaster like a bolt of lightning.

'You're going to rip the whole wall down,' Wolf told her, taking a seat on the dusty floor.

'Ahhhhh!' Baxter cried in frustration.

She flounced over to the other side of the room and slumped down beneath the window.

'Perhaps,' started Wolf, 'this is a good time to—'

'Please don't talk to me,' she cut him off.

She shut her eyes and willed herself to fall asleep.

Thirty-five minutes passed.

Stubbornly, Baxter had kept her eyes closed the entire time, while becoming increasingly irritated by the gentle snores emanating from Wolf, who had dropped off almost immediately.

She huddled up against the chill and cautiously opened one eye: he was sat by the wall, head back and mouth open, exactly where she'd left him. He looked exhausted, even while asleep, neglected: the scraggly beard, his unkempt hair, the way in which his coat was hanging off him, robbing him of the presence that he had always carried so effortlessly. It was as if the 'fire' that had brought him so much heartache over the years had finally gone out. She couldn't help but recall feeling the precise same way about Lethaniel Masse, dressed in his blue boiler suit and handcuffed to a table in Belmarsh Prison.

Even the fiercest blazes are destined to suffocate themselves in the end.

He looked peaceful. She reached over to pick up a stray screw and tossed it across the room at him. Smacking him satisfyingly in the forehead, it bounced across the floor as she feigned sleep once more.

'What the . . . ?' complained Wolf, holding his head while looking around the room in confusion.

'Mind keeping it down over there?' asked Baxter. 'Some of us are trying to sleep.'

Wolf yawned loudly: 'Can I say something?'

'Absolutely not.'

'You have *no right* to be this pissed off with me,' he told her anyway.

'Seriously? *That's* what you're opening with?'

'You're mad at me for leaving . . . but *you* were the one who told me to leave!' said Wolf, not so much angry as exasperated. 'Because I seem to remember a *certain someone* pissing blood all over the floor and me, doing a pretty damned good impression of the "misunderstood hero", prepared to give myself up to save you. *You* told *me* to go!'

'Did it not ever even enter your stupid bloody head that maybe, just maybe, you should never have put me in that situation in the first place?!' countered Baxter, not so much exasperated as angry. 'I didn't hear a *thing* from you for *eighteen* months!'

'What did you expect?' asked Wolf, voice rising. 'After *all* you'd risked to help me? I knew they'd be watching.'

'Do you have *any* idea what I've been through this past month?'

Wolf opened his mouth to answer, but then just nodded sadly. His eyes were drawn back to the stitches and the numerous scabs dotted across her face.

Baxter put her head in her hands.

Hesitantly, Wolf got to his feet to take a seat on the floor beside her.

'That night,' he sighed, resting his head against the wall, 'when you were all over the news . . . I've got that image ingrained in my mind: you standing there, on top of the city, nothing but a few shards of broken glass between you and the world below.' He looked pained. 'He told me to stay away.'

'Finlay?' asked Baxter, clearly hurt.

'I asked him to meet me. He wouldn't. He told me you had someone . . . Thomas?'

She didn't reply.

'Said you had a new partner, the CIA agent and Edmunds, and . . .' Wolf's voice cracked ever so slightly, 'he told me that you'd always have him and Maggie to look out for you.'

They both needed a few seconds.

'Is that why you were so sure?' Baxter asked him.

Wolf shrugged.

'We've both been to enough suicides over the years,' she started, 'to know that people can put on a good show. But that doesn't mean there's not something there . . . in the background . . . something that was there the entire time.'

Wolf nodded and stared at the stained floor in the centre of the room.

He frowned.

'What?' Baxter asked him.

He looked down at where they were sitting, the cogs turning as he got up onto his knees.

'What?' she repeated.

'Why's there a step up into this room?' he asked rhetorically, reaching for a chisel and jamming it between two of the floorboards.

'Wolf!'

The wooden plank sprang up at one end, enabling him to squeeze his fingers beneath and force it up despite Baxter's protests.

'Happy now?' she asked when he predictably only uncovered the wooden joists and metal pipes that ran underneath the flooring. 'Jesus! The minute I think I'm getting through to you . . . What are you doing?!'

He'd moved on to another one in a different part of the room, wedging the tool into the narrow gap between the boards.

'Finlay built this!'

The plank splintered as he ripped it from the floor, again only unearthing the room's wooden foundations.

'Wolf,' said Baxter softly. She couldn't bring herself to be angry with him as she watched this desperate last-ditch attempt to attach some sort of meaning to the loss they had all suffered. 'Finlay took his own life. He left all of us, not just you.'

Wolf didn't appear to even hear her. He had moved into the corner of the room, removed two more floorboards and was working on a third.

'When you left,' started Baxter, having never expected to recite the story, 'Finlay told me that it felt like he'd lost a . . .'

She paused on seeing the look on Wolf's face as he lifted a fourth board away with ease, as if it hadn't even been nailed down in the first place. He got back up and rubbed his dusty chin.

'Reckon that's blood?' he asked her casually.

Baxter slowly walked over to the empty void that he had exposed, just four floorboards in width and not much more than a foot deep. From the neat lines and shiny metal, it was clear that Finlay had built this space into the fabric of the room with a specific purpose in mind, presumably a more secure location to stash an illegal firearm and mounting collection of threatening letters.

Faint red streaks had been smeared across the metallic base.

'Room for a person . . . just about,' remarked Wolf, walking to the window, a confusing mix of anger and relief coursing through him. 'Think perhaps Finlay wasn't alone in here after all?'

Baxter was speechless.

'Can you get forensics down here, please?' he asked her, taking out his own phone. 'And I need to speak to the first officer on scene.'

'Of course,' she replied, unable to tear her eyes from the small empty space that changed absolutely everything, that had been there beneath their feet the entire time. 'Who are you calling?'

'Vanita,' said Wolf, holding his mobile up to his ear. 'Need to tell her I can't go to prison just yet . . . I think we've got a killer to catch.'

CHAPTER 10

Friday 8 January 2016

1.37 p.m.

At least two pounds fifty worth of Swedish meatball splattered onto the pavement as Thomas gawped up at St Paul's crumbling cathedral. Plastic sheets billowed and crumpled noisily, bandages over a wound, while an unsettling drone emitted from somewhere inside as the wind flooded the chambers and halls to roar around its opulent basilica.

He hadn't intended to visit the site at the summit of the city, confident that enough nosy tourists would be congesting the surrounding area, until he happened upon the crater left by the blast. The concrete looked to have burst skywards, as if a volcano had erupted, spewing rubble and rock up at the heavens. Seeing as he was in the vicinity anyway, curiosity had got the better of him, and Thomas had taken his overpriced Pret A Manger wrap to see the main event.

He wished he hadn't.

There was no movie-set glamour to the devastation, no sense of camaraderie to be found among the crowds viewing the world through the screens of their mobile phones, no modern-day virtuosos equipped with pallets and eccentric facial hair meticulously restoring the artwork – just the bleak aftermath of violence and a sea of construction workers sitting around eating Greggs.

Baxter had been a part of this.

Feeling the familiar twist in the pit of his stomach, Thomas remembered the chaos of a city drowning in snow. And seeing this pitiful scene in person had finally made the stories of that surreal night feel real.

It was easier to ignore that in the wake of every good fairy tale lies the rotting corpse of a vanquished monster somewhere in the woods.

Eager to return to his blissful ignorance, he shoved his way out of the crush and re-emerged back out on Ludgate Hill. Able to breathe again, he set off in the direction of his 2 p.m. appointment. Halfway down the road, he stopped outside a jeweller's, recalling that Baxter had lost one of her rarely worn earrings somewhere in St James's Park. He scanned the window display inanely, having no idea what they had even looked like and conscious that his girlfriend's unopened pile of Christmas presents was growing by the day. It had become a lunchtime ritual, scouring the city for the perfect gift, searching for something that might just lift her spirits a little, let her know how much she meant to him, perhaps even rival that absurd stuffed penguin she refused to sleep without anymore.

He made his decision, confident only that he'd got it completely wrong, and headed inside.

'DCI Baxter,' smirked Joe as he stepped into Maggie's hallway, forensics kit in hand. 'If I didn't know better, I'd think you'd been trying to avoid me.'

'You don't know better,' Baxter informed him. 'I was.'

Joe made a cat noise and then followed her up the stairs.

'You don't have to fight your feelings,' he told her. 'We both know there's something between us.'

'There are a great number of things between us . . . and I intend to keep it that way.'

'I'm wearing you down, though,' he smiled. 'I can tell.'

They entered the bare room, where Christian was already waiting for them.

''Scuse me, Gramps,' said Joe, apparently not recognising the commissioner of the Metropolitan Police as he set his case of equipment down beside the gap in the floor.

Heavy footfalls hurried up the stairs behind them and then Wolf appeared in the doorway, phone in hand.

'Still trying to get hold of the first officer on scene,' he announced, moving into the centre of the room. 'So, here's what I'm thinking so far . . . Our killer—'

'Hypothetical killer,' Christian pointed out.

'. . . has just shot and killed Finlay. He's seen photos of Maggie downstairs, her stuff all over the house, so knows someone will be coming home soon. He . . . wipes the gun clean, places it in Finlay's hand and repositions him to make it look like a suicide. He—'

'Or *she*, you sexist bastard,' interjected Baxter.

'. . . closes the door . . . empties a bottle of sealant round the frame . . . climbs down into the compartment, pulling the loose boards over him or her, and waits.' Wolf appeared to be lost in his own imagination for a moment.

'Hello,' smiled Joe.

'Yeah. Hi,' replied Wolf distractedly. 'So, what do you think?'

Christian looked dubious, Baxter even more so.

'*I* think you're forgetting something,' said Christian. 'The text message he sent me. It might as well have been a suicide note.'

'You said he tried phoning you a few minutes before?' said Wolf.

'That's right.'

'Perhaps he was calling for help—'

Christian looked sick: 'Don't tell me that.'

'. . . and then had to make the silent 999 call as the situation got more desperate.'

'Would he *really* have stopped to send me a message in between?'

'Maybe,' mumbled Baxter, staring into space. 'If he was sure he was going to die.'

The three of them fell silent as Joe, oblivious, noisily unpacked his box of toys.

'OK. What have you got for me?' he said, after donning a set
of disposable overalls, tightening the elastic on his face mask and
shooting a forlorn look at the hairnet that wouldn't be required.
He switched on the torch, got down on his front and poked his
head beneath the floorboards. 'Oh yeah! Definitely blood!' he
announced, before gesturing blindly at Christian. 'Scalpel . . .
Scalpel!' he barked when the commissioner failed to comply.

Although clearly tempted to say something, Christian handed
the flailing arm the item requested.

'Box!' ordered Joe, clicking his fingers.

Again, Christian reluctantly obeyed.

They heard the tamper-proof tab snap shut. Joe handed him
back the evidence box without resurfacing.

'Bingo! Looks like scuff-marks!' he shouted unnecessarily.
'Yeah, someone was definitely down here. We've got hair . . .
maybe fabric fibres.' He climbed back out of the hole and pulled
his face mask up onto his shiny head. 'Saunders and Edmunds
about today?'

'Collecting old case files from Scotland,' Wolf answered. 'Why?'

'I'm gonna need DNA samples from each of you to start eliminating evidence,' he explained. 'The sooner the better.'

Baxter's phone started to ring. She glanced down at the screen:

Holly (Vet/Slutty friend)
☎ Incoming call

She should probably change that.

She hurried out onto the landing before answering.

'Hey. Kind of busy right now. Everything all right?' asked
Baxter, choosing her words with care. 'He's what? . . . OK. Calm
down. Yep . . . I'll be there as soon as I can. OK. Bye.'

Everyone was waiting expectantly when she returned to the
room.

'You good?' Wolf asked her.

'Something's come up,' she told them, collecting her things.

'Something more important than this?' Wolf challenged her.

'Uh-huh,' she replied, heading for the door.

'This is probably going to take me a little while anyway,' said Joe, defusing the building tension in the room.

'And . . .' Christian reminded Wolf, 'you've got that press conference to attend.'

Their discovery had bought him a little more time, prompting Vanita to formally announce Wolf's involvement in the case. Deeming 'consultant' a term vague enough to cover the unprecedented, complicated and undoubtedly controversial intricacies of their agreement, she had decided to pre-empt the media savaging.

'I'd be happy to stay with Maggie awhile,' added Christian.

Understandably, she had taken this latest development in the investigation the hardest, and none of them wanted to leave her alone in her current state.

'Shouldn't you be there?' asked Baxter, hovering in the doorway.

'Why would *this* guy be there?' asked Joe.

'This is Vanita's show,' said Christian, ignoring him. 'She's welcome to it . . . Plus, she'll say what I tell her to.'

'Again,' started Joe, now looking understandably uneasy, 'why would this guy be there?'

'After you, Mr Commissioner, Sir,' beamed Joe, standing to attention at the bottom of the stairs with more equipment.

Having said her goodbyes to Maggie, Baxter emerged from the kitchen.

'You could've *bloody* warned me!' Joe hissed at her as she passed him. Standing straight-backed, he saluted as Christian negotiated the final stairs, Wolf following close behind. 'Fawkes,' he nodded professionally.

'Lab guy.'

While Joe retreated back to his work, Christian showed them out, imparting some last-minute words of advice on Wolf regarding what *not* to say in front of the press.

The three of them stepped out into the cold.

'Look after her today,' said Wolf, pausing to speak with Christian.

'You want a lift to the station, Wolf, we're going right now,' barked Baxter as she marched towards the car.

'I will,' Christian assured him. 'You'd better go.'

As Wolf hurried after Baxter, Christian disappeared back inside, closing the door behind him.

'Bollocks!' he said the moment he opened the passenger door, watching the plume of smoke escape Baxter as she huffed.

'What now?'

'Forgot my coat.'

Baxter rolled her eyes, climbed in and switched on the ignition. 'Can you wait just—' began Wolf, before being sprayed with dirty slush as Baxter accelerated away, the passenger door swinging closed as she skidded round the corner. Struck with an overwhelming sense of déjà vu, he wiped his wet trousers and trudged back down the path.

Reaching for the handle, he collided painfully with the solid front door.

'Owww!' he complained, rubbing his head as Christian reappeared in the doorway. Seemingly a little dazed, Wolf took a few moments to speak: 'I forgot my—'

Christian handed him the worn black overcoat with a smile. 'Ta.'

Andrea Hall smiled into Camera 1, while barely defined figures lingered in the shadows beyond.

The 'On Air' sign went dull as the studio lights blazed back to life, reanimating the static audience into an instant frenzy.

'Will someone *please* sort out that shitty teleprompter?!' she hollered at no one in particular.

Downing the dregs of her cold coffee, she got up from behind the news desk as a cloud of hairspray rushed at her, presumably containing her stylist, who treated 'their' trendsetting red and blonde hair with the reverence of a sculptured masterpiece. It was certainly worth as much as one, having transformed Andrea from 'celebrity newsreader' to 'style icon' overnight.

'Who's on later?' she asked her harried assistant.

'Some bishop begging for donations to restore St Paul's.'

She stifled a yawn. 'What's the name of that developer?' Andrea asked her. 'The one who wants to knock the rest down and build offices?'

'Hammond.'

'Yeah. Let's get him on as well. "God versus dick" should keep us all entertained for a few minutes, at least.'

The crew were already setting up for the next interview. Andrea moved aside to let her colleague assume her place in front of the camera. The stern-looking woman took a seat and was immediately accosted with a powdering pad.

'So, what angle are you going with, then?' she asked while contorting her face unattractively. The two women didn't like one another but shared a mutual appreciation for their respective ruthlessness. 'The wolf's on the hunt again? The pack's got its alpha back?'

'I have no idea what you're talking about.'

The woman's eyes lit up despite the sole purpose of her profession being to inform people of things they didn't already know. 'Your ex. He's back. Been spotted with the commissioner and Emily Baxter over in Muswell Hill.'

'Muswell Hill?' Andrea knew precisely where he'd be heading. She grabbed her bag. 'Gotta go.'

'You've got a four o'clock meeting with Elijah,' her assistant reminded her.

'Reschedule it.'

'What about "God versus dick"?'

'I'll be back in time,' Andrea assured her as she pulled her jacket on. 'Oh, and get Jim to sketch us a soulless office block with a basilica on top . . . And one of God sat at a desk on the top floor. That should get things rolling,' she smiled, before rushing out through the doors.

The heavens had opened.

Lost in a forest of stone crosses, Baxter weaved between ranks of moss-covered angels in search of Rouche, Holly or even just the car as the ground dissolved beneath her feet.

Even disregarding recent events, there were few places she would rather have avoided than a cemetery in a thunderstorm.

She very nearly lost a boot to a puddle and was about to kick a gravestone in frustration, before deciding, even by her standards, that was pushing it. Looking around to get her bearings, she spotted a large hooded figure standing a few rows over and was overcome with an irrational urge to hide.

'Grow up, Baxter,' she muttered to herself. However, when she went to call out, she hesitated, wondering why anybody would just be standing there in the freezing rain.

Cautiously, she started to approach, squelching through the mud between graves as she tried to remember what Holly had been wearing. The figure flickered in and out of view as she slowed her pace, remaining perfectly still despite the rain pouring so heavily she could barely keep her eyes open.

Distracted, Baxter slipped, landing in a heap just a few metres from the stranger.

A moment's panic quickly passed on realising that the robed man was made of stone, draped across one of the graves – the very depiction of despair. The empty hood was mesmerising, a gaping black void where a face should have been, as if the statue inside had ripped itself free. She stared deeper still, positive that she could make out a set of eyes—

'Emily?'

Baxter screamed.

Holly screamed louder.

'Jesus Christ!' gasped Baxter, holding her heart.

With an anxious laugh, Holly offered her a hand. 'I don't think I've ever heard you scream before,' she said, pulling Baxter to her feet.

'I just really, really don't like angels.'

'I've found them . . . Not him,' Holly added quickly when a hopeful look appeared on her friend's face.

Keeping one eye on the robed grave marker as they passed, Baxter followed her through to a row of simple headstones, where reserved inscriptions branded uniform marble slabs. Halfway along, they stopped beside one of the modest plots:

Sophie		Elliot
Rouche	&	Rouche
31/07/1982–07/07/2007		08/01/2001–07/07/2007

My everything.

Neither of them spoke for a minute, the two-word message scratched into the plaque a more impassioned declaration of love and loss than all the angels and ornate crosses put together. A fresh bouquet was bleeding petals into the downpour; alongside it, a small stuffed walrus, clearly from the same toy collection as Frankie the penguin.

'He was here,' said Holly. 'It's her birthday.'

Baxter hadn't realised. She had lost track of the days ever since Finlay's death. It all just felt like one long bad dream. Any anger that she might have been harbouring towards Rouche dissipated in a heartbeat.

'Come on,' she said. 'I know where he is.'

With the heater cranked up to maximum, Baxter drove them through the run-down outskirts of the city. She was surprised that Holly had been right about the cemetery, surprised that she had known about it at all for that matter. She had been so distracted with everything that had been going on that she hadn't noticed Rouche and her school friend growing closer. It was obvious now that she thought about it – Holly turning up at the apartment unscheduled, the panic in her voice on discovering him missing, the in-no-way-work-appropriate amount of make-up she always wore.

Baxter made another mental note to edit her friend's details in her phone.

She was pleased that the two of them were getting along, but considering where they had just been, doubted that Rouche would ever be able to give her what she was looking for.

'He's dying, Emily,' blurted Holly. 'I'm watching it happen day by day. We need to get him to a hospital.'

Realising they hadn't said a word to one another since leaving the cemetery, Baxter glanced across at her friend, whose short blonde hair was as perfect as ever, while she looked more like a drowned rat.

'Is there another antibiotic we can try?'

'If the infection turns into full-blown sepsis, all the antibiotics in the world won't save him,' Holly told her firmly. 'We're talking about blood poisoning.'

'I know someone . . . a nurse.' Baxter hadn't wanted to involve Maggie but now wondered whether tending to Rouche might be a welcome distraction for her.

'No,' said Holly, raising her voice. 'Look, we're friends, and I'm probably still a little bit more scared of you than the others are—'

'Who's scared of me?'

'. . . but you are killing him,' she continued despite the look on Baxter's face. 'Rouche was ready to give himself up a fortnight ago. It's only your selfishness that's stopping him.'

'I'm trying to protect him!'

'No, you're trying to hold on to him, and that's not the same thing. I'd rather have him locked up than this.'

'Have you ever been to a prison?' Baxter asked patronisingly.

'I haven't,' conceded Holly as they escaped the depressing High Street and built up some speed. 'But I have been to a graveyard.'

Night had settled by the time they pulled up outside the neglected Rouche family home, but there was still no sign of the rain abating. Baxter climbed out and led the way up the steep driveway towards the house. A solid metal door had been fitted since her last visit, the first unimaginative graffiti tags like a black spot, promising to claim the rest of the forgotten property in due course. Sheltered by overgrown ivy, Holly pushed against the blocked entrance and was surprised when the door swung open.

'I'm going to check round the back,' Baxter told her.

Squeezing past the dustbins, she walked the dark passageway to the side of the property and into the wild back garden, where a warm glow radiated from the Wendy house's plastic window. She smiled in relief and crossed the long grass. Ducking down to avoid the porch, she knocked on the shrunken door before entering.

Rouche looked utterly exhausted, sitting with his head resting against the wall of the empty little house. His grey stubble had aged him, and in an effort to reduce his temperature, he had unbuttoned his shirt, exposing a small selection of his countless wounds.

'Hey,' he greeted her wearily.

Baxter pulled the door closed on the rain and shuffled into the remaining space while attempting to avoid the precarious candles. After a brief spider-check, she made herself comfortable, reaching across to squeeze Rouche's hand. 'You're a dick.'

He laughed, holding his chest in pain.

'You know I'd have brought you here . . . today . . . if you'd asked me?' she said, making it clear that she was aware of the significance of the date.

The rain intensified. The flimsy roof didn't sound as though it was going to hold.

'You've got enough on your plate,' Rouche told her.

She would tell him another time that he didn't even know the half of it . . . that Wolf had been right all along.

'Holly's here,' she revealed. 'In the house. You know she likes you, right?'

Rouche didn't respond, grimacing as he tried to sit up.

'Stay still,' Baxter told him, but he forced himself upright to meet her eye.

'I am *so* sorry.'

'For what?'

'Everything . . . For bringing this mess down upon us . . . For being such a burden on you . . . For all of it.'

'Emily?' Holly called from out in the garden.

'In here!' Baxter shouted back, crawling over to push the door open before embracing Rouche as tightly as she dared: 'You are *not* a burden. We're in this together. And you have nothing to apologise for . . . *nothing*.'

CHAPTER 11

Friday 8 January 2016

5.23 p.m.

Andrea had bought the most expensive bouquet in the shop, forgetting that she somehow needed to fit it on the passenger seat of her baby-blue Porsche. Having removed the insultingly generic 'With sympathies' tag before carrying it up to the front door, she rang the bell.

A light came on. Footsteps approached.

'Hi, Maggie,' she smiled, catching the other woman's look of surprise.

'Andrea!' Maggie exclaimed, overcompensating.

'For you.'

'They are beautiful. Won't you come in out of the rain?' Struggling to manoeuvre the uprooted garden through the doorway, Maggie led the way into the kitchen. She flicked the kettle on and began fussing over the flowers in the sink. 'I was actually going to write you a little note today . . . to say thank you . . . for your card.'

Andrea had received a message at work from a man named Thomas Alcock, who had landed the unenviable task of contacting Finlay's extensive list of friends and acquaintances. She hadn't seen Wolf's mentor in years, not since the incident at his fifty-fifth birthday party, but had always got on well with him and Maggie, and had been genuinely saddened by the news. She had scribbled an uncharacteristically heartfelt message and tucked it into a card along with her personal contact details.

Maggie's reflection in the dark window looked troubled. She started filling a vase with water, but then shut off the tap. Drying her hands on a tea towel, she turned to address her unexpected guest. 'Forgive me for asking, but are you here as a friend . . . or a reporter?'

'A friend,' replied Andrea sincerely.

That was good enough for Maggie: 'Sorry.'

'Don't be. I'm amazed you let me through the door at all.'

'You're looking for Will?'

'I am. He was here?'

'He was. He left a couple of hours ago, I'm afraid.'

'How . . .' Andrea hesitated, conscious that her recent betrayals gave her no right to even ask. 'How is he?'

It was a difficult question to answer. Thinking back, Maggie couldn't recall a time when Wolf hadn't had some form of personal or professional disaster hanging over him.

She shrugged: 'He's Will.'

The answer actually appeared to give Andrea some solace.

They chatted over tea in the snug kitchen, Maggie breaking down at one point, revealing that the police were no longer treating her husband's death as a conclusive suicide.

'Who could ever want to hurt Fin?' she had asked in tearful bewilderment.

Twenty minutes later, Andrea realised she needed to be getting back. Reaching across the table, she took Maggie's hand. 'What can I do?'

Shaking her head, about to refuse the offer, a thought crossed Maggie's mind.

'What is it?' Andrea asked her. 'Anything at all.'

'Will.'

'What about him?'

'He needs our help.'

'He hates me.'

'He could never *hate* you,' laughed Maggie.

Andrea was polite enough not to argue.

'They think I can't hear them talking,' Maggie told her. 'But I can. The moment this is all over, Will's going straight to prison. Let's try to stop that from happening, shall we?' she suggested mischievously.

'You sound like you have a plan?'

Maggie made a non-committal sound.

'I still doubt he'll ever forgive me.'

Maggie patted her arm reassuringly:

'Take it from someone older and wiser: you would be astounded by the things a friendship can withstand.'

'Looks as though I underestimated you once again, Fawkes,' said Vanita, checking her teeth for lipstick as she and Wolf waited to enter the press conference. 'You were right all along.'

He didn't reply, not feeling it much to celebrate. He peered into the room of jaded journalists sent to cover some mundane announcement or other by the Met's camera-craving commander.

Rubbing the pink line away with her thumb, Vanita gave her jet-black hair a ruffle. 'How do I look?'

It felt a loaded question, so Wolf remained quiet.

'Thank you,' Vanita smiled, apparently imagining a compliment. 'Are you ready?'

'I guess.'

'Fawkes, this is what I do,' she told him smugly. 'If I've done my job right, by the time we reach the questions, I'll have shut down every possible avenue they might try. It'll be a tumbleweed moment. So . . . are you ready?' she asked again, as if she'd just delivered one of those generic American-sports-movie-half-time-locker-room pep talks.

Wolf shrugged: 'I guess.'

Vanita deflated. 'Your flies are undone,' she informed him,

flinging the door open and striding confidently into the room.

One trigger-happy photographer was rewarded with an action shot of Wolf zipping himself up before the twice-disgraced ex-detective ambled leisurely towards the front.

The crowd started to recognise him as he passed: 'That's William Fawkes!'

Wolf kept his eyes trained on the vacant seat beside Vanita.

'Shouldn't he be in handcuffs?' someone asked.

He resisted the urge to use his uncuffed hand to give the gobby woman the finger.

'He looked far sexier fat,' added a member of the all-male front row.

Tripping over his own feet, Wolf stumbled into position, taking a seat as the audience held various recording devices above their heads like lighters at a rock concert.

Vanita cleared her throat, thanked the press for attending at such short notice and then proceeded with her carefully composed statement:

'. . . and fresh evidence has come to light regarding the apparent suicide of retired detective sergeant Finlay Shaw, whose death is now being treated as suspicious . . .'

There was little point in trying to conceal Finlay's identity or the fact that he had seemingly taken his own life. Photographs of Wolf, Baxter and the commissioner outside the property were already doing the rounds, meaning that the neighbours had been approached, each no doubt deliberating just how much their loyalty to Maggie was worth.

'DS Shaw will, of course, be known to many of you from his contribution to the Ragdoll investigation,' continued Vanita, edging ever closer to the subject of Wolf's presence beside her.

'He was the doddery old fool who had to be fire-engined down off the embassy roof,' added Wolf with a smirk.

There were chuckles from the audience.

'Quite,' said Vanita, losing her place. Now that every set of eyes in the room were fixed on Wolf, she figured it as good a time as any to get it over with: 'William Fawkes will be working alongside the Metropolitan Police in a consultancy capacity for the duration of the investigation, lending his extensive expertise and long history with the victim to ensure a speedy resolution. His input has already proved invaluable.'

People started calling out questions, but Vanita continued over them.

'At this time, we are unable to go into any detail regarding former Detective Fawkes's movements over the past eighteen months.'

Groans of discontent escaped the audience.

'We have an open investigation that we cannot jeopardise!' she had to shout to make herself heard. She then met Wolf's eye: 'Rest assured, there will be full and frank disclosure in due course.' She looked back at the room. 'That in mind, are there any questions?'

Every hand in the audience went up.

Forgetting that he had a microphone pointed at his face, Wolf swore *under* his breath . . . but *over* the PA system.

'Christ!' gasped Vanita, after stepping through the door of Christian's office. 'You scared me. I thought you'd left for the night.'

Christian wiped his eyes and started hunting through drawers in search of a tissue.

Producing one from her handbag, Vanita made her way over to him.

'Thank you,' he said, dabbing his eyes. Noticing her glance down at the faded Polaroids that littered his desk, he picked one up and handed it to her. 'That's me . . . on the right,' he told her.

She raised her eyebrows: 'Nice ponytail.'

'It was a different time,' laughed Christian. 'That's Fin on the left, looking as gorgeous as ever, and that's his wife, Maggie, standing between us.'

Vanita smiled and gave the photograph back to him.

'I . . . I've found today *challenging*, to say the least,' he admitted.

'He was your friend,' reasoned Vanita. 'I, on the other hand, am not. So I'm probably not the best person to talk to about this.'

'Fair enough,' said Christian, sitting up.

It was no secret that Vanita had thrown her hat into the ring for the commissioner role, having done a sterling job dislodging its previous occupant in the post-Ragdoll-debacle restructure.

'Perhaps you should take some time,' she suggested, tongue in cheek. 'Think about *Christian*. Step back for a while.'

'Oh, Geena, I'd miss the sensation of you nipping at my heels too much,' he grinned at her. 'How did the press conference go?'

'Much as expected.'

'That bad, huh?'

She dropped the file she was carrying into his tray and headed for the door. 'Goodnight,' she called. 'And watch your back.'

'Are we outright threatening each other now?' asked Christian. 'I must have missed the memo.'

She turned back to face him. 'Quite the opposite, actually. Some highly intelligent and clearly very dangerous individual went to an awful lot of trouble to make Shaw's death look like a suicide. We just went public to announce that we're hunting this person, a person who had absolutely no intention of ever running. Who knows how they might respond?'

Christian looked troubled.

Vanita smiled back at him: 'Well, goodnight!'

Wolf took another bite of his pizza as he loitered outside the shabby takeaway. Across the street, a large billboard was brightly lit against its dreary surroundings:

RaGDoLL

It takes a wolf to catch one

Series premiere – 8 p.m., Sunday 28 February

From the poster alone, it was evident that the production company had taken certain liberties. For one, Wolf appeared to have been re-envisioned as a male model. He was dressed in a midnight-blue suit, and judging from the two lumps attempting to burst out of it, they had gone down the 'pec' rather than 'moob' route. A fierce-looking woman stood on one side, arms folded and her back to him; on the other, a beautiful redhead adopting an identical pose.

Making a mental note to be in prison before then, Wolf strolled in the direction of Paddington Green Police Station. He was welcomed 'home' and buzzed into the cells, which were already filling up with the first punchy drunks of the evening. He closed the door behind him to find his freshly pressed shirts hanging up. George had even tidied a little.

Unable to shake the image of his televised self, he abandoned the last slice of pizza in favour of seven and a quarter push-ups. And then, holding a pulled muscle, he walked over to the mirror. Having no use for a disguise any longer, he ran his fingers through his scraggly beard and picked up his razor.

Saunders had fallen asleep in front of the muted television, three empty beer bottles beside his chair and evidence of his 11 p.m. visit to Burger King.

Reduced to couriers for the day, he and Edmunds had boarded two planes, been through three security checks and fallen out with every Scottish customs official on duty to obtain the disintegrating evidence boxes from the police headquarters in Dalmarnock. Spurred on by Wolf's discovery, Edmunds had suggested they make the most of their trip by interviewing two people linked to one of the old cases. Failing to learn anything of value from either of the uncooperative men, the time wasted in their company cost them making their scheduled flight home.

At a little after 3 a.m., Saunders stirred in his sleep, the security light outside his window triggering, as it did whenever anyone came home. There was a soft crack and then the sound of glass showering onto tarmac. Groaning as he got up, he almost turned his ankle on one of the empties. He stumbled over to the window and shivered, peering out over what he could see of the communal parking area. With his breath obscuring the glass, he was about to return to his chair when an alarm went off, orange lights flashing across the wet ground.

'Not again!' he exclaimed, grabbing his keys off the counter and arming himself with a cricket bat as he ran into the corridor.

Wearing only socks, boxer shorts and a T-shirt, Saunders bounded down the stairwell and burst out into the cold. It was indeed his car calling for help, although there was no sign of anybody else in the car park. He cancelled the alarm and cautiously approached, spotting the glittering ground beneath the driver's window. The glovebox was wide open, contents spread across the seats, the satnav missing. Stupidly, he'd left it out on display, too tired to think straight after dropping Edmunds home.

Deciding there was little he could do about it in the middle of the night, he checked each of the doors in turn and then realised that the boot was open.

'Pricks,' he muttered to himself, pushing it closed and heading back up to bed.

CHAPTER 12

Saturday 9 January 2016
7.53 a.m.

No matter how many times Baxter asked Thomas to watch a different news channel, Andrea Hall's flawless *bloody* face seemed permanently plastered to the screen of their television. She picked up the remote control on her way through to the kitchen, her thumb hovering over the 'off' button as she recognised the yellow T-shirt that the woman was wearing. Baxter had the exact same garment buried somewhere at the bottom of her wardrobe:

UNCAGE the WOLF!

Labouring through an interview with a monotonic politician, it was clear that the prominent newsreader had resurrected the campaign that had won Wolf his freedom and even his job back, years earlier. The much-publicised indiscretions that originally sealed Wolf's fate had become heroic deeds of desperation on the morning of the Cremation Killer's final act. Bowing to public outcry at a system *so* broken that it could let a predatory serial killer slip through its fingers, the powers that be had 'reconsidered their position' accordingly, the campaign painting Wolf a true champion of the people.

Baxter, however, knew that the truth lay somewhere in that grey area in between.

'Good morning,' smiled Thomas from the doorway.

He was still in his dressing gown and ridiculous slipper boots. Baxter switched off the television and accepted the cup of coffee he was holding out to her as she joined him in the kitchen.

'I'm really late,' she greeted him, placing her drink back down and pulling on her boots where she had discarded them the night before.

'For the job you're meant to be signed off from,' Thomas pointed out, holding a pain au chocolat up to her face.

She took a bite without even looking at it.

'I saw that Fawkes is back,' he told her, dropping a straw into her black coffee.

'Yeah,' she replied, taking a slurp as she finished buttoning up her coat. 'I was going to tell you.'

Thomas waved it off: 'Are you OK?'

She had never lied to Thomas about her complicated relationship with Wolf but certainly hadn't shared the entire story with him.

'I'm fine,' she said, getting up and giving him a peck on the cheek.

On her way out, she noticed that yet another beautifully wrapped box had been added to the tower of presents beneath the tree.

'I was thinking I'd take the twig to the tip today,' said Thomas when he noticed her looking at it. 'It's starting to smell.'

'Tomorrow?' she suggested.

A wide grin appeared on his face: 'Is it finally Christmas?'

Baxter couldn't help smiling as well. She nodded.

'Roast dinner?' asked Thomas.

'There'd better be.'

'*The Santa Clause 2: The Mrs Clause*?' he called after her excitedly.

'As long as we watch *Home Alone* after,' she shouted back, opening the front door.

'Should I invite my mother round?'
'No!'

Wolf had to be chaperoned at all times while on the premises.
Fortunately, he had arrived at New Scotland Yard at the exact
same time as Saunders, who signed him in and was escorting him
across the lobby when his partner approached them.

'All right, mate?' hollered Saunders. 'Miss me yet?'

'You not been here?' Blake asked him, stopping to chat.
'Honestly hadn't noticed.' He turned to Wolf and nodded in
greeting. 'Really sorry about Finlay,' he said, offering out his hand.

Wolf shook it and then pocketed the colourful Post-it note he'd
just been handed.

Saunders raised his eyebrows: 'Do I even want to know?'

Blake turned to him: 'Probably not.'

There was an uneasy atmosphere in the forensic lab as Wolf,
Baxter, Edmunds, Christian and Saunders all waited for Joe to
return. It was impossible to ignore the fact that their friend's body
was somewhere in the room with them, concealed behind one of
the uniform freezer doors.

Against her will, Baxter's eyes kept returning to Wolf. He looked
a completely different man to the previous day: clean-shaven and
wearing a smart white shirt that didn't strain the buttons. He
looked like the Wolf she remembered from long ago . . . before
the Ragdoll investigation . . . before the Cremation Killer . . .
before everything had gone so very wrong.

She noticed him glance down at a brightly coloured scrap of
paper in his hand but didn't quiz him about it, instead turning
her attention to Saunders, who looked bloody awful, even by his
standards.

'You look bloody awful, even by your standards.'

'Rough night,' he yawned, dark bags under his eyes. 'Car got
broken into again.'

Baxter opened her mouth to say something.

'Not to worry,' Saunders told her. 'Edmunds took all the evidence boxes when I dropped him off.'

'Well, that's a relief,' said Christian, who'd been listening in.

'Doesn't fix my broken window or bring my satnav back,' Saunders pointed out. 'But I'm glad you're happy.'

The door swung open and Joe entered, setting his equipment down: 'Welcome! Welcome!' he greeted them enthusiastically. 'I'm gonna be needing a cheek swab and fingerprints from each of you good people. But first: it's been an interesting night . . .'

He hurried over to a laptop beside a pile of printouts.

'I've got a match for the blood under the floorboards.'

'Already?' asked Edmunds.

'Yes. Because it's Finlay's.'

Christian cleared his throat: 'And that helps us *how*?'

'It doesn't really,' admitted Joe. 'Although the fabric fibres dried into it didn't come from any of the clothes Finlay was wearing when he died.'

'So . . .' started Christian, trying to understand why the strange little man was so excited. 'You think it got there from somebody else?' he asked, stating the obvious.

'I do,' Joe nodded, grinning like a madman and already preparing his next item on the agenda. 'Think about it: all we'd proved before was that someone *could* have been in that locked room with Finlay and that, at some point, somebody had been down in that hidden compartment. But *now* we know that someone with a murdered man's blood on their clothes was down in that hidden compartment *and* could have been in that locked room with Finlay . . . See the difference?'

Five blank faces answered him.

'There's a difference,' Joe assured them.

'Just playing devil's advocate here,' said Christian, 'but couldn't it *still* have been Finlay, wearing something different, on another day? Maybe while building it?'

'In theory, yes . . . but I don't think so,' answered Joe unhelp-fully. 'Bringing me on to my next item.' He donned a pair of disposable gloves and placed a replica gun, similar in size to the one found beside Finlay, onto a tray. 'Wolf . . .'

'Lab guy?'

'Could you please come and pick this gun up?'

Wolf obligingly walked over to Joe. Wrapping his fingers round the handle, he then used his other hand to support the weight as he readjusted to place his finger over the trigger.

'Great,' smiled Joe. 'Back on the tray, please . . . OK. Now check this out.'

He turned off the lights and then flicked a switch on a UV strip, which buzzed in his hand like a lightsabre. The group huddled closer to the purple radiance fending off the darkness; Wolf's fingerprints were glowing brightly, coating both the handle and the barrel of the weapon.

'Covered, right? Now look at Finlay's gun after the same test.' Joe turned the laptop towards them: a relatively tidy row of finger-prints lined the handle, while a smudged partial print painted the trigger. 'Is it just me or does that look a little too neat?'

'Especially for a man who'd been drinking heavily all evening,' Edmunds pointed out.

'You didn't think so the first time round,' Baxter told Joe accusingly.

'He *could* have picked the gun up like that, which seemed the most likely scenario when he was found in a locked room,' shrugged Joe. 'But *you* asked me to look for *anything* that might suggest otherwise, so I thought I might wisely suggest other things.'

Baxter frowned, back in her box.

'And it's the same story on the body,' he continued, oblivious to his audience tensing up at his callousness. 'The minor injuries originally dismissed as general DIY bumps and bangs could *still* just be general DIY bumps and bangs. The only significant trauma is to the cartilage in the nose, but that's completely meaningless because Finlay's been punched in the face almost as many times as Saunders.' He laughed.

No one else did.

'Anyway, someone's done a pretty spectacular job of covering their tracks. It *is* a murder scene, but that's all we know right now. Cards on the table: I'm not sure I'm going to find much more here.'

'Spectacular job or not, this doesn't change a thing,' Wolf told the team on seeing their dejected expressions. 'We carry on exactly as we were: the motive and the gun. Nothing else matters.'

After leaving New Scotland Yard, Christian had driven out to Muswell Hill to check in on Maggie, where she had revealed her intention of selling the house once the investigation was over, explaining that she couldn't bear to stay and could never put her grandchildren in that room now as Finlay had envisioned. Christian had promised to help her with the sale of the property and get her settled somewhere new when the time came. And then, in an ill-fated attempt to cheer her up, he had whipped up one of his 'famous' Marmite omelettes, which, incredibly, tasted even more revolting than it sounded.

'Not a fan, then?' he asked as he scraped the remnants of his masterpiece into the bin. Maggie, meanwhile, was on her third glass of water.

'It's not that. I just can't get the taste out of my mouth,' she laughed.

'You know, many a lucky lady has woken up to one of those in the morning.'

'Did any of them ever come back?'

Christian had to think about it: 'Now that you mention it . . .'

Maggie burst out laughing.

'I've got something for you,' she told him, getting up and disappearing down the hallway.

A few moments passed and then she returned with a cardboard box adorned with the Metropolitan Police Service logo and the word 'EVIDENCE' printed in large red writing.

'What's this?' asked Christian with a frown.

'Oh, excuse the box. Fin used to nick them from work all the time. The garage is full of them. It's just some old photos, some of his police stuff, a few newspaper clippings. I thought you might want to have them.'

'You're sure?' he asked, taking the box from her.

'It's just stuff,' said Maggie. 'It's not him.'

At 12.14 p.m., Christian bid farewell to Maggie and stepped out into the sunshine with his box of keepsakes. One of the neighbours had clearly earned themselves fifty quid by tipping off the press because a small assemblage of journalists now surrounded his Lexus.

Forcing a smile onto his face, he approached the car.

'Mr Commissioner, have there been any breakthroughs in the case yet?'

'Now, you know I can't talk about that,' he chuckled, struggling to open the rear door one-handed.

'What's in the box? Has more evidence been discovered?'

'Or that,' replied Christian. 'Excuse me,' he said, squeezing past a cameraman to open the driver's-side door.

'Mr Commissioner, what message do you have for DS Shaw's killer?'

Christian climbed in and closed the door. He switched on the engine and lowered the window to answer. 'A message? I suppose . . . I'd want to say that Finlay was . . . He was my . . .'

'Mr Commissioner?' the reporter prompted when he trailed off.

'Finlay deserved better than this,' he said vacantly, trapped somewhere between his thoughts and the question. 'Both he and Maggie deserved better cards than life ever dealt them. And the *pathetic* coward responsible for his death deserves to burn for all eternity for what they've done . . . That is all.'

Raising his window on the stunned journalists, Christian slowly pulled away.

CHAPTER 13

Saturday 9 January 2016
12.30 p.m.

Wolf checked his reflection in the tinted window of a Honda Civic.

He reread the address that Blake had obtained for him and looked back up at the smart apartment building doubtfully. The lobby-bound concierge was staring out at him, almost driven to action by Wolf's twenty minutes of deliberation. So, petrol-station bouquet in hand, he entered through the revolving doors and walked up to the desk.

'Ashley Lochlan, please.' He stole a glance at his crumpled Post-it. 'Apartment 114.'

The man behind the desk appeared disinclined to overly exert himself, lifting the phone as though it were a lead weight.

'Name?'

Wolf went to answer and then smiled: 'Fawkes. Just Fawkes.'

Finally recognising him, the man sat up straight and punched in the number, excited to play his small part in reuniting the only survivors of the Ragdoll murders.

'I'm afraid there's no answer,' he told Wolf, infinitely more polite now that he knew he was in the presence of a minor celebrity. 'But . . . and I shouldn't really be telling you this' – he leaned across the desk conspiratorially – 'there's a playground just at the end of the road. Chances are, that's where you'll find them.'

Compensating the man, who fortunately accepted both bus fare and reluctant selfies as payment, Wolf followed his directions to the entrance of a pleasant recreation ground. With his pulse quickening, he started ambling through, scanning the faces of the frozen parents until he saw her. Her long blonde hair was spilling down her shoulders from under a beanie hat, and she looked every bit as beautiful as he remembered. She was sitting on a bench, laughing as a well-dressed man spun a little boy round playfully.

'He's a puker!' she warned the man in her soft Edinburgh accent.

There wasn't a single part of Wolf that had expected her to wait for him to possibly return. And he hadn't any realistic aspiration of rekindling their few days together by showing up like this out of the blue. He had just wanted to explain himself, explain why he hadn't contacted her. He felt that she deserved that much.

He started to approach.

Ashley *really* hoped Jordan wouldn't throw up over Ted's suede shoes, but she wasn't going to intervene. She had never seen him so happy.

She zipped the final inch of her jacket up around her neck as someone walked over to the rubbish bin beside her. When they lingered there for a moment longer than felt natural, she turned to give them an enquiring smile . . .

'Mum! Look!' laughed Jordan, who was definitely looking a little green.

'I know, honey. I am looking!' she called back.

She turned to see a tall man in a long black coat walking away and then noticed the cheap bouquet of flowers poking out from the top of the bin.

Reminded of something . . . of someone . . . Ashley couldn't help but smile to herself.

Edmunds had remained behind with Joe to catalogue the physical entries from the five archived evidence boxes. With each new sealed item, Joe became increasingly excited and soon had every piece of equipment in the lab running tests simultaneously while he darted between them.

Edmunds's phone started to buzz in his pocket. Taking it out, he saw Thomas's name illuminated on the screen. Trapped deep in the bowels of New Scotland Yard, he moved to the opposite side of the room, aware that Joe was listening to his every word.

'Hi . . . No, it's fine . . . OK? . . . O–K? . . . You what?! . . . Tonight?'

Edmunds glanced behind him and frowned at Joe, who was making no effort to disguise that he was eavesdropping. He lowered his voice.

'It's not really . . . It's not really the time . . . Yes, I know that . . . I know that too. I just think it's a bad idea right now . . . Yeah, well . . . Bye.'

He looked down at the screen, shook his head and returned to his seat. After a few moments, he picked his mobile back up to type out a short message:

Sorry. Can we talk about it later?

Ignoring Joe's inquisitive glances, Edmunds attempted to concentrate on his work, but his mind immediately returned to the phone call and this latest looming disaster.

'Shit,' he whispered, rubbing his eyes.

Baxter had spent the majority of the afternoon playing Go Fish with Rouche. Finlay's favourite card game had now become part of the routine during her visits. Perhaps it was wishful thinking, but he had seemed a little more his old self, so she had decided not to bring up the blood-poisoning, organ-failing, next-decade-in-a-prison-cell-themed elephant in the room. With a little over an hour to go until Holly's arrival, she had made him a sandwich and set off back home.

Wolf was sitting out on Maggie's front wall watching the colour drain from the sky when a set of headlight beams rounded the corner. A car pulled up directly in front of the house and a young man climbed out dressed in shredded jeans and trainers.

'Constable Randle?' asked Wolf uncertainly. He looked more like a university student than a police officer.

'Yes,' he smiled, walking over to shake Wolf's hand.

'Thanks for meeting me on your day off. I'm William Fawkes.'

'I know who you are, sir.'

'I won't take up much of your time. Would you be able to take me through your movements, step by step, after arriving here on New Year's Eve?'

'Of course,' said Randle pleasantly. 'Although, I'm not sure I can tell you anything more than was in my statement.'

Wolf shrugged: 'Humour me.'

'Well, I was attending an "emergency concern for welfare" call and parked up in pretty much the exact spot I'm in now,' he started, leading the way down the garden path. 'There was an upstairs light on, so I rang the bell and knocked. I then identified myself by calling through the letter box. When there was no reply, I tried the door to find it locked.'

'Definitely locked?'

'Yes, sir. At which point, I decided to open it with force.'

'How much force?'

'A single kick,' said Randle, pointing to the dent just below the handle.

Wolf opened the door and they stepped into the hallway.

'I called out again and checked each of the ground-floor rooms one by one before moving upstairs.'

The wood creaked beneath their feet as they made their way up.

'I poked my head through each of the open doorways before discovering this room locked.'

Wolf nodded and pushed the door open, stepping up into the crime scene. Randle followed him inside, the young man staring down in bewilderment at the exposed compartment in the floor.

'We believe someone else was in here,' explained Wolf. 'Randle?'

'I . . . I never even thought to . . .' He trailed off.

'No one would. Don't worry – you're not in trouble,' Wolf assured him. 'What happened next?'

Randle closed his eyes as he tried to remember. 'After forcing the door, I saw the body lying face down and the gun beside it. I . . . checked for a pulse and then left the room to call it in.'

'Show me.'

They stepped back out onto the landing, Wolf following him down the stairs and out to the car.

'I radioed it in from here.'

'With the front door wide open like that?' Wolf asked him.

Randle nodded.

'Did you move from this spot at any time?'

'No.'

Wolf looked back at the house. There was no possible way anybody could have escaped out the front without being seen.

'And then what?'

'Ummm . . . The commissioner arrived.'

'OK. From which direction?'

The young man pointed down the street.

'He seemed very distressed. He came up to me and just said: "Finlay?" And then I shook my head and he ran into the house.'

'Where were you?'

'Still here until backup arrived.'

'And then?'

'We all went inside.' Randle headed back into the hallway. 'The commissioner was sitting up on the top stair. He looked shell-shocked. I took him down to the kitchen and offered to make him something to drink. He said no, so I checked all the rooms, doors and windows . . . To be honest, I was just trying to stay out of the detectives' way.'

'Find anything?'

'All secure.'

'Was the key in the lock like that?' asked Wolf, gesturing to the back door.

'Yes. Definitely locked and bolted from the inside.'

'And you checked the garage?'

'Yes.'

Wolf rubbed his face, none the wiser and fast running out of questions.

'You really think it was murder?' Randle asked him.

'Yeah . . . we do.'

'That would mean they were under the floor for hours, wouldn't it?'

Wolf looked confused, still piecing together all these fresh snippets of information.

'I'd have seen anyone leaving through the front,' continued Randle, thinking out loud, 'and all the other exits were secure. To seal the room from the inside, they must have been down there the whole time: when I broke down the door, when the commissioner came running in, the detectives . . . the coroner.'

'Yet didn't leave a trace of evidence,' mumbled Wolf, his head beginning to hurt.

'Pardon?'

'Nothing. Thank you, Constable Randle. You've been extremely helpful.'

CHAPTER 14

Saturday 9 January 2016
8.05 p.m.

Thomas had gone all out for their belated Christmas dinner.

To a backing track of Bing and Mariah, he and Baxter had drunk far too much, eaten more and almost burned the place down with a rogue cracker as it gradually turned dark outside. Abandoning the never-ending job of cleaning up the kitchen, they had changed into their pyjamas and snuggled up with Echo to watch the movie.

Thomas got up to Febreze the tree again, which already had car air-fresheners hanging from its branches like decorations. 'Presents?' he suggested hopefully.

Baxter sprang to life. She paused the movie, filled up their glasses and assumed her position on the floor, reaching for the beautifully wrapped latest addition to the pile.

'Probably save that one until last,' suggested Thomas.

Baxter set it to one side and ripped open another. 'Cluedo,' she said flatly.

'Yeah. Because . . . With you being a detective and all.'

She nodded encouragingly: 'All the fun of work in the comfort of my own home.'

The atmosphere had soured a little.

'Open that one,' she told him.

'Socks!'

'For your feet.'

'Wonderful. Now you go.'

'Earrings! Gold earrings . . . like the ones my mother buys me.'

'You can take them back, but I remembered you said you'd lost one in the snow.'

'One of the few positive things to come out of that night,' mumbled Baxter. 'Oh, that one!'

Thomas tore the wrapping paper open and frowned at the tasteful pair of slippers. 'Why do you hate my slipper boots so much?!'

It carried on like this for a while.

A road sign marked the boundary of Epping Forest and Christian immediately felt himself relax. His drive home never failed to have that effect on him. Situated at the furthest reaches of the sprawling Underground network, the quaint market town was his haven from the oppressive skyscrapers and congested streets of the capital. Regretting his highly unprofessional televised response to what should have been a simple question, he had visited his favourite restaurant, sitting at his usual table to dine alone before heading back to his seven-bedroom woodland excrescence.

He stopped at a mini roundabout and watched a bright set of headlights pull up behind him. Waving apologetically, having paused for no reason, Christian put the car in gear and set off once more. He knew he wasn't driving very well and tried to force himself to concentrate. He indicated and made a left turn, dark trees lining the roadside as, moments later, a white light swept across his dashboard. The vehicle behind closed the gap between them. Christian frowned and sped up a little, but the two blazing suns in his rear-view mirror followed, dazzling him as he negotiated the long stretch of open road.

A car started to approach from the other direction.

The vehicle behind accelerated right up to his bumper before overtaking and speeding away. Christian noted that it was a black

Mitsubishi truck of some sort but was unable to make out the model and had neither the cause nor the energy to memorise the number plate. Slowing back down, he continued on the final few minutes of his journey.

Christian pulled into his road and pushed the button to his electric gate, the nightly routine choreographed to perfection as he passed his neighbours' capacious homes. Ambient lighting climbed the walls and highlighted sections of the landscaped gardens like works of art beneath a star-filled sky, a sight few Londoners ever got to appreciate.

Turning the wheel to enter his driveway, he was suddenly bathed in a stark white light . . .

There was the throaty revving of a powerful engine, the squeal of spinning tyres, and then he felt his head impact the glass. The car rocked. Broken metal clattered onto the road as the black truck reversed a few metres.

Barely conscious, Christian was dragged from his seat and dropped between the two vehicles, headlights blinding him from either side as the violent onslaught commenced. He was kicked and struck from all directions by two faceless silhouettes. All he could do was cover his head and pull himself up into a ball as he prayed for it to end. When one of his attackers stamped on his chest, Christian cried out, hearing his ribs break, and realised they wouldn't cease until he was dead. Kicking out frantically, he managed to scramble underneath the truck, losing a shoe to a grasping hand as it attempted to pull him back out.

Panting mist against the warm chassis, he watched a pair of black boots circle the vehicle. Too experienced to risk anyone hearing their voices, he heard them whistle to one another in code. As one of them searched his destroyed car, pouring the contents of the cardboard box out over the road, the other climbed back into the truck and started to rev the engine, which pulled against the straining handbrake.

With no option left, Christian crawled out and started hobbling towards his electric gates as they slowly began to close.

The truck door slammed behind him.

He could hear footsteps far faster than his own pursuing him. In desperation, he threw himself through the narrowing gap moments before the heavy gates rattled shut.

The silhouette was watching him through the bars, twirling a crowbar teasingly as it regarded the modest wall between them. Lying just a few feet from his attackers, Christian knew that he was utterly spent, that should they choose to clamber over, he wouldn't even try to run.

Blue flashing lights lit the sky above the dark forest.

The figure had seen it too and calmly whistled to its partner. The two shadows then climbed back into their damaged truck and reversed aggressively.

The white light retreating from Christian felt like the tide going back out.

As the truck sped down the road and the red tail-lights disappeared round the corner, he lay back and waited for help to arrive, allowing himself to believe that he might just survive the night after all and appreciating the twinkling stars more than he ever had before.

Baxter stared down at the framed family photograph of Edmunds, Tia and Leila in confusion. She and Thomas had decided to take a break from arguing over each other's presents to argue over other people's instead.

'Why would I want this?' she asked. 'I'm not his gran.'

Thomas took the gift from her, looked at it and pulled a face. 'I actually think it's kind of . . . Yeah,' he conceded, putting it down.

'Am I allowed to open this one yet?' she asked, picking up the small store-wrapped gift even though she didn't have particularly high hopes based on what had preceded it. 'Last one.'

'Go ahead.'

Carefully untying the ribbon, she slid a small box from the wrapping. Puzzled, she flipped the lid open and then gasped at the beautiful diamond ring inside. She didn't notice Thomas getting down on one knee, a sharp crack suggesting Edmunds's family portrait might be beneath it. He gently took the box from her, removed the ring and held it out as she stared open-mouthed at him.

'Emily Lauren Baxter . . . I have never felt so worried, emasculated, irritated, redundant or inadequate as I have this past nine months with you. And I want to feel that way for the rest of my life . . . Will you marry me?'

Baxter appeared to have frozen in place.

Thomas struggled to maintain his hopeful smile, not least because his knee was starting to feel wet. He began to wonder whether Edmunds had been right. For almost an hour, he had tried to dissuade Thomas from proposing, to explain that Baxter wouldn't see the gesture as he did but as an added pressure on top of her already considerable list of burdens.

Her phone went off.

In a daze, Baxter got to her feet and walked into the kitchen, while Thomas patiently remained in his humiliating pose.

'Baxter . . . Shit! . . . Is he— . . . I'll be there soon.'

Heading back into the lounge, she smiled awkwardly down at her boyfriend.

'I, errrm . . . I've got to go. But . . . you know . . . Thanks.'

She gave him a very generous double thumbs-up and then sprinted upstairs to get changed.

CHAPTER 15

Saturday 9 January 2016
9.39 p.m.

'Uncage the Wolf, man!' some waster hollered as Wolf rushed through the entrance of King George Hospital and followed signs for the A&E department.

Maggie had beaten him there and embraced him the moment he stepped into the waiting room. It was obvious that she'd been crying.

'How's he doing? You said he'd been . . . *attacked*?' asked Wolf.

She nodded and led him over to a row of empty seats. 'He's going to be all right. A few broken ribs and he took a nasty knock to the head. The rest is just cuts and bruises . . . a *lot* of cuts and bruises,' she informed him, clearly still shaken up.

'Can we see him?' he asked her.

'They said I could in a little while.'

Squeezing her hand, Wolf settled into his uncomfortable seat for the evening.

Baxter and Saunders were sitting either side of Wolf. Each wore the same vacant expression as they watched the muted television while Maggie was permitted a few minutes with Christian. Details of the incident outside the police commissioner's home had reached the BBC in time for the ten o'clock news. Camera-phone footage, taken through a window from one of the properties opposite, captured the scene just moments after the emergency services' arrival: Christian's Lexus was barely recognisable as it bled oil across the road, crudely dammed to preserve the tyre marks that recounted events like an eyewitness.

'Jesus,' mumbled Saunders. The BBC then regurgitated some VT taken earlier in the day: Christian placing a box of evidence into the back seat of his car before delivering his widely reported message to Finlay's killer. 'Typical press . . . Create a problem . . . film the aftermath.'

Neither Wolf nor Baxter replied, or even noticed him speaking for that matter.

'I'm calling Edmunds,' she told them, getting up. She hadn't wanted him to feel obligated to spend the night in a hospital waiting room with them. After all, he wasn't even a detective anymore, and she knew that the case was already voraciously eating into his family time.

'Hey,' whispered Saunders once Baxter was safely out of sight. 'Wolf? Wolf!' he repeated, nudging him to get his attention.

'What?'

'You good?'

'Yeah. Just . . . got something on my mind.'

'I didn't want to bring this up in front of the others,' started Saunders, leaning in close. 'So, I spent most of the afternoon piecing together a timeline for the night Finlay died.'

'Was murdered,' Wolf corrected him.

'Right. Was murdered. I trawled through Maggie and the commissioner's statements and' – he looked a little guilty for bringing it up – 'there was a small *discrepancy*.'

'Go on.'

'The taxi firm had no record of the commissioner returning to Finlay's after midnight.'

Wolf nodded but didn't appear either surprised or concerned by the news.

'Probably used a different company,' reasoned Saunders. 'But I *am* going to need the name of it. Can't really start questioning him about it at the moment, though, can I?'

'I'll talk to him,' said Wolf as images of Christian's wrecked car returned to the screen of the silent television. 'Can we get hold of Finlay's 999 call?'

'It was silent,' said Saunders, as though he were being thick.

'We should probably double-check that.'

'I'll see what I can do,' Saunders told him, slouching back into his chair.

Maggie had agreed to let Saunders drive her home on the proviso that Wolf remain behind in A&E. With Baxter never having returned from her phone call, he had laid claim to a quiet corner of the waiting room and attempted to get some sleep.

He was jolted awake by the sound of screaming – not an occurrence he was entirely unaccustomed to after a year spent in the company of Léo Dubois and his anarchical network of hired help. Wolf had instinctively raised his arms to protect his head, the most violent of the beatings endured at the hands of his contemporaries still monopolising his dreams.

A woman in labour was wheeled in by her panicking husband and promptly escorted through a set of doors.

Wolf checked his watch. Reasonably confident that he'd had his forty minutes for the night, he got up and decided to stretch his legs. Puddles of light pooled beneath closed doors as he lost himself in the hushed corridors. He hadn't encountered another soul during his aimless wandering. It was as peaceful as watching the rising sun spill over the city at the end of a demanding night shift – like watching a ferocious beast sleep.

Passing the doors to the chapel, he glanced inside and was surprised to find a familiar figure sitting in the front row.

'Baxter?' he asked, knocking politely as he entered the cosily lit room.

She folded up the tatty sheet of paper in her hands and turned to look at him.

'Huh . . . ? I'm fine,' she replied as if he had asked.

Frowning, Wolf pulled the doors to and took a seat on the

opposite side of the aisle, regarding the life-sized and wax-skinned Jesus nailed to a cross between them. A collection of tiny paper balls had accumulated beneath from where Baxter had been using the Son of God for target practice.

'Thought you'd gone,' he told her.

'Just needed some time to think.' She put her face in her hands and exhaled deeply.

'Can't think at home?'

'Can't think at home,' she replied.

Wolf nodded and gazed back at the grotesque statue standing before them. The artist had deemed it necessary to embellish the emaciated body with runs of dark blood to more effectively convey the extent of the sacrifice made and, therefore, debt owed to the Almighty: palms tearing round metal nails, thorns embedded deep into the skin, broken feet pinned together twelve inches above the ground.

A killer sending a mutilated message – the first Ragdoll.

Baxter hadn't moved.

'Want me to leave you alone?' Wolf asked her.

She lifted her head and smiled weakly at him: 'No.'

Interpreting this as an invitation, he removed a handful of Starbucks receipts from his pocket. 'How many points for a headshot?'

'Five. Three for the nappy.'

'I believe it's called a loincloth.'

Baxter pulled a face that suggested she didn't particularly care. 'Ten if you get it to balance on his headband.'

'Crown of thorns,' mumbled Wolf as he screwed up his arsenal of paper pellets. 'Ten points!' he shouted on his third attempt.

'You're sitting at a different angle to me,' Baxter snapped at him, as competitive as ever. 'You're cheating.' She got up and moved into the aisle, taking a seat on the hard floor.

She looked to Wolf expectantly.

'Fine . . . Fair now?' he asked, hip pressing against hers where they filled the narrow space, but Baxter didn't object as the game continued in silence.

'Do you . . . Do you think I could ever do the whole . . . *dad* thing?' he blurted, unable to shake the image of Ashley's delighted face as that Murchison-clad bastard dangled her vomitus seven-year-old over his shoulder.

'*This* is what you want to talk about?' asked Baxter. 'Look, Wolf, I'm still pretty drunk right now, and God knows I have a porous enough filter at the best of times.'

Wolf watched her closely as she turned away to take another shot. The throwaway comment was perhaps the most self-aware thing he had ever heard her say and made him realise just how much had changed in his absence, how much she had changed. Sitting in such unnaturally close proximity, he was able to see the countless scratches concealed beneath her make-up and felt the customary ball of guilt twist in his gut for not being there for her.

'Yeah,' he sighed. 'Me neither.'

Abandoning her shot, Baxter turned to him. 'Think I could ever make an even halfway-passable wife?'

Unfortunately, Wolf's look of horror answered before the rest of him could conjure some tact.

'Yeah,' laughed Baxter bitterly. 'Me neither.'

'Timothy proposed?'

'Thomas.'

'That's a curveball. What did Timothy have to say about that?'

'There is no Timothy, just Thomas.'

'And *he* proposed?' Wolf sounded surprised.

'Yes.'

'To you?'

'Yes. To me!' she snapped. 'You may find this hard to believe, Wolf, but I'm actually a very caring and pleasant person to be around . . . you fucktard.'

A little affronted, Wolf took a shot: 'Three points!'

'That was thigh.'

'What?!'

'That was upper thigh at best.'

'Are you kidding me? That was one hundred per cent deity testicle!'

'Whatever,' conceded Baxter. 'I wasn't keeping score anyway.'

Everything really had changed.

'What are you going to do?' Wolf asked her.

'I have absolutely no idea. Things were fine. Everything was fine. I don't understand why he had to . . .' She trailed off and shook her head. 'Are everyone's lives this complicated?'

Wolf shrugged, his shoulder rubbing against hers.

'I remember me and Chambers talking once . . .' she began, 'about our hopes and dreams, what we wanted out of life.'

Wolf remained quiet, stunned that she would even bring up Chambers's name in his presence.

'I probably said something along the lines of "a fancy new car and a garden for Echo". It doesn't matter. But do you know what he said? What he longed for more than anything else in the world?' Baxter's eyes glistened as she immersed herself in the memory. 'To be bored. That was it. He just wanted a simple, mundane existence, to make it through one *fucking* night without being woken by nightmares, to have *one* conversation with Eve where he could give her his undivided attention. I thought it was stupid at the time.'

She dropped the remainder of her pellets to the floor. The game was over.

'There are no happy endings,' she concluded, staring at the murder scene that presided over the chapel, 'not for people like us. There wasn't for Chambers or Eve. Not even for Finlay.' She started to cry. 'Maggie's life is ruined now. So what hope do we have?'

Wolf took her hand and squeezed it tightly.

'We are cursed,' she whispered. 'Our lives are death and pain, and we *deserve* to be alone.'

As she burst into tears, Wolf put his arms around her, embracing her tightly.

'You are *not* cursed,' he told her softly. 'You are my favourite person on this planet and you *choose* this life of death and pain to spare others from it because you are stronger than the rest of them put together. And when your watch is up, you deserve your happy ending more than any of us.'

Baxter wriggled free. As she rummaged in her pocket for a tissue, she smiled up at Wolf. She looked a beautiful mess: her bloodshot eyes framed in black smudges, her unstraightened hair cascading down her back, her red lips parted as she steadied her breathing . . .

Wolf leaned in, drawn to her, unaware that he was even moving . . .

Baxter's elbow scored an indisputable three-pointer, bringing tears to his eyes.

'What the *hell*, Wolf?!' she yelled, getting up as he rolled onto his side.

'I'm sorry,' he winced, holding himself. 'You're with Timothy.'

'Thomas!'

'Can we just forget this happened? I got caught up in the moment, and you were looking all pretty and sad and . . . I apologise.'

'After everything we've *just* been talking about!' She wasn't prepared to let him ruin the life she had built without him.

'I think I'm going to be sick,' Wolf warned her, still writhing in agony.

'You . . . left . . . me!' said Baxter, hurt. 'You didn't want me.'

He looked confused.

'Over a year, Wolf!'

'We've talked about this,' he said, managing to sit up. 'I wanted to come back.'

'That's bullshit. You were just too much of a coward to face up to what you'd done.'

'That's not it.'

'And in the meantime, Finlay was getting murdered. *I* barely survived a living nightmare. And where were you? Hiding. Just what did *you* have to go through?'

Wolf struggled to his feet: 'If I could've come back to you, I would have.'

'Frankly, I don't believe a word that comes out of— What are you doing?'

He started unbuttoning his shirt.

'Wolf?'

Sliding his shoulders free, he dropped the shirt to the floor and turned his back to her.

She gasped.

His skin was a pallet of purples and blues. An entire area on his flank was peppered with grit, the flesh grated and hard. A line of untidy staples, which no doubt should have been removed long ago, climbed the opposite side of his body. And there, right in the centre of his back, a familiar brand dominated the canvas:

$$\mathcal{L}.\mathcal{A}.\mathcal{D}.$$

Property of Léo Antoine Dubois, the burnt skin blackened and dead – a reminder to those who forgot where their allegiances lay.

'If I could've come back to you, I would have,' Wolf repeated. He turned round to face her and smiled sadly. 'Death and pain, right?'

Very slowly, Baxter walked up to him.

'Shit,' she muttered under her breath.

'I know,' he said self-consciously, his wavy hair hanging over his eyes, a day's worth of rough stubble covering his chin.

'You smell good,' she told him, her voice shaking.

'George bought me some aftershave.'

'Who's George?'

'It's not important right now.'

She inhaled deeply, but then stepped away from him: 'I'm leaving.'

'OK.'

Picking up her bag, she'd made it five steps down the aisle before pausing: 'Shit!'

Wolf watched in confusion as she turned back round and marched up to him.

'Shit! Shit! Shit!' She met his gaze, a pained expression on her face as the internal struggle raged on.

Wolf smiled back nervously.

'No. Do you know what? No!' she said decisively.

Spinning back round, she stormed towards the door.

Wolf bent down to pick up his crumpled shirt.

'Shit.'

Before he had even stood back up, Baxter had thrown herself into him, wrapping her long legs round his waist, kissing him impatiently as he stumbled backwards into the statue, which wobbled teasingly . . . before toppling over with a loud crack.

They both froze, turning just in time to watch Jesus's head roll beneath a pew.

'That's not a sign, is it?' asked Wolf, still holding her.

'Nah,' she said, panting warm breath across his face.

She turned his chin back towards her and then pressed her lips into his as he lowered her to the chapel floor.

Baxter pulled Lethaniel Masse's black coat up over her shoulder.

A moment later, her eyes sprang open and she sat bolt upright, Wolf snoring gently beside her.

'*No!*' she gasped, crawling out from beneath the makeshift blanket to retrieve her underwear, which she inexplicably found three rows back.

There were voices out in the corridor, the squeak of trolley wheels rolling by as she dressed herself as quickly as possible. Stepping over decapitated Jesus, she grabbed her bag and snuck out through the doors. Shielding her eyes from the modest morning light, she followed her route from the previous evening back through the A&E waiting room to the car park.

'Emily!' a voice called after her. 'Emily!'

She turned to see Maggie following her outside and quickly ran her functioning fingers through her tussled hair, which did little to fix the mascara streaked across her cheeks.

'Maggie!' she greeted her enthusiastically.

Her friend looked her up and down: 'Are you quite all right, dear?'

'Me? Fine,' grinned Baxter, who had lipstick on her teeth as well.

'It's just . . . I hope you don't mind me saying, but you look like you've been dragged through a bush.' When Baxter didn't respond, she changed the subject. 'Have you seen Will?'

'Nope. Not seen him.'

'He promised me he'd stay,' said Maggie, looking hurt.

'No . . . He did stay. But . . .'

'But . . . you've not seen him,' Maggie finished, knowingly.

'That is correct,' Baxter answered, as though she were on trial.

'You realise that half of your blouse is hanging open?'

Baxter looked down at her feeble attempt at dressing herself and sighed.

'Come over here,' said Maggie, moving them out of the entranceway. She rebuttoned Baxter's blouse, removed the worst of the mascara from her face and tried to do something with her tangled hair.

'I think I've made a terrible mistake,' whispered Baxter, staring blankly into the distance.

'It's only a mistake if you didn't want to do it,' Maggie told her, working miracles with just a wet wipe and her emergency hairbrush.

'I've ruined everything.'

'There!' she said, admiring her creation. 'Beautiful!' She placed a reassuring hand on Baxter's arm. 'Life is far too short for regrets. If Thomas loves you, he'll forgive you. If you and Will are supposed to be together, then you've taken your first steps.'

'But Thomas . . . You haven't met him. He's so kind and patient with me and generous and handsome; he used to model for the Littlewoods catalogue . . . and he's kind . . .'

'You said that already.'

'What am I going to do?'

'I'm afraid that's not really up to me.'

Baxter looked crushed.

'When the time comes,' Maggie assured her, 'you'll know what to do. It might sound foolish, but there was a moment, this *single* fleeting moment, with Fin when I just *knew* . . . It'll come.'

CHAPTER 16

Friday 16 November 1979

9.18 p.m.

'Barkeep!' Christian yelled across the Clyde and Ship Inn off Bridgegate. 'Keep 'em coming!'

The gruff Scotsman behind the bar shook his head.

'All right. All right,' huffed Christian, who made a show of removing a handful of notes from his wallet before making his unsteady way over to the bar. He tossed the pile in front of the man dismissively: 'And a round for every bastard in here!' he shouted to the approval of the busy pub as he waved and bowed to their applause.

'Remember when you said to tell you when you're being a gobshite?' Finlay asked him quietly. 'You're being a gobshite.'

Christian grinned drunkenly at his friend and pinched his saggy cheek. 'Relax. We're celebrating! You look good, by the way,' he told Finlay with a nod, impressed that he had made the effort to wear a shirt for the occasion. He lit up another cigarette and walked away.

With a sigh, Finlay followed his partner back to their corner of the hazy room where Maggie and five of her co-workers were enjoying the undivided attention of the entire Glasgow Robbery Squad.

Christian pushed through his colleagues to reclaim his spot at her side. 'Looks like you need another drink,' he said pointedly to French, who had been keeping her company in his absence.

'If you're offering?'

'I'm not.'

Either side of Maggie, both men tensed up.

'Looks like *you* need another drink as well,' she told Christian, who regarded his half-full pint of bitter in confusion. Taking it from his hand, she tilted her head back and emptied it in five gulps.

'Good girl!' clapped Christian, flicking cigarette ash all over her. 'Fuck. Sorry!' he said, wiping it with his hand.

'It's fine,' smiled Maggie, excusing herself to clean up her favourite dress.

Finlay saw her weave out of the throng and enter the ladies', noticing that she was wearing a blue bow in her hair the exact same colour as her eyes. He glanced across the snooker table at Christian, who had taken it upon himself to entertain her prettiest friend while she was gone, effortlessly charming her even while drunk. He watched the way that her hands found any excuse to touch his arm and was suddenly acutely aware of the circle of empty space surrounding him.

'Hey, hero.'

Finlay turned round to find Maggie smiling up at him.

Her friend let out a piercingly shrill laugh; half the pub glanced in her direction. Christian had his arms wrapped round her waist as they played some sort of drinking game.

Maggie frowned.

'He's . . . He's being especially . . . *obnoxious* tonight,' Finlay told her. The effort it took to avoid cursing was exhausting.

'It's fine,' said Maggie, turning back to face him. 'I'd much rather talk to you anyway.'

Ten minutes passed, in which Christian drank another pint, smoked two more cigarettes and acquired a phone number up his forearm. Wondering where Maggie had got to, he stumbled across the room and spotted her standing beside the jukebox with Finlay.

'There you are!' he beamed. 'Another drink, anyone?'

'We're fine, thank you,' replied Maggie, raising her glass. 'Fin just bought us one.'

She turned back to Finlay to resume their conversation.

A little bemused, Christian wobbled up to the bar.

'Whisky, my good man,' he asked the bartender, while the jukebox clicked and clunked as it changed record. 'What a song!' he suddenly shouted, downing his drink in one before staggering back over to Maggie. 'You have *got* to dance with me.'

'I'm talking to Fin at the moment,' she smiled.

'Yeah, but it's like . . . my favourite song.'

'She said no,' Finlay told him, his expression a warning.

Raising his hands in surrender, Christian turned to walk away but then grabbed one of Maggie's wrists. 'Come on!'

'No, Christian!'

Finlay stepped round her . . .

'Christian, you're hurting me!'

. . . and then shoved him forcefully into the bar, attracting the attention of the entire pub.

'Take it outside, boys,' ordered the barman.

'No need,' said Finlay, locking eyes with Christian. 'My mate's just had a bit too much to drink. We're done here, aren't we?'

Christian removed another cigarette from his pocket and lit up.

'Aren't we?' repeated Finlay.

'Yeah,' he shrugged, watching smirks appear on the faces of his co-workers at his very public dressing-down. 'Didn't really want to dance with the bitch anyway.'

Finlay had never hit anyone so hard and was astounded when Christian got back up after tumbling into a table. Rubbing his jaw, he picked his cigarette up off the floor, grabbed an upturned bar stool and charged at Finlay, knocking him off his feet as their colleagues rushed in to break it up. When Christian lashed out at French, who threw Wick's drink all over him and the nurse he'd been chatting up, a second fight broke out, prompting the locals to get involved.

'I'm calling the police!' bellowed the barman.

'We're already here, you prick!' someone informed him.

Another stool bounced across the bar, smashing the glass shelf and everything on it as Finlay struggled back to his feet, finishing the fight with a single left hook that knocked Christian out cold.

'You never learn,' he told his unconscious friend.

With a bloody nose, Finlay walked back over to Maggie and offered her his hand. Tentatively placing hers in his, they hurried through the stained-glass doors and out into the chilly November night.

After cleaning himself up in the public conveniences on Saltmarket, Finlay treated Maggie to a night on the town that he could ill afford. They hailed a taxi and somehow convinced La Costiera to stay open while they ordered desserts. He took her dancing at Satellite City and later gave her his jacket as he walked her home along the river.

They eventually arrived at the door to Maggie's shared house and the only illuminated windows on the dark street, where her friends had waited up for her. Finlay waved at one of the angry faces observing from above.

'So . . .' he started awkwardly.

'So . . .' smiled Maggie.

'I'm ignoring the bar brawl when I say this, but it's been a pretty great night.'

She leaned in and gave him a kiss on the cheek. 'There's something I didn't want to tell you earlier because I didn't want to ruin our evening, and I was having such a great time.'

'O–K?'

'I'm starting a new job in a couple of weeks,' Maggie told him.

'OK?' Finlay nodded along, relaxing a little.

'In London.'

'London?'

'I'm sorry I didn't say anything sooner.'

Finlay seemed distracted as he peered down the street.

'Fin?'

'Come with me,' he said, offering his hand once more before leading her to a phone box.

'What are we doing?' she asked.

He dialled a number he knew off by heart and waited for the beep. 'Boss. It's Finlay Shaw . . .'

'Don't call your boss!' Maggie whispered in horror, trying to grab it off him.

'. . . I'm handing in my notice. Call me when you get this.' He went to put the receiver down but then paused: 'I'm transferring to London, by the way . . . for a girl.'

He hung up.

'Fin, are you crazy?!'

He turned to her. 'Look, I don't want you to feel under any pressure from me, and I don't know if anything's going to happen between us, and I don't really know that much about London or if there's even a job for me there,' he explained, struggling to articulate his feelings. 'All I *do* know is that *you* are worth the risk.'

CHAPTER 17

Sunday 10 January 2016
9.10 a.m.

Baxter was sitting on the floor of Thomas's rainfall shower holding the ring that he had given her tightly in her hand. The sensation of the hot water hammering against her head seemed to dull the thoughts she wasn't yet ready to confront. Her fingers had pruned over the course of forty minutes, and Thomas had knocked on the door twice to check on her.

She reached up and turned the knob, feeling the chill of the air on her wet skin. Within seconds, her mind was racing again. Unable to bear it, she twisted the knob back in the opposite direction, letting the tumult subside until the rain was all she could hear.

'Uncage the Wolf, man!'

'Is that guy *still* here?' frowned Wolf, as he and Maggie headed back into the A&E department.

They'd been told Christian had been moved to a private room and that they would be permitted to see him after breakfast, persuading them to brave the hospital canteen for their own. Wolf had questioned Maggie about the sly smile she seemed unable to shift, but she had simply responded that she was relieved Christian was on the mend.

They entered the cramped room. Wolf locked a relaxed expression on his face, underestimating the severity of the attack the commissioner had been subjected to. He empathised, remembering his own apprehension before taking that first look in the mirror to assess the damage. Christian, however, appeared to be in high spirits. The three of them made small talk for a quarter of an hour, Maggie having found yet more old photographs to entertain them with.

'Maggie, I don't want to sound rude . . .' started Wolf.

'But you boys have police stuff to talk about,' she finished on his behalf, sounding a little tired of being evicted from every room she occupied.

Wolf nodded guiltily.

'Say no more.' She got up. 'I'll be in the waiting room.'

After giving Christian a careful hug, she left them alone.

'News?' Christian asked hopefully. One of his eyes was swollen shut and he had burns from the abrasive airbag.

'Nothing new,' replied Wolf. 'Who's looking into your attack?'

'They left a card,' said Christian, gesturing to the bedside counter.

'I'll get in touch.'

'Please do . . . I'm presuming that's not the reason Maggie had to leave, though?'

'It's not,' admitted Wolf. 'Saunders hasn't been able to corroborate your return trip to Finlay's with the taxi company. Perhaps you used a different firm to the one mentioned in your statement or—'

'Yes. Can we go with that?' Christian interrupted him, glancing at the open door.

Wolf got up to close it.

'Wishful thinking, I suppose, hoping this wouldn't come up,' said Christian. 'I drove myself.'

Wolf looked unsurprised by the answer.

'Christ knows how much over the limit I was that night,' he continued. 'I saw that text message, I panicked, and I jumped straight into my car without a second thought. Will, you should do whatever you see fit with this information . . . Admittedly not my finest hour.'

Wolf deliberated for a moment and then stood up.

'A different taxi firm,' he concluded, buttoning up his coat. 'Just as I thought.'

Baxter tensed up on hearing a car door slam.

Edging her coffee cup a few inches to the right, she then decided she had preferred it where it was and moved it back again. Sitting up straight, she watched the front door as a butchered rendition of Ed Sheeran's 'Lego House' grew louder.

'Brrrrr!' shivered Thomas, wiping his shoes on the mat and placing his keys down before noticing her sitting there. 'You're home! You'll be very pleased to hear that the tree is gone,' he informed her, closing his eyes and taking a greedy breath. 'Smell that fresh— I think Echo might have pooed.'

He had.

Thomas walked past the chattering television and gave her a kiss on the forehead, which Baxter accepted without moving a muscle.

'Coffee?' she offered.

'Oh cock,' said Thomas, taking a seat at the table. 'What's wrong?' He hadn't even removed his windbreaker as he reached out to take her hand, which she slid slowly from his grasp. 'Emily, what is it?'

Baxter cleared her throat. 'Do you know how we've all got *those* people?' she started ambiguously, looking ill. '*That* person? The one that got away?'

'I . . . *guess*,' he replied, now mirroring her sickly expression.

'Like that girl at university you told me about,' said Baxter, trying to recall the story. 'Gemma something?'

'Gemma Holland!' nodded Thomas, unable to keep the grin off his face.

'Right. And even though you're with me now and we have our own . . . *thing*, if she walked through that door right this second, how do you think you'd feel?'

'I'm pretty sure she's a *he* now,' said Thomas.

Baxter huffed. 'OK. Bad example. But William Fawkes . . . Wolf

. . . is my "one that got away",' she explained, meeting his eye. 'And the reason I never made it back home last night is because' – she took a steadying breath – 'I was with *him*.'

Thomas looked confused.

'I'm using the word "with" in the biblical sense here,' she clarified.

'I don't think that's a thing.'

'OK. But still—'

'You're thinking of "know".'

'I'm not sure it matters that much right now.'

'No,' he agreed, looking lost. 'I suppose not.'

'I could list you some lame excuses about being freaked out by your proposal or having *way* too much to drink last night. I could blame everything that's happened in the last month for screwing with my head. But that's all they'd be: excuses.'

Thomas nodded as an inappropriately cheery advert sang from the television's speakers.

'I've started packing up my things,' she continued, placing the ring box on the table. She slid it over to him. 'I guess you'll be wanting this back.'

He looked down at it and then back up at her: 'So, that's it, then?'

'Well, I just figured—'

'Don't try to put this on me. I meant it when I said I wanted to spend the rest of my life with you. If that's not what you want, then *you* can be the one to swing the axe. Excuse me,' he said, getting up.

'Where are you going?'

'Out.' Walking over to the sofa, Thomas was the very picture of composure as he picked up the remote control, finding the next advert even more insufferable than the last.

'Out where?'

'For a walk,' he answered distractedly, pushing buttons that didn't appear to be doing anything. In the end, he just pitched the little black box through the screen, which seemed to do the trick. 'Excuse me,' he said again to a stunned Baxter, the television still fizzing electrically as he headed out through the door.

Wolf had finally made it to a shower, which was good news for him, even better for everyone else. He and Saunders had been waylaid, using the afternoon to meet with the detective from Essex Police heading up the investigation into Christian's assault. While unquestionably appalling that the victim of such a crime would be the commissioner of the Metropolitan Police himself, it was hard to deny that it was also rather useful. The detective couldn't do enough for them, bending over backwards to be accommodating, and appeared practically ecstatic at the prospect of having another police force interfering with his work.

There had been little to report overnight, however. The Mitsubishi truck had been found abandoned and torched on a bridal path near Hatfield; forensics were working their way through the wreckage. Having enhanced the neighbour's camera-phone footage, all that had been established was that the two men were almost definitely men, both over six feet tall, muscular and experienced enough to clean up after themselves. The remaining debris had all been collected and taken back for cataloguing.

Smelling better, Wolf wrapped a towel round his waist and strode half-naked through Paddington Green Police Station to settle into his cell for the night.

Edmunds had lost all track of time, working by the light of a broken lamp taped to the top of his lawnmower. Leaving Tia and Leila in front of the Sunday-afternoon movie, he had retreated to the garden to continue with his work. He scribbled himself a note: a reminder to request further files relating to the group operating out of the shipyard warehouse. An entirely separate narcotics-led investigation had been carried out, which he now believed posed a direct bearing upon their own. He leaned back and stretched, joints clicking satisfyingly, when there was a scream from the house.

Kicking over the stool, he bundled out through the door and across his dark patch of garden.

'Alex! Alex!' called Tia, flicking the kitchen light on as Leila wailed in her arms.

The moment he reached the back door, he understood the reason for her alarm: wet boot-prints muddied the lino floor between them, entering from the living room and tracing a leisurely circle round the kitchen before leaving.

'Someone was in the house!' she panted, rocking Leila calm.

'Stay here,' Edmunds told her, pulling the cutlery drawer open and finding a knife.

He stepped through the doorway and felt physically sick when he saw the intruder's route round the sofa on which his fiancée and daughter had been sleeping. Noticing a strange smell in the air, he charged up the stairs, chasing footprints. He checked the wardrobes and then hurried back down, the smell intensifying. A bubbling, hissing sound was emanating from the hallway as he entered. The three boxes of evidence had been rearranged, stacked atop one another; they looked as though they were melting.

Carefully negotiating the dissolving tower, he edged past, checking the bathroom on his right before continuing out into the front garden. Jogging to the roadside, he saw no trace of movement anywhere on the frozen street. He stood there, watching the darkness for almost a minute before heading back inside, kicking what little remained of the boxes over in the hope of salvaging something. As he hurried back to his family, he took out his phone and selected Baxter's number.

'Acid?' asked Saunders as Joe crouched over the gloopy mess on Edmunds's floor.

Shaking a pot in his hand, he held it up to the light, watching the spinning liquid gradually turn red.

'Oh yeah,' replied Joe, standing back up.

Edmunds wore a look of disgust: 'They were carrying this stuff around Leila.'

Wolf watched in astonishment as Baxter reached out to hold Edmunds's hand. She'd walked right past him when she arrived and had been avoiding eye contact ever since.

'Have they gone to her mum's?' she asked.

Edmunds nodded.

'So, we're all now thinking my car gettin' broken into wasn't *just* my car gettin' broken into, right?' asked Saunders. 'Me . . . the commissioner . . . now Edmunds. We're being targeted.'

'Which means we're getting closer,' said Wolf.

'Closer to a toe tag maybe,' mumbled Saunders.

Everyone frowned at him.

'What?' he asked innocently. 'Just sayin'.' Changing the subject, he turned to Baxter: 'Wolf said last night wasn't really worth hangin' around for.'

'Owww!' complained Edmunds when she dug her nails into his hand.

'Just a whole lot of waiting for something that wasn't gonna happen,' he elaborated, sensing the abrupt change in atmosphere. 'Uncomfortable,' he added, unsure whether to keep talking or not.

'He told you what now?!' asked Baxter, by this point most certainly making eye contact with Wolf.

Everyone else turned back to Saunders, none quite sure what he'd said wrong, including Saunders himself.

'Errrr. He said he wanted to . . . *doze off* for a bit but couldn't.'

Baxter's mouth dropped open in outrage.

'I think,' started Wolf, finally catching up, 'he's referring to our night spent on the waiting-room chairs.'

'Well . . . yeah,' shrugged Saunders, confused.

'Oh,' sighed Baxter. 'I didn't stay all night.'

'She left about . . .'

'Eleven?' she suggested.

'. . . two.' Wolf glared at her. 'Two minutes past eleven.'

'Not that you're keeping tabs on me or anything!' fake-laughed Baxter.

'Heavens, no!' replied Wolf, ending the awkward exchange in the most unnatural way possible. He wasn't sure if there was such a thing as a 'suspicious silence', but if there was, this was most definitely one of them. He quickly changed topic: 'I wonder what was in those boxes that was so important.'

Joe puffed out his cheeks as he regarded the puddle of slime at his feet. 'Unfortunately, we'll never know.'

CHAPTER 18

Monday 5 November 1979

Bonfire Night

9.14 p.m.

Finlay fell heavily, scraping his palms on the concrete, the smoke lining his lungs suffocating him slowly from the inside. Struggling to catch his breath, one side of his body was bathed in a warming glow as the first prickles of pain shot across his hands.

'Fin!' yelled Christian from somewhere behind him, his voice getting louder: 'Fin, get your arse up!'

Overladen with his own load, Christian staggered past: several kilo bags of off-white powder, which he dumped atop their growing pile. Finlay got to his knees and started collecting up the bags scattered around him.

'How many more?' he spluttered when Christian jogged over to help.

But Christian didn't answer, saddling him with the bags he'd picked up.

'How many more?' asked Finlay.

'I'm going back in!' Christian shouted, having to shield his eyes when there was an explosion at the far end of the building.

'How many?!' Finlay asked again, but his partner was already running back towards the loading bay. 'Ah!' he grimaced in frustration, half falling into the mountain of heroin as he dropped his contribution against it.

Exhausted, he pushed himself off and hurried back inside to assist with the remainder. Passing through the deformed metal shutter, he rounded the wreckage of the van and then froze, unable to comprehend the situation he'd been presented with: he was standing at the bottom of the metal staircase where Christian had tossed the trolley-load of bags down to him . . . but there were no bags left to carry.

The trolley was gone.

Christian was gone.

'You *bloody* idiot!' spat Finlay, already climbing the steep stairway as he headed back into the fire.

The cool loading bay had lulled Christian into a false sense of security.

Beads of sweat were running into his eyes, the metal structure acting as a giant oven as he pulled the flatbed trolley towards the haze at the end of the corridor. As he passed the furthermost doorway, the heat became unbearable and he considered turning back, the room already claimed, the fire already behind him. Reaching his destination, he struggled to drag the flatbed over the body in the doorway, inadvertently dislodging it.

He fell into the room beyond, hearing the pressurised door slam shut behind him.

'Shit!' he shouted.

The entire back wall was ablaze. He could feel his eyes burning.

Pulling his scarf up over his nose and mouth, he began tossing the neat blocks of cash onto the trolley. Less than thirty seconds later, he was back at the sealed exit. Wrapping his hands round the metal handle, he heard the fizz of his skin blistering before he felt it. He cried out and turned back to the fire, mesmerised by the way in which it rolled in on itself, gorging its way across the ceiling towards him.

An idea came to him: he took out the gun that Finlay had entrusted him with and pointed it at a hinge . . .

'Christian!'

'Fin!' he coughed. 'Fin, I'm trapped!'

There were several loud clunks as Finlay tried in vain to free the door from the other side.

'Fin, hurry!' he called desperately, before watching his blocked escape route in confusion; he heard the distinct hiss of air escaping, felt a rush of warmth pass his ears.

There was a violent slam behind him.

Spinning round, Christian locked eyes with a badly wounded man, his age at most, if not younger. Dressed in casual clothing, he was clearly part of the warehouse operation rather than one of the professional mercenaries responsible for the botched robbery. The stranger appeared equally stunned to see him standing there. As the initial moment of shock began to pass, they each regarded the gun in the other's hand, instinct taking hold . . .

Simultaneously, they raised their weapons. But it was Christian who fired first.

In mortified wonder, he watched the brawny young man fall back into the wall, letting the gun slip from his grasp as he slid to the floor.

Finlay had heard the gunshot on the other side of the door and was frantically calling Christian's name. There was a cry as he finally managed to shove the burning metal open with his bare arm. He looked from his partner to the weapon in his hand, to the crumpled man against the wall as he fought to hold the door.

'Check for a pulse!' he instructed Christian, who just stood there vacantly. 'See if he's still alive!' he shouted, repositioning the body in the doorway and stepping as far into the room as he dared.

Snapping into action, Christian dropped the gun and rushed over to the body, the blazing ceiling beginning to fall in around him. He felt sick when he saw the stranger's eyes following him, because he had already made his decision. Knowing that Finlay was watching, he placed two fingers to the man's throat, feeling the rhythmic beat just below the skin.

'I'm sorry,' he whispered, before turning back to his partner:

'He's dead!'

'Come on, then!' yelled the Scotsman, already at the door.

'The money!' Christian shouted after him.

'Leave it!'

'Fin!'

'Leave it!'

Grasping the handle of the trolley, Christian attempted to pull it through the narrow doorway alone.

'Fin! Help me!' He tugged desperately, unable to roll the wheels over the metal lip, watching helplessly as two blocks of cash slid off the back of the flatbed and were instantly claimed by flames. 'Fin!'

Suddenly, he was back at Christian's side, his thick hands wrapped round the metal handle. And then together they gave the heavy trolley one last heave, finally freeing it of the furnace.

Finlay was standing by the water watching the fireworks.

After all the photographs and bravado, he had seen Christian sitting alone, still failing to steady his bandaged hand. But he hadn't gone over to him.

Their colleagues were wandering about aimlessly, entertaining themselves by watching the fire service do their thing or admiring the bullet holes peppering the bonnet of their Ford Cortina, for the moment, at least, unaware of what he and Christian had crammed into the boot . . . of what they had done. He had never felt so disconnected from them, people he had worked alongside for years; a split-second decision that had changed everything. He wished he could just roll the car into the fire, burn it, burn the money, burn the guilt and shame away.

It would just be ash if we hadn't taken it.

They'd only lock it up in evidence for ever.

No one knows we have it. It's a victimless crime.

Christian's words were rattling around his head. Only, it wasn't a victimless crime at all because *they* had contributed one set of those charred remains.

Finlay removed the handgun from his waistband. He gripped

the handle with a clean bandage so as not to decorate it in any more of his prints. He wasn't entirely sure why he had picked it up off the floor, confident that the fire would have destroyed the evidence anyway.

Better to be safe than sorry, he supposed.

Staring out over the dark water, he reflected on how quickly one deceit could lead to another and started wiping the barrel clean. But then, for reasons that he didn't fully understand himself, he stopped.

Quickly wrapping the gun up in the bandage, he tucked it into the back of his trousers, holding his injured arm as he watched the rest of the display.

CHAPTER 19

Monday 11 January 2016
8.02 a.m.

Joe had listened to the entirety of Pink Floyd's *Dark Side of the Moon*, Led Zeppelin's *III* and Katy Perry's *Teenage Dream* by the time he crashed out on one of the metal gurneys at around 3 a.m. After giving the morning cleaner the fright of her life, he pulled the white sheet off himself and climbed down in search of caffeine.

With bleary eyes, he checked on each of the stations he had left running through the night. Like a nerdy zombie, he trudged between them, flicking through paperwork and typing lethargically into terminals . . . until he reached his fourth screen. Joe set his coffee down on the side, instantly wide awake. He picked up the ream of printouts, shedding paper as he paced the forensic lab.

'I . . . am . . . *amazing*!' he declared, tearing out of the door and colliding with the already jumpy cleaner, who hadn't heard him coming over the sound of the hoover.

Rouche turned his back to the bright window. Feeling sleep rapidly slipping away, he flipped the pillow over and stretched out his legs, his bare foot finding something solid on top of the duvet. After a few moments probing it inquisitively with his toes, he was none the wiser and sat up to discover that he'd been kicking Holly in the face.

She stirred in her sleep as he quickly repositioned his foot.

'Hey,' she smiled, tousling her short blonde hair.

She looked utterly exhausted, curled up like a cat at the bottom of his bed. Checking in on him after work, they had enjoyed a delightful dinner of spaghetti on toast and butterscotch Angel Delight. The cheese course had been replaced with a slightly disappointing fistful of tablets, and then she had settled him in for the night.

'Sorry,' she said, as she sat up in her creased work uniform. 'I only closed my eyes for a few seconds.'

Rouche felt awful. The demands of caring for a deteriorating patient on top of a full-time job were clearly taking their toll on her. Holly was an inherently kind person, the type to naively believe they could actually make a difference in this decaying world, and he was beginning to feel as though he and Baxter were exploiting that side of her nature.

'Why don't you have a night off?' he suggested, wincing as he sat up straight. 'Go out . . . see a movie . . . dinner at Frankie & Benny's perhaps, or whatever it is you crazy kids get up to these days.'

'The pictures and Frankie & Benny's?' laughed Holly. 'Is that your idea of a night on the town?'

'Sounds pretty good to me right now,' he smiled weakly.

'Yeah . . . me too, actually.'

'So do it!' Rouche told her with more energy than she'd seen him display in a fortnight. 'I'd come with, but, you know: FBI . . . helicopters . . . car chase . . . shootout . . . death.'

Laughing, she got up off the bed: 'How are you feeling?'

'Do you know what? Good. Great, in fact.'

'You're not just saying that?'

'Not at all,' replied Rouche, shuffling to the edge of the bed. 'I'm going to make you breakfast.'

'You most certainly are not.'

'Promise to take the night off?' he asked her, dangling his feet, threatening to stand up.

Holly looked torn.

In the end, the deal was struck that Holly would phone once before she went out and once the moment she got home. She agreed to have at least three gin and tonics on the condition that Rouche have some vegetables for dinner. He was to remain in the bedroom at all other times if permitted to join her for breakfast out in the kitchen, with various subclauses involving fire, collecting the post and watching *Bargain Hunt*.

He carried the dirty plates over to the sink before she could protest and had even found her the showing times for some God-awful dying-woman-falls-in-love-with-the-man-whose-organ-could-save-her-life affair that actually made the prospect of an FBI shootout not sound all that bad.

'I've got to go!' said Holly, realising the time. She collected up her things. 'You take it easy.'

'I will,' Rouche promised, making a point of walking her to the door.

They embraced, unaccustomed to the idea of an entire day apart. Holly seemed genuinely happy, however.

'I can't believe the change in you today!' she told him.

Rouche waved her off as she skipped down the stairs. But the moment he closed the door, he slumped against it, gasping in pain as he lowered himself to the floor. The effort it had taken to maintain the façade had rendered him unable to breathe. He could see his pain medication up on the kitchen counter but couldn't bring himself to move. So he just sat there, staring up at the paper bag, his vision blurring as he started to cry.

'What on earth are you doing, William?' asked Maggie while the kettle boiled in the kitchen. 'I'm frozen!'

Wolf was crouched in the hallway beside the open front door, playing with the lock. 'Sorry. One more minute. I promise.'

'Is there something wrong with the door?'

Wolf flicked the handle up and down, checking the mechanism. He shrugged and then pushed it shut.

'It got stuck the other day. Just wanted to check they'd lined it up right when they replaced the frame . . . Checking we can still get in if you ever need us.'

'You're a good boy.'

He looked at her doubtfully.

'Well, you're nice to me, anyway,' she smiled. 'Tea?'

'I'm just going to take the bin out,' he told her, going through to the kitchen to retrieve the half-filled bin bag.

He unbolted the old-fashioned back door, pulling it closed behind him. After dropping the sack into the wheelie bin, he walked the length of the garden, bordered by mature bushes on either side, until he reached the back fence. Climbing the low wall, he peered over the wood into the neglected property behind. Checking no one was about, he scrambled up and over the flimsy panel, landing in an undignified heap on the other side.

'Shit,' he groaned.

His phone started buzzing in his pocket. Not yet ready to move, he groped around for it, feeling underprepared for a proper conversation with Baxter after she'd skipped out on him. But then he sighed in relief. 'Saunders?'

'All right? Joe says he's got somethin'.'

'Who?'

'The lab guy.'

'Ah.'

'Commissioner wants to be kept in the loop, so we're meeting at the hospital at half twelve.'

Wolf checked his watch: 'I'll see you there.'

'Got hold of Finlay's 999 call,' Saunders informed Wolf as they turned the corner into another identical corridor. 'The thing's twenty-four seconds long. The operator asks which emergency service he needs, says she can't hear him twice, then asks him to cough or tap the phone if he's unable to speak. There are two distinct taps; then the line goes dead. There's nothing to indicate if it's actually Finlay asking for help or . . . somebody else entirely.'

'Hmmm,' said Wolf.

'Passed it on to Techie Steve to enhance the audio but don't think we should hold our breath.'

They entered the private room to discover they were the last to arrive.

Christian was propped up in bed, the button for his morphine drip in hand and his various vital signs displayed on the screen behind him for all to see. Baxter had strategically claimed the far corner, thus unburdening herself of the need to make eye contact or engage with any of them. Edmunds, meanwhile, having ill-advisedly broached the subject of Thomas's disastrous proposal, was looking indignant in the opposite corner. And Joe, oblivious to it all, was grinning like an idiot at his own brilliance.

'Ah! Fawkes and Saunders. Please take a seat,' he greeted them, gesturing to the bottom of the commissioner's bed.

Christian hovered his thumb over the morphine button: 'Please don't.'

'We're good,' said Wolf.

'Suit yourselves . . . All feeling happy?' started Joe, illiterately reading the room. 'OK. So, a couple of years back, I applied for funding for a Surface Texture Analysis 3D Mapping System, which they didn't initially want to grant me because—'

Baxter yawned loudly.

'Right. You don't care. But in layman's terms, the closest analogy would be facial recognition for objects . . . objects like . . . . *bullets*,' Joe smiled. 'I spent yesterday inputting the physical evidence from Finlay and Mr Commissioner, Sir's old case files. It took a while, but I finally got a match.'

He held up a clear evidence bag containing a handful of metal shapes. 'Exhibit A: just six of the scores of bullets recovered from the Bonfire Night warehouse bust. All fired from the same weapon.'

'And you know that how?' Saunders asked him.

'Size and make of the bullet?' suggested Edmunds.

'If memory serves,' Christian interjected, 'there were *quite* a lot of guns firing *quite* a lot of bullets that night.'

'I'm glad you asked,' said Joe, indeed appearing glad. He picked up an enlarged photograph of a bullet, colourful lines highlighting arbitrary sections of the creased form. 'Tiny imperfections in the barrel. These leave minuscule scratches on the metal as the bullet travels through; always the same . . . an etched fingerprint, if you will.'

'Not to sound condescending, mate,' Saunders piped up, on his best behaviour with Christian in the room, 'but logic would dictate that, unless completely incompetent, whoever's gun this was would at least get off a few cheeky rounds before receiving one himself. How's this news?'

'Oh, that wasn't my news,' Joe clarified. 'This was simply to establish a baseline.' He held up several other photographs of bullets, all with similarly brightly coloured markings. 'We then started searching for the most frequent indentations.'

'And matched it to Finlay's gun?!' blurted Edmunds excitedly.

'No,' said Joe, sounding a little deflated. 'That really would have been something, though.' He picked up a second evidence bag, this one containing a single tarnished bullet: 'Exhibit B,' he announced. '"B" for "buttocks". *This* is the very same bullet that embedded itself in this great man's left butt cheek' – he gestured to Christian, who waved as if he'd won a prize – 'just days later in George Square. A ninety-two per cent match!'

His audience looked a little bored.

'Is this thing on?' he joked, tapping his chest. 'Do you see what I'm getting at?'

His audience still looked a little bored.

'You don't see? What this means is the weapon that fired *these* bullets was present at *both* crime scenes! So, how did it get there?'

Edmunds and Wolf answered together:

'The Dutchman.'

'Invincible Mullet Man.'

Joe had clearly been waiting for this moment. He held up the bag with the buttock bullet once more. 'The mulletous shit-wad who died an entire two days before *this* bullet was even fired, you mean?!' He was getting excited. 'Conclusion: the Dutchman wasn't the only person to escape the shipyard fire . . . Somebody else got out.'

'That isn't possible,' said Christian, looking even worse than he had five minutes earlier.

Wolf glanced over at him, noticing his heart rate increasing on the monitor.

'It *all* leads back to that warehouse,' Joe told them confidently. 'It's *this* case. And whoever this mysterious second survivor may be, they are now our prime suspect.'

CHAPTER 20

Monday 5 November 1979

Bonfire Night

9.16 p.m.

The sky was burning.

The dying building's metal skeleton groaned as he stared, incapacitated, watching sparks ignite in the air around him; fireflies dancing on the currents. Less than five metres away, what little remained of the tower of money blazed brightly, now nothing more than charred paper and ash. Cruelly, the bullet had missed its mark, embedding itself agonisingly below his shoulder blade, sentencing him to death by fire.

A rehearsal for where he was heading next.

The ceiling continued to crash down around him, allowing a final glimpse up at the stars. And then the collapsing warehouse sang its swansong.

The floor rumbled beneath him.

The pressurised door was ripped from its frame.

He closed his eyes and let himself fall.

Lying among the debris on the factory floor, he wondered whether God was enjoying Himself a little too much. Eyes still shut, he willed it to end as the last of the enormous canisters exploded nearby.

'Come on,' he whispered. 'Come on!'

Feeling a cool breeze on the back of his neck, he opened his eyes; in the corner of the room where the two walls met, a narrow opening had formed. Collecting his handgun from the floor beside him, he dragged himself out into the night. With the dark water at his side, colourful explosions lit up the sky, a sea of blue flashing lights strobing against the cargo containers as he reached the wire fence.

Lost somewhere amid the lights and fireworks, the modest flash of a single camera – capturing Finlay and Christian's moment of glory, capturing Strathclyde Police's largest seize in decades, capturing a five-foot tower of near-pure heroin ready for shipment and the identities of the two men responsible for keeping it off the streets.

CHAPTER 21

Tuesday 12 January 2016

9.06 a.m.

'Hey! Hey! Hey!' a domineering woman called as Wolf and Maggie walked past the nurses' station. 'All visitors need to sign in,' she told them, returning to her phone call.

This was the first that either of them had heard about it. Obediently, Wolf walked over to the book proudly displaying the names of others unfortunate enough to get caught by the boorish woman. He scanned the list and picked up the biro. But then, thinking better of it, he tore her precious page out instead, pocketing the pen for good measure.

'William!' whispered Maggie.

'Sorry. I just didn't like the way she spoke to you,' he said, guiding her away before anyone noticed.

Christian was being discharged, and Wolf had volunteered to accompany Maggie to retrieve him, who had of course gone into full-on nurse mode by kitting out the back of her car like an ambulance. With Wolf at the wheel, they eventually broke free of the conurbation and onto the sun-dappled B-roads that carved a path through the forest. Christian's directions had been unnecessary once they pulled into the private road, the rubber-burnt concrete and overlooked glass that sparkled in the sunshine guiding the way. Entering between the gates, they were presented with an elegant but modern house, a three-floored Scandinavian-style fusion of wood and glass that had been designed to look as though it had grown naturally around the neighbouring trees.

'Wow,' commented Wolf from the driver's seat, his opinion perhaps inconsequential, seeing as he was currently living out of a cell.

They parked up. Christian handed Wolf the keys and gave him the code to the alarm, which blared piercingly around the minimalistic building. The moment he had crossed the threshold, Christian insisted on closing the front door himself, checking it was shut twice before lifting the handle. He twisted the lock and then bolted it top and bottom as Maggie and Wolf watched patiently.

'Forgive my paranoia,' he told them. 'I think it's going to take me a little while to feel safe here again . . . Please,' he said, ushering them into the main living space.

A triple-storey glass wall looked out over the immaculate garden, a quaint wooden gate all that separated it from the forest beyond. A galleried balcony looked as though it were floating above them, drawing the observer's eye up to the magnificent vaulted ceiling.

'My goodness, Christian,' gasped Maggie. 'And I thought your old house was nice! You live here all alone?'

'Regrettably, I do.' He grimaced in pain as he struggled into his favourite chair, Maggie hurrying over to assist him. 'Will, would you please keep me abreast of any further developments?'

Wolf was still looking out over the forest, drinking in the winter sun: 'Huh?'

'Further developments,' repeated Christian. 'You *will* keep me in the loop?'

'You'll be the first to know.'

'He most certainly will not!' snapped Maggie. 'You are on bed rest, mister.'

'All right! All right!' he conceded, giving Wolf a sly wink as Maggie started fussing over pillows and medications, clearly relishing being needed rather than feeling like a burden.

'I'm gonna go,' announced Wolf, tearing himself away from the windows and heading to the door. 'I'll get a taxi to the station.'

'You're sure?' asked Maggie. 'I can run you.'

'No,' he smiled. 'You just keep an eye on Christian.'

The hanging baskets swayed gently in the breeze, sun-starved winter flowers clambering skywards as they choked the life out of each other: survival instinct in all its brutal glory.

Epping Tube Station had to be the strangest that Wolf had ever found himself in, less drained swimming pool, more park pavilion, cared for and devoid of both litter and crowds. He boarded the waiting train and closed his eyes, the carriage gradually filling up around him as they descended underground towards the city.

Resurfacing at St James's Park Station, Wolf made the short journey down the street to New Scotland Yard. He had only just signed in at reception and been told to await his escort when he noticed several of the armed officers mobilise in unison.

'Arrest that man!' one of them barked, pointing towards the busy foyer.

Quite in the mood to watch some unsuspecting idiot get tackled to the floor by five bored DPG officers, Wolf turned to see who they were talking about, which only made life easier for the five bored DPG officers, who proceeded to tackle him to the floor accordingly.

Wolf could have been forgiven for feeling as though he wasn't making an awful lot of progress, given that he was handcuffed again and found himself sitting in the exact same chair, in the exact same interview room he had occupied a week earlier. Fortunately, he didn't have to wait long before Vanita came marching in to take a seat across the table from him.

'Let's keep this short, shall we, Fawkes?' she greeted him. 'I *knew* you couldn't do it. I knew you wouldn't be able to resist flouting the terms of our agreement. I'm only surprised you lasted this long. So kudos for that, I suppose.'

'Thank you,' nodded Wolf, genuinely quite proud of himself. 'And just out of interest, which flouted terms of our agreement do you know about? I mean, are you referring to?' He rolled his eyes, less proud of himself.

Vanita flipped open her file.

'At eight fifty-eight p.m. on Saturday, you left your designated supervised accommodation after curfew and failed to return until the following afternoon.'

'Because I was at the hospital with Christian . . . the commissioner,' he reminded her.

'At which point,' Vanita continued, 'you managed a *whole* four hours before breaking curfew for a second time.'

'To attend a crime scene at Alex Edmunds's home address!' Wolf was getting frustrated now. 'This may come as a surprise to someone who's just enjoyed another pleasant long weekend—'

'I was on a training course.'

'. . . but sometimes, just sometimes, those pesky criminals decide to go beat the living shit out of police commissioners and start throwing corrosive liquids around the place at all sorts of unsociable hours!'

His irritation only made Vanita more smug. 'The others couldn't have handled it?' she asked, turning the page. 'And now it's come to light that on Friday afternoon Detective Constable Aaron Blake carried out an unnecessary, and therefore unlawful, search in order to obtain an Ashley Lochlan's current contact details.' She looked up at him. 'Seriously, Fawkes? One of the Ragdoll list! You *must* have known she'd flag up on our systems?'

Wolf opened his mouth to argue—

'And finally,' she cut him off, looking a little repulsed by the information painted in all-too-vivid black and white before her, 'the chaplain at King George Hospital claims to have discovered you buck-naked inside the chapel' – she frowned – 'lying beside a headless statue of Our Lord and Saviour, Jesus Christ.' She raised her eyebrows: 'An explanation?'

Again Wolf opened his mouth . . . closed it . . . and shook his head.

'I will be detailing your contribution to the Finlay Shaw investigation in my report. Goodbye, Fawkes.' She got up to leave.

'I need to speak to Baxter!'

'Not happening.'

'Then I want to speak to my lawyer.'

Twenty minutes later, Wolf was escorted into an empty room to make his phone call. The officer stepped outside, his shadow lingering in the crack beneath the door, standing guard. Screwing up the details for the Collins & Hunter law firm, the first to come to mind, Wolf dialled one of the few telephone numbers he still remembered off by heart.

'Maggie? It's Will. I need you to do something for me.'

'The hairs retrieved from beneath the floorboards belonged to the commissioner and Baxter,' announced Joe. 'No real surprise there as they'd spent the most time in that room.'

Baxter, Edmunds and Saunders had gathered in the forensic lab and decided not to wait for Wolf, who was now over half an hour late.

'What about the boot-prints at Edmunds's?' tried Baxter.

'Male. Size eleven. Slight instep. Nothing unusual.'

She huffed: 'The acid, then?'

'I'm still running tests on it to establish precisely what it is – most likely some weird home-made concoction. From there, we may possibly have an outside chance of perhaps narrowing down where it might have come from . . . or not.'

'Fine. Me and Edmunds have another morning of knocking on doors ahead of us. See if anyone saw anything remotely useful. Saunders, you—'

There was a crash as Blake hurried into the lab. Looking flustered, he frowned down at the fleshy contents of the tray he'd just upset and subsequently stepped in.

'Is that . . . *brains*?' he asked.

'Not anymore it's not,' tutted Joe.

'God, I *hate* coming down here!' he whined as he wiped his shoe across a clean section of floor.

'Feel free not to . . . anytime you want.'

Blake turned to Baxter: 'Sorry to interrupt, boss.'

'What is it?'

'Wolf.'

'What about him?'

'He's been arrested . . . You know . . . *again*.'

CHAPTER 22

Tuesday 13 November 1979
7.24 p.m.

'Hold still, baby,' she told him, standing in the middle of their tatty kitchenette as she struggled to peel the dressings from his skin.

Gritting his teeth, he took another swig of his beer.

'What's that doctor done to you?' she tutted.

'He's never been much good . . . Guess that's why he's patching up people like me,' he joked, kissing the length of her track-marked inner arm.

'I need to concentrate.'

'So do I,' he said, pulling her onto his lap.

'I'm *trying* to treat you!' she laughed.

'Well, I'm trying to treat *you*!'

There was a knock at the door.

Instantly alert, they both fell silent and got to their feet.

'Go to the bedroom,' he whispered, picking up his gun. 'Yes?!'

'It's Dillon, you bastard! Let me in!'

Relaxing, he hid the weapon under the shirt on the table before opening the door.

'Wow! You look like shit,' Dillon told his shirtless friend as he relocked the door behind him.

'As do you. What's your excuse?'

A moment's tension ended when both men burst out laughing.

'Lorna,' smiled Dillon, noticing her loitering in the bedroom doorway.

'Beer?'

'Why, that'd be lovely.'

Stepping past him to reach the fridge, she saw the handle of a gun protruding from under his jacket but didn't react. Sensing his eyes on her, she removed two beers and went to rejoin the conversation.

'Thank you,' said Dillon, clinking bottles before taking a sip.

'What brings you round, Dillon?' he asked, while assessing one of the more severe burns to his arm.

'Can't a guy simply be checking up on his old buddy, who, by all accounts, should be dead?' he replied, before turning serious. 'It's all gone to shit. The boss, he's . . . he's on the warpath. The warehouse . . . the fire . . . the cops . . . we lost everything.'

'And I'm *trying* to make it right.'

'Is that what the other day in the square was all about?'

'The drugs are gone. The money isn't. I can still get it back.'

'*Actually*, the boss's decided to go with a . . . *different* approach.'

'That doesn't really help me redeem myself.'

'No . . . I suppose it doesn't.'

Dillon reached for his gun, Lorna turning to smash her beer bottle over his head. Leaping onto his back, her childlike frame did little to impede him as her bleeding palms wiped crimson streaks across his jacket. Slamming her viciously against the wall, he removed his weapon just as the first bullet tore through his shoulder. He cried out in pain and raised the gun once more as two more shots were fired.

Dillon dropped to the kitchen floor, Lorna a motionless heap at his side.

'Baby . . . ? Baby?' he gasped, placing the gun down before stepping over his friend as the light left his eyes. 'It's nothing,' he told her, putting pressure over the bullet wound in her thigh.

He reached over and groped at Dillon's corpse until he found the car keys.

'OK, I got you. I got you. Hold on to me,' he whispered, scooping her up in his arms. 'Everything's going to be OK.'

CHAPTER 23

Tuesday 12 January 2016
6.04 p.m.

A door slammed, momentarily distorting Wolf's reflection in the large mirrored window. After hours confined to the interview room, he was as relieved as he was surprised to hear a friendly voice out in the corridor.

'Why don't you go get yourself a coffee?' it suggested to someone in a way that subtly suggested it wasn't in fact a suggestion at all.

He watched the door expectantly as Christian hobbled in. Wolf wondered how many tailored suits one man could possibly need, as the commissioner would have looked as pristine as ever had it not been for the severely battered face.

'Am I glad to see you?!' Wolf told him. 'I didn't mean for you to come down here, though.'

Christian smiled, which looked as if it might have hurt. 'Well, I figured a personal touch might go a long way on this one.' He walked over to the table to unplug the microphones and recording device. 'Vanita's doing, I take it?'

Wolf nodded, the handcuffs scraping against the metal chair at his back.

'You sit tight. I'll sort it.' He turned to leave.

'There's something else!' blurted Wolf, glancing anxiously into the mirror.

'We're alone,' Christian assured him as he walked back over to the table. 'I made sure.'

Wolf relaxed a little. 'I got searched when they arrested me, but I'm pretty sure they didn't find it.'

'Find . . . what?'

'Shirt pocket.'

Puzzled, Christian reached into Wolf's seemingly empty pocket, but then the tips of his fingers found the tiny plastic rectangle.

'Told you,' smiled Wolf in relief, watching Christian examine the memory card in his hand.

'What is this?'

'Alex Edmunds is a *very* careful man,' started Wolf. 'And in his, apparently, not-so-paranoid paranoia, he decided to spend an entire evening photographing *every single* piece of evidence contained within those boxes before they were destroyed.'

Christian looked stunned: 'So . . . we've still got it? All of it?'

'All of it,' nodded Wolf. 'You need to make a copy as soon as . . .'

He trailed off when Christian held his forehead as though he were in pain.

'Are you all right?' Wolf asked him, watching helplessly as the commissioner staggered over to the mirror, reflections warping like disturbed water as he steadied himself against it. 'Christian? Talk to me. What's wrong?'

He was straining to hear what the older man was muttering under his breath and pulled at his handcuffs in vain, unable to help. Finally pushing himself away from the mirror, Christian staggered towards him as if drunk.

'Christian?' asked Wolf in concern, before a violent blow toppled both him and the chair over, his linked hands useless as his head impacted the floor. On the very fringes of consciousness, he gazed up at the ever-dignified man pacing around the small room: restless, frantic . . . desperate.

'*Fuck!* I didn't want this! I never *fucking* . . .'

Wolf dipped in and out of the darkness that waited like a black hole at the edge of his vision, unsure how much time had elapsed lying on the cold linoleum. His skull felt like it had cracked open. His mouth tasted of blood, his vision blurred as the tinnitus built towards a crescendo.

At last, Christian regained enough composure to focus on the more imminent of his problems, crouching over Wolf, who just stared at him vacantly.

'Why couldn't you just have left it alone?' Christian asked him imploringly. 'Why couldn't you just accept it? We could have been friends,' he told him nonsensically. His voice sounded strained, his eyes full of desperate tears. 'I think Fin would have wanted that.'

Wolf didn't respond.

Patting him affectionately, Christian held the memory card out in front of Wolf's face. 'Your investigation,' he announced.

Wolf groaned as he watched the plastic card splinter and break in two.

'Is this over?' Christian asked him. Wolf's furious eyes were fixed on him. 'I'm afraid I'm going to need to hear you say it. Is . . . this . . . over?' He leaned in, his ear to Wolf's lips.

'Fuck you.'

'I knew you'd say that,' Christian smiled sadly. He raised his head to the heavens, gritted his teeth and then struck Wolf again, causing him to black out.

When he came round, he was sitting back upright, Christian dabbing at his face with a bloodstained handkerchief – another crime scene wiped clean.

'Look at me,' demanded Christian, snapping his fingers pugnaciously. 'Look at me!' Grabbing his rough chin, he pulled Wolf's face up and met his burning gaze: 'Your evidence is gone. Your team will be reassigned by morning. Forensics aren't going to find a thing. And you . . . you will spend the foreseeable future behind bars,' he told him. 'It's over.'

CHAPTER 24

Wednesday 13 January 2016
10.20 a.m.

From the comfort of her spacious office, Vanita regarded the furore out on the street below: Andrea Hall's 'Uncage the Wolf' campaign in full swing.

Still reeling from their last encounter, a career-low televised interview that still hindered her sleep, it was impossible to tell whether the destructive reporter was out there somewhere among the crowds. Red hair seemed to dominate the swarm of protestors buzzing around the base of New Scotland Yard, the sheeplike public's aspirations to reinvent themselves on any fleeting trend, cloning Ms Hall's hairstyle, clothing and, apparently, personal values as well for good measure.

Vanita tensed up on hearing her guest get up from his chair to join her beside the window. She watched his reflection take a sip of coffee.

'Christ,' said Wolf, no more pleased than Vanita to see a street full of ex-wife. 'There's dozens of them.'

'There are indeed.'

'That can't be good.'

'No, it can't,' she agreed. 'Well . . . good luck.'

Wolf never imagined a scenario in which he'd deliberate over an invitation to vacate his commander's immediate vicinity but found himself lingering at her side.

'Anything nice planned for this evening?' he tried. 'I saw this recipe for a lemon chicken risott—'

'Fawkes . . .' Vanita interrupted him without taking her eyes off the glass.

'Geena?' he smiled back pleasantly.

'Get out.'

Andrea was performing a soundcheck in preparation to record a segment for her show when there was a sudden roar of excitement from the crowd. Flinging the microphone at her cameraman, Rory, whose disfigured hands made a valiant, if unsuccessful, attempt at catching it, she started pushing through her self-inflicted blockade.

A chorus of howls emanated from all directions.

'There he is!' a strange woman screamed with undue elation.

'Uncage the Wolf!'

Struggling towards the front, Andrea spotted Wolf making a self-conscious dash for a waiting black cab.

'Will!' she called, her voice swallowed up entirely by the din. 'Will!'

Progress halted by the territorial front row, she saw him pause fleetingly to glance into the boisterous crowd.

'Excuse me!' she yelled, elbowing her way through. 'Will!'

There was a slam.

Stumbling into the road a moment too late, Andrea watched the taxi disappear round the corner.

By Wolf's reckoning, the King and Country on Oxford Street held the accolade of being the tenth best pub down the Topshop end of the road (and that was only because someone had once nicked his pint in the Nag's Head). This at least meant that it was quiet, absent of the mobs of bellowing City boys spilling out onto the pavement to drink in the street like the homeless they waved off so dismissively like bothersome flies.

As it turned dark outside, the whole team gathered in a sticky booth in the back corner of the shabby establishment.

'Nag's has got a pinball machine,' Saunders pointed out.

'Do they serve Pritt Sticks here?' asked Baxter, after losing half the wool on her sleeve to the table.

'Look, we're in here *because* it's a shithole!' Wolf explained, noticing the owner clearing glasses from the table next to them too late. He winced and then stared up innocently at the ceiling. 'Is he looking?' he asked Edmunds out of the corner of his mouth without moving a muscle.

'Uh-huh.'

Wolf held his stoic pose.

'You *do* know he's not a T-rex, right? He can see you,' whispered Edmunds. 'OK . . . He's gone.'

While Joe tried in vain to rub a greasy smudge off his glass, Saunders, under the impression they were embarking on a big night out, sank a shot of whisky to the bottom of a fresh pint.

A suitably stunned silence met Wolf's recap of the previous day, when they finally allowed him to speak.

'So . . .' started Saunders, struggling to keep up, 'the memory card was just a bluff?'

'Yeah,' replied Wolf.

'And how did you convince Vanita to release you?' Edmunds asked him.

'I appealed to her better nature,' he deadpanned, taking a swig of his beer. 'I told her the commissioner job would be hers if she just let me finish this.'

'But . . . the commissioner, though?' asked Joe, sure he must have misunderstood.

'I'm afraid so.'

'Mr Commissioner, Sir?'

'Yes!'

'But . . .' said Edmunds, 'didn't Christian arrive on scene *after* the police officer?'

'Yeah,' nodded Wolf.

'So . . . ?'

'He's squeezed himself into the compartment,' started Wolf.

'He hears Constable Randle break down the door and then disappear back downstairs, no doubt in his mind that Finlay was alone in the room. Christian crawls out and replaces the floorboards. He sneaks down the stairs and escapes through the back door while Randle's calling it in. He then climbs over the back fence, exits through the neighbour's garden and "arrives" out front to secure his ironclad alibi. He's the first one back into the house, rebolts the door, thus covering his tracks . . . Simple.'

Saunders squinted at him: 'Could you just repeat the bit . . . where you were talking?'

'No.'

'How did . . . ? When did you know?' Baxter asked him, forgetting that they weren't really talking and clearly a little hurt not to have been kept in the loop.

'I didn't,' shrugged Wolf. 'Not for sure. But I had my suspicions.' He massaged his jaw, which was still bloody painful. 'It was the handle.'

'Spaniel?' slurred Saunders, now three boilermakers in.

'Handle! The door handle. He has a habit,' explained Wolf, picturing Christian securing the door to his mansion the previous morning, 'of pulling the handle up behind him.'

'"A habit of pulling the handle up behind him,"' repeated Baxter, unimpressed.

Wolf ignored her. 'Your police report,' he continued, addressing Saunders. 'It said that Constable Randle had to force entry to the house.'

'Who?'

'Randle.'

'Spaniel?'

'Jesus, Saunders, switch to coffee or something!'

Saunders raised his glass, a drunken smile on his face.

'Well, it did,' said Wolf, giving up and turning back to Baxter. 'So, when have Finlay and Maggie ever locked their front door?'

'Never,' she conceded.

'And they didn't that night either. The handle had just been pulled up . . . from the inside.'

Edmunds nodded. He looked quite impressed: 'You totally Columbo-ed him!'

'I did, didn't I?' grinned Wolf.

'Columbo doesn't usually get punched in the face afterwards, though,' Baxter pointed out before he could get too big-headed.

'Sorry, just going back to the commissioner,' started Joe, bringing the conversation back round to its sombre point. 'Why would he want to murder his best friend?'

Everyone looked to Wolf.

'I don't know,' he admitted. 'And, honestly, I don't really care. He *did* do it. And that's good enough for me.'

They all paused to take a sip of their drinks.

'This is . . . pretty huge,' said Edmunds, hoping to hit the appropriate balance between outrage and excitement. 'Going after the commissioner of the Metropolitan Police for murder.'

'Problematic, more like,' Baxter corrected him.

Rejoining the conversation, Saunders nodded animatedly. 'He knows every way we might come at him . . . We're screwed.'

'So what's our move?' asked Edmunds.

Again everyone turned to Wolf.

'We walk away.'

'What?'

'We walk away,' repeated Wolf, ignoring the look of disgust Baxter shot him. 'Like Saunders said, he's the police commissioner. He knows *every* possible angle we might try to implicate him. We can't win this. Saunders's car was broken into at home. Someone was *inside* Edmunds's house with his sleeping family! And that was before he even knew we suspected him. He attacked me in a building full of police officers, while under arrest, and I *still* can't prove a thing.'

'He's getting reckless,' said Baxter.

'Which only makes him more dangerous,' countered Wolf. 'And let's not forget that he murdered his best friend without leaving a trace of usable evidence. We've backed him into a corner. Maybe Finlay made the same mistake. And none of us know how he might react. It's over.'

'So we just let him kill Finlay and get away with it?' asked Saunders challengingly.

'Of course not,' said Wolf. 'He believes all the evidence was destroyed at Edmunds's house. Whereas, in fact, everything relating to the warehouse and George Square was safely inside the shed.'

'Private detective agency,' Baxter and Edmunds chorused together.

'He thinks he has the upper hand. If he sees us back off as well, his arrogance will do the rest. The surviving case files, along with the forensic work, will all go to Vanita in the morning. She'll take care of the rest.'

'That's it, then?' asked Edmunds.

'That's it. You can bring your family back home.'

Edmunds nodded.

'"Better to be a live coward than a dead hero" my granddad always used to say,' added Saunders, slopping his drink over Edmunds. 'Apparently. I never met the bloke. He stepped on a mine while running away. Doesn't make it any less solid advice, though.'

They all looked a little bemused.

'I *think* that was an OK from you, Saunders . . . Lab guy?' asked Wolf.

Joe nodded begrudgingly.

Finally, Wolf turned to Baxter. Her expression was unreadable. She took a few moments to answer him.

'Whatever you think best,' she responded a little too easily.

Wolf frowned at her.

'What? I'm agreeing with you!'

'Yeah, that's the problem.'

'As long as it gets done, it doesn't really matter who's doing it. You've told her who the killer is, so even *she* shouldn't be able to screw it up. Hand it over to Vanita . . . It's over.'

Wolf watched her suspiciously, but then nodded. He raised his pint in the air.

'To Finlay!' he toasted, hoping that he had lied convincingly enough to protect them.

Andrea was sitting at the desk in her home office, feeling more comfortable surrounded by her work than rattling around the capacious house waiting for Geoffrey to get home. She was on hold while the New Scotland Yard switchboard transferred her through to Homicide and Serious Crime Command. A voice she recognised answered the phone, the same voice she had already spoken with on several occasions.

'Ms Hall! And to what do I owe the pleasure today?'

'Wolf, sorry— William Fawkes, please.'

'I'm afraid that he's neither in the office nor employed by the Metropolitan Police Service any longer, which I may have mentioned yesterday.'

'Are you even giving him my messages?'

'I can assure you that any failure to contact you on his part is in *no* part the failure of our strictly enforced procedures, and thus, we should probably conclude, entirely of his own volition.'

'Who talks like that?! You are *so* irritating!'

'I'm very sorry you feel that way. May I suggest that you—'

'No. You may not. Speak to you tomorrow,' she snapped, hanging up.

Swivelling dizzyingly on her chair, Andrea wondered whether to try Maggie again. But then, suddenly, she stopped. Unlocking her mobile, she scrolled through her extensive list of contacts, praying that an entry she'd had no call to use in years had survived her frequent phone upgrades . . .

Incredibly, it had.

Thomas returned home to the smell of burning, which either meant that the house was on fire or, God help him, Baxter was cooking again. Removing his coat, he followed the sound of early

2000s post-hardcore into the kitchen, the remains of the smoke alarm crunching underfoot as Baxter noticed him standing there.

'Hey!'

'Hi,' replied Thomas, giving her a half-hearted hug before pouring himself the dregs of the wine.

'I made your favourite!' she beamed.

'Literally *anybody* else's cooking?'

Her smile dropped.

'Sorry. Joke. Not funny. Remind me, what's my favourite again?'

'My lemon chicken risotto.'

'Jesus,' he whispered a little too loudly. 'The new One-D?' he asked, tongue in cheek, turning down the terrifying song.

'Glassjaw,' replied Baxter, turning it back up. 'Wine?' she offered, opening another bottle before he'd even had a taste of his own. 'So, I was thinking . . .' she started, determined to build wonky bridges while under the influence. 'My friend Avril. She's quite pretty, right?'

Thomas looked uneasy: 'I suppose.'

'She wears, like . . . nice lady things,' she continued, raising her eyebrows.

'Skirts?' suggested Thomas, finally taking a sip of his drink.

'Yeah, skirts . . . Why don't you do it with her?'

Thomas spluttered wine all over the floor: 'I beg your pardon?!'

'I don't think she'd mind.'

'Well, that's rather by the by, isn't it? Because I think *I* might *bloody* mind!'

Baxter looked confused, suspicions arousing that she might have somehow maybe misjudged the situation. 'I'm just trying to even things out a bit . . . to make them OK again.'

Thomas set his glass down on the worktop.

'I have absolutely no desire to "get even" with you, Emily. I want this to have never happened. You can't just . . .' He trailed off, looking sad. 'I'm sorry. I'm not really hungry tonight,' he said, giving up on the conversation and walking back out of the room. 'Come on, Echo!'

The dozing cat opened his eyes to look up at Baxter.

'Don't even think about it,' she told him, looking stern.

He jumped down from the table and bounded out after Thomas.

Baxter huffed: 'Traitor,' she muttered into her wine glass.

With only five minutes to go until curfew, Wolf leaped off the train at Edgware Road and sprinted up the stairs. As he rounded the corner, he spotted George waiting for him in the entranceway like a concerned parent. Out of breath, he started up the steps to the police station.

'Ten! Nine! Eight!' George counted, ruffling Wolf's hair proudly as he crossed the threshold with an entire seven seconds to spare. 'I was just going to make myself a cup of cocoa. Want one?'

Wolf's breathless answer was incomprehensible.

'I'll make you one.'

After spending ten minutes chatting with George when he came to 'tuck him in', Wolf removed the crumpled hospital sign-in sheet from his pocket. He traced his finger down to the entry that had caught his attention:

Name	Visiting	Date	Time in	Time out
J. Doe	Christian Bellamy	10/01/16	18:35	18:50

Wolf set the piece of paper to one side and scribbled himself a note:

Visitor??? Request CCTV footage
Sunday 6.35 p.m.–6.50 p.m.

This wasn't over.

CHAPTER 25

Sunday 10 January 2016

6.42 p.m.

Christian rolled over in his narrow hospital bed, lingering in that haze between sleep and consciousness. As his sticky eyelids unglued themselves, a blurry figure started to take shape. He stared at it blankly for a moment and then sat bolt upright.

A man was sitting beside his bed, watching him, a bunch of blood-red flowers resting on his lap.

'Did you know you talk in your sleep?' he asked Christian unnervingly, who looked around the room in alarm. 'Shhh. Shhh. Shhh. I just wanted to have a little chat. That's all.'

Composing himself, Christian tried to relax. He leaned back against the pillows.

'You know,' started the man, running his hands through his poorly dyed hair, 'the boys were only ever going to rough you up a bit. After all, you're no good to me dead, are you? But' – he sighed heavily – 'the message doesn't seem to be getting through to that pretty little head of yours: I can't have the Metropolitan Police sniffing around my guys like this. You told me you'd handle it and yet . . .' He shrugged.

'I will . . . I swear,' said Christian, speaking at last.

'Nah. You need to recover your strength. I'll just take care of it my way.'

'No!' Christian blurted before remembering his place. 'You don't have to do that. I'm handling it. I am.'

The bulky man regarded him for a moment.

'Make sure you do. I don't want to have to ask again. We go *way* back, the two of us. I think of you among those I'd call my friends.'

'And I you, Killian.'

'You're important to me, Christian. You know that, don't you?'

Christian smiled.

'But you're *certainly* not indispensable.'

CHAPTER 26

Thursday 14 January 2016
8.46 a.m.

The automatic headlights flickered to life as Vanita pulled into New Scotland Yard's underground car park. Turning into her reserved parking space, she shut off the engine and went to climb out.

'Jesus!' she gasped, hand over her heart, when Christian startled her by catching the door.

Smiling pleasantly through split lips, he leaned in to speak with her.

'Sorry, Geena. Didn't mean to scare you. I saw you park up and thought I'd come over and say hello.'

Vanita laughed nervously. 'I wasn't expecting you in today,' she told him, collecting up her bags and stepping out, only to find herself trapped between his arm and the door.

'I'm not . . . officially. Just have a couple of things to take care of,' he explained, the intensity of his gaze making her uncomfortable.

'Well, I'm glad to see you're feeling better,' she smiled, before looking pointedly at his obstructing arm. 'Excuse me.'

He didn't appear to have heard her. 'Am I right in thinking you released William Fawkes from custody yesterday?'

'You are.'

'I was just wondering what . . . *prompted* that uncharacteristically unorthodox decision.'

'I'd have thought you'd be pleased?'

'Oh, I am. I am. I just wanted to know the reasoning behind it.'

Vanita had to physically push his arm out of her path. She started walking towards the lift on the far side of the deserted car park.

'He had legitimate reasons, on both occasions, for breaking curfew,' she explained, having to force herself to walk at a normal pace. 'I thought he deserved one more chance.'

She pushed the button and heard the mechanism whirr into action somewhere above them. Christian was back at her side.

'No other reason?' he asked, watching her closely.

'Such as?'

He shrugged.

'Look,' started Vanita, knowing that they had both heard the tremble in her voice, 'as acting commissioner, I made a decision and I—'

'You like playing commissioner, don't you, Geena?' he interrupted her, the implication painfully clear.

He knew precisely why she had released Wolf.

Theatrics over, she turned to meet his eye: 'I could get used to it.'

The lift pinged and the metal doors parted. They both stepped inside.

'I'm having a little shindig at my house this evening, to celebrate my return to work. It would look unbecoming on your part not to make an appearance.'

'You *should* enjoy your last bit of freedom,' smirked Vanita. 'Before returning to work, I mean.'

The lift doors sealed and they started their ascent.

'So you'll come?'

'Wouldn't miss it for the world.'

They stopped at the lobby, where two people joined them in the metal box.

'Morning, Mr Commissioner,' one of them smiled.

'Good morning,' Christian nodded back. 'For what it's worth,' he started, addressing Vanita once more, 'I think you made the right decision regarding Will. He *should* see this through to the bitter end . . . wherever it may lead.'

As the lift slowly approached their floor, Vanita turned to face him.

'Wherever it may lead,' she agreed.

Baxter stopped by the flat to check on Rouche, feeling that she had been rather neglecting him with everything going on. She supposed his unconvincing show of improvement earned him a visit free of pandering and concern, so launched into a summary of the past few days instead.

He had reacted to her shocking revelations in the manner he reacted to most things. 'Do they still make those little Kinder Eggs with the toy in?'

'What . . . ? Yes. Do you want me to get you one?'

He thought about it long and hard for a few moments: 'Nah. It's all right.'

'I'll get you one,' she huffed. 'So . . . killer commissioner . . . Thoughts?'

'Oh yeah. That's definitely bad.'

She shook her head. 'Well, now we've got that cleared up, how's it going with Holly?' she asked him, unable to keep the schoolgirl grin off her face.

Rouche waved off the question dismissively.

'What?!' said Baxter. 'She clearly likes you.'

He ignored her.

'They'd want you to be happy,' she told him, glancing at the photograph of Rouche, his wife and daughter atop the bedside table.

'Perhaps . . .' started Rouche, keen to steer the conversation away from his dead family's posthumous wishes, 'Holly might be better off finding someone who won't be either: a) dead; b) in prison; or, c), dead in prison at some point in the next couple of weeks.'

'Oh, don't be so melodramatic,' scoffed Baxter. 'Although, you know, do try not to die,' she added quickly. When her phone buzzed, she instinctively looked down at the screen: 'Son of a bitch!'

'Problem?'

'Son of a *bitch*!' she said again, reading through the offending message. 'That arrogant prick is throwing himself a party tonight!'

'That is arrogant . . . and prickish,' Rouche concurred. 'And he invited *you*?'

'I'm on a managers' mailing list,' she explained. She shook her head and got up.

'You OK?'

'Me? Oh, I'm just dandy. Places to be, though. *I* get the pleasure of informing Maggie that her oldest friend, the man in charge of her husband's murder investigation, the man she's been confiding in and even caring for, is in actual fact the murdering, remorseless, cowardly shit that did this to them.'

Rouche looked at her understandingly. After a few moments, he opened his mouth to say something.

'If this is about your *arsing* Kinder Egg,' Baxter warned him, 'know that I *will* hit you.'

He closed his mouth obediently.

Glaring at him, she picked up her bag and marched out.

At 12.30 p.m., Vanita had been trying to enjoy a joyless salad at her desk when a knock at the door disturbed her.

'Yes!' she called, setting her lunch aside. She relaxed a little on realising it was one of her more professional, and therefore preferred, subordinates. 'And what can I do for you today, Detective?'

'I need a signature, a softer bed and a pass to see the new Tarantino movie one night this week,' Wolf announced, barging past his escort to approach the desk.

'Fine . . . No . . . And I felt it was maybe a little self-indulgent,' she answered efficiently. 'Thank you, Knuckles,' she said, dismissing the short-haired detective.

Wolf frowned as the woman showed herself out: 'Her name's . . . *Knuckles*?'

'Give me,' said Vanita, too tired for his nonsense.

Wolf dropped the IC432-R, otherwise known as a 'cough up the camera footage, you bastards' form, onto her desk, which she signed without even reading.

'You don't want to know what it's for?' asked Wolf in surprise.

'I take it it relates to the investigation?'

'It does.'

'Our esteemed leader caught up with me in the car park this morning,' she explained. 'He knows the only reason I would release you is because you'd shared the truth with me and I'd see it as an opportunity to knock him off his perch. After his ill-advised attempt to intimidate me, I now have absolutely no doubt in my mind that he's as guilty as sin.'

She handed Wolf the autographed sheet.

'Baxter couldn't have done this for you?' she asked as an after-thought when he turned to leave.

'I didn't want her involved.'

Vanita nodded thoughtfully. 'I don't think it's any secret I detest that woman, her appalling attitude, her token title—' She stopped herself before she could get too carried away with the rant. 'But if there's *one* person out there I'd say can look after themselves . . . it's her. And Alex Edmunds, whether in the guise of detective or private investigator, is worth his weight in gold. Something to consider.'

She regretted opening her mouth, however, when Wolf took it as an invitation to sit down. He glanced at the abandoned bowl of leaves between them.

'Your plant's dying.'

'That's my lunch.'

He pulled a face. 'Finlay once told me that the only thing more dangerous than a man with nothing to lose is a man with *everything* to lose. This *is* going to turn nasty.'

'I'm prepared for a fight if you are,' she replied. 'Speaking of which, he's invited me to a cocktail party at his home this evening.'

Wolf looked disgusted but was calm when he spoke. 'Lots of important people going, I presume? People he'd want to impress. Could be an opportunity to apply a little pressure.'

'Or just get him so stinking drunk he confesses to the whole thing,' suggested Vanita.

Wolf considered his options: 'Fancy a "plus-one"?' he asked with a mischievous grin.

'Not if you're planning on wearing *that*,' she told him.

He looked down at his smart outfit and shrugged.

CHAPTER 27

Thursday 14 January 2016

7.44 p.m.

The rented tuxedo smelled of armpit and left very little to the imagination in the posterior but had been the best that Moss Bros could cobble together at such short notice. After several failed attempts, Wolf had given up with the bow tie, which he'd left to hang loose round his neck. He had gone to the trouble of shaving again and even attempted to neaten up his unruly hair.

Sitting in silence in the back of a taxi, he and Vanita wound their way through the forest towards Christian's exclusive postcode. When they eventually arrived, expensive cars littered the length of the private road, their driver scraping a wing mirror as he squeezed through the gap left between an Aston Martin and a poorly parked Range Rover. A professional party planner was waiting at the bottom of the driveway when they pulled up, tray of champagne on hand.

'Welcome!' she smiled through chattering teeth as Wolf climbed out and got the door for Vanita. 'May I take your names?'

'Plus-one,' replied Wolf. 'And Geena Vanita.'

The woman checked her list, hands so frozen it took her several attempts to turn the page. She then handed them each a champagne flute, which appeared to serve as an elaborate hand stamp.

'Please show yourselves up to the house. You'll find Christian with his guests in the main room.'

They crunched along the colourfully lit gravel, past the first immaculate attendees sneaking outside for a smoke and entered through the open front door.

'Wow!' gasped Vanita, experiencing the same reaction everyone did on first laying eyes on the magnificent space: three storeys of glass admiring a star-speckled sky, like the window of a spaceship.

A grand piano had appeared from somewhere, barely audible over the din of upper-upper-class guffawing and self-aggrandising. Even dressed as he was, Wolf was acutely aware that he stuck out like a sore thumb among these people, his weathered face absent of the resting scowl of disdain that the others sported like uniform.

'William Fawkes?' someone bellowed nearby, attracting several inquisitive glances as he marched over to shake Wolf's hand. 'William "Wolf" Fawkes!'

'Fawkes, this is Malcolm Hislop, MP for Chelsea and Fulham, and likely our new mayor come May,' Vanita told him, air-kissing the shiny cheek of the shiny man.

'Geena, always a pleasure,' he said robotically, before turning his attention back to Wolf. 'I wonder . . .' he said theatrically. 'Perhaps I'd be sensible to keep my distance from you, though!' He held up his hands defensively, much to the amusement of their growing audience, a reference to Mayor Turnble, who had agonisingly burned alive from the inside out before Wolf's eyes.

'So . . . we're laughing about that now?' he asked Vanita in bewilderment.

Rapidly catching attention, they inevitably caught Christian's eye on the far side of the room, whose face dropped when he recognised his gatecrashing guest. Ignoring the pompous remarks of the people surrounding him, Wolf raised his glass in toast to their hospitable host. He watched Christian turn away to resume his conversation, but then spotted a familiar figure moving through the crowd towards him.

'Excuse me,' said Wolf, abandoning Vanita to intercept the woman in the black cocktail dress before anybody else could notice her.

Baxter was just three steps from Christian when Wolf gently took her arm and guided her away in the opposite direction.

'What are you doing here?' he whispered through a forced smile as they began to weave out of the festivities.

'You actually thought I'd buy your bullshit "we're gonna walk away" speech?' she asked, fake-laughing as she did so, so as not to arouse suspicion.

The dancing had started, hindering their escape.

'I was *trying* to protect you.'

'Too little, too late,' said Baxter, shrugging off his arm and turning to face him. '*He* killed Finlay. I'm in.'

An important-looking man sauntered over and held his hand out to her: 'May I?'

'May you . . . what?' Baxter frowned, staring at his wrinkled extremity as though it were holding a dead kitten.

The man suddenly looked less confident: 'Have this dance?'

'No, you *may* not. Piss off, perv!'

Smiling apologetically, Wolf swiftly escorted her off the dance floor and towards the nearest door.

'Wolf! Where are we going?' she complained. 'Owww!'

He followed Baxter in and switched on the light. With the door closed, Wolf was pressed right up against her back, a tiny sink jabbing into his side.

'Great. Now we're in the smallest bathroom in history. Happy now?' asked Baxter, elbowing him twice as she struggled to turn round in the confined space.

'This isn't a bathroom,' complained Wolf as he took yet another hit to the solar plexus. 'This is a cupboard in denial.'

Now at least facing one another, Baxter's breasts were pushing firmly into Wolf's chest. To his credit, he really was making a gentlemanly effort not to react.

'You look nice,' he smiled.

'Inappropriate,' she snapped. 'Wolf?'

'Yes?'

'That had better be your phone poking me,' she said dangerously.

'It is,' he assured her, receiving an incredibly ill-timed text alert from his jacket pocket.

'Oh! Gross, Wolf!' she scolded him, climbing up onto the toilet to get away.

'What?! You look nice!'

'You've got ten seconds,' Baxter warned him. 'Why are we in here?'

'OK. I can't convince you not to get involved. And I respect your decision. But maybe you could just do it . . . *quietly*, sort of *act* like you're not involved?'

'I'm not scared of him!'

'Well, maybe you should be!' he bellowed back, making her jump.

He held his hands up in apology, Baxter watching him cautiously.

'I'm not hiding,' she told him.

Wolf's jacket pinged again. Ignoring it, he nodded, knowing that he would never convince her otherwise. 'But it's just us. We keep the others out of it.'

'Agreed.'

There was an urgent knock at the door, and then another.

'Wolf?' someone whispered on the other side. 'Wolf?'

Shooting Baxter a puzzled look, he turned the lock, stumbling back into her as Edmunds came bundling into the cramped room to join them.

'Edmunds?!'

'Baxter?!'

They peered round Wolf to wave at one another.

'Should've known,' he laughed, his scrawny frame drowned by the cheap tuxedo. 'I *was* hoping to protect you from all this.'

'That's sweet of you,' Baxter smiled. 'But I'll be OK. Always am.'

'So, it's "sweet" when *he* does it?' asked Wolf in annoyance.

'You look nice, by the way,' Edmunds told her.

'Thanks.'

Wolf made a frustrated gesture before bruising all three of them by turning round to address Edmunds.

'That had better be your phone poking me,' Wolf told him.

'It is. And I texted you . . . twice. I couldn't see where you'd gone.'

'I take it you're not walking away either, then?'

'Of course not. That bastard killed our friend. Someone working for or with him broke into my home. I need to be part of this. I need to help . . . Saunders and Joe are still in too, by the way.'

Wolf nodded in defeat, but then looked puzzled: 'Joe?'

'Lab guy,' clarified Baxter, rapidly losing patience crouched atop the toilet.

'Anyone spoken to Maggie yet?' Edmunds asked them.

'I did,' she replied.

'And how did she . . . ? Is she OK?'

'Not really. Took it much as expected: said we'd made a mistake, asked why we were trying to make everything worse, accused us of using Christian as a scapegoat to keep Wolf out of prison. And then, finally, everything started to fall into place.'

'Thank you,' said Wolf sincerely, elbowing her in the boob as he spun back round.

'Christ, Wolf!' she complained. 'Could you just tell us what the plan is so we can get out of here?'

'Christian had a visitor while he was in hospital,' he explained, trying his utmost not to look down her dress. 'A couple of hours later, the evidence boxes were destroyed. I confiscated both the sign-in sheet and pen, and I've put in a request for the CCTV footage.'

'This person won't have used their real name,' said Edmunds, before he and Baxter both cried out because Wolf was rotating yet again.

'I know that. But it gave us a time period to work with, a handwriting sample and, if we're incredibly lucky, their finger-prints as well.'

Someone knocked on the door.

'Sorry!'

'Someone's in here!'

'Bugger off!' they all shouted simultaneously.

'So, I've been thinking,' started Edmunds, lowering his voice. 'We always presumed Saunders's car, Christian's attack and the break-in at mine were carried out by the same people. Knowing what we know now, the commissioner getting himself beaten half to death seems somewhat counterproductive.'

'Could've been to throw us off the scent,' suggested Baxter.

Edmunds looked unconvinced.

'There would have been far easier and less painful ways of doing that. You saw his car, his face . . . He could have died.'

'What are you thinking?' Wolf asked him.

Baxter was astounded. Apparently even *he* had registered just how invaluable Edmunds could be.

'Someone working in cahoots with the commissioner, someone *else* carrying out the attack on him. And the threat of this *someone* else likely to be what drove him to murder his best friend. I've already requested more files on the group operating out of the warehouse. Whoever escaped that fire might not be the one who murdered Finlay, but I have no doubt whatsoever they're involved in some way.'

Baxter filled with pride; Edmunds was worth the rest of them put together.

'What do you want me to do?' she asked Wolf. 'Don't turn round!'

'Motive,' he answered with his back to her. 'Something happened in that shipyard we don't know about. Finlay was broke, facing repossession, while Christian's living it up in a mansion. We need to fill in the blanks.'

'Fine,' said Baxter, already climbing down off the toilet. 'Shall we get out there and cause some trouble, then?'

Wolf nodded: 'Why not?'

They fell out into the corridor, ignoring the enquiring looks from their fellow guests, but quickly realised they wouldn't be the only thorns in Christian's side that evening . . .

The dance floor had frozen.

The music had stopped.

All eyes were trained on their host, standing in the centre of his magnificent hall, and the casually dressed woman who had just slapped him across the face.

'Maggie!' gasped Baxter, pushing through the stunned audience to retrieve her.

She looked utterly lost when Baxter reached her, Christian equally so, his hand held up to his cheek in shock, his expression that of a man whose entire world had just collapsed. And when she burst into tears, he even attempted to hold a hand out to her. Batting it away, Baxter led her distraught friend outside.

It took a few moments for Christian to reanimate. He cleared his throat. 'I am terribly sorry about that, everyone!' he smiled. 'Please – drink, dance and be merry. Meanwhile, I'm going to find some ice to put on this!'

Nervous laughs gave way to the hum of conversation starting up once more, the first tinkling notes of the piano filling the silences in between. Still a little dazed, Christian almost walked straight into Edmunds.

'Mr Commissioner,' he smirked, nodding curtly before going to join Vanita, who looked delighted to see him.

Christian continued to the bar, feeling the eyes of his gossiping guests following his every move. He was just about to call the barman over when someone handed him a cloth full of ice cubes.

'Thank y—' he started, looking up to discover Wolf towering over him. He laughed bitterly: 'You told Maggie?'

'You sound surprised?'

'I am . . .' He dropped his voice to no more than a murmur over the din. 'That you'd be so stupid as to not heed my warning.' He placed the cold cloth to his face.

'Oh, I heeded it plenty,' said Wolf, ferocious eyes meeting Christian's gaze. 'Now, why don't you heed mine: you go ahead and hide in your nice palace among the trees. Fill it with all the sycophants and hypocrites you can find. Ply them with your expensive drink and incessant lies . . . It's nothing more than kindling for the day I come to burn it down.'

Christian considered Wolf's threat for a moment. 'Maggie will be safe. You have my *word* on that. As for the rest of you . . .' He shook his head regretfully.

Placing a large hand on his shoulder, Wolf leaned in close to whisper in Christian's ear. 'I know what happened in that warehouse.'

He gave the commissioner a 'Finlay slap' to the back and walked away.

'Everything OK?' a nearby guest asked on noticing the sickly look his host was wearing.

Christian didn't respond as he watched Wolf amble through the party. Edmunds and Vanita were glaring at him from the other side of the room as Baxter re-entered, having seen Maggie off safely.

'I say,' pressed the elderly gentleman, 'is everything quite all right, Christian?'

'Yes . . . Yes, everything's perfectly fine, thank you, Winston. Just the usual pressures of positions such as ours. You know how it is,' he smiled, still watching them . . . watching him. 'The wolves are circling.'

CHAPTER 28

Christian and Finlay had spent the first hour of their shift making stilted conversation. No mention was made of the damage that each of them had inflicted on the other. Christian was limping badly, a wine-red bruise betraying the underlying fracture to his jaw, while Finlay's nose had changed direction yet again, blackening his eyes . . . yet again.

'What are we eating tonight?' Christian asked him, foot to the floor as their new patrol car struggled up the hill past the Cathkin Braes.

'Not fussed,' Finlay replied curtly.

Christian had had enough. He spun the steering wheel, recklessly cutting the corner and bouncing over the verge to turn into the beautiful but notorious 'dogging' spot. Finlay just watched on impassively despite his partner almost killing them. Skidding to a stop, Christian switched off the engine, got out and took a seat on the warm bonnet. With the wind whipping his long hair, he cupped his hands to light a cigarette as the sun began to set over the smoggy city.

Finlay climbed out to join him.

'I was jealous,' said Christian, eyes fixed firmly on the vista. 'I had too much to drink . . . like usual. I was a complete prick

. . . like usual . . . and I'm truly sorry . . . which actually might
be a first.'

Finlay remained quiet.

'Maggie is . . .' Christian shook his head and smiled. 'She's
one in a million, and you two have this amazing *thing* going on.
I was jealous. But you don't have to leave over this!'

'I'm not.'

'Leaving?'

'Oh, I'm leaving. I'm getting on the first plane out of this rainy
bastard of a town and never looking back,' Finlay clarified. 'But
it's got nothing to do with *us*. Maggie's leaving . . . I'm going
with her.'

Christian nodded.

The sun made a break for it, fleetingly bathing the enormous
grey growth on the Scottish countryside in light.

'I've split the money in two,' Christian told him, flicking his
cigarette butt into the bushes before lighting up another.

'It's yours,' replied Finlay.

Christian groaned.

'I don't want a penny of it,' Finlay insisted. 'But what happened
that night . . . and the existence of that money will go to the grave
with me. You have my word.'

'I'm not worried about that!' laughed Christian. 'You saved my
life!' He swung his arm around his friend and shook him affectionately. 'I trust you more than anyone. I just want *you* to be OK.'

'I don't want it,' he reiterated, shrugging off the over-friendly
arm.

'I've been thinking a lot about integrity these past few days,'
started Christian. 'About how it's not this constant thing. How
it's not like a character trait set at some predefined level. It's
more like . . . like an aspiration, always at odds with real life –
testing us, fucking with us, and all the time there's this balancing
act going on behind the scenes: integrity versus what we want,
when what we want is to think of ourselves as having integrity
. . . It's messed up.'

'I wonder,' said Finlay thoughtfully, 'how stupid is the stuff you *don't* say?'

'I'm just saying . . . it's a long life. Half that money is yours whether you want it or not, and on that day, when life finally wears down your integrity, all you have to do is ask. Deal?'

'Never going to happen.'

'So humour me. Deal?'

'Deal.'

CHAPTER 29

Saturday 16 January 2016
11.01 a.m.

The entire dis-disbanded team had gathered in the far corner of the pub, some even chancing the delicacies of the King and Country's depressing breakfast menu. While Wolf attempted to fish out whatever was floating in his coffee, Saunders set to work on his full English. Edmunds, meanwhile, couldn't help but notice Baxter adjusting her bra and then noticed Joe noticing too.

He gave her a subtle nudge.

'Sorry,' she whispered, still not looking particularly comfortable.

Getting his money's worth out of the rented tuxedo, Wolf cleared his throat and got to his feet. 'Morning, everyone. I hope you're all enjoying your' – he glanced at the table of abandoned plates – 'lives. Me, Edmunds and lab guy had a busy day yesterday preparing you a presentation complete with A3 sheets of paper, shocking revelations, different-coloured Sharpies and *even* Edmunds's fiancée's iPad.'

'But please, nobody tell her,' added Edmunds, watching anxiously as Wolf jabbed at the screen with his clumsy fingers.

'CCTV footage from the hospital of Christian's mysterious visitor visiting mysteriously,' announced Wolf, holding it up for all to see.

The video paused when the figure looked directly up at the camera. The image then enlarged, spinning unnecessarily before bouncing around the screen where Wolf had got carried away playing with his new toy.

Baxter glared at him.

'At least I didn't use a sound effect,' he smiled excitedly as the picture finally came to a stop.

Moo!

'Yeah, I did!' he admitted.

The image showed a man of similar age to Finlay but better dressed and with a full head of dark slicked-back hair.

'*That* . . .' Wolf informed them, 'is Killian Caine, the head of the group working out of the shipyard warehouse: drug manufacturing, racketeering, countless accusations of assault, implicated in several murders . . . basically, an utter shit. And yet here he is visiting our police commissioner shortly after a savage beating. Curious, right?'

'And these,' said Edmunds, placing a set of photographs down on the table, 'are his known associates.'

'What do the red crosses mean?' asked Saunders through a mouthful of hash brown.

'That they died in the warehouse fire.'

'And . . .' started Saunders, raising a finger while he swallowed, 'why's some of them just names?'

'Because we don't know what they look like,' answered Edmunds, unsure what he had been expecting. 'This, as far as I can make out, is his entire network.'

'Meaning that the fella who escaped the warehouse fire must be one of them!' announced Saunders, under the impression he had just solved the case.

'Yes,' said Edmunds as patiently as he could. 'So, the mercenaries and the fire wiped out at least half of Caine's crew.' Edmunds removed the crossed pictures from the table. 'I started pulling the files on the rest of them and' – he placed his hand over one of the aged mugshots – '*this* one was murdered just a week after the fire. And that's where Joe comes in.'

Joe attempted to stand up dramatically as both Wolf and

Edmunds had done but found himself wedged securely between the table and the wall. He gave up.

'Two bullets were removed from the body during the post-mortem. And I thought, "Screw it. I've got no plans this year," so I ran them through my machines and guess what? The same indentations back again. It came from the same gun!'

'You think our suspect killed his own man?' asked Baxter.

'I do.'

'And,' Wolf jumped in excitedly, clearly having been waiting for this moment, 'there was a witness's description of someone fleeing the scene.' He wrapped his fingers round the top A3 sheet. 'Enabling me to produce this . . .'

No one spoke for a moment.

Saunders opened his mouth, but then realised that even he was speechless.

'Just one question, Wolf?' started Baxter.

'Yes?'

'What the fuck is that?!'

'"Artist" *is* a bit generous,' commented Saunders as he squinted at the drawing.

'Certainly doesn't look like any of the photos,' said Edmunds as encouragingly as he was able.

'Which means we can discard these,' said Wolf, picking the photographs of Caine's crew up off the table, leaving only the faceless names behind.

'Let me get this straight,' said Saunders, looking confused. 'He killed his fellow gang member *before* or *after* shooting at Finlay and the commissioner in the square?'

'Fear not, my forgetful friend!' smiled Wolf, reaching again for his pile of A3 sheets. 'For I have made us all this handy timeline to help keep track . . .'

'You're an idiot, Wolf,' Baxter told him.

Edmunds looked suitably unimpressed while Saunders laughed out loud.

'Wouldn't a chart or table have been a far more effective way of conveying this information?' asked Joe.

'I'll have you know I put a lot of work into these,' said Wolf, offended. But then he actually thought about it: 'When I say "a lot" . . . Either way, there's one more, if anyone cares to see it?'

Saunders was the only one to raise his hand.

'What's with the rabbit picture?' asked Baxter, unsure why she even cared.

Wolf shrugged: 'I'm just ridiculously good at drawing rabbits.'

'Anyway,' said Edmunds, deciding to take over the meandering meeting. 'Based on *the description*, I've been narrowing down the remaining names, gathering details from snippets of reports, following their various run-ins with the law post-November 1979, and can now say with reasonable confidence that our missing warehouse escapee is . . . Eoghan Kendrick.'

'Case closed!' laughed Saunders, shaking Joe boisterously.

'It would be,' agreed Edmunds, 'had *Eoghan Kendrick* not been a fake name . . . and had the real man with the fake name not disappeared off the face of the earth. Putting together what we *definitely* know, and making some irresponsibly unfounded assumptions, here's what we've got.'

He moved Wolf's drawings aside and held up his own, far more professional, sheet:

- Something happened inside that warehouse.
- Eoghan Kendrick knows what happened.
- Eoghan Kendrick worked for Killian Caine.
- Killian Caine visited Christian in hospital
  (and probably put him there in the first place).
- Christian is suspiciously rich.
- One of Eoghan Kendrick's team attempted to murder him.
- Eoghan Kendrick vanished after that incident.

'Does anybody see *any way* to link those points together to make a coherent theory?' he asked them.

They each looked a little pained as they contemplated the unsolvable puzzle.

'Think I've got it . . .' Saunders piped up, rubbing his chin. 'Christian *is* Eoghan Kendrick!'

'Anybody else?' Edmunds moved on impatiently.

'Just tell us,' Baxter heckled him.

Edmunds attempted an innocent look, but then abandoned the act.

'OK. I've got one theory,' he admitted. 'I think whatever happened that night, Christian and Finlay wanted it kept secret. What they hadn't counted on was Eoghan Kendrick escaping the fire. He tells his boss, Killian Caine, who then uses it as leverage over Christian. Perhaps Finlay was going to expose the truth or use it to blackmail—'

'Finlay wouldn't do that . . .' Baxter interrupted him.

'Let him finish,' said Wolf.

'. . . and that's why they killed him,' continued Edmunds. 'Eoghan Kendrick attempted to rectify his failure at the warehouse but was unsuccessful, prompting Caine to have him eliminated. Instead, Eoghan Kendrick shoots his assassin and goes into hiding. Meaning: the *only* way we're ever really going to know what happened that night is by finding Eoghan Kendrick.'

'If he's even still alive,' Saunders pointed out, now eating Joe's leftovers.

'If he's even still alive,' agreed Edmunds. 'Not to mention that if Christian didn't already know someone else escaped the fire, he certainly does now, and he knows we're looking for them; therefore, we have to presume that Caine and his people are *also* looking for them. It's just a question of who gets to Kendrick first.'

When the meeting adjourned, Edmunds went to take a seat beside Baxter, who was still unashamedly adjusting her cleavage.

'You seem to be having *problems* today,' he said tactfully, making sure Joe wasn't still perving from across the bar.

'Do these look bigger to you?' she asked.

Edmunds resolutely maintained eye contact: 'I wouldn't know.'

'You didn't even look!'

With a hefty sigh, he glanced down at her chest.

'They look the same to me . . . Are you not going to eat that?' he asked of her untouched breakfast toastie, eager to change subject.

'No,' she said, looking a little repulsed by it. 'Smells off to me.'

Taking it from her plate, Edmunds gave it a sniff, then took a bite out of it.

'Want some help today?' she asked him.

'Sure,' he replied with his mouth full. 'Need to pick up a couple of things for Leila on the way, though.'

Boots had run out of raspberry and pomegranate smoothies.

That really pissed Baxter off.

The spotty young man stacking the fridges had perhaps not entirely deserved the concentrated wrath of her foul mood or the very public lesson in supply and demand in which she explained that if every store in the fucking country ran out of raspberry and pomegranate smoothies *every single day,* then maybe, just maybe, someone with the godlike power to make such momentous decisions should perhaps, possibly, cautiously start thinking about stocking a few more. She felt bad, however, when his lip began to quiver and he ran off to have a good cry in the storeroom, setting her off too as she waited for Edmunds to finish shopping.

A few moments later, he emerged from the end of an aisle, face dropping as he hurried over to his sobbing friend.

'Baxter? What happened?'

'Nothing . . . I was just . . . Sorry.'

'Don't apologise. It's my fault. I shouldn't have gone . . . just over there.'

'What is *wrong* with me?' she laughed, wiping her eyes.

Edmunds opened his mouth . . . looked down at the pack of disposable nappies in his arms . . . and then back up at Baxter enquiringly.

'What?' she asked.

He looked a little uneasy.

'What?!'

'Ummm. Feeling tired?'

'Always.'

'How are the boobs now?'

'Weird.'

'Any other foods you've gone off recently?'

'Maybe.'

'Gonna burst into tears again in the middle of Boots?'

'Very possibly.'

'Congratulations.' Tossing the pack of nappies into her arms, Edmunds hurried away.

CHAPTER 30

Saturday 16 January 2016
3.23 p.m.

Wolf was sitting at his old desk in Homicide and Serious Crime Command debating whether or not to risk a Cadbury's Double Decker that had been festering in the drawer since well before the Ragdoll murders. He checked the faded use-by date, which probably should have been an indication in itself:

FEB 2015

With a mouthful of chocolate, he continued with the task at hand: retrieving call records and GPS tracking information stored under Christian's mobile number without alerting those assisting him to whom the phone belonged, which was proving even more problematic than anticipated.

At 3.42 p.m., and getting nowhere fast without Vanita's approval, Wolf received his own phone call that sent a chill up his spine.

'Mum? . . . What do you mean you're an hour away? An hour away from what? . . . Why?! . . . No, of course I do. I just . . . She did what now?' He gritted his teeth. 'Yes. Wasn't that nice of her! . . . No. I'm not actually living there anymore,' he explained, desperately trying to think where to send his parents. 'I'll text you the address . . . Text! . . . Text you!'

A few people in the vicinity glanced in his direction. Wolf mouthed an apology.

'OK. OK. That's just *so* great. I'll see you soon, then. Bye!'

He hung up, stuffed the rest of the discoloured chocolate bar into his mouth and put his head in his hands.

Edmunds had never shouted at Baxter before and they both felt a little weird about it.

They had been trying to work through some case files in his shed when the conversation had inevitably veered off topic and onto Baxter's teary admission that she had made a huge mistake by sleeping with Wolf. In her defence, she *had* already come clean to Thomas, which was something, but less in her favour was the realisation that she was probably pregnant.

Feeling bad, Edmunds sighed: 'Are you going to tell him?'

'Which one?'

'Thomas.'

She shrugged. 'I suppose it might come up at some point when I poop out an angry little baby.'

Edmunds's phone went off. He looked down at the screen and then up at Baxter anxiously. 'I'm just gonna . . .' He didn't finish, disappearing out through the door instead.

A minute passed, in which Baxter composed both herself and an excellent insult for Edmunds to make sure he wouldn't feel like he'd won; however, she forgot it the moment he returned looking perplexed. He put his phone away.

'That was Wolf,' he explained. 'He was asking all these random questions about you and Thomas and where you were currently living and if you had rented out your apartment or not.'

Baxter sat up straight, a look of concern on her face: 'And what did you tell him?'

Edmunds wore the expression of a man faced with no right answer.

'I . . . told him . . . the *truth*?' he replied.

Leaping from her stool, Baxter burst out of the shed.

'We have to stop him!' she yelled back at her confused friend.
'You can phone him on the way!'

'Thank you, spare key!' Wolf thanked his spare key, pleased to
discover that it still opened the outer door to Baxter's building. It was
one of the few things he'd kept, another souvenir from a past life.

He had texted his mother the address on Wimbledon High
Street and then caught the next southbound Tube. Climbing the
stairs up to the landing, he selected a tarnished key and unlocked
the door . . .

The stink of infection hit him instantly.

'*Jesus*, Echo!' he complained, grabbing a can of air freshener
off the side as he entered the main room.

With his sleeve covering his nose, Wolf looked from the worktop
covered in bandages and medicines to the cheery note informing
of a 'tub of Cookie Dough in the freezer!' – to the half-naked,
armed man, watching him from the bedroom doorway. Letting
out an unmanly yelp, Wolf raised his hands, firing a burst of Rose
Petal Paradise into the air.

'Wolf, right?' smiled Rouche, looking clammy and ashen,
lowering the gun to slump against the door frame.

'Right,' replied Wolf in surprise, slowly lowering his hands.
'And you must be the zombie formally known as Damien Rouche?
Saw you on the news. Pleased to meet you.' His eyes dropped to
the blackened word weeping across Rouche's chest.

'I know. Looks bad, doesn't it?'

'Smells worse,' Wolf assured him, hoping Rouche hadn't noticed
he'd been subtly spraying him with rose petal for over twenty
seconds now.

'Is Baxter with you?'

'No. But she *definitely* told me all about you . . . living here
. . . evading capture . . . and so on,' lied Wolf, checking his
watch. 'This is *probably* a good time to mention that we should
be expecting guests imminently.'

'Guests?' asked Rouche, watching as Wolf circled the room, collecting up photographs of Baxter in various states of annoyance at having her picture taken.

'Yeah. But don't worry. You don't have to do a thing . . . apart from tell them this is my flat.'

'Apartment,' Rouche corrected him.

'Even better! And that you're my good friend and room-mate' – he looked long and hard at Rouche – 'Haywood.'

'Haywood?'

'Don't happen to own a top, do you?' Wolf asked him, opening windows as he tidied up.

'I tend to bleed through them,' replied Rouche self-consciously.

'How about a red one, then?' he suggested. The intercom buzzed. 'Oh shit! OK. It's show time!'

Irritatingly, a car had parked in Baxter's space, so she left Blackie abandoned in the driveway and Edmunds sitting there like an idiot in the passenger seat. Sprinting into her building, she tore up the stairs and burst through the door to her apartment. With Wolf gawping back at her, she stormed towards him.

'What do you think you're doing?!'

He looked nervous: 'Baxter, I—'

'You think after everything you've done to me, you can just let yourself in and—'

'Baxter, if you'll just—'

'You are like a *fucking* disease on my life. You realise that? You've already ruined *everything*!'

'Baxter, my pare—'

'I'm late, Wolf!' she yelled, looking sick.

'To be fair, I never *actually* invited you.'

'No, you *shitstick*! *Late*. As in the polite way of saying I think I'm "up the duff" . . . or "You knocked me up" . . . you know, pregnant!'

'*Mazel tov!*' came a voice from the sofa.

She cringed and slowly turned her head to find Mr and Mrs

Fawkes watching them, sitting patiently beside Rouche, who had tactically positioned himself by an open window.

'Beverly!' Baxter beamed.

'Barbara,' Wolf corrected her.

'And Bob!'

'Bill.'

'What an unexpected treat! Can I get you anything?'

'No. No,' replied Mr Fawkes. 'Haywood's been looking after us.'

She couldn't even be bothered to ask.

'You're pregnant?' blurted Wolf, the news finally sinking in.

'Think so,' grinned Baxter, now looking a little manic.

'And . . . we're *absolutely* sure it isn't Thomas's?' he tried hopefully.

'Quite sure! Because Thomas has had "the snip".'

Wolf looked horrified: 'Like a . . . eunuch?'

'No, like a *bloody* vasectomy, you' – she glanced back at his parents listening in – '*fool*.'

'We Fawkeses are *very* fertile,' William Senior chimed in from the sofa as his wife nodded along in agreement.

'Gross, Dad!'

'Well, that's the sort of information that *might* have been useful to know beforehand!' Baxter half shouted.

'I mean, Will here was a *complete* accident!' added Mr Fawkes.

'Did *not* know that, Dad.' Wolf looked a little hurt. 'Thanks for sharing.'

'So, what brings you to London? And specifically, Wimbledon?' asked Baxter, barely holding it together.

'*The Lion King*,' answered Mrs Fawkes.

'*The . . . Lion King*?'

She nodded.

'It was the strangest thing. I was just talking to Ethel the other day when the phone rang and, to my surprise, it was Andrea . . . Do you know Andrea?'

'Oh, I know Andrea!'

'Well, she had been given two top-price tickets and a fancy hotel for the night . . . and she thought of us. Isn't that something?'

'That's *something* all right!'

Baxter and Wolf were both just beginning to ponder the motivation behind his ex-wife's actions when there was a knock at the door.

'I got it!' said Rouche, literally leaping at the opportunity to escape.

With the conversation reaching a strained interlude, they all listened in as Rouche greeted their unidentified visitor.

The click of high heels approached.

'Andrea!' called Mrs Fawkes happily. 'You got my message, then?' she said, getting up to kiss her on the cheek.

'I did!' Andrea turned to Wolf and smiled, having finally tracked him down: 'Will.'

Baxter had been rendered speechless by rage, while Wolf was edging little by little out of the room. The sound of running footsteps thundered up the stairs. Giving up, Rouche just held the door open for Edmunds as he came skidding into the crowded room.

'Andrea's coming!' he announced, panting heavily. Regarding his eclectic audience, he realised he was too late. 'Wait . . . was that . . . *Rouche*?' he asked, turning to Baxter with a look of betrayal.

'Hey!' waved Rouche wearily, noticing Andrea's eyes light up as she recognised the name and then the emaciated CIA agent himself.

'I didn't want you to have to keep any more of my secrets,' Baxter told Edmunds guiltily.

'Why don't you have a seat, love?' Wolf's dad told Andrea, oblivious to the awkward conversation taking place in the middle of the room. 'We're celebrating! Will and Emily are having a baby!'

'Is that *so*?' asked Andrea, turning to them with a smug expression. 'A baby, huh? More often than not, the result of having . . . *sex . . . together.* Now, I know this might look like my "well, well, well, I knew it all along" face, but I assure you this is one hundred per cent my "what a wonderful surprise" face.'

'Must be the Botox clouding the issue,' reasoned Wolf.

'Will!' his mother scolded him.

'I'm going for a lie-down,' announced Rouche, finally having enough.

'Night, Haywood!' Mr Fawkes called after him.

As Baxter took Edmunds to one side, Wolf approached Andrea, interrupting his dad, who had just begun explaining in great detail why the Fawkeses were so fertile.

'Can I borrow you?' Wolf asked her.

Andrea nodded and joined him in the kitchen area. She looked strange: younger, still beautiful, but different to how he remembered her at that age, like a variation on herself spawned from an alternate reality. Unfortunately, she was no less stubborn than he remembered.

'You brought my parents here?'

'You wouldn't return my calls!'

'I was avoiding you! That's what people do when they're avoiding someone!' whispered Wolf. 'It's, like, page one in *The How to Avoid Someone Handbook*: *do not* call them back!'

'I'm not here to argue with you,' she told him calmly. 'I want to help.'

'Help what?'

'You.'

'Help me . . . what?'

'With everything. I am so, so sorry about Finlay. I truly am. And I just want to . . . I want to make up for some of my past indiscretions.'

Wolf shook his head.

'I do! Look . . .' She unzipped her jacket to reveal the updated bright yellow campaign T-shirt and, indirectly, the new breasts beneath:

UNCAGE the WOLF! . . . *again!*

'Notice how I left space for, you know, the next time you spectacularly blow your life to hell,' she smiled.

'Put them away . . . It away,' Wolf quickly corrected himself.
'Put the T-shirt away.'

'You are *so* immature,' Andrea told him, but then she cracked
a smile and embraced him tightly. 'Never do that again!' she
whispered in his ear. 'I've been so worried about you.'

Ignoring the hopeful look on his mother's face, Wolf gently
squeezed her back.

'It's fine,' said Edmunds, speaking to Baxter in private as she
wondered where the photograph of her in Mexico had gone. 'I
was just surprised. That's all.'

'And you could've done *what* to help precisely? Nothing. Which
is why I didn't tell you.'

'A problem shared . . .' started Edmunds.

'Is aiding and abetting,' finished Baxter, winning that round.

'He looks terrible.'

'He's getting better,' Baxter told him, unconvinced by her own
words.

'And your plan was . . . *what*?'

'Get Rouche somewhere safe. He recovers, grows a beard and
lives happily ever after.'

'I thought there are "no happy endings",' said Edmunds, quoting
Baxter and comfortably winning round two.

'He said he's feeling better,' she insisted, having to raise her
voice to compete with Wolf's dad on the other side of the room.

'Even if he is . . . and he does,' started Edmunds, wondering
why it always seemed to fall to him to be the bearer of bad news,
'we now have a serious problem.'

He glanced over at Andrea in concern, who looked to be wedged
between the Fawkeses against her will.

'I'll speak to her.'

'Rouche is wanted for murder, which makes you an accomplice.'

'What do you want me to do? It's Rouche,' she said simply.

'You could go to prison!'

'He *will* go to prison!'

'I'm just saying that a little distance might be prudent. If they find him living in your apartment . . .'

Baxter nodded, at least acknowledging that he had a point. 'Look, it's Rouche. I owe him. He stays.'

Again Edmunds looked over at Andrea: 'Don't you trust her.'

'I won't,' she assured him, taking a deep breath before making her way over to the redheaded reporter. 'Hey,' she said, interrupting Mr Fawkes midway through his rant about the M4 roadworks. 'Could I have a word?'

Looking a little apprehensive, Andrea got up and followed Baxter outside into the hallway, the only place left to speak in private.

'If this is about you and Wolf,' pre-empted Andrea, 'I genuinely don't have a—'

'It's not.'

She looked surprised: 'Then?'

'You are a soulless, shameless, death-mongering mega bitch, and if you keep getting facelifts at the rate you're going, that mark of the beast is going to end up smack bang in the middle of your taut forehead.'

'OK,' replied Andrea. She'd been called worse.

'But whatever problems *we* may have, they've got nothing to do with Rouche. He is a good man who has already lost everythi—'

'Your secret's safe with me,' Andrea cut her off. 'I know you think I betrayed you during the Ragdoll murders, and to some degree that is the case, but the honest-to-God truth is that I chose not to make an *utterly* pointless sacrifice for the sake of our new-found amity. I could have, but I'd have been flushing my career down the toilet, and you *still* wouldn't have liked me that much.'

'You can save the whole "if I hadn't done it, somebody else would" speech.'

'My boss had someone else all set up in the studio *next door* ready to read out the exact same words that I did. I am sorry, but faced with the same choice, I wouldn't do anything differently.'

Baxter laughed bitterly and moved towards the door.

'Congratulations,' blurted Andrea. 'I genuinely mean that.'

For some reason, Baxter paused and turned round.

'Will never wanted children when we were together,' she continued. 'I'm glad he does now.'

'Despite popular belief,' said Baxter accusingly, 'it was a one-time, life-obliterating mistake.'

'And what did he say when he found out?'

'I'm reading between the lines here. Best guess: "Oh look, my evil ex-wife just burst through the door *ten seconds* after Baxter told me and now we haven't had chance to talk about it."'

Andrea looked guilty: 'Oh.'

'I don't really want to talk about this,' said Baxter. 'Especially with you.'

'Fair enough,' Andrea said pleasantly. 'Then let's talk about something else. Like how Damien Rouche ended up squatting in your apartment.'

Baxter shook her head. 'You had more hope with the baby conversation,' she replied, turning her back on Andrea and heading inside.

Baxter watched in wonder as bolt after bolt of lightning struck the same spot, a bridge between the heavens and the earth, tearing the air apart to singe the lid of a Gü chocolate pudding. She'd forgotten to remove the foil before putting it in the microwave and was finally about to do something about it when the appliance saved her the trouble by blowing a fuse.

'Everything OK out there?' called Thomas, still dressed in his badminton kit, having come home to yet another impromptu Baxter dinner.

'Fine!' she lied, serving up the two puddings and carrying them out to the table, ensuring to place the completely uncooked example in front of her. Returning to her seat, she went to take another sip of wine when it dawned on her that it probably wasn't advisable.

She set the glass back down.

'This is nice,' said Thomas. He smiled across at her and then picked up the bottle: 'Would you like more wine?'

Baxter placed her hand over the glass:

'No . . . thank you. And that's actually kind of what I wanted to talk to you about. I have . . . *news*.'

'Oh?' replied Thomas, reaching over to hold her hand . . . his grip unconsciously tightening.

'Look, I'm not very good at this sort of stuff, but . . . I . . .'

Her phone started buzzing across the table.

'. . . love . . .'

She couldn't help but glance down at the screen.

'. . . Wolf.'

Thomas let go of her hand: 'You love . . . *Wolf*?'

'What? No! I love you. I love *you*! Wolf is just calling at a really, really bad . . .' Her hand hovered over the vibrating annoyance.

'But you're not going to answer it . . . *right*?'

'It's my job. Just give me a sec,' she said apologetically before picking up: 'Timing as impeccable as ever, Wolf. What do you want?'

Thomas huffed loudly and folded his arms.

'Christian's phone came up clean. "No location data. No calls beyond normal usage or that couldn't be accounted for,"' Wolf read out loud. 'It was always a long shot. He's too careful to leave a trail.'

'This couldn't have waited?'

'It's for Finlay,' he replied, sounding hurt.

'Sorry. You're right,' she sighed. 'Guess it's unlikely he'd use a computer either, then.' She smiled across at Thomas but only received a glare back in response.

'But he must be communicating with someone,' said Wolf. 'He was in hospital the night of Edmunds's break-in, and I can't really see him jimmying the lock on Saunders's Skoda himself.'

'Could it be Killian Caine and his men?'

'No. I think Edmunds is right. It doesn't really seem their style. Why bother sneaking around the night after beating the shit out of the police commissioner in front of witnesses?'

'So, he must have another phone, then.'

Losing patience, Thomas picked up his spoon and started on his dessert.

'Seems likely,' agreed Wolf. 'And we need to find it. It's either got to be in his home or at the office.'

'That'll be breaking and entering,' Baxter pointed out.

'Only if we get caught. I know the code to his alarm,' said Wolf. 'I'll take the house, but you and Saunders are the only ones who can move freely around New Scotland Yard. And of the two of you, you have the advantage of *not* being Saunders.'

'Can't fault that logic. I'll see what I can do.'

'Thanks. Hey . . . do you think we should maybe talk about—'

Baxter hung up on him.

'Your pudding will be cold,' Thomas told her.

'I don't doubt that,' she mumbled, picking up her wine glass, looking longingly at it and then setting it back down.

'So . . . your *big* news?' he prompted, as if asking an executioner to finish sharpening their blade.

Baxter opened her mouth, shoved in a heaped spoonful of uncooked dessert and shook her head. 'It's nothing.'

CHAPTER 31

Monday 18 January 2016
9.35 a.m.

Baxter had seldom ventured as far into the lion's den.

She had, on occasion, been summoned up to Vanita's office for various tellings-off and had always found the hushed corridors jarring in comparison to the anarchical state of equilibrium that sustained Homicide and Serious Crime.

Wolf had been advised by his new bestie, Vanita, that she had a 9.30 a.m. meeting with the commissioner, presenting a half-hour window in which his office would be standing empty. Armed with an important-looking folder, Baxter strode confidently past the banks of desks. The assorted PAs and administrators paid her little attention, consumed entirely by their own trivial tasks. After a quick glance to the left, to ensure the office was empty, and then to the right, to check she wasn't being watched, she hurried through the door.

'OK,' she whispered, heart racing as she regarded Christian's plush office, the scents of leather and wood complementing the hazy sunshine jabbing through the gaps in the blinds.

She walked over to the large desk and pulled the top drawer open.

Wolf had been inside Christian's Epping Forest mansion for almost an hour.

The damaged electric gate had left room enough to squeeze through, and after a testes-crushing scramble over a wall, he had made it to the back door. Causing as little damage as possible, he forced the lock and then sprinted through to the hallway to punch in the five-digit code that silenced the alarm. There had been no evidence of the party just a few nights earlier, the weak sun warming the rug, chairs and sofa at the nucleus of the vast space. Chess pieces stood poised for action in the centre of the coffee table, and the grand piano had vanished, making Wolf wonder whether he had dreamed the whole thing.

Satisfied that he had thoroughly searched the master bedroom, he moved into the moodily lit walk-in wardrobe, where two rows of bodiless suits stood to attention over their corresponding shoes.

A little unnerved, Wolf checked the time and set to work.

By 9.52 a.m., Baxter had been through every drawer in the desk, the open briefcase beside it and the pockets of the coat on the back of the door. She was aware she only had minutes left and felt desperation setting in. 'Come on, you leathery bastard. Where is it?'

She moved over to the filing cabinet, where the metal tray slid effortlessly from its housing, her mind drifting to orderly drawers of bodies lining morgue walls. She had barely begun flicking through when she heard Vanita's approaching voice.

She froze.

Christian's profile appeared at the window, brow furrowed as they continued their discussion.

Trapped, Baxter gently pushed the filing cabinet shut, looking around the room for somewhere, anywhere, to hide – from the windows that only led to sky to the leafy tree in the corner, from the long coat hanging from a hook to the imposing desk. She realised that Vanita was looking right at her as she stood there ineptly with nowhere to run.

'I knew I'd forget something!' Baxter heard her say on the other side of the glass. Vanita subtly repositioned herself so that

Christian's back was to the window. 'I've got that Pearson email I wanted to go over with you.'

'Of course. Send it across.'

Watching the handle, Baxter backed away from the door.

'Actually, would you mind if we did it now?' asked Vanita, her voice more urgent than she'd intended. 'It's up on my screen anyway and is already considerably overdue.'

'I've got things to—'

'Consider it an olive branch,' she pressed him.

'Well, in that case, of course . . . But let me just grab something.' Christian turned away and swung the door wide open, giving his subordinate an enquiring look when she audibly gasped. He followed her gaze into the empty office. 'I'll be along in a minute,' he told her.

Vanita was still standing there when he pushed the door to. He walked over to the window and pulled the blinds up to bask in the January sunshine for a moment before sitting at his computer.

Christian's knee was just inches from Baxter's face.

Holding her breath, she slowly pulled her boot in close to her, having contorted herself beneath the desk. She watched his smart shoe shuffle towards her and leaned away, pressing herself into the wood as she lifted her body off the floor. As his foot edged beneath her, her legs began to tremble under the strain of the unbearable pose.

Wolf had found something that might have been nothing but was certainly more promising than anything else he'd unearthed in the sparse house: investment certificates dating back as far as June 1981. Unlocking his phone to take photographs, he suddenly realised the time.

Baxter was supposed to be out of Christian's office by 9.55 a.m. at the very latest. She had sworn to message him the moment she was clear to let him know she was safe.

He composed a brief text:

You out???

Hovering his thumb over the 'send' button, he deliberated whether or not to give her another minute.

Baxter could hear Christian tapping away on his keyboard directly above her head as the fabric of his trousers brushed against her arm.

She knew Wolf would be waiting for her message. Conscious of her phone pressing into her hip, she willed him not to call. Reaching three fingers into her trouser pocket, she could feel the metal against her fingertips but was unable to get a firm grasp. Forcing harder, the thin fabric ripped, causing her hand to slip, grazing Christian's shoe.

The typing stopped.

Baxter didn't dare breathe, her eyes wide and alert, her pounding heart trying to betray her. She watched him change position to pick something up off the desk.

'Kessie, could you book me lunch with Malcolm Hislop tomorrow, please?'

Seizing her opportunity, Baxter slid the phone from her pocket and scrolled from 'vibrate' to 'silent' just seconds before the screen lit up with Wolf's text message. She held it to her chest to smother the electric glow.

'Anywhere's fine. Surprise me!' chuckled Christian, ending his call.

She heard him replace the receiver before opening and closing a drawer. He stood back up, flooding the cramped space with light, the sound of his footsteps moving away, followed by a door closing. Baxter slumped onto the carpet, feeling nauseous from maintaining the awkward position for so long, frowning as she noticed the cheap mobile phone taped securely to the underside of the drawer.

Too drained to summon even a hint of triumph or relief, she reached up and ripped it free.

*

At 10.17 a.m., Christian had finished with Vanita and was heading back to his office when his PA intercepted him carrying a very welcome cup of coffee and less-so stack of post.

'Lunch at the Culpeper tomorrow as it's supposed to be sunny and the rooftop greenhouse is to die for!'

'Thank you, Kessie,' he said, carefully taking the hot mug from her.

'Oh, did you see that DCI Baxter dropped something off for you?'

He almost managed to hide his surprise: 'I'm sorry?'

'Emily Baxter,' she clarified, suspecting that she had put her foot in it yet again. 'She came by about three-quarters of an hour ago and went into your office. I just presumed—'

'Oh yes!' Christian smiled.

His PA visibly relaxed.

'Yes, she did. Thank you,' he lied, keeping his smile firmly in place until he'd returned to his office and closed the door.

Hurrying over to his briefcase, he found everything in order. It looked untouched. He then pulled each of the drawers open in turn to discover nothing missing. Finally, he reached beneath the desk and was relieved to find the mobile phone still taped securely in place. Looking down at his desk phone, Christian wondered whether they had tapped it. It was an insult to think he would ever be that careless. He considered the possibility that they had bugged his office in their desperation and was somewhat reassured by that, because that was all they had: their desperation.

He tore the flimsy mobile from the wood, left his office and entered the men's toilets. After splashing some cold water over his face, he ensured he was alone before hesitantly calling the phone's only stored number. It went straight to voicemail. 'It's me. I have a problem I need taking care of.'

CHAPTER 32

Monday 18 January 2016
6.48 p.m.

Rouche had slept through the majority of the day but had set an alarm, just in case, in order to switch the lights on, have a quick wash, tidy-up and general de-stink of the apartment before Holly arrived. Standing in the en-suite bathroom, he stared into the foggy mirror, barely recognising himself anymore – all sunken eyes and hollow cheeks . . .

PUPPET

The letters stood black and proud, looking more like felt-tip on the glass than a reflection of his own chest. He reached out to wipe them away and could almost fool himself into thinking it had worked when his wet thumb blurred the image in the mirror. Bracing himself, he looked down to perform his nightly assessment: prominent blue veins wormed around the dying flesh, knotted just beneath the surface as if retreating from the poison they carried.

There was a noise out in the hallway.

Concerned that Holly was early, Rouche turned off the tap, grabbed a towel and walked to the bedroom doorway. He frowned on hearing a series of clicks and scrapes, picked a jumper up off the floor and pulled it over his head.

There was a sharp clunk, and then, very slowly, the front door swung open.

Taking a step back into the bedroom, he watched as a heavyset man entered the apartment holding a weighty gun in one hand and closing the door behind him with the other. Rouche stared helplessly at his service weapon on the far side of the room, the handle protruding from the holster. He knew he could never cover the distance in time. He considered what resources he had to hand: a pair of Baxter's nail scissors she'd left in the bathroom cabinet, various aerosols, a bottle of bleach. He could snap the head off his toothbrush to form a plastic shiv.

He pushed the door to as the intruder made his way down the hallway. The man looked to be in his mid-sixties from what little Rouche could see through the crack, but had placed a hand over his face to shield from the smell. He paused outside the main bathroom, giving the door a gentle push to ensure it was empty.

Rouche went to dart across the open space, fortunately hesitating just as the man turned back round and entered the kitchen, weapon raised at the open-plan living area. Preparing to make his move again, a creaky floorboard betrayed his location. The man's head immediately whipped round to stare at the bedroom, gun pointed directly at Rouche as he watched, motionless, through the thin crack he'd left between the door and the frame.

He started to approach.

Rouche looked back at the bedroom window in desperation, aware that he would never escape the two-storey fall in any condition to run. He stood a better hope trying to fight, even in his enfeebled state. He watched the man draw nearer, pausing only to glance at the assortment of medications littering the kitchen counter.

Seizing his moment, Rouche pulled the door open just enough to scramble across to the bookcase, the movement attracting the intruder's attention, who was again watching the bedroom door intently.

Rouche didn't dare move, the wall of dark windows reflecting the inside of the apartment like a mirror. Unable to hide from both the gunman and his own reflection, he had nowhere to go, knowing he would be discovered should the man turn his head even a little. The intruder, however, seemed preoccupied with the swaying door, allowing him to shuffle between the furniture to avoid being seen as the gunman cautiously approached the final room.

With his back to the sofa, Rouche could see his holster hanging tantalisingly from the exercise bike but didn't dare reach for it. Not yet.

Holly was early.

She had been looking forward to seeing Rouche all day and had already shopped for dinner in her lunch break, filling the cadaver fridges with wine, diced chicken, cheese and cake.

Her mind had been elsewhere: it didn't register with her that the outer door had been propped ajar. She hadn't noticed the splintered wood on the carpet beneath the broken lock. Hurrying up the stairs, she removed her keys, jangling them against the handle as she struggled with the shopping bags. Pushing the door open with her foot, she stepped inside. She opened her mouth to call a greeting to Rouche when a rough hand covered her face, a constricting arm wrapping round her chest, pinning her in place.

She couldn't breathe, let alone scream, as she struggled against her attacker.

'Shhhh! Shhhh! It's me!' Rouche whispered in her ear.

Holly ceased fighting immediately, allowing him to unwrap his arm from round her and point the gun back down the hallway.

'Go,' he whispered, removing his hand from over her mouth, his eyes fixed firmly on the open bedroom doorway.

Terrified, she did as she was told, turning back to the front door when she sensed Rouche move behind her; firing a single deafening shot, he wrenched her towards him in one fluid motion. Part of the door exploded just above her head as she fell backwards, Rouche unintentionally throttling her as he dragged her into the kitchen, getting off two more rounds as they took cover behind the units.

Everything went quiet for a moment, bar the sound of Holly's panicked breathing.

Rouche looked at her for the first time and smiled, as though they were enjoying a peaceful sit in the park rather than cowering for their lives in Baxter's kitchen. He squeezed her hand but flinched when a set of three gunshots showered glass and broken granite over their heads.

Holly cried out and turned to Rouche with petrified eyes. With shards of Baxter's glassware glittering in his hair, he took each of her hands in turn, placing them over her ears. He winked at her and then sprang up, firing three more shots of his own before dropping to the floor. The intruder made a break for the front door, spraying bullets as he passed, imploding Holly's reflection in the window.

Struggling back to his feet to go after him, Rouche made it just four steps before collapsing to the floor.

'Rouche!' cried Holly, crawling over the jagged sparkles to reach him as he gasped for air, his eyes filling with tears as he held his chest in agony. 'Rouche! What is it? Talk to me!' She frantically checked his body for bullet wounds but found nothing. 'Are you shot?!'

He shook his head: 'Just . . . can't breathe.'

She was already reaching for her mobile when he cried out in pain.

'You're going to be OK,' she promised, holding the phone to her ear. 'Ambulance, please.'

Rouche grasped her hand, his head lolling weakly.

'I'm getting help!' Holly promised him.

He pulled the phone away from her, tears rolling down his cheeks. 'Outside,' he whispered.

She didn't understand.

'Get me . . . outside.'

'You can't move!' she told him, appalled.

He started dragging himself across the floor.

'Rouche!' she cried. 'OK! OK!' She held the phone back up to her ear: 'Wimbledon High Street, opposite the pub. You'll see us. Please hurry. There's a man . . . I think he's dying.'

Baxter had spotted the blue hue radiating over the buildings from half a mile away.

She accelerated harder, grille lights strobing, overtaking the building traffic as she turned onto the High Street. Pulling up illegally a few hundred yards from her building, she switched off the engine and stared in dismay at the scene before her: police vehicles had completely blocked the road. She counted four patrol cars, an Armed Response Unit and various other unmarked resources.

Holly's frantic phone call had prepared her to some degree, but the situation had clearly escalated since then. On discovering Rouche's incriminating wounds, the ambulance staff had requested police backup before leaving the scene, and combined with reports of gunfire in the vicinity, they had sent just about everyone.

Baxter took out her phone and messaged Holly. Less than thirty seconds later, she spotted her weaving out of the crowd before hurrying down the street towards the car. Checking that no one was watching her, she opened the door and climbed into the passenger seat, throwing her arms around Baxter.

'They took him away but wouldn't tell me where!' she sobbed. 'I don't even know if he's still alive!'

Gently easing out of the embrace, Baxter looked at her old school friend: her hair and clothes were covered in tiny specks, and her hands were coated in dried blood.

'You're hurt,' she said.

Holly shook her head: 'Not really. I cut my leg on some glass.'

'What do they know?' Baxter asked her, determined to suppress her own anguish by remaining pragmatic.

'Nothing,' sniffed Holly. 'He made me bring him out onto the street,' she explained shamefully. 'He was thinking about you even when . . . when . . .' She started to cry again, which almost set Baxter off.

'So they don't know about the break-in?'

'No.'

'They don't know that I live there?'

'Of course not.'

'What about the gunshots?'

'Half the street heard them and think the shots came from their buildings.'

'And who do they think you are?'

'Just some crazy emotional bystander who called the ambulance.'

Baxter nodded and patted her friend's arm reassuringly. She had said all the right things so far. It seemed an inopportune moment to warn her that she would have to lie on several more occasions before the police were done with her.

'He saved my life,' whispered Holly, turning to her.

'Mine too.'

'I can't believe he's gone.'

Baxter's eyes were glistening blue as she watched the flashing lights pulse across the windscreen. 'No . . . Neither can I.'

CHAPTER 33

Tuesday 3 May 1994

10.04 a.m.

'. . . Hodgkin's lymphoma,' said the doctor softly. 'A form of cancer.'

Maggie simply nodded, the imperturbable detachment of a career nurse ingrained too deeply into her psyche for anything else. Finlay, on the other hand, was just sitting there open-mouthed.

It was a cruelly beautiful day outside, the breeze teasing the blinds the only sound in the tranquil office.

Maggie had been steadily losing weight since the new year and, at thirty-three, shouldn't have been feeling as perpetually exhausted as she had been, prompting her to ask the advice of a doctor friend, which had quickly escalated into a succession of formal tests and a far bigger fuss than she had wanted.

'Now, Maggie, I know this will come as a shock to you . . . to *both* of you, but I want you to know that—'

'What's the . . . the . . .' Finlay interrupted him, getting stuck when he couldn't remember the correct word. 'What's the prom—'

'Prognosis?' suggested Maggie, smiling at him.

'Yeah, that. What's the promnosis?'

The doctor nodded, clearly expecting the question. 'At this early stage, I can't give you an answer. We need to run tests—'

'More tests,' Finlay tutted.

'. . . to find out *if* and *how far* it's spread.' The man looked to Maggie. 'But she's a tough one and otherwise in perfect health, so I'm going to go out on a limb here and say, "Good."'

Maggie smiled encouragingly at her husband, who appeared slightly comforted by the utterly unfounded and ultimately mean- ingless opinion. She reached over and squeezed his hand.

'Rest assured,' the doctor continued, 'Maggie's going to have the very best that the NHS can afford her.'

Finlay frowned at the comment intended to placate him. And as Maggie and the doctor continued the conversation, his thoughts returned for the first time in years to a car boot full of stolen money, half of which was his.

Christian had remained in Glasgow for almost eighteen months after Finlay's departure until eventually deciding to move back home to Essex. With a little help from his old friend, he secured a job with the Metropolitan Police, even working in the same department for a spell before taking a middle-management role elsewhere. They had gone through various phases of contact but had not spoken in over two years when Finlay called him out of the blue.

Just three days after Maggie's diagnosis, the two men were sitting down in a café together, the enduring sunshine tempting them to a table beside the river.

'Life won,' announced Finlay once the pool of small talk had dried up.

'Come again?'

'Fifteen years ago,' recalled Finlay, 'you told me one day life would wear down my integrity. Well . . . you were right. Life won.'

Christian's brow furrowed.

'I need my half,' Finlay told him.

'Of course. It's yours,' he replied, before pulling a face: 'But it's not quite as simple as just handing you a briefcase.'

Finlay's expression changed.

'Don't worry!' Christian added quickly. 'I've got it all . . . Much more, in fact. But that's sort of the issue. I didn't just bury it in a shoebox in the garden. I invested, diversified: bought stocks and bonds . . . property. I was planning for the long term.'

'I need my *fucking* money!' spat Finlay, slamming his fist down on the table, spilling their drinks.

'And you'll get it,' Christian said evenly, giving the startled waitress a reassuring smile. 'But we have to be clever about this. If I just cash in half my portfolio and hand it over to you, it's going to look a *tad* suspicious. Wouldn't you agree?'

Finlay grunted.

'Why do you think I'm still working like a dog?' Christian asked his friend, who looked crestfallen as he stared out over the water. 'What's going on? If you're *that* desperate, I might have some short-term stock that we won't lose out on too badly.'

'Do it.'

Christian nodded: 'This afternoon . . . but *only* if you tell me what's going on.'

Finlay closed his eyes to steel himself: 'It's Maggie . . . She's not so good.'

CHAPTER 34

Tuesday 19 January 2016
9.03 a.m.

'What the *fuck* happened last night?'

'You *fucking* lied to me. That's what!'

'I told you to keep a low profile, just scare her off. And then I wake up to your botched crime scene all over the news.'

'One unarmed female living there. Is that not what you told me? Not one very-fucking-heavily-armed CIA agent!'

'He was *in* her apartment?'

'He was. And we shot the place up pretty good by the time we'd finished.'

'This is such a mess!'

'I want double.'

'Double?! I'm not paying you single: the job's not done.'

'I got shot! I almost died because of you.'

'Shot? Is it bad?'

'It's not good!'

'Do you need anything?'

'No. I've had worse.'

'Very well: double . . . on completion of the job.'

'Done. So, if she's not living there, where is she?'

'New Scotland Yard. In fact, I'm looking at her right now.'

'I'll head over.'

'Just follow her for now. See where she goes. But if an opportunity presents itself . . .'

'Understood.'

'Black Audi, looks like it's been in an accident. Registration: Romeo, Victor, zero, nine, Hotel, Charlie, Golf.'

'Got it.'

'Update me later.'

Holly hadn't slept at all.

She had spent the whole night googling emerging news stories relating to Rouche's apprehension in the vain hope that one might disclose some fresh detail. She had called in sick to work and, under Baxter's instruction, driven back over to the apartment, lying convincingly enough to fool the officer manning the cordon into believing she lived there. Letting herself in, she hugged herself against the cold, forgetting about the shattered window in the main room and making a mental note to cling-film it up before she left. Unable to do much about the holes in the hallway wall, she entered the kitchen, where Rouche's gun was still lying in the middle of the floor. She unzipped her rucksack and placed it inside, piling all of the medications and dressings on top.

Moving into the bedroom, Holly paused to look at each of the framed photographs in turn, collecting them up along with the wallet, phone, keys and every other trace of Rouche that she could find.

At 9.26 a.m., Baxter received an urgent call from Techie Steve, the technologies officer assisting them with the burner-phone branch of their investigation. Abandoning her meeting with Vanita, she headed down to Homicide and Serious Crime to find Steve as enthused as ever by the most mundane of assignments. He ushered her into a private room, the physical demands of sitting at a computer apparently untucking his coffee-stained shirt.

'I've been getting updates from the network at fifteen-minute intervals since yesterday afternoon,' he started, leaping back into his chair, 'on both the phone you found but won't tell me whose is, and on the stored number you also won't tell me whose is that you found on the phone you found . . . but won't tell me whose is,' he explained, sounding a little bitter. 'Make sense?'

'No.'

'Anyway, they've both been completely dead – i.e. the SIM cards and batteries had been separated from the phones. That was until nine this morning, when I got a ping off the nearest mast. And then, at three minutes past nine, Burner Phone One made a call to Burner Phone Two. Duration: seventy-five seconds. Location: somewhere between Bow Street and Saint Martin's Lane.'

Baxter looked at her watch. Half an hour had passed since then.

'There's more,' continued Steve. 'This isn't the first time that phone has been used in that location. On the eleventh, it was used for a two-minute call in the same area.'

'Meaning you might have found where he's staying!' said Baxter excitedly. 'Is there anything more you can get?'

'Not without a warrant, no. We can gather information on messages and calls made and received but not the *content* contained within those communications.'

'Bloody bureaucrats,' spat Baxter.

'There's been *a lot* of public outcry regarding privacy,' said Steve, surprised.

'If they weren't doing anything wrong, they wouldn't have anything to hide,' surmised Baxter. 'How accurate is that location?'

'Thanks to the number of masts in the city centre, pretty damn accurate. Within a few hundred feet, I'd say.'

'OK. I'll go check it out.' She turned to leave.

'People never tell me anything,' blurted Steve, 'but I couldn't help noticing that the other phone, the one from which the call originated, had a location of . . . well, *here*.'

Baxter nodded thoughtfully. 'Trust me, the less you know . . .'

'Figures,' smiled Steve. 'Well, safe travels!'

*

He had only just parked his motorcycle up when he spotted a black Audi, matching Christian's dilapidated description, exiting the New Scotland Yard car park. Pulling his helmet back on as he returned to the bike, he took off in pursuit, keeping his distance as they negotiated the stop-start traffic along the river. He was conscious that he was making the same journey he had just undertaken, only in reverse, 'conscious' becoming 'concerned' as they passed the enormous banners for *The Lion King* smothering the façade of the Lyceum Theatre before turning off.

The Audi pulled up on Henrietta Street, ignoring the double yellow lines, forcing him to pass to avoid drawing attention to himself. With limited options, and afraid he was going to lose her, he rounded the corner and parked on the pavement outside his guest house. Hurrying back to the junction, he watched Baxter and a man he didn't recognise climb out of the car. They were staring up at the buildings lining the street, searching for something . . .

. . . searching for him.

He quickly pulled the dismantled phone from the pocket of his leather jacket, pieced it together and switched it back on.

'So, I hear you and Wolf are having a pup?'

'Fuck off, Saunders!' snapped Baxter before answering her phone: 'Yeah?'

'Boss, it's Steve . . . Techie Steve.'

'We spoke like half an hour ago. I remember you,' she assured him as they ambled along the busy side street beneath another clear blue sky.

'He just turned his phone back on! It was only a ten-second call, but I was able to get a more precise location.'

'And?'

'He's still there: corner of Henrietta and Bedford Street.'

Baxter glanced up and down the road.

'Good work.' She hung up and turned to Saunders: 'He's here. Get the others.'

*

It had been forty minutes, which Baxter and Saunders had put to good use by visiting hotels, guest houses and cafés in the vicinity. Enquiring after a stocky Caucasian male in his fifties or sixties and probably travelling alone, they took down the details of anyone vaguely matching their description of Christian's accomplice provided to them by Holly.

Edmunds had phoned to say he was five minutes away when Baxter received another call from Techie Steve.

'Baxter,' she answered abruptly.

'He's using the phone again: Henrietta Street.'

She whistled loudly to attract Saunders's attention and then ran round the corner, back onto the road on which they had parked. There were dozens of people moving in both directions: a barrel-chested businessman in a cheap suit, a stray hipster whose elaborate beard appeared to point the way back to Shoreditch, a man in motorcycle leathers, hard-hat-carrying construction workers . . .

'Where is he now?!' she asked as Saunders caught up with her.

'Still Henrietta Street, heading north-east towards Covent Garden.'

'Can you patch the others onto the call?' she asked as she and Saunders proceeded down the road, eliminating people as they entered buildings or changed direction. Patting Blackie as they passed, she checked the windscreen for a parking ticket.

Saunders's phone went off as he joined the conference call.

'Keep going,' Steve advised them.

Increasing their pace, Covent Garden's wide piazza began to open up in front of them.

'Looks like he's stopped,' said Steve. 'Has anybody stopped?'

The famous tourist trap was as bustling as ever, the pillared market hall an island within the sea of cobbles on which street performers captivated the masses. Baxter scanned faces, unsure who she was even looking for.

'I'm here!' announced Edmunds over the phone, sounding out of breath. 'By the Opera House. Where do you need me?'

'OK. He's moving again!' shouted Steve, getting overexcited. 'Towards the market hall and moving fast!'

All three of them sprinted towards the central structure, passing between stone columns to emerge beneath a domed glass roof. Taking a side each, they spread out across the galleried space as a string quartet entertained the people dining below.

'He's stopped again,' Steve told them. 'Hold on . . . Saunders, I'm tracking you.'

'You are?'

'Straight ahead.'

Saunders obeyed, watching everyone he could as he passed the expensive shops.

'Keep going . . . Keep going . . . Stop!'

Again he did as he was told, looking around in confusion at the people walking by. He then peered over the railings in case their target was below him.

'There's no one here!' he yelled over a gaggle of teenage tourists.

'You're right on him! He should be directly in front of you!'

Saunders paced up and down the walkway, desperately searching for anyone matching the description. 'I'm telling you, there's no one within ten feet of me.'

'Ring it,' suggested Edmunds, watching from across the hall. 'Steve, ring it!'

'Boss?' asked Steve anxiously.

'Do it.'

A few tense moments later, a muffled melody started to play.

'Move! Move! Move!' Saunders barked at a group of schoolchildren as he followed the sound over to a rubbish bin. 'He's ditched the phone!' he informed them, rummaging through discarded food packaging and takeaway coffee cups to retrieve it before following the others back outside.

Baxter stared despairingly at the tide of humanity washing in and out of the piazza. Her instincts told her to watch the exit they had entered through, hoping that whatever allure Henrietta

Street held for their suspect might draw him back there one final time. Her eyes fell to a man dressed in full motorcycle leathers, recognising him as one of the people they had followed into the square.

'Sorry I'm late!' said Wolf, finally joining them.

Baxter spotted him over the throngs of people. 'Wolf, guy in black leathers heading straight for you!'

Wolf paused, his pure size enough to redirect the human traffic around him.

Less than ten metres away, their target was staring right at him, had recognised him and immediately changed direction, maintaining his speed so as not to draw attention as he was consumed by the crowds.

Wolf shoved his way through a tour group in pursuit, only to find a heap of leather on the cobblestones.

'Shit! He's removed the jacket,' he told the others. 'I've lost him!'

Edmunds was already following the man when he emerged from the columns of the church.

Keeping his distance, he passed behind a fire-juggling street performer, who had managed to claim a sizeable area from the crowds. Watching their suspect's form distort in the heat from the blazing batons, he lifted his phone to update the team, then hesitated.

Anger and adrenaline rising up inside him, he pictured this unidentified person skulking through the audience doing the very same inside his home, carrying that bottle of corrosive liquid over his sleeping wife and daughter, nightmarish images assaulting him every time he paused to wonder what might have happened had they woken up . . .

Charging across the open space, Edmunds distracted the performer, who dropped his flaming sticks to the ground. Knocking a number of people to the cobbled floor, he locked his arm round their suspect's throat and pulled him down, winded when the heavy man landed on top of him and taking several vicious blows in the process. But, still, Edmunds held firm, tightening his arm round the thick neck.

Saunders was the first to reach them.

'Hell, yeah! Edmunds kicked his arse!' he laughed into the phone, standing over them.

'Little help, please!' gasped Edmunds, now beginning to tire. 'He's *bloody* heavy!'

'Oh, right,' said Saunders, searching for his handcuffs. 'Sorry.'

CHAPTER 35

Tuesday 19 January 2016

11.42 a.m.

The emergency-service vehicles had drawn their own crowd as Edmunds helped load their prisoner into the back of the police van. Flicking through the man's wallet, he rejoined the others, warming themselves with a well-earned cup of coffee in the unseasonable sunshine.

'Joshua French,' announced Edmunds, squinting down at the grubby driving licence. 'I thought I recognised him from somewhere.'

They waited for him to elaborate.

'He came up a few times in the old case files,' he explained. 'Used to work up in Glasgow with Finlay and Christian.'

'Finlay needed some better friends,' mused Saunders, watching the doors close on the sour-faced man.

'He had us,' Wolf pointed out. 'We haven't let him down. We've got Christian's accomplice in custody. This is *so* nearly over.'

'Shall we finish the job, then?' suggested Saunders, pouring the rest of his drink away to snake between the cobbles.

Wolf slapped him affectionately on the back as they started towards the waiting police van. He paused and then turned back to address Baxter, who hadn't moved.

'You don't want to be there for this?' he asked her.

'More than anything,' she replied. 'But I've got a street performer with second-degree burns, a Chinese tourist with a smashed iPad and two bouncy-looking Americans who weren't as bouncy as they looked. You know, boring chief-inspector stuff. You boys go ahead, though. Give him hell for me.'

Wolf nodded: 'I'll call you later?'

'Do,' she told him, waving them off.

It had been unnecessary to walk their prisoner through the lobby of New Scotland Yard, but Wolf had three good reasons for doing so: one, he needed to sign in anyway; two, there was no way on earth he was going to let French out of his sight; and three, he was in a provocative mood.

Everybody in the building knew that he was working the Finlay Shaw 'suicide' case; therefore he had no doubt that news of him marching an arrest through the packed atrium would reach the upper floors even before they did. And that's what he wanted. He wanted Christian to know that he was finished, relished the idea of him sitting alone up in his office afraid to step out. Wolf wanted him to walk shamefully through a gauntlet of judgemental stares from his peers. And as they waited for the lift, he even let himself imagine Christian climbing up onto the window ledge, seeing no other way out, throwing himself towards the distant pavement – a much-deserved and poetic end.

Vanita was waiting for them when the lift doors parted. She had booked Interview Room 1 for the rest of the day and rescheduled the remainder of her engagements. She'd also had a quiet word with her media contacts, forewarning of the possibility of calling a press conference before the day was out.

'I'm not saying a word without my lawyer present,' French informed them, looking quite bored by the whole experience as they escorted him through the office.

'I'll get right on it,' promised Wolf, shoving him through the doorway of the interview room.

'But . . . I haven't given you her name ye—' started French as the door slammed in his face.

Someone more patient had phoned French's lawyer, delaying proceedings, and Wolf was getting restless. It felt wrong sitting there doing nothing with their soon-to-be-implicated murderer awaiting his fate just a few floors above.

'Keep a close eye on him,' Wolf instructed Edmunds and Saunders as he got up.

'Where are you going?' Saunders asked him.

'Taking a walk,' replied Wolf, choosing not to divulge where he was heading or his hope that Christian might elect to throw himself upon his sword in private rather than be slain before the merciless masses.

Christian had been staring into space when Wolf knocked on his door.

'Come in!' he called, picking up a random stack of paperwork to look busy.

He didn't appear at all surprised to see Wolf, who turned out his pockets and lifted his shirt to assure him that their conversation would remain private. Closing the door, he made a show of removing the battery from his phone before approaching the large desk.

'Have a seat,' said Christian wearily, which Wolf graciously accepted.

Lazy sunshine filled the large office, the relaxed atmosphere an unexpected setting for their final act.

'You've had a busy day,' said Christian. 'Fin always told me you were sharp.'

'Nothing to do with me,' admitted Wolf. 'All Baxter.' A look crossed the commissioner's face that he was unable to decipher. 'We're all just waiting around for French's lawyer,' he continued, stifling a yawn. 'He'll cut a deal, no doubt.'

'No doubt,' agreed Christian.

'That in mind . . . I was wondering if you might want to come downstairs with me,' said Wolf pleasantly.

'No. Thank you, but I'll be staying right here.'

'OK,' replied Wolf. 'Just thought I'd ask. I guess we'll be up for you in a bit, then . . . Window there,' he pointed out, just in case Christian had forgotten.

The older man chuckled: 'Just what exactly do you think is going to happen here?'

Wolf let out an exasperated sigh: 'It's over, Christian.'

'Is it?'

'We've taken your pawn.'

'But you sacrificed your queen to do it.'

The words took a moment to sink in.

Wolf was about to respond with something typically irreverent, but there was something about the way in which Christian was smiling at him that felt wrong . . .

Winter flowers throttling one another for their place in the sun . . .

An animal backed into a corner with no way out . . .

Survival above all else.

'What did you do?' Wolf asked him, panic slowing his progress as he reassembled his phone. 'What did you do?!'

Christian leaned back in his chair and smiled.

With his mobile slowly booting back to life, Wolf burst from the room and tore across the office towards the stairwell.

The moment he was out of sight, Christian began to hyperventilate. Sliding onto the floor behind his desk, he tipped out the contents of the waste-paper bin, feeling as though he might be sick.

Baxter was feeling rather proud of herself as she walked back to where she had 'parked' Blackie. She had pointed the Chinese tourist and her smashed iPad in the direction of the Apple Store on the corner, had appeased the two Americans with some lunch and only fallen out with the lawsuit-threatening fire-juggler in the very last breath.

'Lucky for you, this outfit makes me eighty per cent flame-retardant.'

'I'm *pretty sure* you're one hundred per cent retardant.'

That was probably going to come back to bite her.

Tossing her bag onto the passenger seat, she climbed in and checked her phone to see if there had been any progress with French. In the absence of any news, she decided to head back to New Scotland Yard. She switched on the engine to a concerning array of splutters and crunches, especially as she hadn't even gone anywhere yet, and dropped the phone into her bag, missing Wolf's call the moment she pulled away.

Caught up in the one-way system circling the large pedestrianised area, she barely got over ten miles per hour in the lunch-hour traffic. So when she did finally reach the junction with the Strand, in true Baxter form, she accelerated aggressively to jump the lights, hearing an ominous snap as she depressed her foot on the brake.

A moment later, she had hit the scooter in front and was careering into the crossing traffic. She gasped and pumped the brake pedal repeatedly as cars blurred all around her, horns blaring. Wrenching the handbrake on, she miraculously made it through unscathed but was still hurtling towards the busy pavement outside Temple Tube Station. With no time to think, she held her hand down over her own horn, hearing the shouts of the scattering pedestrians as the car plummeted down the wide steps, scraping along the wall as Baxter tried uselessly to control it. Grasping the vibrating gearstick, she ground it into second, the engine screaming in protest yet refusing to slow down.

As the front bumper impacted the pavement below, it sent the car skidding into the four lanes of traffic that lined the river. She was hit side on, the unbalanced car flipping as she was struck again and again, spinning between braking vehicles like a pinball, the murky river growing nearer . . .

Grinding to a stop, the upturned Audi teetered on the edge of the bank, its crumpled bonnet hanging over the freezing water, rocking gently as the first Good Samaritans emerged from their cars to help. Baxter knew she was hurt as she stared dazedly at her phone buzzing against the roof below her:

Wolf (New)
☎ Incoming call

She reached out for it . . . and then felt herself fall.

CHAPTER 36

Wednesday 25 December 2009
Christmas Day
12.25 p.m.

Baxter pushed a handful of popcorn into her face, kernels rolling down her tartan blanket and into the unexplored creases of Finlay and Maggie's wrinkled leather sofa. Over the top of her festive socks, she watched Harry and Marv receive metal paint cans to the face before threatening to snap off an eight-year-old's cojones. It was all getting a bit dark.

'Which one's this again?' asked Finlay from his favourite chair.

'*Home Alone*,' replied Baxter with her mouth full.

'One or Two?'

'One. Two's in New York.'

'So where's this one set?'

'Don't know. I don't think anyone knows. It doesn't matter.'

'Matters if it's New York 'coz that'll mean it's the second one.'

'It's not the *bloody* second one!' Baxter raised her popcorn-loaded hands in exasperation.

'Stop bickering, you two,' said Maggie authoritatively but unable to keep the smile out of her scowl.

She looked worryingly thin, having recently restarted the chemo-therapy, which had again robbed her of her dark hair she loved so much.

A Pringle-dusted hand landed in Baxter's bowl. She turned to Wolf, unimpressed.

'Get your own!' she snapped, flicking some at him, which he pelted back twice as hard.

'Children! Children!' Maggie reprimanded the two detectives. One final popcorn pellet to Wolf's eye and they all returned to the movie.

'I once went to a guy who took a paint can to the face,' blurted Baxter as she reached for her Chocolate Orange.

'Poor man,' said Maggie.

'Nah . . . He was a piece of shit anyway.'

'Language!' Finlay and Maggie chimed in unison, Baxter glaring at her colleague like the potty-mouthed hypocrite he was.

'Was he all right?' asked Maggie.

'Not so much . . . His head imploded!'

'Emily!' frowned Maggie, while Finlay chuckled in the corner.

'That wasn't even the weirdest part, though,' she continued, much to Maggie's disapproval. 'His imploding head out-ploded the contents of the can everywhere. As in, I never saw a single drop of blood, just bubblegum pink running down the walls and dripping from the ceiling like he was an alien or something.'

Wolf turned to her: '*Bull*shit!'

'Language!'

'It's true!' insisted Baxter.

'Where was I?' Wolf asked her.

'Suspended.'

He thought about it for a moment and then nodded, accepting the very plausible answer.

'But,' started Baxter, 'that was *nothing* compared to the guy who—'

'Presents!' Maggie interrupted her. 'How about we do some presents? One might need opening before it can stain my floor again anyway,' she said, giving her husband a significant look.

Sitting up excitedly, Baxter paused the movie and reached into her bag of snacks to produce the first pitifully wrapped gift. She handed it to Wolf.

'Oh, this is awkward,' he told her. 'I never even thought to get you anything.'

Baxter looked hurt.

'Ignore him,' Maggie told her. 'It's upstairs. Why don't you go and get it, Fin?'

Muttering, Finlay made a fuss of getting up out of his chair while Wolf ripped the wrapping paper open.

'You didn't?!' he gasped, holding up the faded Bon Jovi *Keep the Faith* tour T-shirt. 'Where did you find it?'

'eBay.'

He turned to show Maggie. 'I was at this gig but couldn't afford to buy a T-shirt at the time.' He turned back to Baxter. 'I can't believe you remembered! So, you actually *do* listen to me?'

'Only when completely unavoidable.'

'Thank you.' He leaned across to embrace her, Maggie watching Baxter as she closed her eyes and squeezed him back.

'Shame Andrea couldn't make it,' blurted Finlay, having reappeared in the doorway, the smell of dinner cooking following him inside. 'Where did you say she was again?'

Wolf released Baxter and shuffled back over to his side of the sofa: 'Her dad's.'

'And where's he living these days?'

'Hades,' replied Wolf, draping his gift gently over the arm of the sofa. 'Bedworth. I didn't want to go.'

'I don't blame you . . . Shall I bring this in, then?' asked Finlay, carrying the plastic box through by the handle and setting it down on the floor. He unclipped the catches to allow the fluffy cat inside out onto the lounge carpet.

Baxter's eyes lit up.

'You got me a cat!' she shrieked like an excitable child, throwing her arms around Wolf as Maggie laughed at her reaction. 'I can't believe you did this!'

'*He* did this?' asked Finlay bitterly. '*I'm* the mug who's been feeding it the past two weeks!'

Maggie shushed him.

'I just hated the idea of you being in that place all on your own. Now you won't be,' explained Wolf self-consciously. 'He's a rescue cat. Me and Finlay chose him together.'

Baxter's smile became a little forced. 'A *rescue* cat? How about that . . . ? What's wrong with him?'

'Nothing's wrong with him!'

'*Wolf?*'

'He just needs a pill once a day . . .'

'*Wolf?!*'

'. . . up his butt.'

'Gross!' complained Baxter, sliding down onto the floor to meet her new pet.

'Hang on,' said Finlay proudly. 'We've got a trick . . . Hello!' he called, addressing the cat, which meowed back at him. 'Hello!' The cat turned and did it again, making everyone laugh. 'I've been calling him "Echo", but I'm sure you'll think of something much better.'

Baxter got up and gave Finlay a big hug. 'Thank you,' she whispered, looking back at the cat. '"Echo" is perfect.'

Finlay carried Maggie up to bed.

She had lasted for as long as she possibly could but had fallen asleep in her chair by the mid-afternoon. Despite Finlay's insistence that they were welcome to stay, their guests had made their excuses and left them in peace, Baxter heading home to get some rest before her night shift, Wolf needing to phone both Andrea and his parents. Grateful, Finlay had even told his son to postpone his visit until the following evening.

'I, errrm . . . I got you one other present I didn't want to give you in front of the others,' said Finlay nervously. He handed Maggie a plain cardboard box. 'I don't know if it's right or not or . . . Just open it.'

'What's got into you?' she asked suspiciously, lifting the lid and staring in bemusement at the contents. She reached inside, removed the curly dark brown wig and burst out laughing: 'What on *earth* is that?!'

Finlay looked offended: 'It was an expensive one!'

Maggie laughed harder still, wiping tears from her eyes before pulling the synthetic Afro onto her head, at which point Finlay fell into hysterics as well.

'I tried,' he told her, lying on the bed beside her, still chuckling but clearly disappointed.

Maggie squeezed him as tightly as she could and then rested her head against his chest. 'My hero,' she mumbled, already starting to doze off as Finlay stroked her arm.

He pictured the shoebox of cash he had unwrapped in private that morning, another token payment from Christian, not even half a year's worth of medical bills.

'Don't mistake me for the hero,' he whispered softly, listening to Maggie's breathing change as sleep took hold. 'I'd kill every last living thing on earth to save you.'

CHAPTER 37

Tuesday 19 January 2016
3.09 p.m.

Thomas had kicked over an elderly lady's handbag as he sprinted through the corridors towards A&E. It was almost the most dramatic thing he'd ever done, up until the point where he turned back to collect up the contents for her while apologising profusely. Encountering a particularly waspish receptionist, he was pointed in the general direction of a small waiting room to discover that Wolf, Edmunds and Maggie had already beaten him there.

Despite Saunders's protests, Wolf had insisted he remain behind at New Scotland Yard to keep an eye on Joshua French. Unable to look Baxter's boyfriend in the eye, he returned his gaze to the floor.

'You must be Thomas,' said Maggie, getting up to embrace him. She had clearly been crying and moved aside to let Edmunds give him an awkward man-hug.

'Hey.'

'Alex,' replied Thomas expectantly, his eyes flicking back to Wolf in the corner. Unconsciously, he straightened his back to stand a little taller.

'Like I said on the phone, she was in a car crash . . . A bad one.'

'You said they . . . pulled her from the river?'

'It was a bad one,' Edmunds reiterated. 'She hasn't woken up yet—'

'Oh my God!'

'. . . but *only* because they're keeping her under until they've done the MRI. It's normal.'

Thomas nodded and, with nothing left to say, took a seat to wait helplessly with the rest of them.

'How is she?' asked Saunders, speaking on the phone outside the interview room.

French's lawyer had spent almost an hour with her client before disappearing upstairs with Vanita.

'Same,' answered Wolf.

'Well, this might cheer you up a little,' said Saunders, relocating to a quiet corner of the office while keeping the door firmly in sight. 'French is willing to spill his guts: how the commissioner paid him two and a half grand to locate and destroy the evidence boxes, another two and a half to break into Baxter's apartment, which of course is its own can of worms, and . . .' he hesitated, 'how he tampered with her car.'

Someone sent something to the printer, which began to click and buzz loudly, forcing Saunders back towards the interview room.

'What does he want in return?' Wolf asked him.

'Vanita's hashing that out with his lawyer as we speak. But hey! – you should be able to slap some handcuffs on the boss man the moment you get back. That's something, right?'

Wolf didn't respond for a moment: 'Just don't let him out of your sight.'

'Course I won't.'

At 4.46 p.m., a cheerful doctor appeared in the doorway.

Thomas and Edmunds both stood up in anticipation.

'Hi. I'm Doctor Young. I'm looking after Emily. I'm pleased to report that it's all good news so far,' he smiled. 'The MRI looks clear and we've had her on intravenous fluids to bring her temperature back up. We're keeping the neck brace in place *just* as a precaution as we need her compos mentis before we can remove it.'

'Is she awake?' Thomas asked him.

'Yes. And I can allow just *one* of you to see her for a few minutes if you'd like.'

Wolf got up from his seat.

Thomas looked back at him as if he might actually blow.

Edmunds subtly shook his head.

Maggie took his arm and gently pulled him back down.

'Right,' Wolf nodded apologetically. '*You* should probably go,' he told Thomas.

Following the doctor, Thomas was shown through to a room where Baxter lay among the machines and screens that watched over her. It was strange for him to see her in the hospital gown. She looked shrunken, the baggy garment emphasising just how delicate and fragile she really was.

'I'll give you two a minute,' the doctor told him, closing the door.

Thomas sat down beside the bed and squeezed her hand: 'Hey, you.'

Baxter groaned and gently squeezed it back as he talked about trivia for a couple of minutes, lulling her back to sleep. Trapped there holding her hand, Thomas looked around at his uninspiring surroundings. Unable to help himself, he reached across to pull the hospital records from the bottom of the bed and started flicking through.

The doctor had given them an additional two minutes than he should have done, disliking separating relatives from their loved ones. He knocked on the door and then stepped inside to find Baxter alone in the room.

Thomas flung the door open.

Wolf, Edmunds and Maggie all looked up in alarm.

'She's pregnant!' he yelled at Wolf.

'Ummm . . . yeah,' he answered awkwardly.

'You knew?' Thomas asked in disbelief, before glancing at Edmunds and Maggie, who both looked a little uneasy. 'You *all* knew?!'

Finally losing it, Thomas shoved Wolf back against the wall as Edmunds rushed over to intervene.

'Trust me,' Edmunds warned his friend, 'this is one fight you *really* don't want to pick.'

'Look, Thomas, I—' started Wolf, not getting to finish the thought because Baxter's mild-mannered boyfriend had taken an elaborate swing at him, striking him, rather unconventionally, in the ear.

Wolf appeared momentarily confused, but then dropped to the floor in a motionless heap.

'Oh Christ!' Thomas gasped, staring at his throbbing fist in horror. 'I think I've knocked him unconscious. Should I get someone?'

'Let's just walk it off,' suggested Edmunds, ushering him out as Maggie calmly drank her tea.

'Should we put him in the recovery position?'

'Maggie's doing it as we speak,' Edmunds assured him.

Once Thomas was safely out of earshot, he poked his head back round the door to address Wolf.

'You can get up now.'

Baxter couldn't turn her head, the foam neck brace restricting her movement, but had regained enough strength, at least, to pull herself upright. She reached for the cup of water beside the bed but knocked it over, still feeling the effects of the anaesthesia. Steeling herself, she looked down to assess the damage, reassured on finding all limbs present and pointing in their proper directions; however, a moment's relief quickly became unbridled panic.

Ripping the constricting neck brace off, she reached over to pull the bell, surprising herself by her reaction. Seconds later, a fresh-faced nurse came rushing into the room to find her holding both hands over her abdomen.

'Is the baby OK? I mean, I know there isn't really a baby yet, but . . . will it be?' she asked apprehensively.

The woman was clearly out of her depth: 'I'll go get the doctor.'

Saunders watched French's lawyer storm towards him, reasonably confident he hadn't said anything too offensive within her earshot. Stopping just short of him, she grabbed her coat, then marched back out without saying a word.

'What's she so pissy about?' he asked Vanita, who had been following at a more leisurely pace.

'She's just been reassigned by someone more senior at the firm,' she explained, watching the woman leave.

'You think the commissioner's up to something?' asked Saunders.

'She said because of the nature of the allegations and who they involve, her boss thought it advisable to step in. Plausible, but . . .' Vanita shook her head, looking concerned.

Half an hour later, French's new lawyer was shown up to Homicide and Serious Crime Command. The bearded man carried himself with the self-assurance of a career shit and appeared to almost float between the desks on a cloud of his own smugness.

'I *hate* lawyers,' mumbled Saunders.

'Everyone does,' Vanita told him, beaming at their guest as she went to introduce herself.

They escorted him into the interview room.

'Mr French . . . or may I call you Joshua? I'm Luke Preston,' he smiled, taking a step towards his client.

'You're good right there,' Saunders told him, blocking his path.

The lawyer took his hand back and started unpacking his satchel. 'I'll be taking over from Laura, who has done a fine job filling me in on the specifics of your conversation. Now . . . I have eighty thousand things on my plate at the moment, and I'm sure that you have *eighty thousand* questions of your own,' he said, catching French's eye.

Saunders frowned at the unnatural phrasing, as did Vanita. The lawyer, meanwhile, continued to innocently empty his bag.

'So, remind me . . . Am I right in thinking you'll be pleading *guilty* to being the *sole architect* of these crimes, for which you could face up to *two years* in prison?' Again he met his client's eye.

'What the hell are you talkin' about?' snapped Saunders, but the lawyer carried on as though he hadn't spoken.

'That modest sentence, *of course*, taking into account the reasons behind your desperation-driven spate of misdemeanours against the police service, harking back to your *blatantly* unfair dismissal almost thirty years ago.'

'Oi!' barked Saunders, slamming his hand down on the table between the two men.

But it was already too late.

They all turned to French, watching the cogs whirr as he weighed up his limited options. After a short pause, he nodded his head.

'That's right . . . I *will* be pleading guilty.'

Wolf ended his call with Saunders and rubbed his face wearily. He remained there for a minute, just standing out in the insipid corridor staring at the floor. Christian had bought French off right in front of them, and there wasn't a damned thing they could do to prove it, his seemingly boundless influence reaching so far that he was able to derail their entire case against him without even getting up from his desk.

Forcing a concerned smile onto his face, he stepped back into Baxter's private room.

'Good news?' she asked him hopefully the moment he came through the door, her big eyes sparkling with excitement.

He didn't have the heart to tell her, not after all she had been through.

'Still waiting to hear,' he lied, knowing full well that it was over.

Christian had won.

Nine days later . . .

CHAPTER 38

Thursday 28 January 2016

11.58 a.m.

Rouche had been discharged from hospital, which was good, thus meaning he was fit enough to attend Highbury Corner Magistrates' Court, which was bad. He had been permitted brief visits with both Holly and Baxter, which was also good, but would certainly be remanded in custody by the end of the afternoon, which wasn't.

Overall, his day was working out to be pretty average.

After a week spent mostly in bed receiving transfusions, intravenous antibiotics and having necrotic tissue removed, he stood before the judge looking stronger but still not himself. Having lost an entire stone since its last outing, his navy suit swamped him. He had combed back his salt-and-pepper hair, in the way that Baxter liked, and even grown a matching beard for the occasion, which was an utterly pointless formality in order to announce what everybody present already knew.

'Due to the severity of the charges lodged against the defendant and the complexities surrounding the extradition of a British citizen committing a crime on British soil while operating under the remit of the United States government, we refer the matter to the Crown Court Services at a date to be set,' announced the magistrate robotically.

Baxter and Holly were sitting at the back of the uncrowded courtroom, giving them a cheap-seat view of Rouche's back as he too grew weary of his own sentencing and became distracted by a floating piece of lint.

'Again, due to the nature of the charges, the defendant is to be remanded in custody without the option of bail.'

'Sir,' started Rouche's defence lawyer, addressing the judge, 'we would like to request that my client serve his remand period at HMP Woodhill.'

'And the reason?' the man replied, none more animatedly.

'To avoid my client coming into contact with detainees whose arrests he was directly involved in, both in the interests of his upcoming trial and, of course, his personal safety.'

'A reasonable request,' concluded the dour judge, looking to Rouche, who smiled back cheerily when, as hoped, the floating tangle of fluff came down squarely atop the man's balding head. 'Granted. Court adjourned.'

Rouche turned round to wave at Holly. He then gave Baxter a significant nod as the court official escorted him out.

Wolf had driven Maggie to the appointment at her private hospital, disguised as a grand townhouse, just off Harley Street. Taking a seat beside the open fire, he attempted to read a motoring magazine he had next to no interest in, too distracted by the importance of what was occurring in the other room to concentrate.

With all that had been going on, Maggie hadn't wanted to burden any of them with her looming engagement: scans and a biopsy to determine if the cancer was in remission or whether she would be forced back onto a course of chemotherapy to fight for her life all over again. She was putting on a brave face, but it was clear that the prospect of facing her reoccurring battle without Finlay at her side terrified her. Eventually, she had confided in Wolf, making him promise to keep it between them, at least while they awaited the results.

His mind wandered, preparing him for the worst. He pictured Maggie receiving the bad news, surviving just long enough to lose the love of her life at the hands of her most trusted friend before letting the cancer take her, just as it was always going to.

Life was so fucking unfair.

In a moment of rage, Wolf pitched the magazine into the fire, the flames consuming the glossy pages greedily as he got up to pace the room.

Vanita entered Christian's office with the file he'd requested. He was laughing with someone on the phone and waved her in as if summoning a dog.

Ever since Joshua French's abrupt change of heart, life had gradually returned to normal, PR strategies and knife-crime statistics taking precedence over the fact that Vanita knew her superior to be a murderous sociopath who would stop at nothing to protect himself. Pretending as though none of it had ever happened seemed like the best policy. She placed the file in front of him, a few small scabs now all that remained of his vicious beating, and started to walk out.

'Malcolm, I'll have to call you back,' said Christian, putting the phone down. 'Geena!'

She turned to face him.

'Thank you for this,' he said, holding up the file.

'You're very welcome.'

'Where are we at with the Finlay Shaw case?'

Vanita tensed up, unsure whether she was being goaded or tested, or if perhaps the man before her was completely insane. 'I'm sorry?'

'I've got our future mayor asking why William Fawkes is still walking around free when the investigation has quite clearly hit a dead end.'

'He isn't free – he's under curfew, just as he always was,' replied Vanita, struggling to keep her voice even. 'And with all due respect, perhaps this is a *future* concern for our *future* mayor.'

'It's thinking like *that* that held you back from getting the top job,' Christian told her.

She dug her fingernails into her palms.

'So . . . update me, then,' said Christian. 'What *is* the current state of the case?'

Teetering on the verge of challenging him, Vanita hesitated, but then lowered her eyes to the floor submissively.

'Inconclusive,' she answered, hating herself for it. 'Joshua French's refusal to co-operate has brought the investigation to a grinding halt.'

'And is anybody still actively working the case?'

'Just dotting the "i"s and crossing the "t"s,' replied Vanita, politely not pointing out that both letters just so happened to feature in Christian's name.

'Then bring Fawkes in. That's an order.'

She opened her mouth to argue but was gagged by self-preservation once more. 'Yes, sir.'

Baxter was missing Blackie.

She had owned her Audi A1 for four years, had even used it to chase down a cult leader-cum-terrorist and, annoyingly, had left her running shoes on the back seat. She and Blackie had been through a lot together, and she felt he'd deserved a far more dignified send-off than being sunk to the bottom of the River Thames.

Her lack of car had reduced her to catching the bus back to Wimbledon, which, aside from forcing her to share forty minutes with an assortment of weirdos, had given her time to reflect on her fleeting reunion with Rouche. She couldn't put into words what a relief it had been to see him. For nine days, the FBI had obstructed all attempts to track him down, to the point where she had seriously questioned whether he was still alive.

He had taken her tsunami of troubling news with his usual unflappable grace and then spent their final minutes getting Baxter to recap the latest two episodes of *The Walking Dead*. 'So, nothing really happened, then?'

'Nothing.'

After the crash, Baxter had moved back into the apartment. Thomas had insisted that it 'wasn't necessary', which felt a rather different sentiment to not wanting her to go. But she couldn't really blame him, all things considered. She'd had the window replaced, done a bodged job of filling the bullet holes in the wall and was in the middle of repainting to erase all trace of Rouche. It would only be a matter of time before somebody realised he was found directly outside her building and came snooping around.

At 6.25 p.m., the doorbell rang. Setting the roller down, Baxter wiped her hands on her ripped jeans. Peering through the peephole, she was surprised to see Thomas standing there looking as unsure of himself as ever.

'Hey,' she greeted him.

'Hello. I, errrm . . . thought you might like some dinner,' he smiled, holding up a bloated bag of Indian food, the smell nauseating.

'Oh God!' she gagged, already running for the bathroom.

Five minutes later, she returned to find Thomas examining one of the poorly filled bullet holes and was pretty sure she could see him literally biting his tongue as he moved away without comment. A belated awkward hug later, they sat on the dust-sheet-covered floor to eat.

'You know,' started Thomas, swallowing his mouthful, 'they say Indian food can bring on labour.'

Abandoning her naan bread and rice, Baxter wondered what the point had been in the previous twenty minutes skirting the issue making small talk.

'God! I'm so sorry,' he apologised. 'I don't know why that suddenly popped into my head. Well, I do . . . obviously, but I don't know why I decided to say it out loud.'

'It's fine,' Baxter assured him. 'And I think I'm safe for a little while yet.'

Thomas stared down at her belly.

'You're staring at my belly.'

'Sorry,' he said again, while continuing to do so. 'It's just . . . a bit weird, isn't it?'

'Oh, it's definitely a bit weird.'

'I don't want to ruin dinner . . .' he started.

Baxter pulled a face at him.

'. . . any more than I already have,' he added, 'but you realise that this isn't an "I forgive you" curry? This is an "I miss you" curry. A different thing altogether.'

'Noted.'

'You'd know if this was an "I forgive you" curry. There'd be bhajis and samosas and . . . I'm babbling, aren't I?'

Baxter laughed and gave him an unprompted kiss on the cheek.

'What was that for?' asked Thomas.

'Because I miss you too.'

Rouche had spent over an hour with the prison doctor, the generic medical bay somewhat easing his acclimatisation into prison life, but eventually someone came to collect him.

It had been explained to him that, in an ideal world, remanded inmates would be segregated from those tried and charged with a crime. They would be able to wear their own clothes and required to follow a more flexible set of rules to their counterparts.

It was then explained to him that this is not an ideal world.

Like most being escorted through the maze of doors that one by one robbed them of their freedom, Rouche put on a show of bravado. Externally he appeared calm, bored even, when in actual fact he had never been more afraid, unsure himself whether it was his phobia of confined spaces or pure cowardice screaming at him to run, to plead, to bargain his way back outside.

The prison officer stopped outside one of the identical beige doors and pulled it open.

Although he already knew what to expect inside, Rouche was even less inclined to enter as he peered through the widening gap.

The man looked at him.

Apprehensively, he stepped over the threshold, turning back to watch the heavy door close behind him, sealing him inside.

CHAPTER 39

Thursday 31 December 2015

New Year's Eve

6.19 p.m.

Christian looked ill as he watched his friend process his shameful admission.

'What the *fuck* do you mean "There's no money"?' Finlay asked him, his deceptively calm tone purely for Maggie's benefit, who was pottering about somewhere downstairs.

Christian sighed heavily and shook his head: 'I . . . I don't know what to tell you.'

'But . . . I've already spent it! I've got final demands for just about everything stashed all over the house,' Finlay whispered in a rare moment of panic.

'And I swear I *am* going to help you in any way that I can.'

Finlay was too distracted to even register Christian's politician-promise.

'You said you'd have the money ready!'

Conscious of Maggie, Christian cautiously shushed him.

'You said . . .' continued Finlay, 'the day I retired, you'd have the money ready!'

'I know what I said . . . And you've got to believe me, Fin, I wanted to tell you *so* many times, but—'

'What about that big house you're living in?'

'That's not mine!' Christian laughed bitterly. 'None of this' – he pulled at his stylish suit as though it were restricting him – 'is really mine. I am *permitted* to live a certain lifestyle for as long as it is of benefit to *Killian Caine*. The house will be sold in due course, the money laundered and the indisputably honourable tenant moved on to their next project.' He looked utterly lost. 'He got his claws in me a long, long time ago. He *knew* what we'd done.'

'How?'

'I don't know how! We never should have taken the money that night . . . I am *so* sorry.'

'Then we go to the police,' said Finlay decisively. 'Take Caine out of the equation.'

'I'm not doing that.'

'Sorry, I'll rephrase that: *I'll* go to the police.'

'And I'd protect you as much as I could, but there *still* won't be any money. I'd be in prison, and Caine *would* send someone for you.'

Finlay kicked one of the floorboards waiting to be laid across the room.

'Are you boys playing nice up there?' Maggie called up from the bottom of the stairs.

'Course we are!' Finlay shouted down. He turned back to Christian. 'What about Maggie's treatment?' he asked, voice strained.

'We'll work something out.'

'"We'll work something out"?' Finlay echoed, unimpressed, already debating his next move. 'I'll be back in a minute.'

Heading downstairs, he complimented Maggie on her party dress, who knew better than try to persuade him to join her and her friends. New Year was 'nothing but an excuse for everyone to act like a bunch of animals all at once' was his swear-jar-friendly summation of the celebration he had been boycotting for a decade. He disappeared into the garage and emerged a few minutes later holding a dusty plastic bag. Keeping it out of Maggie's sight, he made his way back upstairs.

Stepping back up into the unfinished room, he hesitated before asking, 'Do you know what this is?' Something in his tone made Christian get up off the floor to take a closer look. He reached out to inspect it. 'No. No. No,' said Finlay, pulling it away from him. 'Just look.'

Christian squinted at the yellowed bag and then his eyes widened in surprise. 'It *looks* like a big *fucking* gun!'

'That it is. Not just *any* big fucking gun, mind,' he explained. 'This is a murder weapon . . . still covered in your prints.'

Christian was confused.

'You killed a man, Christian, and *this* is the proof.'

His friend looked betrayed: 'You kept it all these years.'

'What can I say? My gut told me it might come in handy one day,' said Finlay guiltily. 'I'm not greedy. I'm just desperate. A hundred grand by midnight . . .'

'I can't possibly—'

'Another hundred by this time next week and the gun's yours. That's a *fraction* of what you owe me, but it's enough.'

'Fin, it's New Year's Eve!'

'I know that. And I don't care what you have to do: beg, borrow, steal. Just get me my money.' Finlay glanced down at his Casio watch: 'Half six . . . You'd best get a move on.'

At 11.53 p.m., Christian was standing outside the house, the sound of a dozen separate revelries in the air as strangers gleefully taunted him. He could see Finlay inside, working by the light of an exposed bulb in the only illuminated window, and wondered how he was going to break the news to him – that he had only been able to gather a little over a tenth of what had been demanded at such short notice.

With the first impatient fireworks already colouring the sky, Christian let himself into the house, closing the front door behind him.

'It's me!' he called.

'Upstairs!'

Making his way up, Christian entered the chipboard room, which had improved dramatically even in the hours since he had last seen it. Finlay was using a kitchen chair to stand on as he painted the ceiling, the dirty bag sitting temptingly unguarded on the windowsill.

Catching Christian looking at it, he climbed back down.

'Drink?' he offered, picking the bottle of whisky up off the floor.

'Sure.' Unbuttoning his coat, Christian removed four neat wads of cash, which he tossed onto the floor between them.

Finlay handed him his drink: 'What's that?' he asked of the uninspiring pile.

'Eight thousand in cash,' answered Christian. 'And these' – he handed over two debit cards in envelopes – 'are for two accounts no one knows about. You'll be able to withdraw five hundred a day without raising any eyebrows. Thirteen thousand two hundred and fifty in all.'

He held his breath, unsure how Finlay would react.

'It's a start. You can get more?'

'I can. But it's going to take a little time.'

Finlay nodded, apparently satisfied. He kneeled down to collect up the money, stacking it neatly into a corner of the large metal box beneath the floor before getting back up.

'Cheers, then,' he smiled.

Relieved, Christian raised his glass and took a generous sip.

'If you knew what I'd been through to get my hands on that . . .' he laughed, taking a step towards the window.

Finlay stopped him with a firm hand to his chest. 'I said: "It's a start."'

Turning to face his oldest friend, the few seconds of calm already felt a distant memory: 'That gun could ruin me,' said Christian.

'Which is *precisely* why I'll be keeping hold of it.'

'I'm getting you the money!'

'*Because* I have the gun,' Finlay pointed out. 'I'm sorry, but you're making me choose between you and Maggie . . . And I choose her. The gun stays.'

Christian nodded in understanding, waiting until he felt Finlay's hand relax before lunging at the windowsill. Grasping a handful of his clothing, Finlay dragged him backwards, Christian stumbling over a paint can as the older man grabbed the grubby bag. But Christian was on him instantly, forcing his arm behind his back as they wrestled over the incriminating weapon.

It dropped to the floor with a hollow thud.

Seeing an opportunity, Finlay wound up for a left hook, barely glancing Christian as he ducked out of the way before pulling the Scotsman down onto the floor. Rolling on top of Finlay, Christian reached for the bag, feeling the solid metal beneath the plastic, managing to wrap his fingers round it. Lashing out desperately, Finlay took hold of the barrel, hands shaking with the effort, edging the gun down between them as they continued to brawl, rolling again and again as they struggled for position.

The gun went off.

Both men instantly went limp, smoke escaping the small hole in the bag as it dropped back to the wooden floor.

'Fin?' asked Christian, his friend a dead weight on top of him. 'Fin?!' he asked again, beginning to panic as he rolled Finlay off him, revealing the small red hole in his temple. 'Oh my God! Fin! Fin!' Christian felt for a pulse, listening for breathing as a steady trickle of dark blood stained the wood beneath them. 'Fin?' he gasped, hand trembling as he placed it upon his best friend's motionless body.

Starting to hyperventilate, Christian slid back against the wall, eyes transfixed on Finlay in the centre of the room as he took his mobile phone out of his pocket. He went to dial 999 but paused, it suddenly dawning on him how the scene would look: clear signs of a struggle, the offending weapon covered in his prints.

Unsure what else to do, Christian considered leaving and taking the gun with him. But having been one of the last two people to see Finlay alive, and in the absence of a solid alibi, he would still undoubtedly find himself the primary focus of the investigation. And that was before anyone even started looking into his evening of suspicious financial activities. Forcing his gaze away from his friend's warm corpse, he tried to focus. 'Think. Think!'

His car was parked just down the street and he had passed at least three people in varying states of sobriety outside. Someone would remember him. More important than any of that, however, was the simple fact that he couldn't possibly let Maggie come home to find her husband like this.

'Come on!' he shouted at himself in frustration. He needed to think like a cop.

The popping of a hundred distant fireworks signalled the start of the new year, the black sky beyond the window peppered with light. And then it came to him, the realisation that the *only* way to prevent questions being asked to which he had no answers was by ensuring that there was no reason to ask them in the first place . . . such as if the death were considered an unquestionable suicide, for example.

Considering the tools at his disposal, Christian looked from the bagged gun to the dark gap in the floorboards, from the half-empty bottle of whisky to the lonely kitchen chair, from the can of sealant to the lockless door.

Reluctantly crawling over to the body, he retrieved Finlay's phone and slid back over to the wall as quickly as he could. And like the explosions setting fire to the sky outside, beauty born of violence, he laid the first piece of his desperate, imperfect, yet in its own way beautiful, plan:

☎ Calling . . .
Bellamy, Christian

CHAPTER 40

Friday 29 January 2016
6.56 a.m.

Rouche had been staring at the grimy ceiling for hours when the first bangs and voices announced the beginning of a new day.

He had survived his first night.

His cellmate, rather disappointingly, hadn't been named T-Dawg or Deathstar as he'd envisioned but Nigel, a balding, bespectacled, overweight anticlimax of a man. And while probably not Rouche's first choice with whom to share a seven-metre-square room and its exhibitionist toilet, he seemed inoffensive enough.

'Bath time,' yawned Nigel from the bottom bunk, standing up to pull his prison scrubs over his head, which, as a convicted inmate, were slightly different to Rouche's own.

Their door was unlocked, allowing them to join the brightly coloured procession shuffling towards the shower block, Rouche using the time to familiarise himself with the faces of those he was expected to live alongside.

'Need anything?' Nigel asked once inside, offering him a well-used bar of soap from his washbag while standing completely naked.

'No . . . but thanks,' smiled Rouche, averting his eyes as Nigel and his pockmarked posterior wandered off.

Waiting for everybody else to vacate the changing area, Rouche self-consciously removed his clothing, hanging his towel round his neck to cover as much of his chest as possible. Unable to delay it any longer, he followed the sound of running water into the wet room. Choosing the shower furthest away from everyone else, he hung his towel on the peg, hit the button and stepped beneath the hot water.

He closed his eyes.

The spray of the shower drowned out the sound of the other inmates. Rouche smiled, fleetingly able to imagine himself back home, the thump of bubblegum pop music reverberating through the wall from Ellie's room as Sophie did her make-up in the bathroom mirror. He could see her distorted silhouette through the frosted glass and pushed on the door, bursting with anticipation just to see her face—

'What the *fuck* is that?!'

The house dissolved as Rouche was dragged back to reality. Every set of eyes was directed at him, at his chest, at the crudely cut letters scrawled into his skin:

PUPPET

The shower shut off above him, leaving Rouche standing in silence staring back at his unwelcome audience. Some looked fearful of him, some angry, others disgusted. He noticed Nigel hurrying out before anyone had the chance to recall them speaking to one another. Like a pack of dogs waiting for him to run, they watched Rouche's every move as he slowly wrapped his towel round himself and walked confidently towards the exit, bare feet slapping against wet tiles.

Finally, he reached the doorway.

The moment he was out of sight, he grabbed his clothes off the bench and sprinted out of the changing rooms.

Tia was holding her daughter in one arm, her mobile phone in the other, as she pressed a button to pay the gas bill before checking the balance, or lack thereof, in their joint account. Through the kitchen window, she saw her fiancé fall out of the garden shed, quickly closing the door on the cloud of smoke chasing him out. She watched impassively as Edmunds slipped over on the wet grass, desperately trying to plug holes in the woodwork with his fingers.

'What's your daddy done now?' she asked Leila in a playful voice. 'If he's set himself on fire again, we're not putting him out, are we? No, we're not!'

Supposing she had better ask, she ambled out into the drizzle.

'Fumigating,' Edmunds greeted her before noticing the smoke seeping from round the door. 'Maybe don't come any closer,' he suggested. 'It's one Thomas recommended.' Tia looked unimpressed. 'All businesses have teething problems in their first few months,' he told her. 'I'll take care of it.'

Tia swapped Leila to the other arm.

'All businesses find a hornets' nest above the printer, lose a large section of wall and wake up to discover their premises slanting more than the Leaning Tower in the space of a week?' she asked drily as Edmunds pushed his body up against another hole.

'In my defence,' he started, although a little distracted, 'I *only* lost that plank in the wall *because* I threw a brick at the hornets' nest . . . and the agency's only angled as it is *because* I hadn't realised that brick was supporting the foundations.'

'Emily paid you yet?' she asked him for the umpteenth time.

Edmunds looked sheepish: 'Huh?'

'Has Emily paid you yet?'

'No. Not yet. But she will.'

'I'm taking Leila out.'

Edmunds started to choke as the air turned hazy: 'Where?'

'Doctor's.'

'Why?' he coughed.

'Teething problems . . . I'll take care of it,' she told him, walking away.

'OK. Bye!' he called after her, before adding cheerily: 'Don't leave me!'

*

Twenty minutes later, Edmunds was back in his shed packing up Finlay's old case files, concluding there was nothing more to learn from them and no more he could do to assist the investigation.

He paused on reaching a haunting mugshot. Somehow the woman had looked even more emaciated and fragile in the flesh, a lifetime of addiction and poor decisions rendering her no more than a skeletal ghost of a human being. He remembered the smell of body odour radiating from across the table of the greasy spoon, the way in which she could only nibble at the food her body so desperately needed. And he felt guilty for enabling her abuses by handing over the fifty pounds as agreed, knowing that within the hour it would be flowing through her veins.

He stacked the boxes to one side to make room for his new assignment: tracking down a tracksuit-clad gentleman who owed child maintenance to two of the three women he'd had five of his six children with. Apparently, he'd also 'nicked the kids' Xbox', a sign, as if any more were needed, that Edmunds was dealing with a true criminal mastermind.

Feeling unfulfilled by the lack of closure on his former case and unenthused by the triviality of this new one, he grudgingly set to work.

The BBC were showing an old Columbo movie, which Wolf was enjoying with a bag of low-fat crisps from the discomfort of his police-cell bed.

'I totally *did* Columbo him!' he said proudly, watching Peter Falk work his magic.

There was a knock at the door. Ever the gent, Wolf went to the trouble of brushing some of the larger crumbs off his shirt as he sat up.

'I'm decent!' he called.

George entered, closely followed by Vanita.

'You have a visitor,' he revealed needlessly. 'Now, I don't want you to worry or get in one of your moods—'

'What moods?'

'I'm just saying—'

'I'm here to officially arrest you,' blurted Vanita. 'Commissioner's orders.'

George looked exasperated with the blunt woman.

'It smells of feet in here,' she commented, pulling a face.

'That'll be my feet,' Wolf told her, correctly identifying the culprits. 'Arrest me?'

'*Officially*,' Vanita reiterated. 'Perhaps you could get us some chairs?' she asked George, not much liking the look of the unmade bed.

The three of them completed the arrest paperwork together so that she would have something to take back to her superior. While George went off to make a photocopy, Vanita and Wolf had a few moments to talk.

'I'll hold this up for as long as I can,' she told him, 'but you should expect to be transferred in a week at the most. I suppose what I'm saying is that if you're going to do something, you'd better do it now.'

'It's out of my hands,' shrugged Wolf, realising his fingers were still covered in crisp dust and sucking them clean, much to Vanita's disgust.

'Either way, you've got a week. And remember, I've arrested you,' she said, getting up. 'I'm sticking my neck out here. I can't protect you after you leave this building. So, if you do, you had better make it count.'

Visiting hours were from 3 p.m. until 4 p.m.

Rouche had been surprised to be summoned to the large open hall where the real world collided inharmoniously with those trapped in a time capsule: obligatory birthday visits from growing children never failing to shock, parents listing the relatives and neighbours who'd died over the preceding year like a war-memorial roll call, girlfriends attending less and less as real life tempted them away from those who existed like a memory they could call on from time to time.

Rouche spotted Baxter the moment he entered. Waving in her direction, he started to make his way over when he was shoulder-barged so heavily that he fell to the floor.

'My brother was on that train, you fucking freak,' spat the shaven-headed man, intricate tattoos adorning every visible inch of his body up to his jawline, as though he were drowning in them.

'Cut it out!' barked a watching prison officer.

The man held his hands up innocently, inadvertently revealing the swastika inked into his left palm. He smirked and walked out.

Still holding his chest in pain, Rouche struggled back up onto his feet to join Baxter, who looked concerned as he slumped into the chair opposite.

'Making friends already, I see.'

'Yeah, they think I'm a . . .' Rouche paused, not wanting to worry her. 'They think I'm weird.'

'You *are* weird,' she confirmed. 'Beard's looking good,' she preambled before getting to the real reason behind her visit. 'We're getting you the best defence lawyer money can buy. I mean a *real* piece of shit. He's perfect,' she told him. 'My story's not going to change: I didn't think you'd made it out of the station. I chased Keaton to the park, lost him in the whiteout, and by the time I found him, he was already dead.'

'Baxter, I appreciate what you're trying to—'

'*Your* story,' she continued over him: 'you were doing your job. You chased our prime suspect down, believed the device in his hand to be a trigger and had no option but to shoot him when he refused to drop it.'

Rouche looked at her wearily: 'And I disappeared for over three weeks because . . . ?'

'There's not a shrink in the land who wouldn't make a link between that final bomb going off and you losing your family in a similar incident.'

'I don't want to use them like that,' said Rouche, making Baxter feel sick with guilt.

'I don't care what you want. *I* need you around. You're not leaving me . . . You lost it. You weren't thinking clearly. You found somewhere to hole up and blacked out.'

'If we get caught lying,' Rouche told her, 'you'll go to prison as well.'

Baxter shrugged: 'Better lie convincingly, then.'

CHAPTER 41

Friday 29 January 2016
5.21 p.m.

Techie Steve didn't tend to get many visitors, even fewer lady visitors, fewer still important lady visitors, so was quite surprised to hear Baxter down in the IT department asking for him.

'I'm looking for Steve.'

'Who?'

'Steve . . . Techie Steve.'

'*Oh!* In the corner.'

Steve got to his feet as she approached his desk, quickly tucking his crumpled shirt into his boxer shorts.

'Can we speak in private?' Baxter asked him, conscious of the number of bespectacled eyes watching them with interest.

'Sure.' He showed her into an empty room and closed the door. 'So, what's up?'

'If someone was looking for some evidence from the Puppets case . . . such as one of those modified phones that somehow never made it into evidence' – he didn't have much of a poker face – 'would you have a) a working one to lend me and b) the discretion to keep your mouth shut about it?'

Steve looked as awkward as ever, so it was pretty difficult to tell where he was at until he answered. 'Definitely . . . And I might.'

Baxter frowned.

'Wait. No. I meant, I might . . . And definitely,' he corrected himself. 'So, what's in it for me apart from the very real possibility of getting fired?'

'I'll owe you one . . .'

He appeared a little underwhelmed.

'. . . *and* I swear to you I will use the term "suicide text" in *every* interview and press conference from this point on until we get it into *The Oxford Dictionary*.'

Steve's eyes lit up at the idea of being immortalised through his discovery and the name he'd coined for the unrecoverable read-once-only messages those masterminding the murders had been using to communicate with their followers.

'You've got yourself a deal.'

Following his appointment with the prison doctor, Rouche was escorted to the canteen and the selection of troughs containing brown slop of varying shades. Doing nothing to revive his lost appetite, he added a ladle of peas for some colour and then carried his tray into the seating area. People watched him from crowded benches as he passed, heads shaking when he approached the few remaining gaps. He continued to the very back of the room, spotting a table with only a handful of solitary figures spaced out along it, recognising one from the changing rooms that morning.

He took a deep breath and approached.

'Afternoon. Would you mind if I sat here?'

The heavyset man looked to have had a hard life. He was comfortably into his fifties, had sunken features and old scars weaving through the creases of his face.

'That depends. You one of those Puppet people?' he asked in a musical Irish accent.

'No. I'm not,' answered Rouche cheerily. 'It's actually a *pretty* interesting story,' he promised, nodding towards the empty seat.

After a moment's deliberation, the man gestured for him to sit down.

'Damien Rouche,' said Rouche, holding out his hand.

'No offence,' said the man, glancing around, 'but I think shaking your hand might get me shivved.'

'None taken,' smiled Rouche, taking his hand back to try a spoonful of his meal. He pulled a face before pushing the tray away from him.

'You were saying?' the man prompted him.

'Right. So, I'm not a Puppet. I'm a cop . . . Well, was. CIA, in fact.'

Looking up nervously at their neighbours, the older man lowered his voice to a whisper. 'That's worse.'

'Is it?' asked Rouche, absent-mindedly going in for a second spoonful.

'If you *are* a cop, what are you doing with those scars on your chest, and why would you be locked up in here with us degenerates?'

'I was working the Puppets case. I was trying to stop them, and the only way to infiltrate them was to disfigure myself with this,' Rouche answered honestly, holding a hand up to his chest. 'And I'm in here because I was chasing the man behind it all . . .'

'Allegedly. Always say *allegedly*.'

'OK. So I *allegedly* chased the man behind it all from Piccadilly Circus to St James's Park, where I *allegedly* disabled him and then *allegedly* executed the son of an *alleged* bitch with an admittedly excessive number of gunshots to the chest, which led me here, sitting with you, eating . . .' He looked down at his slop in confusion.

'Beef Wellington,' the experienced prisoner revealed.

'. . . eating beef Wellington,' he finished. '*Allegedly*.'

The man regarded Rouche, unsure what to make of him. 'Or maybe you're just another corrupt cop.'

'Maybe,' said Rouche, taking a sip of his watery orange juice. 'God knows there's enough of them out there.' He paused when his neo-Nazi acquaintance walked past the table with a couple of his cronies in tow. 'But you know what? They always get what's coming to them . . . in the end.'

'You *really* believe that?' asked the man, amused.

'I really do.'

He shook his head. 'Optimism! Not heard any of that for a while . . . You're not going to last very long in here.'

'Which is why I could use a friend,' said Rouche, holding out his hand again: 'Damien Rouche.'

His lunch companion hesitated.

'Come on. Don't leave me hanging,' Rouche smiled at him.

With a heavy sigh, and certain he was going to regret it, the man reached across the table to shake his hand. 'Kelly . . . Kelly McLoughlin.'

Baxter really wished she could still drink wine.

At 7.29 p.m., she wondered what the hell she was thinking as she got up to answer the door.

'Andrea.'

'Emily.'

The celebrity reporter followed her through to the living room, where Baxter collapsed onto the sofa. With perfect posture, Andrea took a seat and began unloading her bag onto the coffee table.

'How are you feeling?'

'Shitty,' replied Baxter, looking a bit washed out in comparison to the camera-ready newsreader.

'I brought the stuff you asked for,' Andrea told her, removing the 'Uncage the Wolf' T-shirts of various sizes in preparation for the final push of the campaign.

'Thanks. Vanita's given him a week.'

'And if we can keep him out of prison,' started Andrea carefully. 'Do you think you two will . . . ?'

Baxter groaned and rubbed her face: 'Will what? What do you care anyway?'

'I don't. But I think I'm speaking on behalf of everyone who's ever seen, and will ever see, you and Will in a room together when I say that this little dance you two keep up is getting a *bit* old now.'

'I'm with Thomas!' Baxter snapped, rolling away from her guest in the hope of finding a position that was less painful.

'I know that.'

'He's such a good man.'

'And Will's not,' nodded Andrea. 'But that's sort of his whole *thing*, isn't it?'

Baxter didn't reply.

'You know why things ended between us, don't you?' Andrea asked her. 'The *real* reason, I mean? It was the fact that no matter how much he loved me, and he genuinely did, and no matter how well he took care of me, and he genuinely did that as well, there was no getting past the fact that he was just more in love with someone else . . . with you.'

Baxter pulled a cushion over her head.

'It's none of my business anyway. But why would you be agonising like this if you'd already made the right decision?'

Baxter slowly sat back up to look at Wolf's ex-wife.

'You know life's gone very, very wrong when *you're* the only person I have to talk to about this,' she laughed at herself. 'Screw it. I'll show you.' She got up to retrieve something from her jacket pocket, handing the folded piece of card to Andrea as she sat back down. 'I found this hidden with Finlay's things,' she explained, giving the other woman a few moments to read it. 'To start off with, I was carrying it around in case it was a lead. Now . . . I'm not really sure why. It's his handwriting, but he didn't write it for Maggie. He loved her more than life itself, but he didn't write *this* for her.'

Andrea folded the note up and passed it back to her. 'It sounds quite . . . possessive.'

'It does. And passionate. And angry. And desperate. Can you even imagine loving someone *that* much? Someone loving you *that* fiercely? *This* is what's been messing with my head,' admitted Baxter.

'Finlay and Maggie were happy, though,' Andrea pointed out, 'whoever this note was intended for.'

'Yes, they were,' nodded Baxter, bringing the topic to an inconclusive close. 'Thanks,' she said sarcastically.

'Anytime,' replied Andrea, sorting through the items on the coffee table. 'Did you see Rouche today?'

'I did.'

'That's a story you still haven't shared with me yet,' Andrea reminded her.

Baxter looked torn: 'Can I trust you with it?'

'Of course.'

'Where would you like me to start?'

Andrea thought about it. 'It's 21 December. Night-time. London is suffocating beneath a foot of snow as Lucas Keaton runs through the gates of St James's Park . . .'

Baxter took a deep breath and began to talk.

Behind the stack of cheap T-shirts, a red light flashed excitedly, the palm-sized box listening in, recording her every word.

CHAPTER 42

'You look pretty,' Wolf told Andrea, taking her hand as they sat side by side on the Tube.

'Thanks. So do you,' she smiled, leaning over to adjust the tie she'd made him wear before resting her head against his shoulder, ignoring the stares from their fellow passengers.

With the verdict of the Cremation Killer trial looming after the weekend, it had taken some convincing to get Wolf out of the house. But with the exception of having to leave through a neighbour's garden to avoid being followed by paparazzi, it had felt like a regular Friday night, a much-needed break from the endless controversies and accusations that had been dogging her husband for weeks.

'Tired?' asked Wolf, kissing the top of Andrea's head.

She nodded.

'We'll just make an appearance then get out of there. I'll have you in bed with a peppermint tea and an episode of *Grey's* by ten at the latest.'

She squeezed him tightly as the train attempted to rock her to sleep: 'Promise?'

'Promise.'

Following the balloon breadcrumb trail, they climbed the stairs to the riverside restaurant's private function room, an uncharacteristic extravagance for Wolf's frugal friend.

55 Today!

Maggie was on welcoming duties and embraced them both warmly. 'Get yourselves a drink and then get yourselves out in the sunshine,' she instructed. 'He's out on the terrace . . . drunk as a lord already,' she told them in affectionate exasperation. 'Do you want me to take those for you?' she asked Andrea, who handed over the card and present.

'What did we get him?' whispered Wolf as they headed over to the bar.

'A bottle of that fragrance he always wears.'

Wolf looked puzzled: 'Kebab and cheeky cigarettes?'

Andrea laughed out loud: 'Don't be so horrible!'

Finlay and Wolf had got into a drinking game, which was becoming more boisterous by the second as Andrea and Maggie watched on in concern.

'Shall I break them up?' asked Andrea.

'Might be an idea. It *would* be polite if Fin acknowledged at least *some* of his other guests. He's not even said hello to Benjamin and Eve yet,' said Maggie, as the two women moved in to calm their misbehaving husbands down.

'OK, boys,' said Andrea, taking the shot glass out of Wolf's hand. 'We'll call it a draw. Come on, Will. I want to have a dance.'

Andrea was just leading him to the dance floor when Baxter made her entrance with a floppy-haired man at her side. Breaking free of his wife's grip, Wolf wobbled over to them.

'Baxter!' he beamed, giving her a clumsy hug-pat-boob-graze.

'Emily,' said Andrea.

'Andrea,' replied Baxter.

Oblivious to the frosty atmosphere, Wolf bulldozed on. 'And this must be Gavin!' he said, crushing the smaller man's hand as he shook it. 'You want a drink?' he offered.

'I'm sure they can find their way to the bar without your assistance,' force-laughed Andrea, trying to guide him away. 'Come on. Let's have a dance.'

'Yeah, but,' slurred Wolf, pulling his arm away from her, 'Baxter's got that big case at the moment.'

'No shop talk at a party,' tried Andrea, having appreciated everybody's efforts to skirt the issue of Wolf's new-found fame.

'Oh,' started Gavin, clicking his fingers a little arrogantly as he tried to summon the thought. 'The gay guys they keep pulling out the river?'

'That's the one, Gav,' Wolf told him. 'Wednesday night: Baxter, Chambers, the police speedboat. It's going to be a fun one. I'm jealous.'

Gavin turned to Baxter: 'Don't forget I need you Thursday morning.'

'What's Thursday?' blurted Wolf.

'I think the lowered voices imply something that's none of our business,' Andrea snapped at him.

'It's fine,' said Gavin pleasantly. 'I lost my mum a couple of weeks ago. Thursday's the funeral.'

'Oh,' said Wolf.

'My condolences,' Andrea smiled sadly as she finally managed to pull him away.

Over an hour later, Andrea had persuaded Wolf to take her home. He had taken for ever saying goodbye to people he was going to see the next morning anyway and then stumbled into the toilets for a 'final wee'.

'You're Will, right?' asked the silver-haired gentleman at the next urinal, who sounded a far better shot than him. 'I'm Christian, an old friend of Fin's.'

'*Enchanté*,' replied Wolf, wobbling severely.

'He's told me a lot about you.'

Wolf gave him a drunken smile.

'Well, best of luck for Monday,' Christian told him, graciously giving up on the conversation.

Tripping back out into the main room, Wolf's attention was immediately drawn to the terrace, where Baxter and Gavin were having a heated argument. Like the rest of the party, Andrea was politely pretending not to have noticed and desperately tried to direct her husband towards the stairs.

'It's none of our business, Will.' He didn't even hear her, too consumed with watching Baxter storm away from her dull boyfriend. 'Will!' said Andrea, when he started edging towards the open doors. 'Will!' she called after him helplessly.

He marched outside at the precise moment Gavin took hold of Baxter's arm, which he soon released when Wolf shoved him backwards into a table, sending glasses and candles rolling onto the floor.

'Wolf, stop it!' Baxter yelled at him as he approached the man a second time. 'Wolf!'

Gavin fell heavily to the floor, retreating as he held a hand to his bloody nose.

The rest of the evening was a blur to Wolf. He remembered Baxter being furious with him, his colleagues swarming out onto the terrace to escort him off the premises, Andrea in tears and refusing to utter a single word on the journey home.

But most of all he remembered his naivety at believing the night was over when he collapsed onto the threadbare sofa in the living room.

CHAPTER 43

Saturday 30 January 2016

7.06 a.m.

Rouche hadn't slept again. It was as if he could feel the walls pressing in around him every time he closed his eyes. The darkness combined with the confines of his six-by-three top bunk made the low ceiling feel like the roof of a coffin. His cellmate hadn't spoken to him since seeing the scars the previous morning and got dressed as though Rouche wasn't even there. When their cell door was unlocked, they joined the same shuffling line as they had the day before, along the metal walkway in the direction of the shower block.

There seemed little point in trying to conceal his chest now, so Rouche removed his top first, standing defiant against the stares and insults.

'Still can't believe you did that to yourself,' said Kelly, who had started to undress beside him.

'Well, I had a little help,' Rouche admitted, the tiled changing room somewhat reminiscent of the vile men's bathroom in which Baxter had taken a steak knife to his chest. 'It looks like you've got your own stories, though,' said Rouche, noting the older man's decorated body.

A large, thin scar ran along the inside of his left arm, while an old burn discoloured the other. There remained evidence of several sloppy operations and a perfect circle of raised skin just above his heart.

'How are you even still alive?' Rouche asked, making him chuckle.

'Most of the time I had somebody up there looking out for me.'

'You mean . . . *God*?'

'No. I mean a sniper.'

'Oh.'

'Yeah, I got most of these in the military,' explained Kelly. 'They look worse than they are.'

'Is that a bullet wound?'

'OK. *That* one was pretty bad,' he admitted, rubbing the scar.

'You'll have to tell me the story sometime,' said Rouche, wrapping his towel round him.

'No . . . I won't,' replied Kelly. 'You go ahead. I'll catch up.'

Following the others through the doorway, Rouche had only taken two steps into the shower room when he was struck with something heavy. Slipping on the wet floor, he landed badly, feeling hands all over his body as he was dragged across the rough tiles. Barely conscious, he was propped up against a low wall as the attack intensified, feeling the impacts of the kicks and punches, hearing the ringing in his ears when his head hit the hard floor but unable to fully register the pain.

Kelly entered the wet room. Sensing the tense atmosphere, he instantly knew what was happening: a group of five gathered in a single spot, the water tainted red as it circled the drain. He hesitated, not wanting to get involved, but then cursed under his breath.

'Guard!' he bellowed at the top of his lungs. 'Guard!'

The men dispersed, one pausing to spit on Rouche's incapacitated body where he lay.

Kelly went over to him as the first prison officers came running into the shower block. While one reported the incident, another began evacuating the area, unsure what else to do as they waited for medical assistance.

*

Against the doctor's advice, Rouche had refused to stay in for observation and at 2.55 p.m. staggered down the Med-Bay staircase to the short corridor that led to the visitation hall. Handicapped by only being able to see through one of his swollen eyes, he negotiated the gauntlet of inmates loitering at the bottom of the stairs hoping to have their names called.

'That's the least you deserve,' one sneered.

'You got lucky!' yelled another, throwing something at him.

Ignoring them, Rouche hobbled past.

Baxter's face fell when she saw him approaching. She desperately wanted to go to him, to help him, but knew she would be prevented from doing so.

'Oh God, Rouche,' she gasped, as he slumped into his chair. 'What happened?'

'Got into a fight . . . Not entirely convinced I won,' he joked.

'I'm pulling you out,' she said decisively. 'We'll get you moved somewhere else.'

'No.'

'You can go into solitary confinement until then,' she continued. 'I'll speak to the—'

'No!' he snapped, slamming his hand down on the table.

Two prison officers moved in their direction, but Baxter waved them away.

'I can do this,' Rouche told her.

She wanted to reach out and hold his hand more than anything in the world.

'I *am* going to get you out of here,' she promised him. 'Just hold on a little longer.'

Christian answered his phone: 'Yes?'

'Andrea Hall here to see you, sir,' a voice he didn't recognise informed him, his secretary off enjoying the weekend, just as he should have been.

'Show her in, please.' Getting up from his desk to greet his celebrity visitor, Christian was dressed in a polo shirt and chinos rather than his usual formal attire. 'Ah! Ms Hall. Do come in. Make yourself comfortable,' he said, shaking her hand and dismissing his subordinate with a door to the face. 'So, tell me, what on earth is so important we couldn't do this on Monday?' he asked her.

'Dropping the charges against Will,' she replied simply.

Laughing out loud, Christian sat back down behind his desk. 'And pray tell what would I want to do a thing like that for?'

'You've got nothing against Will,' she said with a dismissive wave. 'You killed one of his closest friends! He *had* to try to take you down. Would you *really* expect anything less?'

He froze.

'I'm not wearing a wire,' Andrea told him. 'And if I were, I'd be implicating myself. I'm here to make you a deal. Will's done. It's over.'

Christian nodded cautiously. 'Kick a dog enough times, it'll learn to stay away,' he said cryptically.

'Oh, and he's got the message. Loud and clear,' Andrea assured him. 'Look, I can't really relate to all these vendettas and emotional crusades. But what I *can* relate to, and respect, is a man doing what he has to to protect his interests.'

Nodding courteously at the compliment, Christian was still very conscious of to whom he was speaking.

'Here's what I propose,' continued Andrea. 'You let Will off with a slap on the wrist; I don't shut this place down with another protest. Plus, I hand you Emily Baxter *and* Damien Rouche on a platter in return. Both now far bigger fish, I'm sure you'll agree.' Christian leaned forward in interest when Andrea produced a mobile phone from her bag. 'A recording of a private conversation between Emily Baxter and myself detailing the events leading up to Lucas Keaton's death, admitting that she was present . . . with Rouche, watched him *execute* their unarmed and incapacitated prisoner, that she was nursing a *murder suspect* back to health at her Wimbledon apartment to ensure he evaded capture.'

'That certainly does sound incriminating,' said Christian, now confident that their conversation wouldn't be shared. 'Too good to be true, perhaps?'

'All I care about is Will. Emily Baxter ruined my marriage. Damien Rouche is nothing to me except a great story.'

'Ahhhh, there's more?' said Christian, sensing where Andrea was heading with this.

'An exclusive interview with Rouche.'

'Done.'

'Before the trial.'

'That might be problematic.'

'Tonight.'

'Now that's impossible.'

Andrea pushed a button on the mobile phone; Baxter's crackling voice started to speak.

'Rouche was ahead of me . . . It was snowing *so* hard. I couldn't keep up. I heard the first gunshot . . . Keaton was badly injured but still alive when I reached him. I tried to stem the bleeding, but—'

Pressing the button once more to pause Baxter's scandalous admission, Andrea held the phone out to him, swinging it like the pendulum of a ticking clock. 'An interview at the prison with Damien Rouche *and* Will released from custody within forty-eight hours. That's my final offer.'

Smiling, Christian regarded the unflinching woman sitting across from him. He reached out and took the phone from her.

'It's locked,' he said.

'You have the recording in your possession. You'll get the password when you've honoured our arrangement.'

'I like you.'

'I don't care. Do we have a deal?' Andrea asked him.

'Yes, Ms Hall . . . We have a deal.'

Rouche dropped his tray, sending his either unappetisingly stringy stew or concerningly thick soup across the canteen floor. To a chorus of spiteful laughter, he got down onto his knees to pick up the cracked bowl.

'Just leave it!' a guard barked at him from across the room.

Taking extra care this time, Rouche had just loaded up another tray when somebody called his name.

In interest, Kelly watched as the governor himself beckoned Rouche over for a quiet word. The conversation lasted a little over a minute; at which point the elusive man in charge disappeared as quickly as he had entered, leaving Rouche in peace to eat his dinner.

'What did the governor want?' Kelly asked him, wincing at the state of his pummelled face. 'Asking about the fight?'

'In part,' replied Rouche, taking a seat. 'There's something he wants me to do . . . An interview.'

'Interview?' asked Kelly in confusion.

'Uh-huh,' nodded Rouche without elaborating.

'OK? So, what did the doctor say?'

'That I got hit in the face . . . quite a lot,' replied Rouche. 'I wanted to thank you for earlier. I heard you calling the guard.'

Kelly waved off his gratitude. 'Even if I didn't hate those Nazi fucks – and believe me, I really, *really* do – there's nothing I dislike more than an unfair fight.'

'Still . . . thank you,' said Rouche as he struggled to eat anything.

'You know, you've got to make this right,' Kelly told him, glaring at the group of shaven-headed clones manhandling each other just a few benches away. 'You can't let these things go unpunished.'

'No,' agreed Rouche, placing a substantial soup-covered shard of broken plastic onto the table between them. 'You can't.'

Kelly looked down dubiously at the sorry excuse for a weapon. 'Well, if you can't win, you can always just burn it all down,' he smiled, passing on the advice that, for better or worse, he had always lived by.

Rouche nodded and placed his napkin over the makeshift blade before leaning in conspiratorially. 'Look, I haven't got an awful lot of time . . . There's something we need to discuss.'

CHAPTER 44

Sunday 31 January 2016

8.37 a.m.

'The interview is a go!' Andrea called across the studio to anyone within earshot. 'I need Rory, sound and lighting at Woodhill Prison by six a.m. tomorrow to set up, a live feed from seven and the space to run it every hour throughout the day!'

'Damien Rouche is month-old news now,' her editor-in-chief pointed out, coffee in hand as he emerged from the adjoining office.

'Just trust me on this,' Andrea smiled across at him. 'When have I ever let you down?'

'Oh, I've seen *that* look before,' her boss chuckled. 'Who'd you screw over this time?'

'No one who didn't already have it coming.'

'Guard!' yelled Rouche. 'Help me! Please!' he shouted desperately as the concrete tainted the spilt blood a rich wine colour. He pressed his hands over the wound in Kelly's side as a crowd started to gather. 'Guard!'

An experienced prison officer came sprinting across the crowded recreation yard.

'Get back!' he yelled at the growing crowd, already radioing in for assistance. 'Get back! *You* stay there,' he ordered Rouche, recognising that he was trying to help. 'I need a medic down here and we need to clear the yard. There's a lot of blood. Looks like a stab wound.' He turned back to Rouche: 'What happened?'

'I didn't see anything,' answered Rouche, with no choice but to follow prison etiquette with so many ears listening in. Beneath his hands, Kelly was writhing in agony. 'You're going to be all right,' Rouche assured him, dark stains already soaking their way up his sleeves.

The cavalry arrived, herding the inmates to allow the doctor to attend to his patient.

'We need to get him up to the medical bay now!' he told the guards.

Wiping his bloody hands on his top, Rouche was ordered to join his fellow prisoners at the far end of the yard to watch helplessly as his one ally was heaved onto a stretcher and carried away.

Baxter was in the bath. Hoping that a visit from Holly would lift Rouche's spirits, she had been free to spend the entire day with Thomas, who had turned up on her doorstep wearing a cheap gift-shop T-shirt:

I ♥ LONDON

Baxter had, of course, outright refused to wear hers but had agreed to his plan of visiting all the usual tourist traps that residents of the city tended to avoid at all cost.

Donning her garish hat and gloves, they had queued for over an hour in the cold to get into the Tower of London and then taken an obligatory selfie outside Buckingham Palace. After lunch at Hard Rock Cafe, they had strolled around the grounds of Kensington Palace with takeaway coffees to keep them warm, a reminder that despite all the horrors, death and malevolence eating away at its foundations, a historic and enthralling city resolutely weathered the storm.

It had already been the best day Baxter could remember, even before discovering the small black box that Thomas had left on

her pillow. Trying her engagement ring on for size, she felt a huge
weight finally lift off her shoulders. Closing her eyes, she dunked
her head under the water: she had made her decision.

It was a lonely walk for Rouche as he found a quiet spot to eat
his evening meal. He had deliberately dragged his feet getting
to the food hall to minimise his time in there. The Nazis were
watching him from their usual table but soon lost interest when
a black inmate ill-advisedly walked too close to them, inviting a
torrent of racial abuse.

Making the most of this brief respite, Rouche tried to force
down some food. But he wasn't the remotest bit hungry, not
because of his painful jaw on this occasion but due to guilt.
He had been standing in the entrance to the visitation hall at 3
p.m. expecting to find Baxter, but on seeing Holly's anxious face
glancing around the room instead, he had walked away, unable
to bear her seeing him in such a sorry state. Regretting his decision, he pushed his meal away and sat there silently, watching
the food hall gradually empty out.

The Nazi table was among the last to get up, the less imposing
men unconsciously circling their alpha as they jostled for position,
one seeking approval by shoving another inmate into a wall.

Rouche calmly removed a rolled-up facecloth from the waistband of his trousers, unwrapping the bloodstained shard of
plastic in his lap. He picked up his tray and ambled between
the empty tables on his way to the exit, pausing momentarily to
place the offending weapon on the bench where the group had
been gathered.

And then, whistling innocently, he followed them out.

Christian was in a very good mood by the time he arrived home.
Locking the front door behind him, he paused when he instinctively went to lift the handle, deciding it one habit he could probably live without. Setting the alarm, he strode through the moonlit
main room to the tap of freezing rain against the windows. He

poured himself a large Scotch and then took a seat in his favourite chair, positioned at the very centre of his silent palace.

Although certainly not the weekend he had planned, he had satisfied his assurances to Andrea Hall by arranging her unfeasible interview and lodging the initial release papers for William Fawkes. He had submitted the phone containing the incriminating recording to evidence and scheduled an urgent meeting with Professional Standards to discuss Detective Chief Inspector Baxter. He had also spoken with Devon Sinclair, the FBI agent tasked with the unenviable job of tying up the Lucas Keaton fiasco, both to share the good news and to express his expectations of being publicly credited for his contribution.

Whatever the tenacious journalist could get out of Rouche in the morning would only further cement the case against him.

Taking another sip of his Scotch, Christian regarded the chessboard set up expectantly atop the coffee table, assigning each of his enemies a piece as he repositioned his own round them . . . all but one.

Killian Caine and his crew were still searching for Eoghan Kendrick, a man who in all likelihood was no longer even alive and who, in over thirty years, had not come forward with his outrageous story of corrupt cops and missing millions.

He was of little consequence.

Feeling as though he could finally breathe, Christian raised his glass in toast to the chessboard: 'Checkmate.'

CHAPTER 45

Monday 1 February 2016

6.26 a.m.

Even Andrea looked tired, her crew worse, Rory as though he might actually die, as a commendably thorough or just farcically anal prison officer unscrewed a metal plate on the television camera.

'That's the warranty voided, then,' Rory told him through a coffee-tainted yawn.

Ignoring him, the man prised the panel away in order to inspect the innards of the wildly expensive piece of equipment for anything illicit.

After their debilitating early start to reach Woodhill Prison by 6 a.m., they had travelled approximately ten feet in twenty-six minutes, running into a roadblock at the security gate as each individual item of their kit was unpacked and scrutinised in turn.

'Is this going to take much longer?' snapped Andrea, conscious that she was due live on air in just over half an hour's time.

The man looked up at her, shrugged and then set to work removing another panel.

Exhaustion had finally got the better of Rouche, who had managed to steal almost five hours of sleep but was wide awake when he heard footsteps approaching his cell at 6.53 a.m., shortly before the morning prisoner movements. Keen to reach his destination before then, he climbed down from his bunk and was already waiting in the centre of the room when the guard came to collect him.

He was escorted down the stairs, his bright blue uniform the only spark of colour as he walked the length of the deserted cell block. Unlocking and relocking doors as they passed through, they finally reached the corridor to the visitation hall. Rouche glanced up at the dark medical bay, remembering the look in Kelly's eyes when he had slipped the jagged shard into the soft skin just below his ribcage.

'Oi!' his escort called, holding the door for him.

'Sorry,' apologised Rouche, thankful to have been pulled from the memory.

'Wall,' the caffeine-starved prison officer barked on reaching the final door.

Rouche compliantly turned to face the taupe wall as the guard punched in a five-digit code, swiping his identification card through the reader before pulling the door open. They entered the familiar space, where the TV crew were still setting up their equipment while Andrea fixed her make-up in a compact mirror.

'Your interviewee!' announced the man, clearly a little star-struck by the world-famous reporter.

Andrea got to her feet and nodded in greeting to the man she had sold out to their common enemy. Rouche, being Rouche, smiled back and returned the gesture with a cheery wave.

By 6.59 a.m., Doctor Yuán was nearing the end of his fourth consecutive night shift and had never been more excited by the prospect of two days off and a decent sleep. Just as the weekends seemed to awake something in those beyond the walls – an illusion of diminished responsibility, an indulgence of excess they felt deprived of during the week, confidence in raucous numbers – Friday and Saturday nights within the walls were unfailingly eventful: seven fights, one head injury requiring transfer to an external facility, one set of slit wrists and a stabbing.

He was exhausted.

Tidying up in anticipation of his colleague's arrival, God willing before anybody else could injure themselves, Doctor Yuán looked in on his three overnight patients, all of whom were still sleeping peacefully, doing nothing to alleviate his own tiredness. Lit by the cosy glow of the equipment and screens singing their monotonic lullabies, he very nearly dozed off in the doorway. Snoring himself awake, the doctor rubbed his stinging eyes, immediately aware that something had changed.

He took a step forward, squinting to focus in the low light, frowning as he regarded the middle of the three beds, eyes growing wide as he realised it now stood empty.

He turned to run, not realising that a figure had appeared in the doorway behind him.

Kelly stepped out into the light, a large scalpel in his hand.

'Don't even think about it, Doc,' he said calmly when the man glanced at the panic button on the wall. 'No need to fret. I don't want to hurt you, and I won't, so long as you don't do anything stupid.'

The doctor raised his hands.

'Better,' Kelly told him, collecting his personal possessions from the tray beside him. 'Got your ID card handy?'

'Yes. But it won't do you any good,' replied the doctor, his exhaustion dulling the effects of the adrenaline. 'I only have limited access.'

'Is that so?' asked Kelly, disinterested.

'Yes. For eventualities such as this.'

'Smoke?'

'I'm sorry?'

'Do . . . you . . . smoke?'

The doctor shook his head.

'Matches? A lighter?'

'Second drawer down,' he told Kelly, pointing him in the right direction.

Without taking his eyes off the doctor, Kelly backed towards the unit, rummaging around until he found the box of matches.

Striking half a dozen at once, he held them to the smoke detector above his head.

'There's no way you'll ever make it out,' the doctor told him, watching the injured man struggle to hold the flame steady.

The shrill alarm triggered, followed by another close by and then another. Seconds later, the terrifying roar of hundreds of trapped inmates answered the call.

'Good job we're not breaking out, then,' smiled Kelly, taking a firm hold of the doctor's arm. 'We're breaking *in*.'

'Heat and smoke sensors: East Sector!' called one of the control-room staff, leaping up from his monitor.

Several CCTV feeds showed prisoners out on the walkways, growing increasingly agitated as the outnumbered guards struggled to contain the situation.

'We need urgent backup!' another member of the team broadcast over the radio. 'All available personnel to the cell block immediately!'

Abandoning the feed of Rouche sitting opposite Andrea and her crew, the young man brought up an alternative view of the cell block, which was on the verge of erupting into violence.

'Shit!' he said, watching the screens. 'We've got to get more people down there!'

The rumble of the building pandemonium had reached the visitation hall, an unwelcome memory of one of the most terrifying ordeals of Rouche's life inevitably returning to him. On this occasion, however, sitting across from Andrea and her television camera, it was precisely what he wanted to hear. He watched as his escort deliberated over what to do, listening in to his colleagues' radio exchanges becoming more frantic as the commotion steadily grew louder.

'Stay put. I'll be right back,' he told them, already running for the door.

Looking understandably anxious, Andrea and her team waited with their equipment at the ready, ignoring the screaming in their ears as the producers back at the studio demanded to know why they weren't broadcasting.

Rouche slowly got to his feet: 'I guess it's that time.'

Kelly had led the doctor down the Med-Bay staircase and through the first door on their left, which had opened with his ID card alone. The alarm, situated halfway along the corridor, was deafening as they hurried beneath it and approached another sealed door, reinforced with a keypad entry system.

'OK, Doc,' Kelly shouted over the noise. 'You're up.'

The red light on the lock turned green as the door swung open, revealing first the perplexed doctor and then the scarred and wrinkled face of his abductor.

Rouche grinned: 'Wasn't sure you were coming.'

Kelly handed him the scalpel as they traded places. Apologising sincerely, Rouche raised the blade to the doctor's throat.

'Kelly McLoughlin, meet Andrea Hall,' Rouche introduced them. 'You can trust her. She's one of us. Andrea Hall, meet Kelly McLoughlin, otherwise known as Eoghan Kendrick. I think the two of you have a lot to talk about and not a lot of time.'

'We're all set up for you over here,' Andrea told Kelly.

He looked uncertain and turned back to Rouche. 'You aren't screwing me, are you?'

'No,' said Rouche honestly. 'I swear. This came from the commander of the Metropolitan Police herself. You're putting yourself in harm's way to help bring down a murderer. We're in your debt for this, and that's a very good position for you to be in.'

He nodded, allowing Andrea to lead him over to the others.

'Hey, Kelly!'

He paused to look back.

Rouche smiled: 'Burn it all down!'

CHAPTER 46

Monday 1 February 2016
7.11 a.m.

The sun was yet to rise on another frosty morning.

The darkness outside and one celebratory Scotch too many had persuaded Christian to hit the 'snooze' button twice. Letting out a hungover groan, he groped blindly for his mobile when the incessant device started buzzing atop his bedside table. Squinting at the screen, he sat up, instantly wide awake.

'Killian! To what do I owe the pleasure?' he answered, switching on a lamp but unable to disguise a trace of concern at the unsociably timed call.

'Did I wake you?' the influential career criminal asked calmly.

'No! Well, yes. But I was just about to get up anyway, so don't worry.'

'I wasn't.'

Unsure how to respond, Christian waited for him to continue. A long, exasperated sigh filled the pause, only putting him further on edge.

'That man we spoke about . . . Eoghan Kendrick. I thought you'd want to know we found him.'

'That's fantastic news! Isn't it?' Christian asked, confused by the downbeat tone.

'Is it?'

Again he waited for the other man to elaborate.

'He is, at this very moment, being broadcast live from Woodhill Prison, spilling his guts about *my* operation, you, the dead detective *and* the missing money.'

The news hit Christian like a physical blow. He wanted to simultaneously vomit, cry and scream.

'Woodhill Prison?' he mumbled, beginning to put the pieces together, the realisation dawning on him that he, himself, had played an integral part in his enemies' plan against him. 'How's that even possible?' he asked, feigning ignorance.

'I was wondering that myself.' Caine's calm tone was unnerving. 'It turns out that *you* set up the interview. *You* granted the most famous reporter in the country access to the prison and, consequently, the *one* person who could destroy us both. Ultimately, Mr Commissioner, the buck stops . . . with you.'

'Killian, I—'

'You'll be hearing from us.'

'Wait! I can still fix this!'

The line went dead.

Shell-shocked, Christian just sat there for a moment, staring at the phone in his hand as though it were a severed safety rope. Feeling light-headed, he climbed out of bed and pulled his dressing gown on over his pyjamas. He hurried downstairs, where the sky beyond the towering windows had turned an inky blue, the trees below standing perfectly still, featureless black shapes like a painted background on a stage. Crossing the room, he picked up the remote control to switch on his enormous television, its unnatural glow bathing him in light as he started flicking through the channels . . .

He recognised the man immediately despite the thirty-year interlude. Christian staggered to stay upright as memories flooded back to him: the heat of the fire, the groan of the failing building, the weight of the gun in his hand, the look in the very same man's eyes as he abandoned him to die in one of the worst ways imaginable in favour of his own greed.

On screen, Kelly lifted his top to reveal evidence of the bullet wound, of the act that Christian was most ashamed. Putting his face in his hands, Christian laughed bitterly, at long last understanding how Killian Caine had known the things he had.

'It's over,' a deep voice announced from somewhere within the room, reverberating all the way up to the rafters.

Christian didn't turn round immediately, lowering his head in defeat.

'How did you find him?' he asked.

'I didn't,' admitted Wolf, his voice closer now. 'Edmunds did . . . a while ago.'

Christian rubbed his face: 'Caine's *entire* network couldn't find him.'

'Perhaps they should've been looking for the girlfriend instead.'

'And how did you persuade him to talk?'

'Again, I didn't. Rouche did. You think it was an accident he wound up in Woodhill?'

Nodding, Christian switched off the television: 'Ms Hall?' he asked.

'Not quite the heartless bitch we'd all taken her for,' replied Wolf.

'And the recording?'

'Staged. And deleted the moment you listened to it.' He didn't elaborate further, having barely understood a word of Baxter and Andrea's convoluted plan involving 'suicide texts', chipped phones and clone messenger apps.

'Just you, I notice,' said Christian.

'Just me,' nodded Wolf, emerging from the dying shadows as the sky outside grew brighter by the second.

Christian turned round to face him: 'Old habits die hard, I suppose.'

'If I was going to hurt you, I'd have done it a long time ago.'

He tossed a pair of handcuffs onto the sofa beside Christian.

'You know I never wanted any of this?' he told Wolf, showing no indication of picking up the metal binds. 'I would have rather *died* than *ever* hurt Fin and Maggie.'

Wolf edged towards him: 'I don't care.'

Christian glanced back at the tranquil garden.

'Don't make me chase you down,' said Wolf, pausing where he stood.

Christian smiled wearily. 'You should know better than anyone, Will . . . everybody runs.'

Upsetting the chessboard as he leaped over the coffee table, Christian reached the glass doors. Falling out onto the icy patio, he scrambled across the frozen lawn.

Watching him disappear through the gate at the bottom of the garden, Wolf calmly held his phone up to his ear. 'He's heading right for you.'

Christian wondered whether he was still asleep as he ran barefoot through a carpet of dead leaves. With the freezing air tearing at his lungs, the first slivers of sunlight found a path through the trees of the hoarfrost forest, a surreally beautiful dreamscape by anyone's standards.

Within the space of five minutes, his life had changed irrevocably.

All he could do was keep running, to abandon everything and everyone that had come before, to start afresh, because he would do it all so very differently if only given another chance – the irrational bargaining of a desperate man, the fear-induced delusion that he could actually disappear all he had left to hold on to, the notion of escape all-consuming.

He fell heavily, hands sinking into the damp earth beneath the debris discarded by a forest shedding its skin.

There was a rustle nearby . . .

With fearful eyes, Christian watched the trees.

A loud snap from somewhere else . . .

He was disorientated, unsure from which direction he had even come as he calmed his breathing and listened intently: the thud of running footfalls emerged from the silence, a dark figure flickering between the trees. Scrambling to his feet, Christian was gripped by fear as he spotted another shape approaching from the other side. Choosing his route, he broke into a frantic sprint, the sound of his pursuers intensifying all around him as yet another joined the hunt.

He fell again, exhaustion and panic impeding his co-ordination. With no option left, he went to ground, crawling through the dirt and beneath a fallen tree. He watched as two silhouettes tore past, disappearing as quickly as they had come into the dawn-lit forest. A third, however, slowed to a walking pace. Christian closed his eyes, willing them to move on, listening helplessly to them padding across the forest floor in search of him. He huddled up tighter . . .

The rustling drew nearer.

He held his breath.

They approached his felled tree, sending brittle leaves spiralling to the ground in front of his face . . .

Bursting out from his hiding place, Christian sprinted blindly into a clearing, hearing a set of heavy footfalls rush towards him.

The impact knocked him clean off his feet as someone landed on top of him.

'Over here!' Wolf called to the others, a feral look in his eyes as Christian stared up at him, utterly spent.

Edmunds suddenly appeared to his left and then Saunders to his right. Moments later, Baxter limped into view above his head, each of them regarding him with the same dispassionate look. Surrounded by his enemies, Christian started to laugh.

'This was never an arrest . . . was it?' he asked them, his silver hair dark with dirt and leaves. 'You *wanted* me out here alone!'

Wolf tightened his grip on his struggling prisoner.

'No witnesses, right?!' shouted Christian manically, straining to look up at Baxter. 'Get it over with, then!' he goaded Wolf, meeting his eye. 'Come on!'

'You ain't gettin' off that easy, mate,' Saunders told him just as the sound of sirens filled the morning air.

As he finally accepted his fate, Christian let his body go limp, submitting entirely to Wolf. With the sirens drawing ever closer, one by one his captors dispersed, leaving him and Wolf alone in the clearing. Rolling him onto his front, Wolf handcuffed Christian's wrists behind his back. And then, savouring each and every one of the words he had been waiting to speak, he read the commissioner his rights.

'Christian Bellamy, I am arresting you for the murder of Detective Sergeant Finlay Shaw. You do not have to say anything, but it may harm your defence if you do not mention when questioned something which you later rely on in court. Anything you *do* say may be given as evidence. Do you understand?'

Overcome with emotion, Wolf pulled his prisoner up onto his feet and, with blue eyes glistening, marched him towards the dancing lights in the distance.

CHAPTER 47

Monday 1 February 2016

2.34 p.m.

Edmunds was late.

The anticlimactic realities of police work had absorbed most of the day as the team meticulously logged evidence, gave detailed statements and were forced to attend a meeting with the insufferable PR department; focused on damage control, it felt as though they had arrived with a mop and bucket to tackle the aftermath of a publicity nuke going off.

Sneaking through the doors, he spotted Wolf leaning against the wall as a jubilant Vanita addressed the audience of her hastily organised press conference. Edmunds quietly went over to join him.

'. . . While we obviously cannot discuss any of the details surrounding our ongoing investigation,' Vanita told the room firmly, 'it would be naive to pretend that you're not already well aware of the accusations being levelled against Christian Bellamy and the seriousness with which we are treating them. That in mind, *I* will be standing in as acting commissioner for the time being . . .'

A few reporters shouted out questions that Vanita wouldn't have been allowed to answer even had she heard them.

'Hey,' whispered Edmunds, squeezing in beside Wolf.

'Hey.'

'Where are the others?'

'Not coming.'

Edmunds frowned, having been told by Wolf himself that it was imperative he attend.

'. . . And in that capacity,' Vanita continued, 'I would like to acknowledge the *truly* inspiring and courageous work of the team involved, both civilian and representatives of the Metropolitan Police alike.'

Turning to give Wolf and Edmunds a scripted smile, she read out her list of names:

'Detective Chief Inspector Emily Baxter, Detective Constable Jake Saunders, former Detective Constable Alex Edmunds, former Detective Sergeant William Layton-Fawkes . . .'

Wolf winced.

'. . . former CIA Agent Damien Rouche and friend of the police Andrea Hall.'

Prompted by Vanita, the room broke into an obliging applause.

'So how does it feel?' Edmunds asked Wolf, able to raise his voice as they clapped along to their own half-hearted ovation. 'To be the man who took down the commissioner of the Metropolitan Police?'

'I think I cried a bit,' admitted Wolf.

Edmunds nodded, only a little judgementally: 'That's understandable.'

'I *needed* to be the one to arrest him,' said Wolf, lowering his voice as the applause subsided. '*That* was for me. The rest is *all* you,' he told Edmunds cryptically as Vanita returned to the microphone.

'I'm going to hand you over to a member of that team now, who will answer your *pre-approved* questions regarding the investigation . . .'

Wolf pushed himself off the wall in the direction of the limelight to which he was so accustomed. But then he turned to Edmunds, giving him an affectionate slap to the back. 'You got this, *right*?'

he smiled before casually walking out.

Vanita's expression mirrored Edmunds's own as she quickly recovered. '. . . Errrm . . . Ladies and gentlemen, former Metropolitan detective and now private investigator . . . Alex Edmunds!' she announced, leading another reluctant applause.

With cameras flashing in time to a chorus of unintelligible questions, Edmunds blundered towards the podium, almost kicking over a television camera in the process. Instantly becoming the face of the team responsible for exposing the biggest scandal in years, he shook Vanita's hand enthusiastically before stepping up to the microphone.

He cleared his throat. 'Good afternoon . . . Are there any questions?'

CHAPTER 48

Wednesday 3 February 2016
4.49 p.m.

Christian's arrest had felt like an ending, but with Finlay's body being held until after the trial, it would still be a little longer before they could give him a proper funeral. However, Maggie had wanted to do something. Inviting only those closest to her husband, she had arranged an informal memorial service in her back garden, insisting it be a happy occasion, a chance for them all to finally say goodbye. Timed to coincide with the fleeting winter dusk, Wolf, Baxter, Edmunds, Saunders and Andrea joined a handful of others in huddling round the fire pit to share their favourite stories by candlelight.

When Ben E. King's 'Stand by Me' crackled through the record player, Wolf offered Maggie his hand, standing in for her husband as they danced to Finlay's favourite song.

Friday 21 May 2010
Finlay's birthday
23.58 p.m.

Wolf was passed out on the sofa of his and Andrea's poky Stoke Newington cottage, blissfully unaware that he had completely ruined Finlay's birthday party. He had upset Maggie, knocked out one of Baxter's boyfriend's teeth and caused a huge row between the two of them. Far more importantly, however, he hadn't gone to his wife, who had spent the previous half-hour crying on the bed wishing that he cared enough to check on her.

There was a crash out in the hallway.

Falling off the sofa, Wolf stumbled to his feet. Still dressed in his crumpled shirt and tie, he entered the hallway just in time to receive a work shoe to the head.

'Jesus Christ!' he complained, holding his forehead in pain while regarding the sum of his worldly possessions strewn all over the stairs. 'What the fuck?!' he called up to Andrea, who was standing on the landing with another load.

'You're moving out,' she informed him with make-up all over her face. 'Tonight.'

'Uh-huh,' nodded Wolf. 'Just one thing, though . . . I'm going back to sleep.'

The second shoe hurt even more than the first.

'Would you *please . . . stop . . .* throwing things at me!'

'Get out!'

'No.'

Andrea disappeared for a moment. Wolf couldn't be sure whether that was a good thing or a bad thing. His gut told him bad . . .

She returned to the top of the stairs holding his Fender Telecaster.

'Get out,' she said again.

'Now, let's not do anything rash,' he smiled up at her.

'Get out!' She dangled the guitar over the stairs.

'Don't . . . you . . . *fucking* . . . dare!'

She released her grip, sending the blue flame-burst guitar crashing down the staircase.

'What is your problem?!' he bellowed.

'You are! I've had it with you! I've had it with her! I've had it with this whole screwed-up situation! I just want it over!'

'This is *my* house too!' shouted Wolf, throwing things back up at her but looking a little scared when she suddenly stormed down the stairs towards him.

'Get out!' she screamed, shoving him towards the door.

'Andie—'

She pulled the front door open, driving him out into the mild night illuminated by the flashing lights of the police car parked in front of the house.

'And what do you want?!' Wolf yelled at the two officers hurrying through the gate.

'Sir, I'm going to need you to calm down,' one of them told him. 'Could you step away from the lady for me?'

'This is my house!' he spat at the man, shrugging off his hand and heading back in.

'Sir!' The officer grabbed his shoulder.

Wolf spun on the spot, striking the man in the face, immediately knowing it was a mistake.

Bursting into tears, Andrea ran back inside: 'I can't do this anymore!'

'Andie!' he called after her as the front door slammed. Calming down too late, he turned back to the police officer and his fresh bloody lip: 'I'm sorry . . . I don't suppose there's anything I could say to convince you not to arrest me?'

'Nothing at all.'

'Fantastic.'

Wednesday 3 February 2016

5.20 p.m.

Wolf and Maggie had been joined by another older couple as they wobbled along to the song. Picking up her hot chocolate, Baxter went over to stand with Andrea, who was working her way through the photographs pinned up around the garden.

'Emily.'

'Andrea.'

'This is nice.'

'Yeah . . . it is.'

They stood in silence for a moment looking at the photo of Finlay and Wolf mid-drinking game at his fifty-fifth birthday party, approximately an hour before it all went so horribly wrong.

'You know he got himself arrested that night?' sighed Andrea.

'Yeah, I heard.'

'Being an idiot, like usual,' she said, smiling as she watched him spin Maggie dangerously close to the frail old couple, who now looked to be holding on to one another just to stay upright. 'I taught him that move,' she told Baxter proudly. 'How's Rouche?'

'No idea. After co-ordinating a mini jailbreak and abducting the prison doctor, they're not letting me see him,' she said, looking worried.

'Just stick to your story,' Andrea reassured her. 'They've got nothing on him and they know it. It's just your word against theirs.'

Baxter nodded.

'What about Will?'

'Going to prison,' replied Baxter matter-of-factly. 'But a nice one. And not for very long. Vanita looks to be keeping her word.'

Although a little stilted, the conversation was going incredibly well by their standards.

'And . . .' Andrea hesitated, wondering whether she was over-stepping the mark, 'any decisions on the *other* thing?'

Baxter glanced around to ensure no one was listening in. 'Thomas gave me back the engagement ring.'

'And?'

'And what?'

'Did you say "yes"?'

'No. Not yet. But I'm going to.'

'Really?'

'Really.'

Andrea beamed and gave her an awkward hug. 'Congratulations! I'm really happy for you. And' – she looked over at Wolf as he made Maggie laugh out loud – 'you're making the sensible choice. So, when are you going to tell Thomas?'

'Tonight. There's just one thing I need to do first.'

Saturday 22 May 2010
1.42 a.m.

Lying on top of the police-cell mattress, Wolf wished he could shut his brain off, just for a little while, a thousand different thoughts racing through his mind at once.

He was still in shock after what had happened, by the ferocity of Andrea's fury, by the depths of her unhappiness: unspoken feelings left to ferment far too long. They'd had fights before, of course, big ones, but nothing quite like this. Recently, it had seemed as though he couldn't put a foot right where she was concerned, but there was a finality in the air now, which felt as much a relief as it was heartbreaking.

He wasn't even entirely sure which police station he was in, but one of the officers had recognised him, extending him the comforts of his own cell and the offer of getting hold of anyone he wanted them to.

A door slammed and then a set of unhurried footsteps approached.

'You stupid, stupid shit,' a rasping voice greeted him.

Pulling up a chair, Finlay took a seat on the other side of the bars.

'Yeah,' replied Wolf, sitting up. 'I know. I know. What are you doing here?'

'Well, some prick got into such a row with his wife the neighbours called the police, who he then decided to assault before putting *me* down as his emergency contact . . . On my birthday . . . which he'd already ruined.'

Wolf stood up. 'One, I didn't expect them to call you *tonight*. Two, thanks for coming down, though. And three, I *had* to do something back at the party. You saw the way that guy grabbed Baxter, right?'

Finlay looked both a little drunk and exhausted. He yawned. '*I* saw a perfectly nice bloke gently take his girlfriend's arm because he didn't want her to leave.'

'Well, you're old,' reasoned Wolf. 'Your eyes don't work properly.'

'You were just looking for an excuse, Will,' Finlay told him in exasperation. 'If it hadn't been the arm thing, it would've been something else. Whoever turned up with Emily tonight was gonna wind up getting hit.'

Wolf waved off his friend's theory dismissively.

'Look,' Finlay continued, in no mood for an argument, 'I've smoothed things over with the custody officer and there won't be any follow-up because the colleague you hit has agreed to show you some professional courtesy . . . You're welcome.'

'Let's go, then.'

'Oh, you're still spending the night,' Finlay told him. 'My suggestion. *I* think you need to sleep this one off.'

Wolf slumped drunkenly onto the bed. 'Got nowhere to go anyway. I think me and Andrea are done.'

'You can still fix things.'

Wolf shook his head: 'What if I don't want to?'

'She's your wife!'

'We're not like you and Maggie! The two of you are meant to be together. Maybe me and Andrea just . . . aren't.'

Finlay rubbed his tired face. 'You and Emily would be a disaster. Everyone thinks so. You have a wife. You owe it to her to at least try.'

'What do you mean, "everyone"?' slurred Wolf.

'I mean everyone! We *all* watch the two of you pulling each other's pigtails all day every day. You're not exactly subtle about it. And Andrea's had to watch it with the rest of us.'

'Well, if I'm such a *shitty* human being, what are you still doing here?'

'Know what? I was just wondering that myself,' said Finlay, standing up and walking out.

Wednesday 3 February 2016
5.23 p.m.

Balancing her hot chocolate on a fence post, Baxter walked over to Maggie and Wolf. 'Mind if I borrow him?' she asked.

'Be my guest!' laughed Maggie. 'He's trodden on my feet *quite* enough for one night.'

Leading Wolf to the far end of the garden, Baxter perched on the wall between two flickering candles.

'I need to tell you . . .' she started, abruptly changing the subject to buy herself a little more time: 'Maggie seems happy . . . Well, not happy exactly, but . . .'

'She is. As much as she can be.' He checked to make sure they were alone. 'She got her first clear scan from the hospital yesterday,' he whispered through a smile. 'She didn't tell anyone because she wanted tonight to be about Finlay.'

'That's great news,' said Baxter a little flatly.

'What's wrong?' he asked, taking a swig of his beer.

'Nothing. It's just . . . He's not around to see it, is he? And they're saying all these things about him in the news.'

Wolf nodded. 'But that's not the point, is it? Think Finlay would give two shits about people calling him names? Maggie isn't safe now through luck or fate or God. She's alive because of *him*, because only the *very* best was ever good enough for her, *because* he compromised everything he was to save her.'

Baxter smiled sadly. 'You've always been good at warping things into what you want them to be.'

'And you've always been really bad at it,' he told her.

'I just think sometimes people need to admit when they've made a mistake . . . Like I did that night in the chapel.' Wolf frowned as Baxter took a deep breath: 'Thomas asked me to marry him again.'

'Oh.'

'And I'm going to say "yes". I got confused there for a little while with everything going on and the proposal freaking me out and finding that stupid note, but I know what I want now.'

'Note?' asked Wolf, shivering against the cold, the glow of the fire pit on the patio not helping.

'It doesn't matter now.'

'It obviously did, though,' he pushed her.

Baxter huffed. 'I found something Finlay wrote among his things . . . A love letter, of sorts, that he didn't write for Maggie. And it just really got to me, the idea of him feeling that way about another woman when he had Maggie, and . . .' She paused on noticing Wolf's guilty expression. 'Oh my God! *You* know who he wrote it for, don't you?'

'I don't know what you're talking about.'

'Liar!'

'I think perhaps some things are best left in the past.'

Not taking 'no' for an answer, Baxter removed the crumpled piece of card from her pocket, unfolding it to read aloud.

'Still no name for me?'

Wolf didn't respond.

She shrugged: 'Maybe *this* will jog your memory . . .'

Saturday 22 May 2010

1.46 a.m.

'Finlay, wait!' called Wolf, hurrying over to the bars.

After leaving him to squirm for a few moments, Finlay ambled back over.

'I'm sorry.'

'It's fine,' replied the Scotsman, emotional exchanges making him uncomfortable.

'Before you arrived, I was just lying there' – Wolf started pacing the small cell, running his hands through his hair as he struggled to verbalise what was in his head – 'just thinking about all of it, about things I've wanted to say for a long time but couldn't . . .

about how now might be the *only* time to say them. You're right: me and Baxter are a mess; me and Andrea are a mess. The whole situation's a complete mess and something's got to give . . . Will you give her a message from me?'

'Andrea?'

'Baxter.'

Finlay rolled his eyes: 'Have you not listened to a single word I said?'

'Just one message,' Wolf slurred. 'And if she's not interested, then I'll know, won't I? I'll be able to move on with my life one way or another.'

Finlay groaned: 'Why me?'

'You think she's going to talk to *me* after tonight?'

'No,' he conceded.

Borrowing the biro from the visitors' sheet, he removed a creased birthday card from his back pocket and ripped it in half. As Wolf continued to pace, going over the words he'd been practising over and over in his head, Finlay sat back down, pen poised. 'So what's the message?'

Wednesday 3 February 2016

5.27 p.m.

'"How do you still not *fucking* get this yet?"'

By the light of the dying candles, Baxter read the words that she realised were already for ever ingrained in her memory.

'Baxter, I—'

'"I don't just love you. I unreservedly, unremittingly and hope-lessly *adore* you. You . . . are . . . mine."'

'Baxter, I need to tell you something.'

'"And none of these fucking people, none of the horrible shit that's happened between us, not even these *fucking* bars, are going to keep us apart . . ."'

'Baxter!' snapped Wolf, snatching the note from her and drop-ping it to the ground.

He hesitated and then slowly crouched down to meet her eye, tentatively reaching out to take her hand.

He took a deep breath. 'Because no one is ever, *ever* taking you away from me.'

Baxter's annoyed scowl gradually softened into something resembling irked confusion before settling somewhere in the vicinity of dumbfounded shock.

'He never gave it to you?' asked Wolf.

Speechless, Baxter just shook her head.

Wolf nodded, unsurprised: 'He always was a bastard.'

EPILOGUE

Thursday 15 December 2016
7.34 p.m.

'What did the witness say?' asked Baxter, phone clamped between her shoulder and ear as she rooted around for her keys. '*Nooo!* And forensics? . . . *Nooo!*' She had rushed home from work. The moment she crossed the threshold, she called up the stairs: 'Is she still awake?!'

'Just about!'

Tossing her bag at the Christmas tree, she kicked off her boots and ascended the staircase, pulling her blouse over her head rather than waste valuable seconds fiddling about with buttons. She put the phone back to her ear.

'Whose?! Don't say the dead guy's fingerprints?! . . . *Nooo!* . . . What? Yes, they still make them . . . I don't know – Tesco? I'll get you one. Look, I'm back now. I need to go . . . Fine . . . *Fine!* I've got to go . . . I'm hanging up. Bye!'

'She's starting to doze off!' the voice called as she stumbled out of her trousers and fell into the shower.

'Then prod her or something!' Baxter shouted back, throwing on her tartan pyjamas as she rushed into the bedroom.

'Just in time,' Wolf greeted her, a bedtime story in his hands.

'Move your arse! You've had her all day!' she barked as they swapped places, reaching down into the cot, where Finlay Elliot

Baxter was on the verge of sleep, her tiny hand grasping Frankie the Penguin's worn wing.

'What dead guy's fingerprints?' Wolf asked in an excited whisper.

Baxter frowned at him: '*Perhaps* we should talk about it later?' she suggested.

'Was that Rouche?'

'Yes. And it sounds like he and Edmunds have caught a juicy one, which I'll tell you about . . . *later*.'

'But what are they thinking? Faked death or that someone removed the dead guy's fingers?'

'*Christ*, Wolf! Later!' Gently scooping her daughter up, Baxter's smile dropped as she regarded his handiwork for the day: 'Errr, Wolf?' she started, in the same tone she normally reserved for words such as 'arsehole'. ''S'up with the wallpaper?'

'Nice, right?' he said proudly. 'Spent all day on it.'

She carried baby Finlay over to a section of wall where a cartoon crocodile looked to have been spliced with the rear end of a giraffe. She turned back to him and frowned.

'Thing is, they don't expect you to match these things up perfectly,' he told her.

'Where's this elephant's head?'

He glanced around the room, it admittedly looking a tad more terrifying now than it had in the daylight. 'There,' he said smugly, pointing somewhere above the doorway.

'It's . . . ' She mouthed the word 'shit'. 'Do it again.'

'*You* do it again!'

'It looks like a taxidermist's nightmare!'

'Whatever. I didn't see what was wrong with the angels we had before.'

'I don't . . . *do* . . . angels! How many times?!'

Baby Finlay started to cry. Baxter gently rocked her to sleep before placing her back in her cot.

'I'm not doing it again. End of,' whispered Wolf, folding his arms defiantly.

'That zebra over there has the head of a snake and the paws of a lion. It *almost* looks like it's been joined that way.'

Wolf's arms slowly unfolded the longer he stared at the offending abomination.

'Remind you of anything?' she asked him.

He sighed heavily: 'I'll do it again.'

'Thank you. Where did you get up to?' she whispered, picking up the storybook.

'Does it matter?' he asked.

She shot him a look.

'He just defeated the sword-wielding monster,' he informed her, heading out of the room. 'I'll go get started on dinner.'

'Duck à l'orange?'

'Spaghetti on toast.'

'I hate you!' she called after him with a smile.

'I hate you more!'

She flicked through to the final pages, squinting to make out the words as the Lullaby Light Show threw colourful shapes across the walls.

'"The gates splintered and snapped! . . . The king's men were inside! 'Run!' the princess told the knight as the clatter of armour filled the tower. 'Please, for me. Run!' The brave knight didn't want to leave but did as his princess commanded, climbing from the highest window of the tallest tower so that he may one day return to her . . . So she waited and she waited some more, and one day, many, many months later . . . he did.'"

Baxter turned the final page.

'"And they lived happily ever after."'

Loved Endgame?
Here is what you've missed . . .

IIIIIIIIIIIIIIIIIIIIIIIIIIIIIIIIIIIIIIIIIIIIIIIIIIIIIIIIIIIIIIIIIIIIIIIIIIIIIIIIIIIIIIIIIIIIIIIIIIIIIIIIIII

Start with *Ragdoll* . . .

A body is discovered with the dismembered parts of six victims stitched together, nicknamed by the press as the 'Ragdoll'. Assigned to the shocking case are Detective William 'Wolf' Fawkes, recently reinstated to the London Met, and his former partner Detective Emily Baxter.

THE GLOBAL BESTSELLER

'SURPRISING AND ORIGINAL'
Sophie Hannah

'SUPERB THRILLER WRITING'
Peter Robinson

RAGDOLL

ONE BODY.
SIX VICTIMS.
NO SUSPECTS.

'A BRILLIANT, BREATHLESS THRILLER'
M J Arlidge

'A STAR IS BORN'
Simon Toyne

DANIEL COLE

The 'Ragdoll Killer' taunts the police by releasing a list of names to the media, and the dates on which he intends to murder them. With six people to save, can Fawkes and Baxter catch a killer when the world is watching their every move?

Devour *Hangman* . . .

A body is found hanging from Brooklyn Bridge, the word 'BAIT' carved into the chest.

In London a copycat killer strikes, branded with the word 'PUPPET', forcing DCI Emily Baxter into an uneasy partnership with the detectives on the case, Special Agents Rouche and Curtis.

Each time they trace a suspect, the killer is one step ahead. With the body count rising on both sides of the Atlantic, can they learn to trust each other and identify who is holding the strings before it is too late?

Then tell us what you thought!

'Superb thriller writing' Peter Robinson
'A brilliant, breathless thriller' M.J. Arlidge
'A high concept solution to a mystery' Sophie Hannah

Go back to where it all began . . .

Read on for an extract from
Ragdoll

CHAPTER 1

Saturday 28 June 2014

3.50 a.m.

Wolf groped blindly for his mobile phone, which was edging further across the laminate floor with every vibration. Slowly the darkness began to disassemble itself into the unfamiliar shapes of his new apartment. The sweat-sodden sheet clung to his skin as he crawled off the mattress and over to the buzzing annoyance.

'Wolf,' he answered, relieved that he had at least got that right as he searched the wall for a light switch.

'It's Simmons.'

Wolf flicked a switch and sighed heavily when the weak yellow light reminded him where he was; he was tempted to turn it off again. The tiny bedroom consisted of four walls, a worn double mattress on the floor and a solitary light bulb. The claustrophobic box was sweltering thanks to his landlord, who still had not chased the previous tenant up for a window key. Normally this would not have been such an issue in London; however, Wolf had managed to coincide his move with one of England's uncharacteristic heatwaves, which had been dragging on for almost two weeks.

'Don't sound so pleased,' said Simmons.

'What time is it?' yawned Wolf.

'Ten to four.'

'Aren't I off this weekend?'

'Not any more. I need you to join me at a crime scene.'

'Next to your desk?' asked Wolf, only half-joking as he hadn't seen his boss leave the office in years.

'Funny. They let me out for this one.'

'That bad, huh?'

There was a pause on the other end of the line before Simmons answered: 'It's pretty bad. Got a pen?'

Wolf rummaged through one of the stacked boxes in the doorway and found a biro to scribble on the back of his hand with.

'OK. Go ahead.'

Out of the corner of his eye, he noticed a light flickering across his kitchen cupboard.

'Flat 108 . . .' started Simmons.

As Wolf walked into his ill-equipped kitchenette, he was dazzled by blue flashing lights strobing through the small window.

'. . . Trinity Towers—'

'Hibbard Road, Kentish Town?' Wolf interrupted, peering down over dozens of police cars, reporters, and the evacuated residents of the block opposite.

'How the hell did you know that?'

'I *am* a detective.'

'Well, you can also be our number one suspect then. Get down here.'

'Will do. I just need to . . .' Wolf trailed off, realising that Simmons had already hung up.

Between the intermittent flashes, he noticed the steady orange light coming from the washing machine and remembered that he had put his work clothes in before going to bed. He looked around at the dozens of identical cardboard boxes lining the walls:

'Bollocks.'

Five minutes later Wolf was pushing his way through the crowd of spectators that had congregated outside his building. He approached a police officer and flashed his warrant card, expecting to stroll straight through the cordon; however, the young constable snatched the card out of his hand and examined it closely, glancing up sceptically at the imposing figure dressed in swimming shorts and a faded '93 Bon Jovi: *Keep the Faith* tour T-shirt.

'Officer Layton-Fawkes?' the constable asked doubtfully.

Wolf winced at the sound of his own pretentious name:

'Detective Sergeant Fawkes, yes.'

'As in – Courtroom-Massacre Fawkes?'

'It's pronounced William . . . May I?' Wolf gestured towards the apartment building.

The young man handed Wolf's warrant card back and held the tape up for him to pass under.

'Need me to show you up?' he asked.

Wolf glanced down at his floral shorts, bare knees and work shoes.

'You know what? I think I'm doing pretty well by myself.'

The officer grinned.

'Fourth floor,' he told Wolf. 'And be careful heading up there alone; it's a shitty neighbourhood.'

Wolf sighed heavily once more, entered through the bleach-fragranced hallway, and stepped into the lift. The buttons for the second and fifth floors were missing and a brown liquid had dried over the remainder of the control panel. Using all of his detective skills to ascertain that it was either poo, rust or Coca-Cola, he used the bottom of his T-shirt, Richie Sambora's face, to push the button.

He had been in hundreds of identical lifts in his time: a seamless metal box, installed by councils all over the country. It had no floor covering, no mirrors and no protruding lights or fixtures. There was absolutely nothing for the underprivileged residents to destroy or steal from their own life-enriching piece of equipment, so they had settled for spray-painting obscenities all over the walls instead. Wolf only had time to learn that Johnny Ratcliff was both 'ere' and 'a gay' before the doors scraped open at the fourth floor.

Over a dozen people were scattered along the silent corridor. Most looked a little shaken and eyed Wolf's outfit disapprovingly, except for one scruffy man wearing a forensics badge, who nodded in approval and gave him a thumbs up as he passed. A very faint but familiar smell intensified as Wolf approached the open doorway at the end of the hallway. It was the unmistakable smell of death. People who work around such things quickly become attuned to the unique mix of stale air, shit, piss and putrefying flesh.

Wolf took a step back from the door when he heard running footsteps from inside. A young woman burst out through the open doorway, dropped to her knees and then vomited in the corridor in front of him. He waited politely for an opportune moment to ask her to move when another set of footsteps approached. He instinctively took another step back before Detective Sergeant Emily Baxter came skidding into the corridor.

'Wolf! I thought I saw you lurking out here,' she roared across the hushed hallway. 'Seriously, how cool is this?'

She glanced down at the woman retching on the floor between them.

'Could you puke somewhere else, please?'

The woman sheepishly crawled out of their way. Baxter grabbed Wolf by the arm and excitedly led him into the apartment. Nearly a decade his junior, Baxter was almost as tall as him. Her dark brown hair turned black under the gloom of the unimpressive entrance hall and, as always, she wore dark make-up that made her attractive eyes appear abnormally large. Dressed in a fitted shirt and smart trousers, she looked him up and down with a mischievous grin.

'No one told me it was a mufti day.'

Wolf refused to rise to the bait, knowing that she would quickly lose interest if he only remained quiet.

'How pissed is Chambers gonna be he's missed this?' she beamed.

'Personally I'd take the Caribbean cruise over a dead body too,' said Wolf, bored.

Baxter's huge eyes widened in surprise: 'Simmons didn't tell you?'

'Tell me what?'

She led him through the crowded apartment, which had been dimly lit in the glow of a dozen strategically placed torches. Although not overpowering, the smell grew steadily stronger. Wolf could tell that the fetid source was close by because of the number of flies zipping about feverishly above his head.

The flat had high ceilings, contained no furniture, and was considerably larger than Wolf's own, but was no more pleasant. The yellowed walls were peppered with holes through which the antiquated wiring and dusty insulation bled freely onto the bare floor. Neither the bathroom suite nor the kitchen looked to have been updated since the 1960s.

'Tell me what?' he asked her again.

'This is the *one*, Wolf,' said Baxter, ignoring the question, 'a once-in-a-career case.'

Wolf was distracted, mentally sizing up the second bedroom and wondering whether he was being overcharged for his poxy box of a flat across the road. They rounded the corner into the crowded main room and he automatically scanned the floor, between the assorted equipment and pairs of legs, for a body.

'Baxter!'

She stopped and turned to him impatiently.

'What didn't Simmons tell me?'

Behind her, a group of people, standing in front of the large floor-to-ceiling window that dominated the room, moved aside. Before she could answer, Wolf had stumbled away, his eyes fixed on a point somewhere above them: the one light source that the police had not brought with them: a spotlight on a dark stage . . .

The naked body, contorted into an unnatural pose, appeared to be floating a foot above the uneven floorboards. It had its back to the room, looking out through the enormous window. Hundreds of almost invisible threads held the figure in place, which, in turn, were anchored by two industrial metal hooks.

It took Wolf a moment to identify the most unnerving feature of the surreal scene before him: the black leg attached to the white torso. Unable to comprehend what he was seeing, he pushed his way further into the room. As he drew closer, he noticed the huge stitches binding the mismatched body parts together, the skin tented where the material punctured through: one black male leg, one white; a large male hand on one side, a tanned female counterpart on the other; tangled jet-black hair hanging unsettlingly over a pale, freckled, slender, female torso.

Baxter was back at his side, clearly relishing the look of revulsion on his face:

'He didn't tell you . . . One dead body – six victims!' she whispered gleefully in his ear.

Wolf's gaze dropped to the floor. He was standing on the shadow cast by the grotesque corpse and, in this simplified state, the proportions appeared even more jarring, gaps of light distorting the joins between the limbs and body.

'What the hell are the press doing out there already?' Wolf heard his chief shout at no one in particular. 'I swear, this department has got more leaks than the *Titanic*. If I find anyone talking to them, they'll be suspended!'

Wolf smiled, knowing full well that Simmons was only play-acting the part of the stereotypical boss. They had known one another for over a decade and, until the Khalid incident, Wolf had considered him a friend. Beneath the forced bravado, Simmons was in fact an intelligent, caring, and competent police officer.

'Fawkes!' Simmons strode over to them. He often struggled not to address his staff by their nicknames. He was almost a foot shorter than Wolf, was now in his fifties, and had developed a managerial belly. 'Nobody told me it was a mufti day.'

Wolf heard Baxter snigger. He decided to adopt the same tactic that he had used on her by ignoring the comment. After an uncomfortable silence, Simmons turned to Baxter.

'Where's Adams?' he asked.

'Who?'

'Adams. Your new protégé.'

'Edmunds?'

'Right. Edmunds.'

'How am I supposed to know?'

'Edmunds!' Simmons bellowed across the busy room.

'Work with him a lot now?' asked Wolf quietly, unable to hide the hint of jealousy in his voice, which made Baxter smile.

'Babysitting duty,' she whispered. 'He's the transfer from Fraud, only seen a few dead bodies. He might even cry later on.'

The young man bumbling through the crowd towards them was only twenty-five years old, stick-thin and immaculately presented, apart from his scruffy strawberry-blond hair. He was holding a notebook at the ready and smiled eagerly at the chief inspector.

'Where are forensics up to?' asked Simmons.

Edmunds flicked back a few pages in his book.

'Helen said that her team still haven't found a single drop of blood anywhere in the apartment. They have confirmed that all six body parts are from different victims and were roughly amputated, probably with a hacksaw.'

'Did *Helen* mention anything we didn't already know?' spat Simmons.

'Actually, yes. Due to the absence of blood and lack of constriction of the blood vessels around the amputation wounds . . .'

Simmons rolled his eyes and checked his watch.

'. . . we can be certain that the parts were removed post-mortem,' finished Edmunds, looking pleased with himself.

'That's some fantastic police work, Edmunds,' said Simmons sarcastically before shouting out: 'Could someone please cancel the milk carton ad for the man missing a head? Thank you!'

Edmunds' smile vanished. Wolf caught Simmons' eye and smirked. They had both been on the receiving end of similar putdowns in their time. It was all part of the training.

'I just meant that whoever the arms and legs belonged to are definitely dead as well. They will know more once they get the body back to the lab,' Edmunds mumbled self-consciously.

Wolf noticed the reflection of the body in the dark windows. Realising that he had not yet seen it from the front, he moved round to look.

'What have *you* got, Baxter?' asked Simmons.

'Not a lot. Slight damage to the keyhole, possibly picked. We've got officers questioning the neighbours outside, but so far no one's seen or heard a thing. Oh, and there's nothing wrong with the electrics – every bulb in the apartment's been removed except for the one above the victim . . . s, like it's on show or something.'

'What about you Fawkes, any ideas? Fawkes?'

Wolf was gazing up at the body's dark-skinned face.

'I'm sorry, are we boring you?'

'No. Sorry. Even in this heat, this thing's only just beginning to stink, which means the killer either murdered all six victims last night, which seems unlikely, or he's had the bodies on ice.'

'Agreed. We'll get someone to look into recent break-ins at cold-storage units, supermarkets, restaurants, anywhere with an industrial-sized freezer room,' said Simmons.

'And see if any of the neighbours heard drilling,' said Wolf.

'Drilling is a reasonably common sound,' blurted Edmunds, who regretted the outburst when three pairs of angry eyes turned on him.

'If this is the killer's masterpiece,' continued Wolf, 'there's no way they would risk it dropping out of the ceiling and just being a pile of bits by the time we got here. Those hooks will be drilled into load-bearing metal beams. Someone should have heard it.'

Simmons nodded: 'Baxter, get someone on it.'

'Chief, could I borrow you a moment?' asked Wolf as Baxter and Edmunds moved away. He pulled on a pair of disposable gloves and lifted a handful of knotted black hair away from the gruesome figure's face. It was male. The eyes were open, the expression unnervingly calm considering the victim's clearly violent end. 'Look familiar?'

Simmons walked round to join Wolf by the chilly window and crouched down to better examine the dark face. After a few moments, he shrugged.

'It's Khalid,' said Wolf.

'That's impossible.'

'Is it?'

Simmons looked up again at the lifeless face. Gradually his expression of scepticism transformed into one of deep concern.

'Baxter!' he shouted. 'I need you and Adams—'

'*Edmunds*.'

'. . . over at Belmarsh Prison. Ask the governor to take you directly to Naguib Khalid.'

'Khalid?' Baxter asked in shock, involuntarily glancing at Wolf.

'Yes, Khalid. Phone me the moment you've seen him alive. Go!'

Wolf looked out towards his block opposite. Many of the windows remained dark, others contained excited faces filming the spectacle below on their mobile phones, presumably hoping to capture something grisly to entertain their friends with in the morning. Apparently they were unable to see into the dimly lit murder scene that they would otherwise have had front row seats for.

Wolf was able to see into his own flat, a few windows over. In his hurry, he had left all of the lights on. He spotted a cardboard box, at the bottom of a pile, with the words 'Trousers and Shirts' scrawled across it.

'*Aha*!'

Simmons walked back over to Wolf and rubbed his tired eyes. They stood quietly, either side of the suspended body, watching the first signs of morning pollute the dark sky. Even over the noise of the room, they could hear the peaceful sound of bird-song outside.

'So, most disturbing thing you've ever seen then?' Simmons joked wearily.

'A close second,' replied Wolf without taking his eyes off the growing patch of deep blue sky.

'Second? Do I even want to know what tops this – this thing?' Simmons took another reluctant look at the hanging collection of dismemberments.

Wolf gently tapped the figure's outstretched right arm. The palm looked pale in comparison to the rest of the tanned skin and the perfectly manicured purple nails. Dozens of silk-like threads supported the outstretched hand and a dozen more held the extended index finger in place.

He checked that no one was listening in to their conversation and then leaned across to whisper to Simmons.

'It's pointing into my apartment window.'